69

Part 1
The Fake it Till ya
Make it Emperor

B. McGraw

This is dedicated to all the people out there thinking about
the Roman Empire once a day

CONTENTS

ACKNOWLEDGMENTS

I acknowledge that I wrote this book by finding a free online copy of Tacitus and re-writing it in my own words only filling in the gaps with rumors spread by Suetonius, Plutarch, and my own imagination. Also have to acknowledge Mike Duncan's phenomenal podcasting ability. I got the idea for this book listening to his *The History of Rome* podcast.

1 OTHO JOINS UPPER SOCIETY

Great men aren't born great; they are pushed into it by their parents. In ancient times, before competitive preschools, parents conspired with their friends, who conspired with an army of mystical old men, augurs, and soothsayers to inspire confidence. Maybe an auspicious bird landed on their ancestral grave at birth, or a natural disaster forecasted a turbulent life. They cleared the path to greatness by predicting greatness. Next, an entire network of parents, grandparents, cousins, friends, political allies, work colleagues, and sometimes even suspiciously convenient deaths would conspire to get that child into the right schools, military positions, jobs, and political offices until they were a shoo-in for great things. None of these things happened for Marcus Salvius Otho. Nonetheless, he dreamed of great things. Otho was a well-off patrician, but his upbringing was far from fulfilling his desire for greatness.

One night in Rome, Otho entered an upscale

party that permanently changed his life and the course of the Roman Empire for upwards of three months. Otho walked down a wide cobblestone road with his friend, who was striding with pride. The light traffic signaled the end of the workday.

"Otho, how do you keep scoring invites to these dope-culus[1] parties?" asked Claudius Senecio, a twenty-three-year-old man sporting a tunic with ripped-off sleeves for the gun show. These two men might have been Roman, but they were living the Greek life.

"I met some hot lady of influence a few months back. She has connections, so I've been trying to milk it for all it's worth," Otho replied with feigned confidence. He was a generic-looking white Roman in his mid-twenties. These two young men were so exceptionally average that it took their friends three introductions before they could put the correct name to their vanilla-bland faces. It made little sense that they were strutting down the streets of Rome like they owned the city. Otho and Senecio didn't even own their homes. They had the same boring bowl cuts displayed on the busts in museums. The only noticeable difference between the two was Otho's slightly shorter build and less pronounced cheekbones. What Otho had that Senecio didn't was confidence and an energy undeserving of a man of his meager skills and talents.

"Now just be cool, and I can get you in with me."

The two walked down a dim Roman street to

---

[1] Inappropriate language was left in Latin so this book does not end up on a banned book list. Please familiarize yourself with all of the ways Futuere (To F&*#) can be conjugated

an upscale neighborhood and approached an armed guard standing at a door. The noise inside indicated a good time. As they swaggered up to the guard, Otho said, "Salve[2], I am Marcus Salvius Otho. This is my guest Claudius Senecio, and I believe I'm on the list." Otho introduced himself with a flourish. He acted so much like he belonged it was obvious he didn't. Just in case, he double-checked his small bag of sesterces.

"Oh, yeah! You're on the list. Cornelia's been wondering where her boy toy is," the guard replied with a guttural laugh. Standing tall and intimidating, the guard looked down on Senecio. "She didn't mention anything about you bringing a guest. Does he come with any girls or wine?"

"I think I can satisfactorily compensate you," Otho replied, shaking his coin purse.

"Not with that tiny nut sack you can't," the guard jabbed. He leaned on the house's threshold and threw a flat-faced stare at Senecio until their confidence was broken.

"I don't have to join ya, Otho," Senecio backed down. "I'll just see you tomorrow." Defeated, Senecio began to walk away. He shrugged his shoulders high to soften the blow.

The guard lost his composure and keeled over laughing. "I'm just messing with you guys. Cornelia said you could have a guest. Come on in, futueris pueris!"

Relieved that Senecio could join, the two took a deep breath and walked into the party villa. Just before making it past the crowded atrium, they heard a passing, "Hey, stupid," from behind.

---

[2] Salve means *hello* in Latin, the guard's name is not *Hello* as far as we know

Otho and Senecio were the only two in the atrium to look back at the guard like a couple of plebs, only to see him ROFL'ing at their shallow insecurities.

"Ya just don't look back when someone says 'hey, stupid . . .'"

The two dude-man-bros felt a temporary crush to their spirits. Objective One was to rally fast to recover their evening. They went straight to the wine—and they drank with a purpose.

"Ya know, it won't be long before we run this town, and we'll never get disrespected like that again," Otho proclaimed after wiping residual red liquid off a wispy mustache.

"How do ya figure that?" Senecio questioned. "That's a pretty tall order, considering, you know, we're not like millionaire rich."

"You don't need a ton of money to get power in Rome. You just need to look like you have money. Once you get the right connections, you're in—and the money will come," Otho mansplained to Senecio before taking another big gulp from his red solo goblet. "That's why we're at this party."

"Ha, I thought we just came to pick up chicks and get sloshed off fortified wine," Senecio said. "Hey! Where's your girl, Cornelia? By the way you described her, I figured you'd be with her all night on your way to some evening temple worship, if ya catch my drift. Ya can't wait too long; you could get some wine-induced performance issues," Senecio teased before flicking Otho's phallus.

"Futue off, man," Otho said, swiping away Senecio's hand and keeping a low profile. "Yeah, I don't know. I haven't seen her yet. I still need to do some networking. These are my friends."

"Yeah, like, who's your friend here?" Senecio asked. Across the room, no one appeared to make eye contact with the two young men except a silver-haired woman. She seemed to be aging before their very eyes; they could almost taste the must. "Looks like you've at least got one friend over there. Who's she, your old wet nurse?"

"Oh, uh, something like that—" The woman walked over, swaying her hips with the veracity of a puma in heat, her once-youthful arms now wrinkled and swaying. "Salve, Cornelia. Thanks for the invite."

"If it isn't Otho, my strapping young man in the city. Show me a good time like you did the other day, and I'll invite you to any party in the city," Cornelia said, placing her hand on his shoulder for a casual side hug. "And who's this? A friend of yours?" Cornelia began mentally undressing Senecio, entering an imaginative world of carnal delights.

"This is an old friend of mine, Senecio," Otho introduced his drinking companion. "He likes to party just as hard. You gotta watch out for this guy. I usually have to stop him from getting too crazy most nights. I thought you'd love to meet him since he's your type of company."

"A man who likes to party even harder than Otho?" Cornelia swooned, fueled by countless nights of repressed postmenopausal hormones. "Do tell me, Senecio, how easily do you get motion sickness?" Cornelia interrogated her new interest, pouring wine into Senecio's goblet until it overflowed onto the floor.

Otho, realizing his work was done, stepped away to relocate to another crowded room.

Looking back at his unwilling wingman, Senecio stood paralyzed with Cornelia hanging off one of his motionless arms, staring deeply into his hazel eyes. Senecio did not immediately exchange glances but made parting contact with Otho. Senecio's eyes spoke to Otho's with one articulate, stern glance: *You pelusia magna. Between this and distracting that girl's dad who was obsessed with the potentially catastrophic dangers of currency debasement on the Roman economy, you're gonna owe me big. I had my ear talked off, with absolutely no futuendi warning, for five hours about the value retention of precious metals not even a week ago. But tonight, I'm taking a real arrow for you, man! If you don't make this disgusting sexual escapade worth my while, our friendship is over. This is an unhealthy pattern, and I think my mom is right. This might be a one-way relationship.*

I will never forget your sacrifice! I'll come back for you! Otho's eyes replied as he slipped through the loud party to distance himself physically (and morally) from his total betrayal of Senecio's lingering trust.

Recharging his goblet of wine from a nearby servant, Otho was well on his way to achieving his primary goal of filling his tank with leaded fuel. He wasn't in the mood to climb the ladder just yet. He had to get in just the right mood to be an effective introvert for some facetime with Rome's movers and shakers, but there was no gas in the tank for long, tedious conversations. Hopefully, wine would help. Otho was tired of having the same old stuffy conversation with the old farts of Roman high society. They were all so boring he had to pre-game for it.

Maybe he could find someone else; it wasn't all old people. There must be some important person's son or someone more interesting to hang with to feel like he was doing something other than getting drunk at someone else's expense.

Otho scanned the room for some youthful energy but mostly came up short. A good portion of the party consisted of middle-aged, high-society hedonists marked by their unnecessarily heavy breathing and cumulative eating and drinking damage to their bodies. Besides the high concentration of slaves serving food and drink, many of the young men capable of a good, fun time were military men or rising politicians who were likely mild-mannered Boy Scouts, far too stuffy to talk to. Good connections for the day, but not good company after the sun sets. If a war story from Germania or the Far East came up, that was the end of the conversation for Otho. They all usually kept to themselves.

Just when all hope seemed to be lost, a spritely young man was spotted across the room pouring wine over the head of a slave before kneeing him in the nuts. Probably some important dude's son. Who else could get away with that? Otho chugged what wine he had and procured two more goblets on his way over.

"Yo," Otho uttered, handing over one of the full glasses of wine. From a closer glance at the fellow upper-class, spoiled delinquent, Otho realized he may have hit the jackpot. It was Nero. He took out a coin and covertly matched it to his face; it was him. This was the ultimate connection to the upper crust.

"Thanks, this culus spilled mine. You just can't find good help in the city anymore," Nero said, toasting Otho. "You a fan of music?"

"Who isn't?" Otho replied, knowing full well Nero was a bit of a nerd about that stuff. "I never miss a good performance."

"Who's your favorite singer these days?" Nero asked.

"Uhhhh, tough one. Really putting me on the spot here. I'd have to go with, uh, *fukghpughus*." Otho mumbled something that sounded like it could be a name and hoped Nero was too far gone to notice.

"Oh stercus, that dude's my futuendi muse," Nero replied, only hearing the artist he was hoping to hear. "I tell you what—"

Nero prodded some drunk couple making out off a nearby couch. He jumped up in the cleared space and stood tall above the crowd in the high-vaulted room. "Everyone shut the futuus up!" he commanded.

The crowd, aware of who he was, indeed shut the futuus up. "My friend here wants to hear 'The Waywardly Harlots of the North Appian Way' written by his favorite singer. Coincidentally, I know the song and can sing it flawlessly. I'm gonna need silence to do this justice!"

Preceded by whispers, a wave of silence washed over the entire party throughout every room of the villa. Nero, at the time, was only seventeen years old but had been proclaimed emperor of Rome at sixteen upon the controversial death of his father-in-law, Claudius. With such a naive man in extreme power, it was the golden age of suck-ups. Otho knew this.

Once the party became Nero's captive audience, he began the song with a tearful verse about women trapped in the harems and brothels along the Appian Way. Doing the song's opening slow meter justice, everyone began to feel for the plight of these women. It was a good break from the jingoistic propaganda songs typically heard about serving Rome, the Gods, and family, which had flooded the markets ever since the elite learned how to weaponize them.

Maintaining a strong, slow pace, Nero's singing touched the hearts of everyone in the room. He was kind of good, maybe even Athens good. The crowd was moved and began to rethink the way they treated their prostitutes.

Once Nero finished the ballad, there was a short pause while everyone waited to make sure the song was over. It wasn't clear if the pause was for dramatic effect or if he was trying to remember the words. Nero didn't remember the rest and motioned with his arm in a side bow that he was done.

Applause and finger whistling filled the room. Nero accepted his public admiration, feigned or sincere, and stepped off the couch.

"Technically, that was masterful. Very true to the original artist," Otho said. "You almost had me believing you were a sensitive artist."

"Thank you," Nero replied. "What sort of artist would I be if I could not enter another man's skin? I'm practicing so that I can sing it at Athens City Limits music festival next year."

Otho continued to pepper the right number of compliments with interesting sophomoric conversation about art, life, and hedonistic philosophy, just like a couple of college freshmen getting way too high and listening to some Pink Floyd. Except Otho was just the RA that was four years older trying to be chill. Nero began to take a liking to him, and they both became engrossed in each other's company. After an hour and three wine refills, they were primed for some real fun.

"Nero, when was the last time you partook in some old-fashioned shenanigans?" Otho asked, perking up Nero's ears. "It feels like you're under a lot of stress. This party is past its peak, and there's a certain senator's villa we're planning on vandalizing tonight. You should join us." Not many had left the party; it was still mostly old people, but a handful had already begun passing out.

"Which senator?"

"Piso," Otho answered.

"Oh, futuus yeah, I hate that guy. Let's go." Nero agreed to an evening of delinquency. On the way out the door of the villa, Otho spotted Senecio across the room, propped into a corner with Cornelia's leg vigorously rubbing against his like two sticks attempting to ignite a campfire on a desert island.

Fulfilling his promise to come back for him, Otho grabbed Senecio's shoulder and pulled him away from his desperate predicament. Cornelia, temporarily stuck in her gyrotastic motion, let out a disappointed moan and eyed Otho desperately for him to give Senecio back.

"Cornelia, you're a disgusting crone. Go find another futueris pueris," Otho insulted her. If tonight was a success, he wouldn't need her anymore. "Your cunnus smells like a newborn goat. Don't write me anymore."

Leading the newly formed trio through the atrium, Otho entered the streets with Nero and Senecio without looking back to see the flames from the bridge he had just Molotov'd.

With the sun well below the horizon, no moonlight, and the three lit torches they snagged on the way out, there was only enough illumination to not run into a wall or walk off a ledge. After three turns into the city, Otho had led the group into the darkness with nothing but an abyss outside of their immediate reach as the surrounding buildings shadowed any residual light produced by the stars. While Nero may have been followed by the Praetorian Guard upon leaving the party, there was no telling if anyone would save the young emperor in a pinch.

"My mom's gonna be so mad at me if she knew I was doing this," Nero whispered to his new friends as they ventured deeper into the labyrinth.

"Futue her, dude," Otho replied softly. "You're a grown-culus man."

Despite the potential social consequences, Senecio began snickering, having lost his inhibitions from the massive amount of wine Cornelia had funneled into him.

"Ha, you're afraid of your mom," Senecio mocked Nero. "Who are you, by the way?"

"Nero, and I'm your futuendi emperor, dude."

"Woah . . ." Senecio exclaimed, realizing he was hanging out with the one teenager in charge of the whole empire. "The emperor of Rome and all of the Mediterranean is futuendi afraid of his mom . . ."

"Shut the futuus up," Nero said, trying to save face. "It's a little more complicated than that."

"Shhhh," Otho interrupted. "I think I see some people out here. Daggers out . . ."

The group became silent once again. It sounded like two men were in the alley. The three slowly approached the unaware homeless men. Otho drew a seven-inch dagger from underneath his tunic. Senecio reached down and pulled out a four-inch blade. While it was shorter than Otho's, it was much thicker with substantial weight. While Otho and Senecio were very aware of each other's daggers, there was much anticipation as Nero jiggled his belt and dug his secret dagger from the mysterious unknown within his tunic; he revealed a massive nine-inch blade. Not only was it nine inches, but it also featured an elaborate integral guard, an exotic style usually seen around Judaea. Many blacksmiths did not have the heart to snip off that much of their blades to create an integral guard like this. Rumors circulated that this practice produced smaller daggers with less striking power. At least Otho and Senecio knew that rumor was absolute bull stercus.

The three came upon the two harmless men wearing brown blankets that specks of faded fabric revealed were not always brown. They didn't realize it, but running into them sleeping on the street gave them the element of surprise. With unified force, the three began kicking the homeless men and shouting.

Startled from their uneasy slumber, the men wriggled along the ground, scrambling to stand up and shouting coarse obscenities.

"What the futuus are you doin' in my alleyway?" Nero yelled. The two homeless men were too confused to do anything other than slip and fall against each other, stand up, and run away. Looking intimidating with their massive daggers, who were these men to question their authority?

"Dang, that was close. We almost got attacked!" Nero said.

They couldn't figure out where the two homeless men had gone.

"Okay, let's get out of here," Otho signaled to the others to GTFO. "They could have friends!"

Otho was the first to start sprinting back in the direction they came. The two others made a quick pivot, testing the grip and dexterity of their street sandals, and followed Otho by the fire of his torch, which began to roar in the wind as they dashed away from the scene. As the two caught up with Otho, his torch led them through a few turns and into a main street where they slowed to an ambling pace.

"I don't know. I don't think anyone would give a stercus enough to chase after us," Otho stated with absolute authority to the group catching up.

"Man, did you see the looks on those guys' faces?" Senecio slurred. "They were like, 'Woah, what's going on?' Man, those street trash are . . . uh . . . dead," said the street trash with more money.

"That was a helluva lot better than that lame party we were at," Nero said, catching his breath. "I haven't done anything like that since my XVth birthday. So glad ya dragged me out of that stuffy room with all those old fogies. Where to now?"

"Well, I got a buddy who told me they just took down the scaffolding on Piso's house, who's apparently kind of a culus," Otho replied. "We're meeting him there with some paint for graffiti. I walked by it earlier today, and it was just asking for it."

"Yeah, Piso's an absolute culus," Nero said. "He causes me more work than the rest of the Senate combined, and I get absolutely no imperial respect from him. I can always tell he thinks he can do a better job than me!"

***

After a methodical thirty-minute trek through the dark, including two wrong turns and another daggers-out moment, the three approached a flickering speck. The ember presumably belonged to Otho's friend's torch with the paint awaiting to join in on the shenanigans. Piso was an increasingly successful statesman in the city, and his villa in Rome proved he had substantial power and influence. It had more than a three-chariot garage, a ten-foot wall blocking a squash-court-sized garden entrance to a three-story complex of vaulted rooms, spacious balconies, and courtyards filled with fountains, foliage, and statues perfect for strolls to discuss political intrigue. That much money displayed to the world was unquestionably asking for it. These four youths couldn't ignore this obscene display of Piso's enormous dagger.

"Did you get the stuff?" Otho asked his skeezy-looking friend standing by a small cart in a dark hooded cloak.

"Oh, I got it all right . . . here!" The friend snapped a sheet off the cart and pointed to four large jugs. "Never miss an opportunity for a late night of art. The problem is, I haven't found a way into the courtyard yet. We may only be able to graffiti the outside."

The news was too disappointing to believe.

After a quick lap around the villa, everyone confirmed they would have to settle for the outer wall. Nero and the crew took out some brushes and began drawing a crude painting of a man on all fours with his mouth open. They couldn't hold back their snickering as they predictably drew two erect men on both sides of the dude on all fours. The quality of the painting was a little better than stick figures. Nero finished the drawing by captioning the man in the middle as "Piso pleasing the Senate." Without an established street tag, Nero then signed his name at the bottom, taking credit.

The four stepped back and began to admire their work.

"You sure about putting your name on there? Not worried Piso'll get angry?" Senecio asked.

"Futuus no, I'm the godsdamn emperor," Nero replied. "What's he gonna do, stage a coup? He doesn't have it in him."

"Hey, bet I climb that wall and see tha' other side. Don't tell me what I can't do!" Senecio responded to no one's criticism. "I'll find some stuff . . . climb up to on the other side. You see. Can do."

The drunk Senecio was full of wonderful ideas and energy as his wine buzz transitioned from stumbling and useless to fun and a catalyst for a good time. He motioned around as if he was evaluating some impressive equations, then tossed his torch over the other side and stepped back from the wall an estimated four—never mind, not far enough—six feet.

In a quick sprint and a parkour jump off a corner of the wall, Senecio grabbed the top of the wall and pulled himself up, swinging up a leg and straddling both sides. He began offering his hand to everyone for a pull up to the top. Otho took it and began climbing.

After a glance over the wall, Otho noticed an

ablaze gazebo beside Senecio's torch's inconvenient landing zone, comprised of some dry brush.

"Aight, it's time to bounce," Otho said as he jumped down to the street, pulling Senecio, who tumbled and rolled backward.

The two started running.

"I think we just woke up the guards." Otho gasped for air.

The others were soon to follow as they smelled the smoke, saw a glow, and heard the crackle of the burning gazebo.

As a matter of fact, Piso did plot a coup against Nero involving an assassination only to be betrayed from within. While there's no evidence the coup was started by Nero drawing Piso getting sodomized from both ends, angering the senator to such drastic action, there's also no evidence that he didn't.

The four hooligans darted away, led by the delinquently drunk Senecio who didn't have a torch. This worked to his advantage as another fire might push him into felony drunk. Soon enough, Senecio led everyone into an alleyway. After running into the dead end, he paused long enough to catch his breath and collect the dizzying thoughts he would not remember the next day. After everyone caught up with Senecio, Otho felt the excitement peak for the night and decided this was a natural end for the shenanigans.

Leading the street gang out of the alley, Otho's hooded friend peeled off into his own neighborhood, and Senecio passed out somewhere in another dead-end alley once his adrenaline stopped carrying his energy through his drunken stupor.

Otho kneeled to grab Senecio's personal sack of coin. "Better grab this for his own safekeeping," Otho said. "It'll either be me or the thieves anyway," he added before leaving the alley.

Once Otho and Nero made it to a main road, their deep knowledge of the meandering, twisty roads of Rome eventually led their way to Nero's palace.

"Is, uhh, Senecio gonna be alright back there?" Nero snickered.

"Oh, he does this all the time," Otho answered calmly. "He's always fine. He's passed out in stranger places than this and showed up the next day. Just remember to tell him he had a great time when he asks what happened."

"Gotcha, so how often are his nights as memorable as this?" Nero asked with eyes aglow.

"Pretty often. Between me and him, we have a pretty fun time."

"I certainly could use this sort of company these days," Nero added.

"Yeah, how's that?"

"My mom's just a culus, man, and I need to get some friends to get away." Nero began to open up. "She always expects a lot from me, but whenever I want to make my own decisions, she talks all my political advisors out of it, whatever it is. She has way too much influence in my life. I haven't quite found a way of getting rid of her. Like, leave me alone, fine, or let me be emperor, whatever, just pick one . . ."

"Futuus, family can suck sometimes," Otho said, feeling for the guy. "I'm sorry to hear all that. Sucks it's your mom too. That's gotta be weird. It's not like she's your dad though, just tell her what's up, dude."

"I've been trying to stand my ground more with her, but it's hard to assert authority safely," Nero elaborated.

"Safely? What do you mean?"

"It's just rumors around the palace, but we're all pretty sure Mom killed my stepdad when he started seeing what she was up to," Nero answered, being careful about how loud he talked. The two arrived at the palace, and Nero led Otho into his personal playground. "Yeah, follow me, got something to show you, and keep your voice down about my mom."

Nero led Otho through a long hallway and into his personal bath. It was well lit by a line of torches and kept warm by a round-the-clock furnace. The floor of the bath was decorated with an ornate mosaic of a nude man wrestling another, slightly visible through the water.

Nero grabbed a special copper vase from a corner and popped off the lid. The fruity lavender air filled the cozy, humid room. It smelled like a Bed Bath & Beyond or some shop where you buy candles for Mother's Day. They stripped off their clothes, and Nero shut the door. He began rubbing the oil over his acne-speckled, mildly athletic body while making *mmmmmmnn* noises, teasing Otho with the oil's quality.

"I got this oil from an Egyptian merchant, and I've never found anything more soothing than the feel and aroma of this stuff."

Nero dipped his hand in the aromatic oil and lightly sprinkled an expensive mist over Otho's youthfully taut body, one slowly transitioning into a drinking-induced dad bod. Otho then made a high orgasmic sigh as he rubbed the oil in.

"You're going to have to tell me about your dealer so I can get some. I could get some serious business deals done with this stuff," Otho replied before making a much needed segue back to the previous conversation. "So, Agrippina killed Claudius? I heard those rumors, but I didn't believe them."

"Yeah, at least, that's what we all think. So, after Claudius declared me his heir, his friends and advisors started getting concerned," Nero explained. "Mom already was convincing him to do whatever she wanted. She really has a way with men," Nero said with a concerned grimace.

He continued, "A day or so before Claudius kicked the bucket, some servants saw my mom delivering a special bag of mushrooms to the palace kitchen. I don't think they were the fun kind. Supposedly, they were only served to Claudius. Putting two and two together, it's pretty obvious what happened, man."

"Stercus, dude, that's so futuatis up!" Otho replied. "I can't say I'm that surprised given all the rumors going around about her."

"Yeah, this one girl I've been futuendi for a while has been bugging me about how I'm too afraid of my mom and why I won't marry her. She doesn't know the half of it. Mom's a freaky woman," Nero continued. "Now, do not repeat what I'm about to tell you, or I swear to the Gods I'll feed your family to the lions for the next games. It won't even be a main event, just an intermission while the crowd warms up."

"I swear, man, you can trust me," Otho promised.

"Okay," Nero went on. "When I started getting real sick of my mom, especially when I started seeing that girl—Poppaea's her name . . ." Nero paused, thinking about something, feeling for the words. "I started not giving a stercus what she thought. There's not much she can do to me; I'm the emperor now. Once or twice a month, after I get real drunk in the palace, my futuendi Mom tricks me into futuendi her . . ."

"That's futui!"

"Yeah, when I'm drunk and can't control myself."

"Fuuutuus!"

"Five times now," Nero affirmed his story. "I know she's got all the real political influence in Rome and all that, but her days are numbered here."

"Yeah, you gotta get rid of that crazy psycho cunnus."

"I know! Thanks for listening," Nero told Otho. "We'll be doing more of this, I'm sure. Hanging out, that is. I just gotta complain about it, ya know . . ."

The two continued bathing for another hour before retiring for the night. Otho was so excited that he couldn't go to sleep. This was the connection of a lifetime, and someone he could have fun with. Win-win! Otho, with just one night of hot, steamy, very heterosexual bromanship, knew he should go the extra mile to secure Nero's friendship and loyalty. If Nero was an oil nerd, Otho was fixin' to become the president, treasurer, secretary, and the master of ceremonies of the oil fan club.

***

Not even a full day after their first meeting, Otho was leading a blindfolded Nero down a hallway of a local bath.

"I'm very curious now. Not many surprises warrant a blindfold," Nero said, eager with anticipation.

"Oh, you'll just have to judge for yourself in a few moments," Otho answered, guiding Nero towards his own hot and steamy room. Nero felt the humidity increase to 110 percent, which Roman science had yet to discover was impossible. He could taste the delicious surprise waiting for him in the air. Otho just had to remove the blindfold. "Okay, removing in three . . . two . . . one."

Nero's eyes needed no time to adjust to the softly lit room. Beyond one door was a standard hot tub, but unlike most Roman baths, this was far beyond the deluxe model men buy during a mid-life crisis, which only creates relentless nagging from their wives for years. A tub like this would have cost a middle-aged man his marriage and required refinancing of his suburban villa. Not only were there pipes creating a quintessential modern-day hot tub effect, but silver, bronze, and gold pipes pointed inward from all directions within the room above the water, slowly spewing fine oils into the bath. Each pipe of the luxurious, hygienic pipe organ contraption gurgled in different low, spurting tones, creating a euphony of soothing steampunk sounds straight from the little engine that just couldn't even. Some believed they were in A major while others only heard the chords they wanted to hear. Not even Dr. Seuss and

Willy Wonka teamed up could conceive such an elaborately unneeded bath design showcasing both luxury and imagination as did this wealth-gap-induced monstrosity.

Nero was at a loss for words. His hedonistic processing power maxed out due to the stimulus overload. The look of the intricately designed pipes, the aroma caused by the waterfall of fine oils, the feel of the suds slowly falling into the bath, and the water jets within the bath hitting all those special places left Nero in a state of earthly pleasure he had not heretofore dreamed of.

Once the shock and awe had subsided, both Nero and Otho spared no more time in stripping their clothes, tossing them toward the door, and easing into the bubbling suds. Otho had found the absolute jackpot with this one. Ten minutes passed without a single word as time stood still within Rome's premier hot, sudsy pool-oil-pipe-organ contraption fitting of the word thingamajig. Nero looked at Otho, took a deep breath, and forgot what he was about to say as he nodded his head while a jet found another one of those sweet spots.

A few minutes later, Nero had built up enough control over his own pleasure to utter into the water, "This is the steeeercus . . . blrghl blrghl."

Nero struggled to comment before sinking back below the suds into the hot tub, yet again ensconced by earthly delight. After another thirty minutes of their silent, leisurely soak, Nero finally worked up the energy to say something, "Otho, how in the futuus did you find this place?"

"It helps to know people. I still had to pull some favors—I've been meaning to check it out. I figured you liked oils and baths, and I thought you'd enjoy it," Otho humbly responded, eliciting simultaneous laughter from both.

Otho not only pulled favors; he used every connection he could and leveraged a few of his friends' homes without them knowing for access to the hot tub. The collateral on the oil-bath-organ-thing was unfinanceable by Roman insurance standards.

Looking over, Nero held out a fist hanging half a foot above the water. In that moment, Otho knew he had really earned Nero's respect. This was not a light occasion by any means. Otho raised his hand into a fist for Nero to lean over and bump it.

"Listen! I have a plan you may be perfect for," Nero proposed to his best new bud. "I mentioned how I've been seeing that one girl and how I'm married to my cousin, Octavia, that I don't care for."

"Yeah," Otho responded. "You're seeing Poppaea, right? That's kinda an open secret these days."

"I know, but I can't seem to make it happen with my lame mom lording over me right now," the teenager said with much angst. "I've got a plan to do it, but it's gonna take some time, and probably some luck. Just got to get rid of my mom. Apparently, according to her, I have no legitimacy if I'm not married to Octavia or some garbage, according to that witch. Considering she was Claudius's daughter, it does concern me a little bit with the old fogies in the Senate."

Nero paused for a thought. "It's a little hard to get rid of Octavia. Gonna take careful planning if I want to survive. Problem is, Poppaea is pretty futuendi thirsty. I don't think I can keep her available in the meantime."

"Yeah, from what I've heard, she's the sort that gets around," Otho agreed.

"At first, I was like, yeah, that's pretty hot—a lot of threesomes in my future. But she's ambitious, too. and is pushing for marriage and something more permanent. I mean, I don't really care that much, but if I don't figure something out soon, she says she's going to marry someone who can be more committed. Ya know what I mean?" Nero rambled.

"Yeah, they just want to lock you down like that, I know how it is," Otho agreed.

"She could be the key to getting away from my futuendi mom. She's from a rich family, so marrying her will make some political sense. She's not just hot. So, here's what I'm thinking," Nero transitioned to the plan. "You're obviously a man of ambition and can hold on to her. If you marry her now, you can have a fun time and keep her while I find a safe way of getting rid of Octavia."

"Seems like quite a commitment on my end," Otho noted.

"Yeah, but dude," Nero exclaimed, drawing Otho in, "she's like crazy hot. I'm almost doing you a favor here. I don't really mind her seeing other guys and stuff, it's kind of more fun that way. We can even enjoy her together, if you know what I mean. Besides, I'll be sure to take care of you in the meantime."

"Okay, okay, okay . . ." Otho quickly agreed to the plan he was hoping would solidify his new powerful connection. "I'll do it. I'll marry your hot mistress and have totally awesome sex while you get rid of your current wife. You've convinced me."

"So . . ." Nero added after Otho agreed to the

proposal. "There's another problem. Poppaea's already married, so we need to find some way to get her to divorce her current husband."

"Yeah . . . Wait, you said you were worried about her getting married?"

"You can hardly call it a marriage. Politically speaking, he's on the way out. Almost no influence, so absolutely no chance he can hold on to a woman like her," he explained.

"Okay . . ." Otho responded skeptically. "That's still a little bit more complicated. Who is it?"

"He's Rufrius Crispinus, the head of the Praetorian Guard," Nero said with a wince.

Otho raised an eyebrow at the surprise of such an ambitious plan. "Well, he was the head of the Praetorians, so it shouldn't be too hard. The way I hear it, they've never had too much of a love life either."

"That's not too hard then, especially if Poppaea's the go-getting type. Won't want to stay with someone who's out of a job," Otho speculated.

The two shook hands, and Otho had not only officially become Nero's closest friend, but an integral part of his five-year life plan. Otho was going to marry Poppaea and enjoy some pretty awesome sex. Historians couldn't agree on much regarding Poppaea, but they all agreed that she was a ten out of ten in the looks department.

2 THE DINNER PARTY

One night in Rome, Nero and Otho decided to throw a dinner party. They had been scheming to abduct Poppaea from her eleven-year loveless marriage and, on empty stomachs, determined that a classic, Roman show-off-your-wealth dinner party was the best way to do it. When a house slave dropped a plate of food and took an extra hour to fix a dish of olives and boiled eggs, hunger set in, and the dinner party was the only thing on their minds. They meticulously laid out their plan with careful guest placement.

Despite the amount of work that went into crafting the seating list, there was an unexpected dinner guest Nero couldn't refuse. Agrippina wasn't even supposed to be in town that day. Despite Nero's attempts to push his meddling mother out of his life by kicking her out of the palace and hiring men to harass her with catcalls and frivolous lawsuits, she still seemed to show up just in time to kill his vibe. Nero couldn't stand her constant nagging about how to be a better emperor. What did she know about being the emperor? She was only married to one and ruled behind the scenes. The eighteen-year-old Nero, of course, thought he knew better than his mom because he was not only the actual emperor, but also a more stable and benevolent leader than his mom. At least, so he thought.

Nero and Agrippina had a super weird relationship. Buckle up for some classic Hapsburg-level royal incest. Agrippina was a daughter of the Julio-Claudian dynasty by means of Agrippina the Elder and Germanicus. They were politically influential in Rome until their son, Agrippina the Younger's brother, Caligula, got super paranoid and executed/murdered most of his own family to prevent anyone with hereditary legitimacy from taking the throne. The elder Agrippina told the younger that it would always be her destiny to take back the throne for their line of Julio-Claudians. Germanicus and Agrippina the Younger did the dirty deed and had Nero during their Caligula-caused political exile. When Caligula died and Claudius took power, most of the Julio-Claudians were able to reenter the political elite of Rome. Agrippina the Younger found a perfect opportunity to get close with her good ol' Uncle Claudius, the new emperor. She stayed away from being too influential until her husband died, and then Claudius's wife died too.

Agrippina, despite being independently wealthy at the time, figured she could use a life upgrade and seduced her Uncle Claudius into marriage. After some significant political maneuvering, Agrippina gained power in Rome through Claudius and allowed her son, Nero, to be the heir to the throne over Claudius's blood son, Brittanicus, because Nero was older than Brittanicus by a few years. The extra heir to the throne made Claudius seemingly more invulnerable to assassins, so it appeared to be a win-win for him. However, Claudius saw the power-hungry machinations of Agrippina and became suspicious of her ambitions for securing her hold on the throne. Once Agrippina became aware of Claudius's suspicions, she *allegedly* fed her uncle-husband some poison mushrooms and committed uncle-husbandcide.

With Claudius out of the picture, the teenager Nero became the emperor, with Agrippina the Younger ruling the empire through parental lectures and the Senate from behind a curtain. Agrippina the Elder would be proud. Unfortunately for Agrippina the Younger, she didn't have as much control over her own son as she thought. While she was able to get her son to marry her niece/daughter-in-law, Octavia, Nero was not sexually happy in a marriage with his cousin/wife/sister-in-law. Seneca the Elder, a mentor, proposed that Nero should funnel his hormone-driven sexual energy toward someone else. Nero chose a freed woman, Claudia Acte, for his wild sexual exploits. When Nero began spending all his energy on Claudia and not Octavia to make future little son/nephew/cousins to rule Rome, Agrippina became disheartened at Nero's interest in a lower-class woman and not his cousin/wife/sister-in-law. Valuing family line and political legitimacy over not enjoying incest and possibly more carnal reasons, Agrippina lectured the young Nero on how involving himself with an ex-slave was political suicide. This is where the rift in their mother/mother-in-law/aunt–son/son-in-law/nephew relationship began. In case you're wondering if incest was more normal during Roman society, it wasn't, except for the Julio-Claudians.

Nero reportedly had a close relationship with his mother. Some would say the relationship was a little too close. Not only was she lording over his political policies and his propensity for spending the imperial treasury, but she was also dictating his sex life. Normally, when a man becomes an adult, he would move out of his parents' house. But in the case of Nero and Agrippina, that house was the imperial palace, so Nero kicked his mom out of the palace. To further drive his mom away from meddling in his professional and social bizness, Nero paid Roman citizens a pretty penny to aggressively catcall her in the city of Rome. If that wasn't enough, he also commissioned law-savvy citizens to berate Agrippina with frivolous lawsuits, driving his mom further away from the political center of the empire and his life. Agrippina's plan to secure power and control Rome through her son turned out to be fundamentally flawed. Despite Nero's attempts to drive away his mother, she still popped in for short meetings. Typically, unannounced.

A cold wind blew from the east wing. "Nero, what is wrong with you?" Agrippina stormed into the palace dining room. "I didn't risk my life giving birth and spend the better part of seventeen years raising you—"

"Seventeen, Mother," Nero corrected.

"Seventeen years raising you to throw a dinner party with these subpar recliners, this decade-old carpet, or these low-class plates." Agrippina began listing Nero's party planning shortcomings. Before a deep exhale to catch her breath, Agrippina snatched an empty chalice and began violently waving it, her overly bangled wrists a-clanking, signaling to the nearest slave that a fill-up was desperately needed. "Do not tell me you were planning on using these candles. They're not even scented!"

"No one's going to care, mom." Nero attempted to counter her unwanted helicopter parenting. "Just chill out and wait for the party. I have it under control. You don't even need to be here."

"Not be here!" She half-laughed in frightened surprise. "This better not be like the time you were thirteen and wanted to throw your own Floralia celebration. I still can't believe you picked out flowers that wilted halfway through the festivities." Agrippina belittled Nero as a slave filled her glass. "I have known you your whole life, and I know how much you need me to not screw this up. I don't care how ready you think you are; I'm going to check in on the kitchen to see what you chose for food."

Just as wild and fast as she arrived and ruined everyone's mood, Hurricane Agrippina stormed off to go harass the kitchen staff.

"Dude, this screws up the whole plan! How are we going to make a positive impression on Poppaea when your mom's here?" Otho panicked.

"This actually may be a blessing in disguise," Nero answered while thoughtfully scratching his neckbeard (and avoiding picking at any new acne). "You know who my mom really hates . . . and who hates my mom? Rufrius."

"Poppaea's husband? Why?" Otho inquired.

"So, Rufrius *was* the leader of the Praetorian Guard . . ." Nero emphasized the "was" with obvious insinuation, but it wasn't clear enough for Otho. "Rufrius was the leader under Claudius until Agrippina wanted someone from her bodyguards she trusted more. For some reason, she's always kinda hated him, so she got him fired. Rufrius has never forgiven her. As soon as he shows up, they'll be at each other's throats, giving you a chance to chat up Poppaea."

"Oh, yeah, dude," Otho said, understanding the stercus-storm Rufrius was in for tonight. "If I knew that, we would have invited your mom earlier."

Calm returned briefly before yelling echoed through the hallways—Agrippina's sharp criticisms of the kitchen staff's grilled chicken and hors d'oeuvre pairing choices. "Well . . ." Nero interjected amid her grating micromanaging, "even then I wouldn't have intervened because there are trade-offs."

Despite despising his mother's helicopter parenting, Nero could have used it. Although his goals were clear, his dinner party would have been a mess. In the gap between Claudius and Nero's slightly more adult reign, Agrippina proved capable of ruling the empire from behind the scenes. Though she married her way into power and allegedly killed her husband/uncle with mushrooms, she was a competent leader.

With Agrippina's unwanted help, Nero's scheming dinner party was about to become a successful show of power, aiming to lure Poppaea from Rufrius's waning influence. The food, decor, and atmosphere were *divine*. Nero didn't plan a full palace show of luxury, just a kickback that would be a good time.

The guests were met by a line of twenty

servants greeting them before entering a warm environment of aromatic candles illuminating endless wall frescos and intricate mosaics. Now, it was time to follow through on their plan—with one extra diversion.

"Okay, so the plan is," Otho rehearsed, "I'll be seated next to Poppaea and her soon-to-be-distracted husband. I'll then have enough time to seduce her with my wealth and political influence. Next, Rufrius's sabotaged recliner will collapse. Being a gentleman, Rufrius would offer Poppaea the intact recliner. A servant will then 'accidentally' spill wine on Rufrius's tunic." Otho took a breath. "The slave will insist on taking him to get a new tunic, leading him all over the palace, giving me plenty of time to display my superior Big Dagger Energy."

"Yup, all set up," Nero said. "Also . . . I found a way to make you super interesting and alluring. Surrounding you will be boring political wannabees. They'll be so dull that you'll be the only person Poppaea would even consider interacting with. I hired actors to play the boring politicians and the slave for the Rufrius distraction plan. Next to me will be young sycophants laughing at my jokes and hanging off my every word: also actors. They wanted the exposure, so I didn't have to pay them. Just don't let them talk to the boring politician actors because they are getting paid."

It was go time. The guests filed into the dining room, chatting through the luxuriously decorated hallways of the imperial palace. Conversations buzzed about the beautiful artwork strategically positioned according to Agrippina's orders. It was a successful show of power to Poppaea, Rufrius, and a bunch of actors.

The chitter-chatter was interrupted by Nero's announcement: "Welcome to the dinner party! Please, relax and take to your recliners."

To avoid giving away the plan to the actual guests, the actors were instructed to sit so Poppaea and Rufrius couldn't sit close to Nero, leaving one open seat near Poppaea for Otho. Despite vague instructions, it almost fell apart. No one knew where to sit, leading to a game of musical chairs.

Fumbling about, the actors hesitated, waiting to see where everyone else sat. Once Nero sat down, the sycophants filled in around him. Not knowing who else was a sycophant, they fought over seats, counteracting the boring politician actors who struggled to decide where to sit. One actor ended up on the wrong side of the table, resulting in forced cross-table conversations and awkwardly missed opportunities to laugh at Nero's jokes. By sheer dumb luck, they left an open seat for Otho next to Poppaea, so it wasn't a complete wash.

Agrippina found herself among the boring politicians but across the table from Rufrius. This didn't stop her from seeing him and verbally assaulting him for his audacious attempt at regaining imperial influence.

"Who the futuus invited you?" Agrippina questioned Rufrius without any polite inhibitions. She was already four wines in at the beginning of the dinner and was waving her chalice around, splattering nearby partygoers. "I thought I got rid of you. Think you can have an in with my son while I'm not involved? Well, mister, think again."

"Yes, your son invited me and my beautiful

wife. What are you gonna do about it?" Rufrius sparred.

Meanwhile, the paid actors, uninformed of the new plan with Rufrius, struggled to determine how to react to the unfolding drama. At first, they kept to themselves and tried to ignore the verbal lashings until it was revealed that no one removed the faulty recliner or updated the wine-spilling actor on the change of plans. Agrippina had the recliner. She fell and spilled wine on herself before more wine was spilled on her by the servant actor. With no planned execution on seating, there was no telling who would have gotten the rigged recliner.

Agrippina stood up and shoved the acting slave against the wall. "What the futuus do you think you're doing being so clumsy, and who let me sit in a faulty recliner?" Agrippina berated the disguised thespian. "I know it was you. I watched you set up the furniture tonight. A slave like you belongs in the galley where you can't futuisti up this badly!"

"You don't understand, ma'am," the slave replied. "I'm an actor! I'm not really a slave."

"Ha! I've never heard that one before," Agrippina scoffed. "Nero, what's wrong with this palace slave?"

"He's always been trouble," Nero said, maintaining character. "I had no idea he was delusional too. A slave like this certainly belongs at the bottom of a trireme."

"Guards!" Agrippina shrieked, and two Praetorians stepped into the room. "See to it that this slave is delivered to the docks to be sold into his new life. Keep the change."

Two heavy-set guards took the slave

impersonator away to a new life of permanent method acting. Agrippina, now doubly red-wine stained, took her primal energy and resumed yelling at that snake in the grass, Rufrius. With the heightened energy of the room and Agrippina now standing in a dominant posture, Rufrius had no choice but to stand and match her aggression. The two political outcasts burst from the table and battled it out into the hallway.

"So anyway . . . a man, standing before a censor, is about to testify whether he has a wife," Nero interrupted the dinner party's silence as everyone eavesdropped on the loud argument diminishing down the hallway. "The censor asks: do you have, in all your honesty, a wife?" After a quick pause where one sycophant actor laughed too early, Nero delivered the punch line, "The man replied: I surely do, but not in all my honesty." The sycophants lost their stercus, the boring actors golf clapped, and Poppaea snickered while Otho had next to no reaction to the joke he had heard a half dozen times[3]. Everyone uses that joke; it's overdone and, for the English speakers, a pun on honesty and wife.

The event finally became a proper dinner party. Nero began entertaining his guests. While his attention was primarily directed toward the sycophants, the boring politician actors kept to themselves and discussed made-up tax procedures because that's what they imagined politicians talked about.

It was up to Otho to start the conversation with

---

[3] This joke has been overused for centuries and is a play on the phrase often used in oaths 'in all honesty' which can also be understood as 'to your liking'. It was probably funny for a few years but not anymore.

Poppaea. Normally quite charming, Otho had not realized how attractive Poppaea actually was, and it was totally throwing off his game. She had all the right stuff in all the right places, and you could tell she knew it. His nervousness had been building throughout the beginning of the dinner party. While most were transfixed by the creatively unique insults Agrippina was throwing at Rufrius down the hall, Otho's heartbeat steadily increased as he tried to think of a clever opening. As the disasters began to settle down, he had to think of something. The longer he waited, the weirder it would be.

"So, guess I'll be your date with your husband out of the picture," Otho jumped feet first into the plan with his choice of opener.

Poppaea, between processing the recent events and the lingering weird vibe in the room, noticed Otho and his strange comment. Many of the actors found themselves unintentionally rudely staring at Poppaea while trying to refocus on their paid roles as sycophants. Used to receiving disproportionate attention at social gatherings, Poppaea chose a tenuous response, "I guess . . ."

What the futuus did that mean? Otho thought. Poppaea grabbed a bite of bread and an olive, took a swig of wine, and blankly stared at the other end of the table. Without a smartphone equipped with a freemium game, this was the most she could do to express her desire to be left alone and wait out the party. Otho needed to collect himself and think of something clever to say. Thinking of a joke that killed the other day at the bathhouse, Otho turned his head to Poppaea and opened his mouth before losing the courage and closing it again. *No, there's no way she'd get that reference; I forgot it was an inside joke. Oh shoot, I'm still staring! Look away, Otho, look away! Damn, she's hot.* Poppaea was the only girl, and the vibe couldn't be worse for Otho.

Maybe I could try something casual, Otho thought. He went for something less risky: "The wine's pretty good, right?"

"Yeah . . ." Poppaea articulately responded.

"I really just love these dry reds we've been purchasing this year. It's been a really great season. This particular wine comes from Pompeii; that's where the best wine comes from. Ever been?" Otho elaborated.

"I've spent some time there." Poppaea mustered a full sentence in the mostly one-way conversation while avoiding eye contact with Otho or, worse, the strangers around her.

"I started going there a few years ago regularly for wine tasting parties. I have a very sophisticated palate," Otho bragged.

"Oh . . . I grew up there. Those places are tourist traps," Poppaea responded, now with two sentences. Despite her tone, Otho was making some progress.

"Oh, you must be sick of those places," he said, recovering. Now that he knew Poppaea grew up in Pompeii, Otho became careful to stop mentioning the city and looking foolish. He had never actually been there but wanted her to think he could afford it. From now on, Otho's main strategy would be his go-to for any social situation: flaunt wealthiness. Without Instagram to post pictures of himself leaning on sports cars, eating at fancy restaurants, or inside luxurious palaces on expensive vacations, Otho had to rely on bragging.

"I can see that. Usually, I spend more time in my other summer home up north near the mountains," Otho flaunted another luxury.

"That must be a beautiful place to spend a summer." Poppaea even smirked, giving Otho a break from carrying the conversation. "I wouldn't mind taking a trip up north to see the mountains."

"So, what was going on with your husband there? That was a pretty wild scene," Otho said, letting his curiosity get the better of him.

"Soooooo . . . Agrippina and Rufrius have never gotten along. It started with an argument years ago and spiraled until Rufrius vowed to get rid of her in this palace. He says she's a security risk or something," Poppaea explained, feeling more comfortable now. She knew Otho wasn't just a dirty commoner trying to deflower her. At worst, he was a wealthy commoner trying to deflower her. "I don't know why he thinks that, but he believes Agrippina killed people. A lot of people think she killed Claudius, but Rufrius always rants about some Julian hit squad conspiracy, taking out respectable citizens and covering it up. I'm just sick of hearing about it! I thought the conspiracy theories were credible until they hyped up the focaccia-gate conspiracy. I was lost at that one. I mean, like what? There's absolutely no evidence, and it's absolutely ridiculous. At this point, just move on; you won't be able to prove anything."

"I don't even remember what focaccia-gate was all about," Otho inquired. "I remember hearing a lot about it and how people had strong opinions, but I never actually knew what it was about."

"Well, let me tell you, I have some really

strong opinions that it was complete and utter bull stercus. Anyway, there was this focaccia restaurant in Rome and in the basement, supposedly . . ." Poppaea began but was interrupted by a strange scene. "Isn't that . . . ?" she said, pointing at a girl who looked like a younger Agrippina. From her hair, face, and legs, she was Agrippina's doppelganger but with more youthful skin. By the way the woman stood and interacted with Nero, you could tell it wasn't her. Agrippina's crossed arms, jerky gesticulations, and accidental wine spills were replaced with this other woman's meek shrugs, soft facial expressions, and calming aura. Agrippina didn't have any rebellious daughters, so there was no chance of a *Freaky Friday* scenario.

The doppelganger whispered something into Nero's ear, to which he smirked, whispered a few presumably juicy sentences back, and slapped her on the culus. The sycophant actors played their roles too well to point out how creepy the situation was. Instead, Nero received tacit nods followed by vocalized "nice" responses. The boring politician actors just appeared confused, realizing ogling at such juicy gossip would discredit their roles as total squares. Otho, on the other hand, was ready to pocket the occasion for later. *Boy, is that gonna be irreplaceable trash talk. Nero is never gonna live this one down*, Otho thought.

"Jesus Christ, is this family futuendi weird or what," Poppaea said, both of them staring with gaping jaws.

"Jesus who?" Otho anachronistically questioned.

"Some guy that new cult from Judaea talks

about all the time. I hang out with a bunch of Jews, so he comes up a lot. I'm not sure why, but it just rolls off the tongue," Poppaea explained. "Jesus Christ . . ." she said with a flourish.

"Yeah, it kinda does," Otho agreed. "I may be stealing that. I hope you don't mind."

"Oh, not at all. I stole it from someone else. The phrase has been catching on fast."

"Yeah, I've gotten pretty close with Nero. We're kinda bros," Otho preempted his Julian family credibility while softly pounding his chest a couple of times. "I've never hung out with him without him trash-talking his mom at one point or another. But, I mean, he's a teenager, so I thought it was just that." Otho paused and looked around. "This is the first time I've met his mom, and she is something else," he said earnestly.

"It's a weird relationship. Trust me, I've heard all about it from Rufrius. Yeah, crazy he's got all that power and money, probably doesn't even know what to do with it," Poppaea said. "And you're friends with him?"

"Yeah, I'm basically the head of his entourage right now," Otho reassured Poppaea. "I'm pretty much the closest influence on the most powerful man in Rome right here." Otho gave two thumbs up to himself.

"Wow, so you're, like, kinda important then . . ." Poppaea spoke in an Apennine Valley–girl accent. Upon the revelation that Otho was not only rich but influential, Poppaea did the only thing she could. She took her hand off her wine glass, reached over to Otho and, knowing her own effect on men, placed it on Otho's mid-thigh—not his lower thigh, nor his upper thigh (which have been a bit too aggressive), but mid-thigh—showing the most interest she could have ever expressed in this one moment without causing a noticeable erection but only a modicum of chubbing. It wasn't accidental; she touched his mid-thigh with full intent and knowledge of the implications.

It was practically official now. Poppaea divorced the old deadbeat Rufrius and started shacking up with Otho—she just needed to do the paperwork. They were a couple now, essentially the moment she touched Otho's thigh.

Otho, trying to maintain his success of the night, tried as hard as he could to contain himself. Not only was she hot and talking to him, but she was also interested. Feeling Poppaea's hand on his mid-thigh and looking over to her, Otho could only imagine the wonderfully dirty, sexy things he was about to experience. He had been putting his time in with old cougars to enter upper society, and now he got to play the power game, all while knocking boots with the most beautiful girl he'd ever met. Despite Poppaea's careful hand placement, Otho still got an erection lasting longer than four hours.

3 MILK BATHS

"Sooooooo . . . how did it go?" Nero asked, causing an echo within the organ bath.

The elaborate bath arrangement Otho had discovered was so beloved by Nero that the contraption had been recreated and improved within the palace. Many parties ended in the bath complex Nero had created, but only the elite could ever enter the inner sanctum of the oil-spewing bath pipe organ. The sauna sanctum never failed to impress newcomers.

For Nero and Otho, however, any other bath would always feel lacking. Whenever they ended up in a lesser bath at a friend or colleague's place, they would complain about how it wasn't as good. The two hedonists were always left wanting.

"I'm still having trouble maintaining my cool around her," Otho replied. "Just when I think I'm used to her sexiness, she finds some unexpected new way to poke me under a table, suggestively chew on some food, or just give me those damn eyes. I'm having trouble hiding my own excitement."

"Sounds like a real problem ya got there," Nero said with a forced grin.

"Oh, shut the futuus up," Otho said. "Anyway, thanks for letting me and Poppaea stay at the palace. It's been really annoying how long it's been taking for the workmen to finish the renovations at my place."

"Oh, it's no problem at all," Nero accepted Otho's gratitude. "It works in my favor with Poppaea so close. Y'all can stay as long as ya want. You're a real brother helpin' me out here. Don't feel like you owe me anything."

A month after the dinner party, Poppaea had split up with Rufrius and hastily married Otho. Their young love had become the talk of the town, and their fiery honeymoon period in Poppaea's hometown of Pompeii was a subject of gossip. Many said that you could feel their lovemaking shake the entire city. At least, that's what Otho told everyone. The rumblings were in no way caused by tremors indicating volcanic activity of a soon-to-erupt volcano. Nope, just really great sex.

Upon their return to Rome, Otho had to renovate his home in the capital. It was a real bachelor pad, and he had to get rid of all his awesome man cave stuff to make way for Poppaea's womanly needs—or at least, that's what he told everyone.

In the meantime, the young couple stayed at Nero's palace. Nero and Otho were having a good time bro-ing out more often, so there were no complaints. Poppaea enjoyed the decadence and proximity to power. Nero took advantage of how easy it was to show off his power and personally perceived sexiness in front of Poppaea. He was doing a lot more self-flattering arm stretches—the ones where he'd stretch up, lean back, suck in his gut, and flex his arms all at once. Otho, it turned out, was not a fan of that.

"I can't thank ya enough," Otho continued. "I'm young; it's not a big deal. It's just a lot of construction, adding the new wing and extra gardens. Poppaea's a delicate flower. Especially after taking her from Rufrius's pad, I couldn't subject her to all that commotion on a daily basis."

"It has been taking a long time; that's gotta get old," Nero replied. "What contractors are you using?"

"Oh, some people a close friend recommended," Otho answered vaguely. "I've used them before—no problem. I just don't think they've ever tackled something so luxurious before. I may have to start using new people for the next addition. I can't get rid of them now; I've already paid them."

"Sunk cost fallacy."

"What's that?"

"I heard it one time from some nerd; it's what you're doing," Nero explained.

"Ah, sounds bad."

"Well, if they keep taking their sweet-culus time, let me know," Nero said. "Don't ever think I'm trying to get rid of ya, but there's only so much customer loyalty a man can have."

Only one other member of the palace was a regular of the bath's inner sanctum, and without much warning, there she was.

"You guys having a good soak without me?" Poppaea announced herself.

Women were not typically invited to the baths, let alone the inner sanctum, but Poppaea did what

Poppaea wanted, and no one questioned her place.

"Yeah . . . uhhh . . . sure, hop on in," Otho invited her, yanking on a cord to turn on the turbojets to hide his excitement with the gurgling.

"Why do you always turn on the jets when your wife arrives?" Nero questioned.

"Hope I'm not interrupting anything important," Poppaea said, disrobing and sitting between the two men.

Otho didn't have a good comeback to Nero's question he hadn't already used, so he had to dig for one he had been saving. "So, what's the deal with that servant that looks like your mom?"

"Cornelia is a fine servant, and I have no idea what you're talking about," Nero answered.

"I really love what y'all have done with the place, but I can't wait until I get my milk baths like I've been asking for," Poppaea said, looking at Otho wantonly.

"I don't even know why you want those milk baths; they sound ridiculous," Otho said while rubbing into one of his five pleasure pipes spewing half of his daily recommended essential oils. "It won't be long before you'll have your bath with all the milk you want."

"You said that a month ago," Poppaea said, questioning Otho's unanswered promise. "I need my milk baths, or my skin won't be as wonderfully youthful, clear, and smooth. Don't you love my skin and want it to stay this silky smooth forever?" Poppaea asked, raising her leg in front of Otho's face.

"Could you please not do that here," Otho asked, holding back oh so many desires.

"Why? Nero loves to watch, and you love my

legs . . ." Poppaea answered, switching legs, causing Nero to develop a steady nosebleed. "Why don't you just relax and enjoy them?"

Otho was already on the brink of losing control in front of Nero and didn't want to do anything sexual in front of his bestie. Nero was always a fan, but it was a little too weird for Otho. At least, it was weird with Poppaea.

Otho had to leave the room. He quickly pulled himself out of the bath and threw on his robe faster than anyone could look. "I gotta go take care of some, uh, business stuff."

"What business stuff?" Nero said.

"It's after dark. Come back, honey," Poppaea called.

"BUSINESS, woman!"

He retreated from the bath, leaving Nero and Poppaea alone. Even after a month of living in the palace, this was the first time Nero and Poppaea were hanging out without Otho. They had spent plenty of nights drinking, bathing, partying, participating in festive orgies, abusing servants, and generally enjoying being rich together, but this was the first time Otho was not in the picture. You'd think after how wild it got in the last orgy when they brought out the dice and the sea slugs, the two would be familiar with each other. But they weren't.

Nah, that's stupid. She'll think I'm an idiot, or sexist, or too violent, or have an unnatural hatred of Egyptians. I'll settle on something about those milk baths. I have no idea what those are and am legitimately curious. Also, she seems to care a lot. This could be a good opener.

"So . . . milk baths?" Nero asked, overthinking

his question to break the silence.

Poppaea made no effort to think of an opener, not because she didn't like Nero or wasn't clever or interesting, but because she knew it didn't matter. Luckily for the two, the man with the oily, sudsy neckbeard thought of something. It only took fifteen minutes while he stopped his nosebleed from making too much of a mess. Poppaea wasn't a servant girl; she wasn't poor either, not even middle class. Even better, she wasn't a relative. Coming from an upper-class family in Rome, Nero wasn't too sure how to approach her without being stupid, creepy, or weird. A man could have all the power in Rome, but even that couldn't armor his ego against the gaze of such a beautiful woman. Maybe if he was in his mid-twenties, he could fully utilize the power of his status.

"Yeah, I was talking to this priestess, and she was telling me about it," Poppaea replied. "She was in her sixties, but her skin was flawless! I asked her what her secret was, and I couldn't believe it. You won't believe it either; it's wild! She said if you wanted to look young forever, you had to bathe in milk. I've been around for a while, I know a lot of people who take this stuff seriously, and I've never even heard of such a thing. I was like, please tell me more! Apparently, Cleopatra took regular milk baths. If they're good enough for that sexy queen, they're good enough for me. I know it seems silly, but that woman, just wow, they must work. She got with two emperors!"

"Huh . . . fair enough," Nero replied. "If there's any way we can keep you looking the way you do, I'll see to it that the servants here arrange a bath for ya whenever ya want."

"Thank you for the compliment and the offer, wow, thanks!" Poppaea said, scooting closer to Nero within the hot tub. With so many oil horns jutting out in every which way, her scooting wasn't as smooth as she liked and involved some ducking and weaving. After much effort through sloshing, oily water slightly stained from Nero's nosebleed, she worked her way next to him.

"You're a really nice friend to have, ya know that?" Poppaea said, staring into his eyes and twirling her oily, wet hair with her index finger.

"You could say I'm kinda in charge here," Nero replied.

"I do love having powerful friends treating me to nice things," Poppaea elaborated. "My last husband was able to for a while . . . but when he lost his job, I had to go back to Pompeii and treat myself. That's no way a woman should have to live. Look at me now, in a . . . wait, what do you call this thing?"

"We're still debating on the name," Nero replied. "Otho is pushing for the Oilatorium, but I like the Hot Steamy Dream Boogaloo. I would just go with that, but I'm undecided, mostly because I couldn't get anyone to carve that whole name over the entrance. Too many words, all the craftsmen say."

"Well, whatever it is, it's really something, and I do appreciate you providing so much for me and Otho," Poppaea said, trying to get back to her point. "I'd love to return the favor, I'm just not sure how."

That's when everything in Nero's head clicked. Normally, by this point in a conversation with a woman, Nero would already be taking the express highway to poundtown, but the combination of Poppaea's beauty and the amount of planning that went into the moment had him second-guessing. Worried about scaring her off, Nero reached up and wrapped his arm around her.

Poppaea, losing patience, promptly placed his palm on her tit. She didn't have time for that tame stuff. Moving her hips over Nero, well, that was it. They started humping. Poppaea at least had some of the sturdier pipes to maintain her balance during the jerky moments, whipping the Oilatorium into a frenzy. The pipes buckled half an inch, and she moved her hands to his shoulders. Poppaea stared blankly at Nero's forehead while maintaining a passable smile. Nero, on the other hand, was staring blankly at Poppaea's rockin' boobs with his mouth slightly ajar. He wasn't thinking about much more than that. Nero moaned and started saying, "Oh gosh, oh gosh, oh gosh" to the sound of water splashing on and off the surrounding tile bath and a silent Poppaea.

Nero slipped into the water, and Poppaea went back to grabbing the pipes. After making waves in the hot tub for about a minute or two, Nero was done in the normal amount of time it takes teenagers. Poppaea then moved aside and stopped thanking Nero in her special way. Sitting down beside Nero and breathing a little heavier, the water's oscillations slowly diminished until any evidence was masked by the rolling bubbles of the gurgling pipes.

"That was amazing," Nero said over the wheezing pipes, much sooner than Poppaea anticipated.

"Not what I was expecting tonight, but I'd welcome it any time." Nero slow-clapped , but with him, it could have been for his own performance.

"You're kinda in charge, like you said, so I

didn't have much choice," Poppaea said. "Why only kinda in charge? Why not totally in charge? What's that about your mom?" she asked derisively.

"I'm in the process of doing something about that, actually," Nero explained. "It's just too tricky with my mom. I've been trying to get rid of her, but she has too much power in this city. She's killed more men who got in her way than disease this year. Allegedly, she's killed more men. I can never seem to prove it, but she's pretty dangerous . . . that cunnus." Poppaea poked a nerve with that question.

"She is a real cunnus. I've heard a lot about that," Poppaea agreed. "Such a shame you can't just permanently get rid of her somehow. It would open a whole world of possibilities with her out of the way. She's only your mom. Can't be that hard, right?"

"She just ruins everything," Nero kept complaining. "The only reason I can't enjoy myself all the time is her constant nagging about running the country or whatever. Like there's more to life than politics and money. That's what nerdy slaves and senators are for. Don't even get me started on Octavia."

"I wasn't planning on it."

"That girl just acts like she deserves everything, and she's not even that good looking." Nero's rant could not be stopped. Poppaea had reached the point of no return. "I mean, I deserve a woman like you, not Octavia. She'd never hang out in here and do fun stuff like this."

"Yeah, it's a real shame you aren't in control of your own life with your mom involved," Poppaea said. "I'd drop Otho and marry you in a heartbeat if I could, but I guess that will never happen with your mom in the picture."

With Nero now in deep thought, Poppaea felt a natural conclusion to the evening and retired. Wiping off with a cloth and putting her chiton on, she said, "Say hi to Octavia for me," on her way out.

Nero was left alone in his refractory period in the Oilatorium. Numb to any more pleasure for the night, he began to come down from the apex of his evening. In his daze, he had a lot to think about while his skin pruned and his silent thoughts rebounded against the vaulted ceiling of the Oilatorium.

We're going with Hot Steamy Dream Boogaloo, he concluded . . . among other things.

Nero continued to meditate on what his life could be like without Agrippina throughout the next day. He was uncharacteristically pensive during his daily routines and social interactions, speaking only a few sentences to his friends and servants, who assumed he had a hangover. With Otho's help, Nero's mood would soon be lifted as the evening approached with liquid spirits and a fun vibe.

As the day neared sunset, the party crew filed into the palace as they did most nights. A troupe of actors—minus the one sent to the galleys the night before—a group of musicians, some socialites, athletes, and, of course, a bunch of slinky women and hot studs arrived. With Otho at the head of Nero's entourage, the palace parties had reached new levels of general shenanigans. Seeing his friend in a depressed state, Otho made sure Nero always had some wine in hand among other distractions.

"You want to participate or what?" Otho asked, replacing yet another glass in Nero's hand.

"Usually, probably, yes. What is it?" Nero

asked, getting out of his head.

Otho began pulling the sloppy and raging Nero from his funk as he guided him to a long hall where loud jeering echoed from the other end. A group of young women and men were fighting over a three-foot bow at the entrance. One man shoved another aside and began aiming.

"What is this new game here? I want to play," Nero said, entering the fray of upper-class delinquents. "How does this work?"

"It's basically exactly what it looks like," Otho answered.

What it looked like was a drunken archer aiming a fully drawn arrow at a green vase on top of the head of a slave ten yards down the hallway. There were some splotches of red on the ground and wall that looked too dark to be wine.

The archer wobbled, took a breath, held steady, then expertly shot his arrow through the vase, shattering it into a hundred pieces and making a satisfying sound. The slave made a different sort of satisfied sound. Cheers abounded.

"Okay, it's my turn," Nero shouted, downing the rest of his wine before snatching the bow from the archer and drawing a new arrow from a group stashed in another vase. The slave stood tall and placed another vase on his head with a trembling hand. Nero held his draw, wavering from one direction to another as his empty cup toppled to the floor, rolling to his right. Closing one eye, Nero dialed in on his target before letting loose his arrow directly into the slave's right shoulder. Writhing in pain, the slave hunched over, dropping the vase to the ground. Eyeing his shot, Nero handed the bow back to the original contestant. "I don't see why this game is that hard. That slave is a huge target from this distance. Better luck with your next shot."

Nervous silence turned into sycophantic laughter as Nero walked back into the main room of the party, regaining positive vibes from his win. Dodging a poet puking next to the door and a gladiator chugging wine while doing a handstand over a topless girl catching the spilled wine off the man's chin, Nero and Otho rejoined the main party.

"Finally, there's the Nero I know," Otho welcomed him back to the land of spoiled rich people. "What's up, dude? You've been in a mood."

"I fucked Poppaea last night after you left," Nero blurted out. "It was awesome. She orgasmed like four times. Probably should have the Hot Steamy Dream Boogaloo cleaned before we go back in tonight. She was so goddamn sexy I really don't know how you focus on anything else with her around."

"First off, nice," Otho replied to the news, swallowing some feelings. "Second off, I still think we should call it the Oilatorium. That name is way catchier. Hot Steamy Dream Boogaloo is way too much of a mouthful."

Nero giggled. "Mouthful."

"Anyhow, I imagined it would only be a matter of time. Is that why you've been acting weird today?"

"Well," Nero took a breath. "It wasn't as much the sex as much as it was me realizing I haven't figured out how to kill Agrippina yet."

"Jesus Christ, I thought you just wanted to get rid of her. Are those lawyers not bothering her enough?" Otho replied. "I didn't know you were planning on killing her."

"Yeah—wait," Nero interrupted himself, "Jesus who?"

"He's some Jew Poppaea told me about," Otho answered. "Apparently, he leads a bunch of cannibals in some new cult from the East."

"Wow, that's totally metal. I'm stealing that. Anyway," Nero explained, "I realized I can't do much while she's around at all. I started thinking today about how I'd do it. A simple plan won't work; I'm going to have to think of something with my better actor friends and use Cornelia as a body double. I just haven't found a way to make Cornelia realistically old enough to pass for Agrippina. Haven't found the right makeup guy, so I've been threatening her with execution and generally stressing her out as much as I can to maybe get some natural gray streaks in her hair. That's just the start of the plan, though. I'm going to have to come up with one of the more elaborate schemes for this one if she's not gonna see it coming. I don't actually know how I'm going to use Cornelia, but it's just too clever using her as a double not to."

"Well, this is moving a bit fast. I thought I'd get some more time with Poppaea," Otho replied to the news of the expedited schedule. "You're going to have to do that elaborate planning. Going after Agrippina can be dangerous. Do too much planning, and she might find out. You know how it is."

"Yes, but I finally figured it out," Nero replied. "She needs me more than I need her. With Britannicus dead, she can't threaten me much. I don't know why it took me so long to figure that out. I probably would have been long gone if it weren't for those poisonous mushrooms he ate."

"Poisonous mushrooms, you really do take after her."

"Shut up."

"Yeah . . . good thing, you got lucky there, him going so young, and naturally too," Otho replied slowly. "Anyway, I think I'm gonna grab some food. See ya in a minute." Otho walked away, not quite sure how he felt about the change of pace. Nero's lethargy just transferred to Otho. Walking into the dining room, Otho thought it all over with a plate of cured meats and olives. During his public stress eating, Otho caught a glimpse of Poppaea in another room being chatted up by some random YOLO-bro.

Putting down the plate of food, Otho walked over to Poppaea and wedged himself into the conversation after the YOLO-bro attempted to block him with a wide stance and far-reaching arm movements.

"So, there I was, facing down a ferocious lion on this huge mountain . . ." the YOLO-bro said.

"Mind if I have a word with MY WIFE?" Otho pushed through the YOLO-bro blockade.

"Your wife . . . ? Yeah, sure." The YOLO-bro said before walking away, mumbling, "Every futuendi time" under his breath and letting his gut relax. He had been sucking it in for the entire conversation, not knowing that gives you acid reflux.

"Sounds like you had an interesting night with Nero after I left. An interesting night four times, he said," Otho opened the conversation without any subtlety.

"Ha, is that what he told you? Maybe if his night continued after I left, four times for him,"

Poppaea answered without confirming the number. "There wasn't much more to do. He said he'd get me my milk baths set up. I was just being nice. He's not exactly a gift basket kind of guy; I figured it was a good way to thank him."

"Hmmm."

"What?"

Otho wavered.

"I'd really rather you not," Otho said, realizing there wasn't much he could do to stop her. "I know him pretty well. Playing with him is playing with fire, okay? It would be better not to go all the way with him."

"Oh, how bad can it be?" Poppaea asked.

"Well . . . for instance . . . after last night, he's started making plans to kill his mom. He's a little too easily influenced when you play with him like that. It makes him hard to predict," Otho answered. "You're venturing into dangerous territory. I would at least limit yourself to half-assed hand jobs. Otherwise, there's no telling what he'd do. Did he mention what he's been doing with Cornelia? Giving her death threats?"

"Otho . . ." Poppaea placed a hand on his shoulder. "You're not getting jealous, are you?"

Otho, placing his hands on her hips and staring back into her eyes, said, "No, I trust you. I just don't want to lose this."

"Thank you, I'll be fine," Poppaea reassured him. "Well, this gal's gonna have one helluva time tomorrow when I can finally start up my beauty regime like I've been wanting," she bragged, doing a jig with little kicks and her thumbs pointed at herself as the winner of a contest only she competed in while she jerkily jogged in place in celebration.

"What is that?" Otho pointed at her. "You don't ever dance like that while we're hanging out. Is that all I needed to do? Give you those milk baths? You gotta tell me these things. I can get you your milk baths. Though I still don't quite get the point, it doesn't exactly sound beautifying . . . whatever. I just want to keep you happy."

"Tell you? I've been bringing it up constantly! You'll be far more pleased once I can finally look as beautiful as you deserve. You treat me plenty anyway," Poppaea assured him while maintaining her jig. Otho did a double-take around the room and looked back at Poppaea, driving her to the wall and making out with her, high-school style, feeling her rhythmic vibrations caught between the wall and himself.

Otho forgot to go back to Nero and continued playing tonsil hockey with Poppaea further into the night. Maybe she would be fine after her night alone with Nero. He decided not to leave her side that night and was put at ease as he enjoyed his youthful marital bliss for the remainder of the evening.

***

The next day around early afternoon, Poppaea was lounging in her room at the palace. Her lazy day was interrupted by a half dozen slaves transporting supplies she had requested earlier that morning when Nero gathered details for her unusual bathing request. Surprised by the speediness of her fulfilled demand, Poppaea led the dairy-laden servants to her bath. With all the supplies in the palace apartment and her bath sufficiently filled with fresh milk, she dismissed all but one of the female servants. Flavia was quickly becoming her most trusted slave. She was attentive and had enough intelligence to assist Poppaea in expertly guiding the personalities of the palace. After quickly learning how to anticipate her behavior and needs, Poppaea made sure to communicate her palace requests through Flavia and only her. "Empty half of that jar of honey and a quarter of that jar of oil into the bath," she calmly ordered Flavia.

Poppaea began disrobing and tossed her clothes over a nearby couch. With the bath prepared, she eased into the drawn milk bath, enjoying the cool, creamy liquid enveloping her body. "Toss those petals over me and stand over there," Poppaea continued ordering her favorite slave.

Flavia delicately tossed a colorful assortment of flower petals over Poppaea's submerged body as if she were in a directionless perfume ad. Poppaea dipped down into the bath, going fully submerged for moments before surfacing and stroking the essence of the bath into her face and hair a few times. She finally had the bath she had been dreaming about since she was a little girl. With Flavia appropriately distanced from the bath and minding her own business solving sudoku puzzles or something, Poppaea could just lay in her long-awaited, vitamin-C-fortified soak in peace.

That was until an unexpected visitor arrived. After at least fifteen minutes of bliss, Poppaea's serenity was interrupted by a knock at the door. Luckily, the servant was well attuned to palace life and knew when it was appropriate to take some initiative. Before Poppaea even had the chance to stop relaxing, Flavia answered the door to prevent a disruptive distraction. This was one of the reasons she was Poppaea's favorite. It was neckbeard himself.

"Who is it?" Flavia inquired as she cracked open the door to see who it was.

"Whoa, hey ugg—"

"Flavia."

"Flavia, right," Nero said after jumping back half a cubit upon seeing his own reflection in Flavia's shiny forehead poking through the door crack.

"Poppaea is not taking visitors at the moment," she said before he had a chance to say anything. Nero was visibly irked. He squinted his entire face in confusion at such an inconvenience. He wanted some, but now it just felt like he was an annoyance. Flavia just had that way about her to disarm people. She was not a pushover. Today, Flavia's dirty work was allowing Poppaea to enjoy her bath without any futueris pueris interruptions. Nero got his wits about him and realized she must not realize that she has yet another amazing opportunity to have sex.

"You want me to deliver any messages to Poppaea?" Flavia asked Nero. "I can do that."

"Yes, tell her it's go time. She should know what that means by now, heh heh," Nero told her fully confident, two days after their first one-on-one bath time encounter.

"Okay," Flavia replied shortly before closing and locking the door. Walking over to Poppaea in the milk bath but standing at the door to the bath and looking the other way for her privacy, Flavia relayed the message. "It's Nero. He wants to futuere."

Flavia was met with silence. She couldn't hear

any movement in the bath either. Maybe she had fallen asleep. Or maybe she wasn't quite sure how to answer. Flavia knew to be patient and waited a few minutes before speaking again. "What should I tell him?"

"Ughhhhhhhhh . . . hmmm . . . godsdamnit . . ." Poppaea responded once pressured. Dipping her mouth down into the milk, Flavia could hear her making gurgling noises as she thought about what to do. "Is he still there?"

Flavia tiptoed back to the door and stealthily approached to listen for Nero's heavy breathing without alerting him. Silently shuffling back to the bath, Flavia apologetically answered, "Yeah, he's still there. I'm sorry."

"Uuuuugghghhh, just tell him I'm too busy then," Poppaea moaned. "Please, just get him out of here. I'm not in the mood."

Flavia walked back over to the door, not stealthily at all. "She's too busy. You'll have to come back later," she told Nero through the cracked door. The conversation was not over due to Nero's sturdy foot placement in the crack of the door.

"What could possibly be keeping her so busy she can't spend some quality alone time with her favorite emperor?" Nero questioned.

Flavia looked at Nero. Nero looked at Flavia. *Just futuendi ask her*, Nero said with his eyes.

Futuus off! Fine. I'll be back, Flavia said by rolling her eyes back.

Pushing Nero's foot out of the crack and locking the door again, Flavia made her way back to Poppaea.

"He wants to know why you're too busy,"

Flavia said. "I don't know what to tell him. We could just wait him out."

"No, I have a feeling that won't work," Poppaea thought out loud. "You'd be going back and forth all day. He's too dense; he won't get the hint that easily." She continued pondering and realized there was only one way to get rid of a thirsty guy. "Just tell him Otho's here, we're having sex, and if he asks if he can join, tell him Otho doesn't want a three way right now." As Flavia walked to the door, Poppaea began making unnecessarily loud fake orgasm noises.

"Otho's here, and they're enjoying a little private time," Flavia said, this time with her foot in the crack for more door-control dominance.

"Sweet, I wanna join," Nero said, excited.

"No," Flavia quickly extinguished his hopes.

"Jesus Christ, why the futuus not?" Nero questioned with his dagger chubbing up.

"Otho isn't in the mood for a three way, I'm afraid." Flavia pushed his chest away from the crack and locked the door. She waited and listened for evidence that Nero had finally left, tuning out Poppaea's high-pitched moaning and "oh yes" whines. While she waited, she wondered, *Nero didn't seem like the Christian type. How does he know who Jesus is? This could be good news. I'll have to spread it to the church. We may be more accepted by the state after all. Nero of all people . . . who would have known?*

Eventually, Flavia heard Nero walk away and let a minute pass before motioning to Poppaea that she could stop. She sat down and relaxed while Poppaea continued her milk bath uninterrupted.

Finally, Poppaea could lay back and absorb all the antioxidants and essential oils into her skin. She didn't know what they were. All she knew was that they were good for her.

4 MYSTERY MEAT

The next day, Nero and Otho arrived at the
Circus Maximus for a day of races. It was a beautiful,
clear day with highs in the mid-seventies, just after a
low-pressure system cleared out for the weekend.
Low humidity and a gentle two-mile-per-hour wind
moving in from the south with occasional gusts up to
ten, created the perfect day to sit outside and watch
chariots race around in a circle. Nero and Otho took
advantage, planning a long day at the Circus Maximus
before a nasty high-pressure system would move in
later that week. After reading some entrails and
interpreting a rapidly dropping dew index, the augurs
predicted a week of nasty rain moving into the area
from a wet and cold front sometime later that evening
after sundown. Anyone in Rome would have regretted
missing out on enjoying the weather while they still
could.

The two best buds sat in special boxed seats
reserved for the emperor. It was just north of the
center of the circuit. Raised on a platform, the box had

a good view of the finish line even while lounging. A sizable smorgasbord of food befitting an annual Methodist potluck fundraiser[4] prevented any excuse of leaving the box until the games were over. Unfortunately for the two, they showed up on time for the events of the Circus Maximus and had to suffer through some dumb parades. They would be bloated and rip-roarin' drunk before anything interesting happened. They showed up at the time the doors opened—no one does that!

"What the futuus is this?" Otho pointed to some chunky white concoction of dairy products, unknown meat, topped with a garnish of something green.

"I don't know, but I can't stop eating it," Nero replied, stuffing his face, one dipped piece of bread at a time. "We're going to run out at this rate. Go get more!" Nero yelled to a nearby slave.

"Why'd we show up so early?" Otho questioned while fighting Nero for the remaining dip. "When the circus says doors open at one, races at two, they actually start at three. Openers always suck. We should have shown up fashionably late, like most people."

"Usually I'd agree with you," Nero replied, "but there's this flute player who's playing at the end of the parade. He's a master."

"How good could he possibly be?" Otho asked.

"I was traveling across town in my litter when I heard him playing a sweet melody so upbeat with

---

[4] Methodist churches have the best potlucks, and it was the only accurate descriptor for the large amount and variety of comfort food Otho and Nero had access to.

nonconventional rhythms I had to stop and listen," Nero said. "I was so impressed I found a top-of-the-line flute from a temple of Apollo in Boeotia. It's made of silver and holds a perfect tune. The thing cost me ten thousand sesterces."

"For a flute? Who's your flute guy?" Otho asked.

"They're all that expensive at that level of quality. He deserved it; it was a tragedy to see him playing on what he had," Nero explained. "I told him if he did well, I'd permanently commission him for the palace. I have to see how he plays under pressure."

"Wow . . . I guess we'll see if he plays as well as you say," Otho replied. "We'll just have to suffer through some dumb parades in the meantime."

With the white mystery meat dip depleted, Nero and Otho tried some other food in their spread and quickly lost interest after one bite per dish. After ten or so minutes, it was clear nothing could compare. They were learning that life was not complete without that dip. The parade continued with cavalry troops parading behind military men in full armor. Every so often, there was an exotic animal or a troupe of ladies dressed in feathers showing a PG-13 amount of skin like they were about to charge fifty dollars for a picture on the Vegas strip. However, the mediocre performances were vastly outmatched by a less-than-mediocre crowd. Most people knew to show up at least two hours late. The only people there on time had nothing better to do and were just there to hang out.

"Jesus Christ, is this over yet? Where's your flute player?" Otho asked Nero as he watched another group of soldiers walk from one end of the track to the other. Just when it looked like the parades were over, a new contingent of Vestal Virgins strolled across the track, slowly waving to the sparse, sleepy audience. Once the Virgins had made it to the other end of the track, collecting brown dust at the bottom of their dresses, a lone flautist appeared on the horizon.

"See, there he is!" Nero pointed to the man who was walking to center stage. The flautist began playing, but it wasn't the best auditorium for a flute player. He couldn't get that loud even with a ten-thousand-sesterces flute, and no one could hear the musician. Even if Nero could hear the emotionally charged flute performance, it would have been overshadowed by the slaves bringing a new bowl of that meaty, white dip. The nutritional label on the bowl would have said it was four servings, but that wasn't even a quarter of a serving for Otho and Nero.

"Futuus yeah, more dip!" Otho exclaimed as they began digging into their new favorite food after deflowering the dip of its green garnish. No one cared about the presentation here.

"So, you must have had a real fun time with Poppaea yesterday," Nero suggestively mentioned to Otho, elbow deep into the fresh bowl of dip.

"Uh, yeah, always have fun with her," Otho commented, not quite sure what Nero was getting at.

"I'm sure she was really happy with the milk bath I provided for her. Just wish y'all would have let me join in the fun," Nero said more suggestively, poking two index fingers into the two ends of a piece of bread.

"Ummm, okay, I'm a little confused. I'm not

sure what exactly you're getting at."

"I thought we'd be going to town on her together. All the time. Don't tell me you're above a three way with your best friend," Nero escalated the conversation.

"I had no idea you were interested in something like that yesterday," Otho replied, even more confused but trying to de-escalate whatever this was about.

Nero didn't know what to say to his best bro. The box became silent. Nothing was heard except the open-mouthed chewing of dip and the slightly audible flute ballad coming to the climax of a song. The flute player finished his song and walked off center stage to no crowd reaction and no palace commission. He gave it his heart and came up short. The Circus Maximus was silent, and neither Nero nor Otho knew how to break it.

When the new bowl of dip was empty, Nero took the bowl, scraped it clean, and overhand tossed the void dish at the nearest slave. They were now left without any more distractions. They both laid down on recliners at the viewing area of the box where they sat staring straight ahead. There were more military parades and some more exotic animals.

"Can't they just bring a bigger futuendi bowl?" Otho said, breaking the silence. "I can't eat the rest of the garbage they brought us."

"Maybe if you weren't hogging all the dip," Nero accused Otho. "That's just like you."

"Okay dude, what's up? What's your futuendi problem?" Otho had now lost his cool.

"If I get a taste of something . . . and I like it . . . and I don't have it all the time, there will be problems until I get my way! That's all I'm saying." Nero raised his tone to forcefulness.

"Stercus, man, just tell me and we won't have problems. We'll get more dip." Otho tried to calm Nero down with his words, but not his tone.

"Sometimes, there's only enough dip for one person," Nero said with a calm voice but murderous eyes. A servant placed a new bowl of dip on the table. Nero, with a deliberate motion, got up, grabbed the bowl and a loaf of bread, and sat back down, holding his bowl of dip closely. He looked back at Otho. "I think it would be best if you left. I know you, and I know how you operate."

Otho didn't say anything. He had no idea what he could say because he still wasn't sure what was going on. Leaving Nero's observation box, he gradually increased his speed away from that strange interaction. Skipping every other step on the way down, Otho made it to the streets and began his walk back to the palace. He and Nero had been friends for some time, but he had never had an interaction like that. Nero was irked about something. The interaction was so unexpected that Otho went into deeply introspective thought as he walked back to the palace. He paid minimal attention to his surroundings as he began problem solving, only thinking about how he was going to get home and thinking backward to the last time Nero was acting normal. At least, normal for himself. He bumped into dozens of people, nearly tripping down some stairs twice.

What the futuus was all that about? That dip wasn't that great. I mean, it was pretty futuendi good with that creamy sauce and tender whatever meat that was. It didn't taste like lamb, but it had that consistency. Maybe it was beef? No, it was definitely lamb. I didn't even get to stay for the actual races, Otho thought to himself, his internal chatter growing progressively intense. He began mouthing some of his most worrying thoughts like a crazy person. He concluded that there must have been something else going on, seeing that there was no obvious explanation for Nero's attitude. There rarely was, but this seemed more urgent. Dangerous.

Now, I remember saying some jokes the other day about that slave Cornelia. He is definitely sensitive about his mommy issues, but he usually blows those off. I mean, Agrippina is kinda good looking for her age, and Cornelia definitely does all that stuff you wouldn't expect girls to be down for. I mean, the thing she did with the candlestick the other day, that was wild. Although, he probably made that up. That can't be it. Maybe it was the other day when I mocked him singing behind his back at that party a week ago by lip-syncing. I didn't even realize I was doing it until some people started laughing. Well, that could be it, but I don't think so. That dip stuff was awfully specific. There's no way he interpreted that as me being jealous of his singing skills. It had to be something else—something we're sharing, I guess. I mean, we're sharing the palace, but he hasn't had a problem with it so far. I know I've been there for a while, but he wouldn't suddenly get mad about that.

Otho stopped in the middle of the street once he had figured it out, remembering Nero's story of him in the bath the other night, and yelled at himself, "Futuus, futuus, what the futuus did Poppaea do!"

Upon his realization, Otho sprinted towards the palace. The sprint turned into a very slow jog after twenty cubits. His stomach began to protest, and he had a feeling the white dip wouldn't taste too great a second time. He was physically limited by his stomach sloshing from side to side, but he knew he had just lost his handle on the Poppaea situation and needed to figure out how to strategize damage control fast from whatever Poppaea did.

After a dramatic and very uncomfortable run back to the palace, Otho made it to Poppaea. He had slipped on some smooth stones three times and stopped five times to catch his breath on his way, settling on an unsteady run/jog, but he had made it. His face and toga had been well misted in sweat as his cardio prevented him from becoming drenched at a steady pace. His cheeks were still flushed with blood, and he had some open cuts on his legs and knees from a misguided attempt to hop a row of bushes. Otho was a hot mess.

Without announcing himself, Otho entered Poppaea's room and bent over his knees to catch his breath. He didn't see Poppaea, but he did see Flavia, and where Flavia was, Poppaea was. After a few dry heaves, he fought back the dip and regained enough composure to speak. "Flavia, get the futuus out. I have to talk to my wife in private." Flavia left in a hurry, partly from Otho's request but primarily from his strong musk blitzkrieging from his open armpit throughout the unventilated room. Otho was in decent shape considering he had spent years drinking and overeating, but the party life had left a toll, and there's only so much you can do to prepare for running on a full stomach of dairy and meat.

The room was empty, and Otho locked the door. "Jesus, who is that? Is that you, Otho?" Poppaea said from her milk bath. The ensemble of aromas from the bath combatted Otho's stench and saved Poppaea from being slightly uncomfortable as he approached the bath. "What's going on? Did something happen at the races?"

"Yeah, something weird happened, and I'm trying to get to the bottom of it," Otho replied, pulling out a stool to sit down and calming down a little. "Two days ago, Nero seemed mostly normal except for all the 'killing his mom' stuff. I mean, that's kind of normal for him, just a little more drive and planning to his normal weird goals."

Otho paused as he tried to find a way to phrase things without accusing Poppaea. He knew it had something to do with her. He just needed to get the facts and not hurt her feelings. By the way their conversation ended a couple of nights ago after she and Nero started futuendi, it could have been anything. "Did anything happen between you and Nero yesterday?"

"Well . . ." Poppaea started in deliberately careful speech. It did not matter though; Otho had stopped listening at that one word. She may have said something to set Nero off unintentionally, but it wouldn't have mattered. What was done was done. "He was like trying to come in and have a quick futuus or something like that . . ." Otho caught some of the story. Something did happen. How was he going to smooth things over? Maybe it wasn't that serious. "Anyway, I was in a milk bath and wasn't in the mood, and he would not leave me alone. You also told me to try and not futuat him anymore, I guess I kinda get why . . . had no idea he was so needy." Otho tried to listen, but millions of thoughts and social interaction simulations were playing through his head. He was paralyzed in thought. "So, I told Flavia to tell him you were here. I don't know how else I would have gotten rid of him."

"So. Let me rehash this so I know I understand," Otho attempted to calmly regroup his thoughts. "Nero wanted to futuere, you didn't want to, and you told him I told him to leave?"

"That's about the gist of it," Poppaea confirmed. "Flavia did all the talking through the door, so I don't know exactly how Nero reacted to it all. It didn't seem like a big deal; you did tell me not to futuere him, and I didn't want to anyway. What exactly happened today?"

"I'm not completely sure yet. He wasn't speaking openly about all this, but I think he's really mad at me about the whole thing," Otho replied, leaning back and rubbing his temples. "Fuuuuutuus. Thanks for telling me. He must have been pretty horny and took it personally. At least I know what I'm dealing with now."

"I wasn't trying to blame you; I just didn't know how else I could say no and get him to leave." Poppaea explained. "I don't know what else I could have done. I'm okay. I can futuat him if it causes more problems. It's not really a big deal for me."

"That may be the path forward if I get through this. I'm not completely sure how to handle it all," Otho replied.

"What do you think he's going to do?" Poppaea asked with a concerned look.

"I have absolutely no idea, but nothing good," Otho replied. Standing up and walking back to the bedroom to lie down. "I need to lie down for a moment and think this through. Don't get up. Enjoy your bath," Otho said, dragging his feet into the adjacent bedroom. He threw himself onto the bed, still sticky with cold sweat, but he didn't care. Confirming the source of Nero's oddly misplaced jealousy did nothing to calm his mind. Lying on his back, he allowed his thoughts to spiral towards every potential negative outcome, ignoring any positive ones.

I don't even know how I can smooth this one over. Usually, Nero's pretty chill about stuff, but damn, he turned into a jealous monster fast on this one, Otho thought, turning his head toward the open door and catching a glimpse of Poppaea's leg sticking out of the bath.

No, I'm as good as futuatis on this one. How could I even talk my way out of this? Even if I told him Poppaea was lying, how would he understand that after the great time they had three nights ago? Futuus. I should have known I was playing with fire when I got involved with this dude, let alone marrying his crush. I should have known better.

Otho continued pitying himself and failed to come up with a game plan as he lay on his back, staring at the ceiling. Poppaea didn't dare get out of the bath to confront the mess she may have caused. She didn't feel guilty, but she felt bad enough to stay in the bath for a while. Her skin would have been incredibly pruny by this point, but that vitamin E worked wonders.

Otho stayed motionless on the bed, not knowing where to go, what to think, or what to do. He lay there long enough for a knock to sound on the door. "Otho, are you still in there?" a voice called out. Otho didn't recognize it, which was not a good sign.

"Yes, who's asking?" Otho replied.

"Nero requests your presence in the throne room," the voice answered.

This is it. I may as well deal with it, Otho thought as he rose from bed with diminishing hope. *Not much I can do now.*

Poppaea didn't know what to say and dared not guess. Otho slowly approached the door and cracked it open to see an armed guard. This did not calm his spirit.

"Right this way," the guard said, pushing the door fully open.

Otho, without hope of escape or any room for social maneuvering, followed the guard to Nero's throne room. His thoughts-per-minute went from a headache-inducing speed to panic attack level. It didn't show because men of such stature were not allowed to visibly display such troubling emotions. Otho swallowed and metabolized his stress into a stomach ulcer he'd later blame on a bad diet. He maintained his cool by wearing a straight face and crossing his arms to stabilize his shaking hands.

Otho made it to the throne room slightly more collected than when he left his bedroom. The long hallways gave him time to accept his fate. Nero was sitting on his throne, leaning to his right and surrounded by guards. On both sides of the room stood important-looking old men, mixing bewilderment and boredom. No one seemed to know what was going on except for Nero. Light shone through the room from a large open door, illuminating the visibly impatient crowd. Otho was not alone in his uncertainty.

The guards led Otho to the center of the throne

room. He had been there at night with Nero while it was empty—drunk, screwing around with youthful shenanigans, and tolerating Nero's excessive use of the acoustics provided by the high vaulted ceiling and stony interior. The memories of good times escaping stale parties in the throne room to sober up while tolerating Nero's drunken singing faded into an unexpected and unfortunate new memory.

Nero stood up from his throne and broke the stale silence. "Congratulations on your promotion, Otho," he said, raising his arms together into a clap. "Everybody, clap. Please clap!" he ordered the important-looking old dudes surrounding the room.

Otho was welcomed with a roomful of forced, half-hearted applause.

"I was unaware I was up for a promotion," Otho said as the applause died down.

"Yes! You have been such a loyal friend. I made sure you would be awarded with a duty suiting someone of such high trust," Nero said in an unfamiliarly formal tone. "By order of me and the Senate," Nero eyed his captive audience, "I'm giving you the governorship of Lusitania."

Holding off a transparent verbal pause, Otho mustered a confused and unsure response. "Thank you, I will serve the empire with honor."

Nero raised his hands again, and Otho was met with more half-hearted clapping as he stood in shock at the news.

"I have made the necessary arrangements. You will be leaving by the end of the week," Nero continued. "Lusitania is a very important province, and I need my best man on the task."

"I will serve the empire with honor," Otho

repeated. The assignment was so unexpected, he couldn't think of anything else to say, let alone anything that wouldn't get him into more trouble.

"Well, that's it. Better run along, prepare for the trip, and say your goodbyes to all your friends!" Nero dismissed Otho. "Lusitania's a loooong way away."

Otho traded his stress for malcontent, expressed through forceful steps out of the room. After exiting the throne room and creating enough distance, he stopped, sighed, and muttered to himself, "Futuus! Lusitania's in the sticks!" He kept walking at a deliberate march back to the bedroom.

Otho entered the bedroom while spewing profanity. By now, Poppaea had exited her bath, dried off, gotten dressed, and was engaged in beautification activities involving a hairbrush, some citrus fruit, and a fig branch. A loose pile of drained fruit suggested she had been at it for some time.

Otho sat down on the bed and gave a hard look at Poppaea before telling her the news. "You really futuatis me over, I hope you know that."

"Well, you're still alive and not imprisoned, so it can't be that bad," Poppaea replied to Otho's poutiness.

"No, it's worse!" Otho said, his tone angsty. "He's made me governor of Lusitania."

"That's not bad news—that's great news, Otho!" Poppaea attempted to cheer him up before squeezing more lemon juice on her fig branch and hairbrush. A bit of juice and pulp flew into her face, causing a short squeal and a lot of blinking.

"What the futuus are you doing?" Otho asked. "And for your information, Lusitania is over fifteen hundred miles east and two mountain ranges away from here. It is hardly developed. I'll basically be a glorified slave master, and it is the most cut-off region in the empire. There's not even combat there! Between the distance and absolutely no chance for military glory, it's going to be the end of my political career before I even have one. Trust me, you're going to hate it there."

"Fifteen hundred miles away? Futue that noise, I think I'm going to pass on that wonderfully stercus opportunity," Poppaea quickly replied while tediously straining her hair through the fig branch and the brush, dripping juice everywhere. "And for your information, I'm keeping my hair perfect by cleaning out all the negative energy and removing all the bad spirits . . . duh."

"Is that why . . . futuus woman, I couldn't give a stercus anymore," Otho said, exasperated. "At this point, I don't know how I'm going to make it out there without you."

"It's going to be real tough," Poppaea replied. She couldn't bear to look Otho directly in the eyes, between her accidental betrayal and the lemon-pulp-induced blinking. "There's no way I'm going to Lusitania."

"Wow, I'm going to need you out there!" Otho pleaded with more desperation.

"That's too big of a request for me. I can't see how I can maintain this lifestyle out there . . ." Poppaea said, growing even more distant.

"This is it for us, then, I suppose. This is it for me," Otho said, a single tear dripping down his face, washing all his stoicism away. "We had Nero eating out of the palms of our hands. With this banishment and you out of the picture, I have no political footing. We could have made so much money; we could have been securely wealthy for the rest of our lives." At that moment, he grabbed a few items, collected what loose change he could find, and left the room, then the palace, and finally the eternal city. He didn't even want to wait a week to leave.

Besides formal reports and insulting drunk poetry sent by Nero, that was the last time Otho had any contact with the emperor or Poppaea. Marriage law in Rome was very informal and quick. The only damage it could have caused was temporarily harmful rumors. Roman marriage, like many ancient marriages, was never about love; it was only about status, wealth, political influence, and having sons to collect that wealth before any poor people could get their hands on it. Otho no longer had any of those things, and the divorce was quick. Poppaea faced zero repercussions from the divorce other than being murdered by her next husband, Nero, while pregnant with his child.

5 OTHO'S SECOND CHANCE

Otho had taken a huge hit to his pride, but he soldiered on. Through remarkably mediocre leadership, he served as a fine governor of Lusitania for a decade. He was notably okay and not much more. Lusitania was not easily accessible and generally out of the way for many Romans. It did not border the Mediterranean and was about as far west as you could get without getting wet. Unlike other remote provinces of the Roman Empire, Lusitania did not see any military action. The most excitement Otho saw as a leader was making tight bureaucratic deadlines and overseeing tax collection. One time, he had to respond to six budget requests within eight business days! It was an incredibly dull time with nothing to screw up or succeed in.

He had grown accustomed to his new way of life in the boonies. Primarily residing in the capital city of Augusta Emerita, Otho had access to most normal Roman amenities such as theaters, occasional games, and most importantly, a bathhouse. Yeah, it had everything. But the small-town pace of the people and the day-to-day life left Otho always wanting more. After Poppaea and the hustle and bustle of Rome, Otho couldn't bring himself to settle in. He hadn't been on one date, preferring to remain single rather than stoop to the level of those country bumpkins. He became a generally unpleasant sore loser.

Despite his uppity attitude, the locals still tried to be friends with him. "Hey Otho, want to go to the whatever festival[5]?" they would ask.

"Not really. Once you've gone to the whatever festival in Rome, anything else is just depressing," Otho would respond like some hipster who moved out of New York City when they found out that not everyone could write the next great American novel and the bar tips just weren't covering rent. Now, they're living somewhere boring and can never enjoy pizza again because it's just not the same. Otho was a stewing mess of resentment, and it wasn't a good look.

That annoying type of superiority complex, coupled with a major life failure, alienated him from everyone. The only person who could stand him long enough to make it through a full conversation was a slave working in his office named Onomastus. Some assumed it was because he had to be there, but many other slaves found ways of feigning enough incompetence to be reassigned. Onomastus stuck

---

[5] The Lusitanians prided themselves in their neighborhood festivals. There was about one every other week during the spring and fall. After you go to three they all started to blend in together with the same shops, foods, drinks served and all of the same people participated in the parades.

around. The slave was a tanned, broad-shouldered man with medium-length curly hair. Though he's tried shaving every other morning, his dark facial hair could not be fought, so he unwillingly wore a full beard.

Onomastus felt the pain in Otho's heart and, despite his insufferableness, reached out. While many slaves and colleagues just waited for Otho to finish complaining, Onomastus practiced active listening. He responded with "That sucks," "Oh man, I hate it when people do that," "Wow, you're right, what an interesting point of view," "Yeah, I hate this place too," "I can't believe Karen said that," and most importantly, "Yeah, Nero's a real culus." It helped that Onomastus occasionally complained about his own life and was antisocial enough in Lusitania to relate on a genuinely personal level. He was well-versed in reading and writing, which earned him an administrative position in Otho's office.

Onomastus was a blessing to Otho's governorship. Otho managed to avoid many office dramas thanks to Onomastus's thoughtful observations discovered from his lonely desk in the corner of the office. He provided Otho with next-level insight he would never have been able to fathom. In industry terms, he was a real force multiplier. That intrapersonal insight made him so loyal to Otho. He could tell Otho wasn't meant to spend his life in Lusitania and would move on to greater things. He wasn't just loyal to Otho; he believed in him and his ambition.

They had become so acquainted that Onomastus was Otho's closest friend at the time. They were both very comfortable around each other, and the barrier between master and slave had diminished to scandalously low levels. Otho had always had the legal right to do whatever he wanted with him, but the human connection he had developed in their friendship was the only comfort he had in his time in Lusitania. Onomastus knew this and grew comfortable with that knowledge. They could talk plainly and casually. Otho could reveal all his deepest feelings without any regret. They trusted each other.

One day in the administrative quarters of the governor's mansion, Onomastus was sifting through administrative letters when he came across interesting news. It was a silent, ordinary, unassuming day they would never forget.

"Hey Otho, there's some interesting information here about Nero," Onomastus said.

Otho replied, not correctly reading Onomastus's tone, "Jesus, what's that mother futuebatur up to now?" Otho asked, using his favorite insult because he believed Nero was literally a mother futuebatur.

"It looks like there's a rebellion growing against him," Onomastus replied. "Some dude, Vindex, is leading an insurrection in Gaul and they've proclaimed Galba the new emperor."

Otho stiffened, dropped the letter he was reading, sat straight up, raised an eyebrow, and eyed Onomastus. "You're futues with me, right?"

Onomastus looked back. "No, sir, this looks legit." He took a closer look. "Yeah, this is Vindex's seal right here, and he's not exactly a joker. He's asking for support from other governors in the rebellion."

Otho sat back in his chair, trusting the letter's

legitimacy and beginning a detailed daydream of finally getting back at his old friend. "Well, stercus, if this is real, I've been waiting for an opportunity like this since I got sent out here."

"He wants a response," Onomastus continued. "This really looks like something Vindex would write, but this could be a loyalty test. There's no way to know right now. Responding affirmatively could be a trap."

"I don't give a futuus if it is," Otho replied. "What's Nero gonna do, send an army out here? If it is a loyalty test, I want Nero to know I still hate his guts. I say we respond and send Galba some gold or something for support of the rebellion."

"We don't have much to send right now," Onomastus replied. "Most of our treasury's tied up in public works projects."

"Well, we should send something." Otho thought about the liquidity of his assets. "I want to be at the head of this thing. Let's just get whatever unnecessary gold we have lying around. It doesn't have to be in coin form to help."

"What? Like, send silverware or cups or whatever lying around the palace?"

"Yeah, they can melt those down, and we don't need it all," Otho elaborated. "They just might be the first of the Galba coins! That'll give us time to find some more capital for real financial support. Think about it, if we're first to send support, we'll have some major brownie points when Nero finally gets deposed. It's about time. That dude is a maniac."

"Alright!" Onomastus agreed. "By the way you've been talking about him, it was only a matter of time."

"Go, grab another slave and a bag. We've got no time to waste!" Otho ordered Onomastus with some uncharacteristic and unexpected excitement.

Moments later, Onomastus returned with the nearest slave he could find and a large, empty brown sack. The fit, young male slave barely spoke and was fairly confused but looked ready to haul a lot of gold. If potatoes were a thing back then in Rome, the bag would have been perfect for a bunch of them. Just to save you the Google search, potatoes are New World crops and didn't make their way over until Muslims forced Western Europe to make better boats.

"That looks perfect. Let's do this! Start here in the office. Come over and hold that thing open," Otho commanded.

The slave walked over to Otho's desk and held the bag open. Otho began tossing desk ornaments into the bag.

"Don't need this, don't need that," Otho verbalized his anti-hoarding state of mind while tossing anything with gold or other valuable-looking metals into the sack. Candlesticks, ceremonial-looking knives, plates, cups, and anything shiny went into the bag. Otho guided the bag-toting slave through every adorned surface in his office.

Next, Otho led the slave into the hallway, depositing more jewelry into the bag. They moved from room to room, filling the bag with valuable items. He snagged more cups and dishware from the dining room, then his bedroom, and continued filling the bag in a lounge until it was practically overflowing. Only a few candle holders didn't make it in because they were too long.

The slave could hardly keep up with Otho

towards the end. His arms shook as he struggled to keep the bag off the ground.

"That should do it for now. Find a chest or two to hold it all and get it ready for delivery." Otho ordered the slave into his courtyard.

"Isn't this a little rash?" Onomastus questioned after following the personal ransacking through the governor's mansion.

"Not rash enough, if you ask me!" Otho replied glibly. "If I'm supporting a rebellion against Nero, I'm going to do everything in my power to fund it! There's one last thing we should do; call the house slaves."

"Okay . . . I'll be right back," Onomastus replied, heading back into the mansion.

Otho waited, tapping his feet for about fifteen minutes before Onomastus returned with about fifty slaves in tow. Onomastus motioned everyone to one side of the courtyard and returned to Otho. "Here they all are."

"Perfect! Onomastus, which of these is necessary for the villa? And I mean absolutely necessary," Otho asked.

"Oh no, really?"

"Yeah, not holding back here."

"Okay, well . . ." Onomastus began pointing at individuals in the crowd and motioning them to the other side of the courtyard like a pickup basketball game. "Him, Mr. Muscles there, that cook, that dude, her, you, baldy—yeah, you—blue eyes and, yeah, I don't want to do all that laundry, get over here. These guys ought to be able to maintain this place just fine."

"See to it that the rest and this gold get sent to Galba in Hispania with a letter pledging our support in the war effort. Tell him he can smelt these fine pieces into coinage for immediate funding and use these slaves any way he sees fit," Otho commanded Onomastus. "Send a letter to Vindex as well. I imagine sending resources to Galba will be better suited for distribution to the greater rebellion."

Additionally, Otho figured it would be better to gain more favor with the presumed replacement emperor than Vindex. By the end of the day, Otho managed to fill another bag full of trinkets and golden doodads before the package had been sent to the (hopefully) future emperor. Otho's dinner parties from here on out would be devoid of any glamour— but he didn't care.

***

The first person to stand up to the tyrant Nero was Gaius Julius Vindex, pronounced like the window cleaner. He was a Romanized Gaul[6] who started the revolt. While he quickly assembled an army of a hundred thousand men, he failed at coordinating nearly anywhere else. Not even Otho's support reached the North fast enough. After sending many letters to other provincial governors, every recipient had turned the letter in to the relevant authorities

---

[6] After Gaul had been conquered by the Romans, some became accustomed to Roman ways of living and abandoned their Gallic culture entirely such as Vindex. There was widespread resistance to this phenomenon led by the infamous warrior poets Asterix and Obelix who not only fought the Romans but maintained a close connection to their Gallic heritage. They did not care about Nero.

except Servius Sulpicius Galba, the governor of Hispania. While Galba did not turn Vindex in, he did ghost Vindex by not responding for a while. Like horny young men on online dating apps, Vindex interpreted Galba's ghosting as an affirmative.

In the most egregious double-texting incident of the decade, Vindex sent another letter asking Galba to lead the revolt and, because he knew his heritage would prohibit him from becoming emperor himself, suggesting Galba proclaim himself emperor. Before Galba had a chance to respond, the one-way correspondence was intercepted by Nero's spies, and Galba was declared a public enemy. Galba, not seeing any other options, presumably said, "Fine, I agree, Nero sucks, and I'll be emperor." Vindex continued with his rebellion.

Believing he would get much more political support, Vindex started his power grab by attempting to take Lugdunum. Despite his optimistic prediction, the city leaders did not open their gates. This is because—and the liberal media who love dishing on Nero will never tell you this—Nero helped them out in a pinch after a citywide fire with money and a heartfelt thank you note for contributing money to his pleasure palace. When the gates didn't open, Vindex began a siege, only to be abruptly distracted by the Germania Superior Army arriving in Gaul. While Vindex was the only leader who hated Nero enough to do anything about it, this particular German army was the only force loyal enough to defend Nero. None of the other generals or armies cared much either way, and generally, the rebellion had a low turnout on both sides.

Accordingly, Vindex peeled off a sizable force

from the siege at Lugdunum to meet the German army. Many men deserted because they realized that there may be considerable fighting involved and weren't that committed—like the many armies who didn't show up for either side. Before the whole fighting rumor spread around, it just sounded like a fun pastime, or they got peer pressured into showing up by the popular kids. It was the most apathetic rebellion on record.

A still-optimistic Vindex led a thirty-thousand-man army of Gallian rebels armed with his passionate hatred of Nero. He sat on top of a horse in a scuffed metal helmet and a leather breastplate. The piece even had an etched chest, protruding nipples, and eight-pack abs to generously curve around his torso, which did not have eight-pack abs. He was surrounded by six different officers on horseback watching over their men. They managed to keep most of their men together and in some degree of military formation. They had a few more fair-weather friends than anyone anticipated, especially Vindex.

"At least we outnumber them a little," one commander mumbled.

"I don't like the looks of it. We should've brought more men from the siege. I didn't think so many would desert when we found out there might be actual fighting. Besides, those are experienced legionnaires. We just have a bunch of untrained rebels," another officer counseled Vindex.

"It's really not a good idea to meet in a field battle," another one added.

Gaius Julius Vindex listened to his leadership intently. "No, this is an opportunity for victory! I'm going to parley. This commander's probably gonna be reasonable. We're on the right side. I'm sure he'd be as happy to fight against Nero as we are: no one likes that guy. I invited him to the uprising. He only ratted me out to cover his culus. I don't think anyone wants to fight today."

Vindex rode off between the two forces to meet the commander of the Germania Superior army, Lucius Verginius Rufus. It is, after all, tradition. The men approached Rufus dressed to the nines in his standard-issue metal football pads[7] and leather skirts. His square jaw extended out of his helmet and was covered in dark stubble rough enough to scrape the paint off a metal fence.

"Salve," greeted Vindex. Before Rufus could respond, Vindex launched into his elevator pitch. "Listen: let's not get played here. I know you want to get rid of Nero as much as I do. Why fight over this guy? After all his boring, mandatory lyre concerts in Rome, that guy's days are numbered."

Rufus crossed his arms in thought. "Where's Galba? Isn't he supposed to be leading this thing? Doesn't seem like much of a rebellion. Just ten, maybe twenty thousand untrained men. Pretty tough to take Rome with an 'army' like that." Rufus gestured with air quotes.

"Galba's holding up the rear, he's fast on his way with reinforcements, and we have many, many more," Vindex responded. "Besides, I know you're pissed about that stunt Nero pulled. You and the rest of the commanders lost some prime downtown real estate in that fire. Do you really think the Christians did that? Follow the money, man. It's so obvious it's not even a conspiracy at this point. Don't be a sheep,

---

[7] Or *Lorica segmentate* for nerds

Rufus."

"I did spend the better part of my youthful XXs forcing my neighbors out of their apartments so I could build that nice dining room extension. I am still pretty ticked off about that." The bitterness in Rufus's voice was clear.

"Yeah, those Christians are weird as stercus, but pretty much no one thinks they started that fire. Did you know that cult drinks blood? Freakin' weird, dude. Yeah, Nero's the worst. I doubt he'll last the decade at this rate. But what's in it for me? I'm going to need a little more assurance I'm not gonna get 'exiled' like Nero's first wife. I'm just trying to do my job here."

"With our two forces, more people will join in. We're on the right side of history," Vindex reasoned. "You can help lead the coup with me and Galba, and it will only be a matter of months or even days before the tide is in our favor. Yeah, it's a bit of a risk, but not as dangerous as you think. Would you like to be on the wrong side of this revolt and get stiffed by the new leadership? Let's not get a bunch of our men killed for a lost cause here."

After about a minute of thought on the proposal, Rufus made up his mind. "Okay, this battle's off. Let our armies meet, and we can talk details with our officers." Rufus agreed with a handshake. The two commanders rode back to their forces to disseminate the news to their respective armies: no fighting today!

Vindex rode back to his officers with a smile. His men cheered as he rode through a gap in their ranks.

"Well, what did he say?" asked one of

Vindex's officers.

"He's joining the fight against Nero!" shouted Vindex. "We're on our way to victory. Move the troops in, and we'll pick our next move together." The Gallic rebel army began to march toward the German legionaries at ease. The tension was gone, and the battle was over without a drop of blood spilled.

"Well, what did he say? Do they still want to fight?" asked an officer in Rufus's group.

"They don't want to fight, and he made some good points about going after Nero. They're marching over now to join forces, and we'll discuss it later." As the Gallic rebels approached, so did the legionaries in tight formation.

"Well, I suppose we should let our troops know not to attack," Rufus thought out loud to his men. "Ya know, Vindex is really on to something here. At this point, just about anyone could be declared emperor and have a better shot than Nero. It wouldn't take much to just wipe this army out and start our own revolt without having to deal with Galba. Remember how annoying he was when he was in Germany? 'Uhhh, is that helmet regulation? I'm gonna have to write you up for that. We can't have an officer being a bad example for the troops.' Screw you, Galba, that helmet with the horns and face plate was fierce. I had to barter away a month's worth of provisions for that thing only to get it confiscated because it didn't follow regulations."

Murmurs of agreement resounded as other officers recalled similar stories of Galba's Germanic tour.

"One time, he made me run drills with my men for five hours just because I suggested a quicker way to build ramparts for a new camp," one man complained. "Apparently, making everyone's life better isn't a traditional way of building a fortification and I'm a teeeeerrible person for thinking outside the box."

The crowd got louder as the armies slowly approached each other, only to divert into more Galba storytelling.

"No, no, no, no, you think that was bad," interrupted another officer. "I knew a guy that was under his command for years, even followed him to Africa. Not even once did Galba pay him a bonus. I mean, that's unprecedented. Apparently, discipline alone is enough to hold an army together, he always says!"

"Shoot, those rebels are getting really close now," one officer pointed out. "We should call off our men, right?"

Rufus saw the situation before him. "On the one hand, we could call our men off and work with Vindex like I said I would. But . . . I'm not so sure Galba's much better than Nero. On the other hand, we could just let this happen. I mean, look at those guys over there: that guy's spear is just a sharpened stick. They're gonna get wr3ck'd."

Rufus considered the trade-offs between Galba and Nero. "Nah, let's just let this battle happen and we'll start our own revolt, or coup, or something with blackjack and hookers. Vindex is holding us back. He's only first-generation senatorial rank, for Jupiter's sake. No wonder nobody's out here helping him. He sent letters to pretty much everyone in his Rolodex, and Galba was the only guy who responded.

This is a sinking ship if I've ever seen one. Let's be the iceberg."

***

"Uhhhh, why are they in tight formation over there?" questioned one of Vindex's officers riding behind the rear of the Gallic rebels.

"Do you know if you can trust this guy to keep his word?"

"I'm not sure now," Vindex said nervously before barking some orders when he saw a group of the Germans launch a volley of javelins.

As the two forces met, the loose formation of Gallic rebels soon discovered there was no ceasefire. Despite quickly attempting to cobble together something of a formation, they were torn to shreds by the professionally trained and equipped legionnaires. The defeat was quick and decisive, resulting in the death of twenty thousand Gallic rebels and the suicide of Vindex.

According to tradition in such politically unstable times, Rufus was immediately proclaimed emperor by his own men—but then he refused— which is usually tradition. For the first time, at least.

***

After Otho's initial contact with the rebellion, he entered a waiting game for news from the war effort. Weeks passed with no updates, and his heart broke when he learned that Vindex had failed in liberating Gaul and was crushed so thoroughly. Some hope remained since no serious forces had yet been deployed to depose Galba. Otho often spiraled into negativity: Was this a lost cause? Did he back the wrong leader? Was this too early and needed more planning and coordination? What could he have done to ensure the success of the rebellion?

Otho tortured himself with regret, his head spinning with endless, made-up debates he always lost. He became even more depressed than before the attempted rebellion and his brief taste of hope. For months, Otho stared across fields at sundown while quoting sad poetry because emo bands had not been invented yet.

But one day, just before his life became unnoteworthy again, he finally received good news in another letter.

"Otho, you're not gonna believe this," Onomastus told him in his office, "Nero killed himself, and the Senate has proclaimed Galba the emperor."

"Nah man, don't mess with me, I'm not in the mood." He was too depressed to believe again.

"Nah dude, it's real."

"Futuus . . . no way!" Otho became less downtrodden.

"Yeah way, dude!"

"No futuendi way, dude!"

"Yeah, dude, this thing's real. Legit seal from the Senate. I think this is it. Good thing you backed Galba," Onomastus verified.

"Yeah, but that's just a seal."

"Hey, it's my job to know what a real and not real senate seal looks like. Otherwise, you'd have lost all your money to another Northern African prince scheme."

"Seriously! This is just too good, and they went with Galba after we gave him all that money. With that early support, I've gotta be able to get in close with him. From what we heard, it didn't sound like a lot of people supported Vindex or Galba when the whole rebellion thing kicked off," Otho reasoned in an elevated voice. "I'm gonna get plenty of political points with him. Probably get some super high political positions."

"Ya know . . ." Onomastus paused, "Galba doesn't have any sons, and . . . he's really old."

"You're kidding me."

"Nope."

"So, you mean—"

"Yup!"

"Well, Jesus Christ. I gotta get over there and show my face while I have the chance. This could be it for me!" Otho's excitement grew through the roof.

"My thoughts exactly." Onomastus met Otho's excitement. "We gotta pay our respects to Galba. Make our way out to Rome, ride this momentum."

"Nothing goes on out here. Yeah, that deputy governor dude, whatever his name is, can totally handle everything in the meantime," Otho replied. "So, what do we have to lose? Are we going to get to Hispania in time before Galba leaves?"

"I don't know. An appointment like that, he's probably already on his way. We don't have time to delay, so we must leave tomorrow if we're going to have any chance," Onomastus responded.

"Well, that's settled. Get the arrangements together. We're shooting for tomorrow. We're heading for Hispania," Otho ordered Onomastus, "and then, for Rome."

Onomastus got right to organizing the trip. He first leased an open-air carriage at zero down, 0 percent APR, and didn't even have to worry about any payments for another twelve months. Then, he peeled off a small contingent of cavalry for security, passed administrative work off to Otho's chosen replacements, grabbed some of Otho's favorite snacks for the road, and canceled all future restaurant reservations. Onomastus had prepared for many work trips in the past, but none this last minute or important.

Otho, on the other hand, could only focus just enough to pack his belongings. It took him all night because of how many times he distracted himself with happy daydreams—even folding all his clothes took thirty minutes. He was not just thinking about finally putting the Nero-centric trauma behind him but also about never coming back to Lusitania ever again. This was his second chance to climb up that political ladder. Few even got one chance, so he wasn't about to waste his second.

Otho eventually got packed, and Onomastus had expertly made all the last-minute arrangements for their trip. Before the sun came up, their carriage was loaded and ready for the one-way journey back east. Onomastus sent an order for the small cavalry to be in formation thirty minutes before sunrise, so the commander told the officer of the thirty-man unit to show up an hour before sunrise. Subsequently, the junior commander told all of the men to show up an hour and a half before sunrise, so all of the men were in formation an hour and thirty-one minutes before sunrise, give or take a minute.

All Otho had to do was roll out of bed, hop in the carriage, and hit the road. Pepped with energy, Otho exited his mansion one last time, followed by four slaves carrying two medium-sized chests. Otho packed light. One chest was full of clothes and other belongings, while the more reinforced chest contained his personal treasury. Onomastus was right behind him with his own chest of paperwork and all the office supplies he would need for the journey and beyond.

Both men mounted the carriage, with Onomastus at the lead of the reins. Everything was set, and Onomastus commanded the horses forward. "Hold on! We forgot the goat jerky!" Otho interrupted the journey after a minute of movement. "Hold everything!"

Onomastus held up a large, chunky bag he had placed in the carriage, right behind his back. "You mean this? I wouldn't forget that."

"Thank goodness!" Otho grabbed the bag and opened it for a long sniff of the dehydrated meat. "No road trip is complete without goat jerky."

"It's a last-minute trip, but I knew what the priorities were," Onomastus assured him.

"Could you imagine how awful it would have been if we had forgotten it? I just don't even want to think about that."

Otho looked at a nearby horseman who was heavily slouching while maintaining pace with the carriage. "Hail, legionnaire! So, how early did your commander make y'all form up for this stercus patrol?"

"Sir! We were told to form up nearly two hours ago, sir!" the legionnaire replied.

"Damn, that late? Also, that better be your last 'sir' sandwich." Otho replied. "It sure helps to have a short chain of command!" he joshed the cavalryman, who then elicited a tired laugh. Otho ripped off some pieces of jerky and tossed them to the soldier and a few others within range.

Otho had always been good with soldiers. He had never been one, but he knew enough to bro out with the guards and men on leave in Rome. He heard all the stories, knew the language, and how to talk to them. Sometimes it was all about just being a bro.

They were all going to get very comfortable with each other. It was a two- or three-week journey to Tarraco, where Galba would (hopefully) still be located by the time they got there. The men would only stop each night with just enough time before sundown to feed the horses and make dinner. Otho didn't mind camping on the road, and it was generally a pleasant journey that was hasty—but not too rushed. The quiet of the road across the scenery of the Iberian Peninsula would provide good mental respite.

***

One day on the journey, around noon, Onomastus broke the silence of travel. "So, what's the plan when we get to Tarraco?"

"Well, generally, it's to suck up to Galba, play it by ear, make friends, and hope for the best," Otho answered.

"Sounds very thought out. What exactly does all that mean in practice, though?"

"I'm not exactly sure. It's gonna be tricky.

Galba's not exactly the bribe-friendly sort, from what I've heard."

"Yeah, that's not usually standard practice for the conservative types like Galba."

"I know." Otho scratched his chin. "I'm not gonna lie, Onomastus, you may see a side of me you haven't seen before in Lusitania."

"Oh? What do you mean exactly?" he asked.

"I told you about my time in Rome with Nero and Poppaea, right?"

"Yeah, you did. Sounded like a wild time until it was all over."

"So, before that, to even get into that social circle, I had to do a lot of, uh, upper-class socializing. It's not as fun as you'd think—especially with the older guys like Galba," Otho explained.

"Oh, you poor thing, hanging out at the bath, drinking wine, and going to fancy dinner parties with all the rich people. However did you survive?" Onomastus teased.

"Yeah, yeah, that's what it looks like. But you gotta say the right things and act a certain way, otherwise, you'll get nowhere. The snootier the crowd, the more dangerous. If you ever stop signaling wealth and class, it's over! That city gossiped if you even spoke out of turn or were caught hanging out with the wrong class. Why do you think they all hated Nero so much?" Otho asked, rhetorically.

" 'Cause he was a psychopath, maybe," Onomastus answered.

"No! They're all psychopaths. How else would they all get so rich? That wasn't the issue. They hated Nero because he was young and didn't get brainwashed by all the upper-class twits, despite his mom's best efforts. He cared about lower-class things like music, drinking, and games instead of politics and diversifying his financial portfolio. Yeah, he was a psychopath, but he was a down-to-earth psychopath. I felt lucky when I met him because I didn't have to go through the whole rigmarole of upper-class garbage I normally did. Before that, I had to play the game just to get into the same room," Otho explained.

"So, how did you play the game?" Onomastus asked.

"Hanging out at the bath, drinking wine, and going to fancy dinner parties with all the rich people." Onomastus set Otho up.

"Haha, no, but really, what do you mean?"

"I've been very kind to you, Onomastus, but when we get to Tarraco, I'm going to have to be a total culus. I'm gonna yell at you for stupid stercus, insult you, and give you a lot more dirty work. It's all a weird alpha game I gotta play. I promise it'll be worth it, but just roll with whatever happens. I'll need your eyes and ears on the ground with the other slaves to figure out what's going on if we're going to get anywhere. I have no idea what the situation is in Galba's administration, but we're gonna find out and exploit whoever the hell is calling the shots. There's no way that old man is running everything. We really are going to have to play it by ear, Onomastus," Otho elaborated. "Galba may not take bribes, but someone near him does, I assure you. Until then, I gotta play the part."

"Ah, yeah. For some reason, I didn't think about all that, but it makes sense. I get it. Thanks for the heads up. I'll try and look all pathetic and whatever for you to cultivate that alpha energy,"

Onomastus confirmed.

"I knew I could count on you. Even when we get to Rome, this—" Otho finger-gunned Onomastus and himself back and forth "—is only gonna happen in private. Even with other slaves around, we can't get rumors started. I promise I'm not a culus, but as soon as we get to Tarraco, we're strictly professional in front of anybody. Aight?"

"Got it," Onomastus replied with a fist bump.

"Now pass me more of that goat jerky," Otho requested, "This leg of the journey is the last time we'll get to relax for a while."

With their mutual understanding, the two sat back and relaxed for the rest of the trip to Tarraco. Otho continued to tell stories of his experience in Rome to prepare Onomastus for the tribulations ahead. He shared multiple stories of his sycophantic past, warning Onomastus of how pompous he was about to get. Otho even shared stories of his cougar-chasing years before Poppaea with women such as Cornelia. While Otho's stories showed the darker side of upper-class Rome, Onomastus began to quit hating the game and started respecting the player.

***

After a couple of weeks, Otho and Onomastus finally reached Tarraco on a cool, early afternoon. They sent a couple of cavalrymen to make arrangements for their arrival a day prior. Upon entering the gates of the city, Otho was met by two of their soldiers who led them to a room for the night. While he did not expect to stay in Tarraco long, Otho was surprised to learn that Galba hadn't even left for Rome yet. He didn't know how long he'd be in Tarraco.

Wasting no time, Otho had his belongings unloaded into his room for the night and made his way toward the governor's villa at a quick pace after making sure his room was livable and not one of those dingy hotels you pack your college buddies in on an unplanned spring break trip. He arrived at the door of the governor's villa with Onomastus and took a deep breath before knocking forcefully.

Upon opening the door, the two were met by a male house slave. "Salve, what can I do for you, sir?" the slave inquired with the door fully open.

"I am Marcus Salvius Otho and have arrived to pay my respects to Galba and offer my services in his new administra—wait a second, you look familiar," Otho interrupted himself.

"Yes! You sent me here a while back with all that gold," the slave responded.

"Ah, yes. I did do that. Hope you were able to help the rebellion," Otho recalled, unable to remember his name. It was Lucius.

"Well, Galba didn't have much use for us on that front unfortunately. He sold most of my friends and my wife to save on money," Lucius answered. "Anyway, I'm sorry to say, but Galba is not available right now. If you wait over here, I can find out for sure."

Otho and Onomastus entered the mansion and sat down on some couches in the atrium while the slave spoke to another in an adjacent room and returned to the atrium. "So, Lucius! How's life in Villa Galba?" Onomastus asked Lucius while Otho waited silently.

"Eh, it's alright," Lucius responded, "It hasn't been too different until Galba became the emperor. Now, it's been a little bit busier with all the people coming to visit and suck up. I'm not gonna lie, y'all probably won't get to see him today."

"Shoot, really?" Onomastus replied.

"Yeah, he and his close advisors are in some secret underground meeting, not to be disturbed," Lucius replied. Lucius leaned in and whispered, "I think it's a sex cult," to an unsurprised Otho.

"If not now, then when?" Otho interrupted.

"I don't know, and I think everyone's actually leaving for Rome soon," Lucius replied. "I will say, if you want your best shot, meet up with one of the pedagogues; I hear Vinius is the easiest to convince if you're in a hurry."

"Pedagogues, Vinius, who's that?" Onomastus asked.

"There are three men who Galba trusts in this town to run his administration. Laco, his legal advisor, Icelus, who, uhh, just keeps Galba happy, and Vinius. He's one of the more influential members of the pedagogy. He has control of the legion. From what I've heard, I'm pretty sure he's the mastermind of the revolt. Luckily, he's also the most easily influenced with the right motivation," Lucius explained. His eyes roved over to the adjacent room at the slave monitoring Galba's meeting, looked back, and by Lucius's face: no luck. "Yup, he's still doing that cult stercus."

"Gotcha, we'll look into that. I did write a letter in the eventuality we weren't able to meet Galba." Otho handed Lucius a letter.

"I'll put it with the other letters." Lucius grabbed the letter and placed it in a three-foot-deep basket full of letters. "I'd just talk to Vinius. This isn't even perfumed."

Otho and Onomastus left the villa and headed back to their room for the night. "Right, so Vinius it is then," Onomastus commented.

"Yeah, I guess so. I was hoping I'd already have some favor. Just a road bump, but I think I know what to do," Otho assured Onomastus.

"Yeah . . ." Onomastus replied, "You've done this sort of thing before. I'm sure you can do it again."

"Yup. Anyway, you head back. I've got someone I need to visit first," Otho said.

"Okay, I'll see you later then," Onomastus waved Otho away.

Otho headed towards his contact's place, guided by an address from a friend in Rome. Pulling out the letter, he mumbled to himself, "Right here, second house on the left. Here it is, with the statue of Venus, just like it says," Otho mumbled to himself, staring at a four-foot marble statue of the goddess with exposed nameplate covered in bird stercus. "Uhh, this statue's seen better days."

Otho knocked on the door and waited for a response. "Who's there?" a voice answered through a cracked door.

"Yo, Gaius, it's Otho," he replied.

"Otho, what the futuus are you doing here?" Gaius asked, letting him in. "Hey, go grab some wine, it's Otho!" Gaius shouted at a six-year-old boy running around hitting the wall with a stick. The kid stopped and stared at his dad silently. "In the kitchen. Don't make me ask again."

"I thought you were the pullout king," Otho joked as the child ran into the other room.

"I swear I didn't mess up, but this one girl was just extra fertile." Gaius laughed. "Nah, it was time. I love that kid. He's weird as stercus, though, always handing me random rocks. What brings you here to Tarraco? Galba, I assume?"

"You know me too well," Otho answered.

"Ha, you and everyone on this side of the empire right now," Gaius said. "I've made a killing renting out my spare room. You lucky enough to actually see him?"

"Well, I was lucky enough to support the rebellion at the beginning, so I'm joining his journey to Rome and his administration," Otho responded. "We should be leaving soon, so I had to pay a visit."

"No kidding. Well, stercus, congrats, man. That's a big step up from Lusitania governor. You must be excited to get back to the city," Gaius said, grabbing wine from his kid and pouring drinks for the two of them. "Glad you were able to stop by."

"Yeah, well, I do have a small favor to ask," Otho began. "I made it over from Lusitania, but I'm a tad short on coin for the journey. The trip lasted much longer than I had anticipated. You know how these roads can be."

"Oh man, I know how it is. How short are you?" Gaius asked.

"A few thousand sesterces, at least. I have plenty of assets in Rome and Lusitania. I'm just in a bind, and I think we're about to leave soon. I'll pay you back, don't worry," Otho assured Gaius.

"Gosh, that is quite a bind," Gaius agreed. "Well, if you're gonna be on Galba's administration, I don't think I have to worry about getting paid back. Just remember me when you've hit it big." Gaius laughed.

"Thanks, man, you're the best," Otho said before toasting their wine. "I got you man . . . with interest, don't you worry."

"Hey, Primus," Gaius called to the small child who had quit slapping his stick at the wall and was now stabbing it. Primus stopped his attack to stare at his dad intently. "Never mind, I don't think you're strong enough." Gaius stood up and walked upstairs, followed by Primus.

Otho waited for Gaius to return. A minute later, Gaius emerged with a small chest at the top of the stairwell. He walked down slowly, with Gaius's two hands on both ends and his son on the lower step supporting the center. Gaius was unwilling to trample his own son and descended at a step a second. He then placed the chest in front of Otho. "This should hold you off till you get to your assets in Rome."

Otho opened and closed the chest. "Yes, you, my friend, are a lifesaver. I promise, as soon as I get back to Rome. Especially with this new job, you know I'm good for it."

Otho stayed for a few more rounds of wine before noticing the outside light dimming. "Oof, I've got to go before I can't find my way back."

"Aight, see ya next time," Gaius said. "Don't be a stranger. Probably next time I'm in Rome more likely!"

Otho grabbed the chest and exited the door. "See ya, Primus. Take care of your dad for me." Gaius laughed and closed the door. Otho hustled down the street, holding the trunk just below his chest. The wine told him to quit hustling, but the valuable-looking chest and dimming sunlight in a strange street urged him to hurry. He was luckily only blocks away from his room and didn't have to work up too much of a sweat.

Otho entered the room with the chest. "Salve," he greeted Onomastus.

"Salve," Onomastus responded, giving Otho an inquisitive look about the chest.

Otho ignored the look, set the chest down, and pulled out his other chest. He opened both chests and stared at their contents for two and a half moments. He ran his hand through the coin, stood up, and stared at the two open chests for another moment. He grabbed the smaller one, poured some gold into the larger, and sat it down in the same spot. Going through the same procedure, he laser-focused on eyeballing the quantity, felt around, and looked back. Some advanced financial calculus was afoot. He traded his previous large pour for handfuls of gold back and forth as he repeated the process. He then began moving individual pieces of gold and trinkets for another moment before standing up and observing the two containers and kicking one, then the other. Tilted both up together. He then bent over and shook the smaller chest before taking out three more pieces of gold for the larger one.

"Yup, that oughta do it," Otho said finally, looking at Onomastus.

"Where did—what . . . ?" Onomastus began.

"Don't ask. Just bring this to Vinius tomorrow and get me some time with Galba," Otho instructed.

6 THE MIDDLE SEAT

Vinius received the package, and it was sufficient. Onomastus explained everything and secured face time with the big man. It was lucky for Otho he showed up in Tarraco before everyone important had left and happened to find out exactly who to grease for his influence. It was even luckier that Otho had a friend in town he could borrow money from. Between Otho's ambition, the clear opportunity, and his experience, it would never be over until Otho had absolutely nothing left.

A few days later, Galba, his forces, and his entourage finally left for Rome. Many months of administrative planning and logistics had prepared for an old man to ride in a carriage from Hispania to Rome. Vinius, at the head of the entourage and in contact with Onomastus, arranged for Otho to ride in Galba's carriage on the first day.

For solidarity, the cavalry had been absorbed into Galba's forces, and only Onomastus was within Otho's direct influence in the large force marching to

Rome. Onomastus would be walking most of the way alongside the slow-moving force. After purchasing the most expensive travel fare without complimentary free drinks and a hot towel, Otho entered Galba's carriage and awaited his destiny.

Within the cabin of the carriage were Galba's pedagogues: Vinius, Laco, and Icelus. Two old and crabby, one young and out of place. You could hang a picture off Vinius' hooked nose between his grimacing face. Laco, however, looked stern and lost in thought, probably thinking about what he was going to say tomorrow or what he should have said yesterday. Icelus just looked bored and tired. Before Otho had a chance to sit next to Icelus, Vinius interrupted, "That seat's for Galba," and patted the middle seat.

There were no middle seat armrest rules in ancient Rome, so Otho was going to have to fight for every inch of space he had. He would attempt to be polite, being new to the group, so it was a fight he would lose. Three minutes after he sat down, Galba finally arrived. The door of the carriage was held open by a soldier as Galba slowly climbed into the carriage and sat to the right of Icelus, making some old man groaning noises only solved by high-tech hip replacement surgery. There was no room to spare between the two, but plenty on Galba's right. Icelus was pinned.

Vinius was a Roman politician experienced at accumulating wealth to a degree exceeded by few other Romans. True to his miserly nature, Vinius had amassed quite a retirement account by skimming capital off the top of some slush funds he set up during Galba's reign as governor in Hispania while also being the commander of a legion. His lust for riches proved so strong that he even tried the previous emperor Claudius's tolerance. According to those who knew him closely, Vinius had kleptomaniacal tendencies—such that when dining with the emperor Claudius, he pocketed the dinnerware (and was caught). Luckily, Claudius was not a murderous psychopath like his predecessor and successor. The good-natured emperor punished Vinius with peasant dishware at the next dinner, embarrassing the up-and-coming politician.

Vinius was also famous for his love of loose women. In one story from his first military campaign, Vinius snuck in his own commander's floozy wife by dressing her up as a soldier and sneaking her into the general's quarters at night. According to Plutarch, Vinius then proceeded to have "commerce with her" (and I just cannot come up with a better euphemism for a loose woman secretly meeting up with a money-grubbing Roman than that). This apparently got Vinius thrown in prison and almost killed. He was, however, quickly released instead of serving his due sentence. Presumably, the commander's reasoning was, proverbially speaking, "you don't hate the player, you hate the game."

The less famous or infamous members of the vehicle were the legal advisor, Laco, who was all things crafty in finding loopholes in obscure Roman laws or twisting words in just the right ways. Then there was the young and handsome freedman, Icelus, who Galba liked to keep around to fulfill other needs best left to the imagination. Somehow, Icelus would become the least controversial of the pedagogues.

Before the caravan began moving, the silence

was broken. "Who are you?" Galba pointed at Otho. "I don't recognize you. Have we met?"

"I'm Marcus Salvius Otho. You may remember me from my letters during the rebellion. I've come to join you in your reclaiming of Rome from Nero's sadistic stranglehold," Otho replied.

"That name does sound familiar," Galba grumbled. "Hmmmm, did we fight in the war together?" He scratched at his fuzzy decades of memory.

"I sent financial aid for the rebellion, some slaves too," Otho tried to jog his memory.

"He did send money," Vinius backed up Otho. "He was one of the only governors to support us before you were proclaimed emperor."

"Ahhhhh," Galba acknowledged Otho. "I still don't recall, but I'll trust Vinius's word that you are loyal."

"I'm more than loyal," Otho said. "I'm a capable administrator, excellent at navigating the politics of Rome, and I would do anything to further establish a stable post-Nero regime." Otho knew this was his first impression and went full elevator pitch to a hiring manager after being unemployed for months. It was clear he had been practicing his own elevator pitch daily. "Before I was governor of Lusitania, I was an established figurehead in the imperial administration. I still know a lot of the movers and shakers in the city. If you want a clean transition in Rome, I'm one of the top men for the job."

Otho awaited a response from Galba. The rocking carriage moved the elderly emperor back into his seat like a rag doll. Galba sat up briefly, revealing closed eyes and an open drooling mouth. Otho waited another thirty seconds on the edge of his seat until he heard Galba begin to softly snore.

"I'm not sure how much of that he heard, but welcome aboard," Vinius told Otho. "Maybe you'll get some more face time after lunch. He's very tired from all the administrative work he's been doing to set up the Hispania governorship and the transition here."

"So, who is this guy?" Laco questioned Otho's credentials. "I don't remember hearing about him or receiving financial aid."

"You may have not seen the aid because I've been taking the liberty of handling the finances since the rebellion. He was the governor of Lusitania. Now he's joining us," Vinius defended Otho. "If he has the influence I observed yesterday, he'll be invaluable." Vinius cleared his throat to make himself clear to Otho.

Otho already knew what he meant and hoped he had enough in his chest for the journey. He subtly nodded to Vinius in agreement. Icelus failed to respond as Galba had already begun leaning over to rest his head, shoulders, and hand on all parts of Icelus. The freedman was completely pinned under total imperial authority like a disobedient province full of tax dodgers and could not make a sudden move or sound to avoid waking Galba. That was the cozy side of the carriage.

On the not-so-cozy side of the carriage, Laco was still not convinced. "I'm not convinced," Laco said sternly. Skeptically, he continued "I'm skeptical. Galba becomes emperor, we finally make our way to Rome, and this guy shows up like he's one of us. I know you're a tad shadier than most, Vinius, but you're at least the type of shady I know."

"I've checked him out. He has no ill will. There's plenty of room for the three of us," Vinius told Laco across Otho, smooshed between the two. Icelus then grunted a couple of times at Vinius through Galba's snoring. "My apologies, there's plenty of room for the four of us."

"Well, I'm just happy to be here," Otho interjected. "I've been itching to get back at Nero and his regime since they sent me out to Lusitania a decade ago. I don't believe we've all met just yet."

"I'm Cornelius Laco. I handle all the legal matters," Laco said shortly, still skeptical of Otho.

"As you know, I'm Vinius, I handle finances. That over there is Icelus, and you can kinda see what he does. He, uhh, keeps the boss happy," Vinius said without further explanation.

"Well, I'm Otho, as I mentioned earlier. I'll help with the politics in Rome and interfacing with the legions and the Praetorian Guard," Otho said, giving himself responsibility.

"That's an expensive job there," Vinius told Otho. "I hope you have the personal means to accomplish that."

"Oh, I have plenty of means in Rome. That's not an issue," Otho assured them.

"Wait, weren't you the guy that was all buddy-buddy with Nero a long time ago and was married to his second wife, Poppaea?" Laco questioned. "I knew your name sounded familiar."

"Yeah, that's, uhh, me," Otho replied. "Obviously, you know how that went. Can't trust that guy. Not that it matters anymore. Between having it for my wife, just trying to use me, and not folding to his will all the time like some other spineless sycophants in the city, my days were numbered in Rome."

"I hope that's the case," Laco said, trying to read Otho's virtue signaling. "Because I don't think there will be much place in Rome for friends of Nero, past or present."

"I am by no means a friend of Nero. You can trust me," Otho answered Laco's criticism.

"Did you ever remarry?" Vinius asked.

"No, I'm still single," Otho answered.

"Interesting, because my daughter is available if you really do want to be part of the team," Vinius said, the Poppaea story giving him ideas.

Laco and Vinius temporarily ended the introduction, and transitioned to some boring, unproductive, and circular debate about a senator named Marcelus, primarily between Laco and Vinius. They argued back and forth like it was a tennis match but eventually began to relax. It would be a long journey to Rome. Otho was stuck in a particularly physically and socially uncomfortable journey. His money felt wasted as the man he wanted to get face time with was asleep or out of it in the close comfort of Icelus's warm embrace. Even among the conscious members of the carriage, Otho was constantly playing the third wheel to Vinius and Laco and the fifth wheel to the group as a whole. This wasn't the type of third wheel that leads the tricycle either; it was one of those weird third wheels at the back of one of those weird stingray motorized tricycles people drive that want the feel of a motorcycle but not the risk of one.

Without social and political context, and because of the many years Vinius and Laco had been working together, Otho was like an intern sitting in at meetings after being told to take notes. He had trouble following what the two were talking about for a full day of sitting in that carriage. All Otho could tell was that Laco and Vinius were usually in disagreement but never while Galba was awake. It was almost always a polite, healthy disagreement, but it was never primarily about policy. Instead, it was about winning the argument. Between Laco's keen eye for colorful interpretations of laws and Vinius' manipulative tendencies, the arguments were unnecessarily tedious, semantic, and long-winded.

It was a real task to follow, and Otho questioned his own intellect in his passive listening role. This was no reason to feel dumb or inferior, but the feeling of inferiority made Otho want to prove himself. He had to prove his intelligence by understanding what was going on and providing value at the risk of sounding dumb. Because of this, he felt he could not ask questions. Asking obvious questions that even the freedman/gigolo, Icelus, seemed to know the answers to would immediately reveal his own ignorance. Otho tried to avoid asking simple questions. Instead, he would pose the questions as long-winded and tediously worded as Laco and Vinius's. This kept him ignorant far longer than necessary, at a greater risk of sounding dumb. For Otho's purposes, it was not okay to be perceived as the new guy.

***

One month of travelling later and not much had changed. Galba was asleep, but Otho could at least build rapport with Laco and Vinius outside of chests of cash. Periodically, he would work up the confidence to say something. He was typically met with quick, dismissive criticisms or, worse, laughter—not with him but at his naive comments. Trying to sell himself, he would occasionally relate topics of political discussion to personal experience to display value. Without fail, Otho was met with a "cool story, bro" type of response. To make it worse, he had a middle seat for the equivalent of a month's worth of international flights. At least Galba's overactive bladder required frequent stops.

It was a nightmare hybrid between a job interview he wasn't ready for and an endlessly confusing meeting he had to try and follow. Otho bought this experience with his good friend's money, and it was worth every piece of gold. He may not have been providing the impression he wanted toward the pedagogues, but he observed and understood enough to get valuable exposure to the Galba regime no one else would see. The fact that he was there in that carriage most of the trip revealed Vinius's greed as the major weakness of the regime.

"I've got to grab some air," Otho told them. He could not spend every hour of every day of the trip in these suffocating conditions. "I'm gonna step out for a bit. Spring a leak, stretch my legs."

"We're not stopping," Laco told Otho. "You're gonna have to wait."

"I don't need this thing to stop. I'm gonna combat roll," Otho answered Laco's dumb criticism with authority. He may have been struggling to keep up intellectually, but Otho knew how to emanate that BDE (Big Dagger Energy). Laco interpreted his BDE for young jock overconfidence but didn't care enough to say anything.

"Aight, see ya in a bit," Otho said, stepping over an annoyed Laco, opening the door, and timing for a nice patch of grass to land on. He made a short hop with bent knees and executed his combat roll like a professional. As a man in his mid-thirties, he groaned while walking off the unnecessary physical jolt to his unstretched tendons, which was unwelcoming to such gross acts of youthfulness.

"Woah, sick roll, dude," one legionnaire commented on Otho's stunt.

Otho had to hide the pain. He quit groaning and bounced back up to a walking position. "Gotta keep limber," Otho told the men as he maintained his composure to the laughing soldiers. He jogged to a nice open location overlooking the countryside of southern Gaul as they were in between mountain ranges. Otho lifted his toga and let loose his dagger, relieving himself into an open field while soldiers and the rest of the caravan walked by.

"Uhhhhh," Otho moaned to himself, enjoying the moment of release while he felt the warmth of the sun where it normally didn't shine. The break from the carriage and the pristine countryside was just the breather he needed. Some things will always be sacred, and urinating outdoors to a beautiful view will never stop being one of them.

After pinching it off, Otho jogged back into the caravan along the road and toward Onomastus, walking an appropriate distance behind the imperial carriage. "How's it been going in there?" Onomastus asked.

"It's the same ol' same ol'," Otho replied as he slowed to Onomastus's walking pace. "Galba's asleep, Icelus is his travel pillow, Laco and Vinius have been arguing over finances and policies all day, and I've been just struggling to follow."

"I'm sure it'd be nice to sit back and relax in that carriage, but I still do not envy that arrangement," Onomastus commented on Otho's road life. "I am hearing some interesting stories out here."

"Oh, like what?" Otho asked.

"Well, just ask them," Onomastus told Otho, nodding back at the soldiers marching behind them.

"How's the march? Being treated well?" Otho asked the soldiers who had laughed at his clumsy combat roll.

"It's business as usual, sir," one soldier in the front responded. "Gonna try to get out of this unit as soon as I'm able to. I could be making more as a godsdamn pleb," the soldier cursed.

"What? Soldiers get paid better than most men in the empire. I don't like the sound of that," Otho commented.

"Yeah, in most legions," the soldier said, "We haven't had to risk our lives yet, but even my friends in more peaceful parts of the empire at least get bonuses."

"No bonuses? That's unheard of," Otho sympathized. "How's that even possible?"

"Galba's a cheap bastard," the soldier answered. "You're part of his entourage now, can't you fix this? I can't even imagine this unit's morale without any pay increases."

"Ya gotta be kidding me," Otho said,

immediately taking the soldiers' side. Paying soldiers bonuses was common practice. It was general knowledge that you wanted the men with pointy things to be happy and well paid. "I'm sure it's a financial problem or a misunderstanding," Otho shouted to the unit. "You will all get bonuses once we get to Rome. You all deserve your fair share for securing the empire!"

The soldiers cheered. "Can you even promise that yet?" Onomastus questioned Otho under his breath.

"I'll find a way. That's insane. Who doesn't pay their soldiers?" Otho asked rhetorically.

"Apparently Galba. Every soldier I've talked to on this trip has had the exact same complaint," Onomastus said.

"Wow, that's just stupid. What the hell is wrong with him?" Otho thought aloud to Onomastus. "He's just asking for another revolt."

"I've certainly never heard of it."

"If that's the case, I think I've found my second opportunity here," Otho said.

"Second?" Onomastus asked for clarification.

"Yeah, between the soldiers and Vinius, when we get to Rome, influence is going to have a very defined price. This is going to be easy," Otho explained.

"You sound like you know what you're doing," Onomastus said as Otho jogged back to the carriage with a rejuvenating new plan. "I hope you have more of those chests and friends of yours when you get to Rome . . ."

Otho knew exactly how many chests he had in Rome. "Anyway, see ya later. Break's over, I'm afraid."

"Aight, good luck in there," Onomastus told Otho as he jogged back to the carriage.

Otho maintained speed, knocked on the door as a warning before opening it up and hopping in. The open door introduced a brief, slow gust of dusty wind kicked up by the soldiers. His expected intrusion interrupted whatever was happening inside as he climbed over Laco to reclaim his seat. There was some elbow encroachment past the middle seat border, so Otho had some work ahead of him to reclaim long-fought-over ground.

"Have a good stretch?" Laco questioned Otho as his elbow firmly stood its ground.

"The best," Otho replied.

The commotion and the dust awoke Galba. "Ahh, welcome back from another urination break, I assume," Galba coughed from the dust. "How are the troops doing out there?"

"They're holding up, sir. Generally good morale," Otho answered. "They are good men. You have been training them well."

"Did I ever tell you of my time in Germania?" Galba asked.

"You've mentioned it a few times."

"I would march alongside a unit like this on foot at three . . . no . . . four times this speed . . ." Galba yawned through his story. ". . . That right there is how you command the army. These days, commanders would never know the first thing about gaining loyalty."

"It's a real tricky job," Otho agreed.

"Do you know . . ." Galba paused, ". . . most commanders these days just bribe their men?" he scoffed. "Can you believe that?"

"I have heard of the practice," Otho said, giving a disgusted look. "Absolutely no class if you ask me."

"You know what I always say?" Galba paused, unanswered because everyone knew what he was about to say, "I choose my soldiers, I do not buy them." The occupants of the carriage nodded their heads along with the rhythm of Galba's go-to phrase to justify being cheap. "I am absolutely pooped. Those looky-loos yesterday in Narbo really wore me out." Galba excused himself back into dreamland. The group, now well acquainted with Galba, smiled and nodded at their fearless sleepy leader before getting back to business.

***

The convoy slowed upon the ascent of the Alps. Soldiers, in full gear, were driven to an unreasonable speed up a mountain pass that would leave any man winded, no matter the altitude. The pass was in the beautiful heart of the Swiss Alps, with green hills curving exponentially upward to snowcapped peaks. Each man was carrying at least forty-five pounds of gear, not including a backpack of rations, which for some soldiers were quickly running low. All the while, each formation was critiqued on their uniform or marching pace by military leadership at the insistence of Galba's love of discipline. Nothing ruins a beautiful view faster than being criticized.

The sun was quickly approaching the edge of the valley, and the convoy halted to set up camp.

First, toiling away for the imperial tent, then erecting quarters for the men, the soldiers didn't even have a moment to catch their breath. After stopping short of the top of the pass by some unknown distance, the rest of the grueling journey would have to wait for the morning. With the camp pitched and two men starting a fire, the rest were finally able to kick back and relax while they waited for dinner to finish cooking.

"Oh man, my dogs are barking," one moaned, leaning back on his backpack and propping up his feet on a rock.

"I hear that dude," another soldier joined in the complaining.

This was when Otho decided to pop in and see how all the common folk were doing. He had heard more complaints from the soldiers and from Onomastus and decided to show his friendly face. "Hey, mess mates, what's cookin'?"

"Hey, it's the combat roll guy," one soldier recognized Otho. The other soldiers who witnessed Otho's great feat laughed. "What the futuus are you doing out here and not in the bougie tent? That's where I'd be."

"Dude, you have no godsdamn idea," Otho played to the position of maximum suffering. "The bougie tent and the bougie carriage are absolute mental futuendi torture."

"Yeah, so you came to hang out and take our food?" Otho was teased by the reclined soldier.

"It wouldn't be very patrician of me if I didn't come bearing gifts, now would it?" Otho replied, holding up two dead chickens in each hand. He handed them over to the young man stuck with cooking duty and Slav-squatted next to the fire. "Wish

I could just march with you guys, really."

"Oh, bull stercus, no way anyone would prefer marching up this mountain to sitting in a covered carriage," the soldier replied. "Brutus, by the way."

"That's what I thought, too, but after a week of this, I'd prefer the physical pain in my legs to a persistent, throbbing headache. And it's Otho, the combat roll guy." Otho laughed at himself with everyone.

"So, how much further till the top of the pass?" Brutus asked.

"I don't know, I've never been on this pass before," Otho replied.

"Why's that?"

"Because I sailed to Hispania," Otho answered.

"Ex-futuendi-actly," Brutus replied to murmurs of agreement from the rest of the men. "Why the futuus aren't we just sailing to Rome? I've been in the army for ten years now, and I ain't ever marched through the Alps."

Otho wasn't there during the planning of the trip, but he wasn't about to say "I don't know" in front of his men. He chose another leadership tactic. "Galba's just old-fashioned like that."

"Old-fashioned," the soldier replied. "When was it normal to march through a mountain range when you can just take a three-day boat ride?"

"I wouldn't know, I'm not very old-fashioned." Otho answered. "That just seems to be Galba's answer for everything."

"Is it also old-fashioned to be as annoyingly strict as possible and not give us enough rations for the march?" Brutus pried further into his upper rung of leadership. "We are mess mates, after all."

Otho nodded through Brutus's griping, backed by the agreement of the rest of the men. "I'll see what I can do. I'm not gonna lie to ya, Brutus, we're most of the way up a mountain right now. I can complain up for ya, but I don't think we're gonna see any more supplies till we're off this hill. I'll tell ya what, though, I can at least get y'all some bonuses in Rome."

"We could deal with that," Brutus agreed. "I do appreciate the straight talk."

Otho was able to quell some of the grumblings of the troops with his promises. There was no telling if they believed him or if he would be able to get those bonuses. More soldiers each night knew Otho by name toward the end of the journey, and Otho increased his rapport with the men from acquaintance to friendly nod to finally "waddup, futuebatur" level friendship. As the rapport built, Otho had a harder and harder time hanging out with Galba and the pedagogues in the cabin, and his urination breaks became more and more frequent.

Day in, day out, Otho's experience was the same: passively enduring intricately aggressive arguments between Laco and Vinius, taking a break, and then popping back in. It was all a blur of political chitchat and watching other important men pay homage or commanders parade their troops in front of Galba in hopes of a sign-on bonus. It was all very boring until they were about to make it to Rome.

***

On the journey to Rome, Galba's contingent encountered many irregular armies ready to pledge loyalty to the new emperor. Galba often threatened these troops with decimation to deter their behavior, but this did not stop every unit from seeking that sweet, sweet bribe to avoid starting a new rebellion. The carriage suddenly stopped.

Galba and his men were only twenty-five furlongs away from Rome—or fifty-five football fields for Americans—when they were surrounded by a group of rowdy men carrying the standard of Nero. Galba did not know what to make of these men. Though they might have acted like soldiers, the consensus among the procurators was that they were a loose gaggle of armed men. They looked more like highway robbers than an army. Most of the men wielded weaponized farming equipment and protected themselves with shanty armor and kitchen pans as shields. Their standards were tattered and fixed atop the straightest branches they could find in the nearby forest. Galba, Otho, and the pedagogues stepped out of the carriage to see what was going on.

One of the men—a veritable salty dog—approached Galba's carriage but was stopped short by some soldiers. He was a tall, swarthy, and weathered man with an eye patch and hair so wild you'd lose two combs trying to tame it. He wore a piece-meal set of armor assembled from kitchenware scraps, protecting a crimson cape that reached his ankles. One hand was replaced with a hook, and the other held a six-foot spear topped with a serrated blade. It was unclear whether he was for or against the Roman empire. Before hocking up a generous loogie and spitting a solid four cubits to his left, the seasoned sailor let out a grand, "Ahoy, we are part of th' Nero-established soldiers of maritime misfortune. I'm Captain Nigrus Barbatus, leader o' this crew. Aye, we have come fer our new standards."

"What unit is this? Your unit does not seem conventional at all," Galba questioned with reasonable suspicion.

The unit commander then made his proposition to Galba, insinuating the dire consequences of not controlling this sizable force just outside of Rome. "I like th' cut of yer jib. Aye, we were a group of seamen who lost most our crew on th' open seas. 'Twas Nero that made us an official legion of Rome. We're here for our rightful pay and new standards. You wouldn't want any units running around with rebel insignias during these difficult times, would ye?"

Galba and his men found themselves in quite the pickle. There they were, surrounded by an "army" demanding pay and legitimacy. The rest had asked nicely and looked far less threatening. It would have been an easy decision for most Romans to buy their way out and legitimize the reasonably questionable collection of armed sea dogs. While this would normally be an easy score for the group of men, they completely underestimated the gods-level frugality Galba had practiced his entire life.

After hesitating, Galba said, "I see you are quite patriotic for the security of the empire. I'm afraid that I am not well-versed in the financial state of the empire, let alone the legitimate units of legionnaires employed in the protection of Rome. Why don't you get in touch with my folks at the standards and practices office once I get to Rome, and we can look into awarding you your rights as soldiers."

Immediate silence met Galba. The tall man representing the group furrowed his grizzled brow in surprise at the response. He was not angry, sad, or vindictive—but he was caught off guard and did not quite know how to respond or what his next move would be. The swarthy spokesman then responded, "Ye talk . . . later, eh? I've met a lot of politicians in my time in the long forty years on this earth. Sounds more like ye are just using this to deny our rightful privilege as soldiers, methinks!" The hook-handed spokesman gripped the hilt of his sword, which had clearly seen better days, and started eyeing Galba.

Galba would rather risk life and limb than unnecessarily spend money and responded accordingly. "No, you just need to follow the proper protocol, and maybe look a little more presentable if you are, in fact, soldiers of Rome. I'm not denying your request—though I'm certainly not accepting it at this point in time, either." Galba again dug in his heels.

The tall, spaghetti-strainer-armored man's furrowed brow turned into a stare of utmost suspicion, countering Galba's discriminating glance directly. The seaman gripped his weapon even tighter, making a point of doing so visibly. They both knew where this was going—or at least, they thought they did. Each man had severely misread the expectations of the other and was heading into dangerous territory.

The hook-handed seaman knew his own intentions—hence the sword-grabbing display—and believed Galba's words surely meant a deal heading south. On the other hand, Galba, blinded by his frugality, was merely going through the motions of saving a few denarii.

The leader of the seamen raised his sword towards Galba and shouted some sailor nonsense like, "Aye, ye ain't no spittin' image o' Neptune, matey. Ye're a barnacle chafin' at me side . . ." He took a quick breath and snarled before finishing his complex thought: "Aight, you old breath o' mist in me broadside. Negotiate—or we be sewin' yer name in yonder sails!" The surrounding seamen grew restless, shouting to back their fearless commander in front of the emperor.

Galba broke his stare, glancing at his commander of bodyguards, who quickly motioned to the auxiliary cavalry to surround the seamen. A readied flaming arrow shot up into the sky, and Galba was surrounded by a close contingent of bodyguards, all with broad shields ready for the fight. While the group of seamen rattled their sabers, distance quickly grew between the ragtag army and Galba's forces just before the battle commenced.

Without a motion to rally the loosely formed troops of seamen into a defensible position, the auxiliary cavalry sounded their battle horns and closed in. Before the troops threatening the emperor clashed with the bodyguards' shields for ten seconds, Nero's standards were dropped, and the seamen began to run for the hills. The men were in an immediate rout, and the tall man with the hook for a hand was nowhere to be found. Many of the men died either from being trampled or from the swift stabs of the spear-skilled cavalry. Thousands died, and many of the men were not even armed.

Subsequently, the remaining men who

surrendered were rounded up and presented to the emperor. Galba saw only one fitting punishment for these men: decimation, the indiscriminate killing of one out of every ten men. This punishment had rarely seen the light of day since the infamous slave rebellion led by Spartacus and the inadequate army charged with subduing it.

Word swiftly reached Rome of the quick and brutal subjugation of the seaman army, and Galba entered the city with a new reputation—not as a senile old man who would hold the place of emperor, but as the man to bring the soldiers of Rome to toe the line.

Galba, Otho, and the pedagogues had, at last, reached Rome. The rumors of the brutal onslaught so close to Rome filled the air of the imperial city with fear and incredulity among the many men stationed in and around Rome. Nero himself had recalled a Spanish legion—a full fleet—and detachments from Germany, Britain, and Illyricum from the Caspian gates to Rome to deal with Vindex's rebellion. With the patchwork army lying dormant in the vicinity, soldiers itching their palms waiting for bribes, and confusion over the leadership, Rome was a tinderbox ready for one spark to create yet another bloody civil war. Galba would need to win the hearts of the people to prevent another violent overthrow from taking his new position and maintaining peace. For now, at least, Galba was leaning towards the Machiavellian "better feared than loved" model of leadership. Otho, however, smelled the chaos in the air and sensed opportunity.

7 THE SEARCH FOR THE LEG LAMP

Galba arrived in Rome with one goal in mind. Unfortunately for the Senate, it wasn't the shared goal of stabilizing the empire—it was to make as much money as possible. The empire was in deep debt after the spendthrift rule of Nero. In the days before fiat currency and fractional reserve banking, this concerned the sort of people who freak out about things like debt-to-GDP ratios. Under the influence of the legally crafty Laco, Galba and his advisors came up with fundraising plans better described as schemes. They raised as many taxes as they could, including a urine tax. He stopped bribing officials, soldiers, and guards. He even began demanding back the many gifts Nero had given out. Somehow, much of the funds raised would disappear overnight under the careful watch of Vinius, who, perchance, was becoming one of Rome's wealthiest men overnight around the same time.

Vinius, always looking out for his coffers, was waiting at a table full of scrolls in a basket at the head of a line of carts and a large troupe of soldiers personally overseeing the Nero gift repo squad. "Everybody, take a cart and a list," Vinius called out to a crowd of armored guards in a mid-city outdoor warehouse. Between the clean toga he wore, the rings on his hand, and the visible lack of arm strength, he appeared as a man of privilege—more privilege than normal. It was a cool fall day. "Each of these items is listed with a monetary value and an address. You all will recollect each gift or an equivalent monetary value. Do not take no for an answer!"

"What if they refuse? This doesn't sound legal," one of the equites called out.

"It is, in fact, legal," Vinius rehearsed, "not just because it's an order from Galba himself but because the previous emperor Nero has been proclaimed a public enemy. Therefore, all of the gifts purchased with imperial funds on this list were illegal and can be repossessed. So go on and get back those gifts! For the glory of Rome!"

The equites started to pair up. One older eques tapped on the shoulder of a younger man with a scroll. "Let's go, we'll take this district. I know it well." The young man nodded in response.

Tributus was a young, inexperienced eques, but where he didn't have experience, he made up for in spunk. He had the sort of youthful energy you'd just feel bad about ruining with your own cynicism. Tributus wore lighter armor made up of some metal plates and mostly leather strapping. His sword appeared so new that it likely had not yet seen action. Accompanying Tributus was his street partner, the older Languidus. He had served under three Caesars personally. There wasn't much in the streets of Rome

Languidus hadn't encountered in his lifetime of service keeping the city safe from malarkey. In contrast to Tributus, Languidus had been in a scrape or two and opted for the full set of iron Praetorian armor. "You don't see as much as I've seen and not use protection," he always told everyone.

They led their horse-pulled cart out into a main roadway. "What's first on the list?" asked Tributus.

"Looks like this house 'ere. Says Nero gave this man a rare flute from a temple of Apollo in Boeotia. Made of silver and holds a perfect tune," responded Languidus. The two men approached a run-down villa in the arts district. The neighborhood was lined with three-story townhomes that looked like they were packed to the brim with tenants.

"Why'd we have to get the artists?" commented Tributus. "Always getting the stercus assignments. Do you really think we'll get anything valuable out of a place like this?" Tributus groaned, not looking forward to dealing with the unpredictable personalities artists might have. Easy to intimidate, but volatile.

"Nero hung out with a lot of these losers," replied Languidus. "I'm pretty sure we'll find some of that junk here. Can't imagine they'll put up much of a fight either."

The two equites arrived at their first stop. They knew they were at the right place because they heard the faint sounds of a concert flautist on the other side of the door. "Open up in the name of the emperor," Languidus commanded after five loud, spaced-out knocks. The fluting immediately ceased at their presence.

"Just a minute," the tenant responded. A bit of rumbling was heard from the other side of the door. It wasn't the sort of rummaging for a clean tunic but more like the sort of rummaging after your parents get home while you were doing something dubious. The two equites looked at each other, preparing themselves for whatever nonsense this was all about.

"Salve, fine gentlemen. How may I help you?" asked a scrawny man in an oversized tunic. His head was adorned with some sort of crown made from backyard weeds and a couple of wilted flowers. They looked like they used to be yellow but were now clearly Dijon-mustard brown. The room behind him was a mess of junk and half-finished art. Most of the art consisted of repurposed junk and must have been used to model future projects because postmodernism had not yet hit the Roman art scene.

"Good morning," Languidus started, reading from a scroll. "By order of Emperor Galba, the previous Emperor Nero has been declared a criminal by the state. According to Roman law, any gifts purchased with Nero's access to the imperial treasury have been declared illegal and must be immediately repossessed by the offices of Emperor Galba for instant auction."

Tributus pulled out a scroll and skimmed through it until he found the current resident on his list. "According to our records, you are in possession of one silver flute, which reportedly will hold a perfect pitch, blessed by a Greek priestess, and estimated to be worth ten thousand sesterces. We have orders to acquire the flute or nine-tenths of its equivalent value."

The scrawny man was not expecting such an

unpleasant visit from the taxman and his face went from calm to panic. "I can't pay that much money!"

"Then give up the flute. It's just a flute. We know you have it; we heard you playing it just now," responded Tributus. "Let's not make this harder than it needs to be."

"Okay, okay, let me get it for you." The flautist began rustling through a pile of junk, nervously looking for the silver flute. "It's around here somewhere."

"You were just playing it; how come it's taking you so long to find the thing?" questioned an already impatient Languidus.

"Here it is, right here," the scrawny man jumped up with a rusty silver flute. "I got it, no need for trouble here." He handed the flute to Tributus, who was about to mark it off his list before being stopped by Languidus.

"Hold on, let's hear a note before we go," requested Languidus. "The flute's supposed to hold a perfect pitch. We should verify we're getting the correct instrument, right? This could be any old flute for all we know . . ."

Tributus handed the flute back to the artist for a quick goodbye song. The flautist gripped the flute with his quivering hands, puckered up his lips, and began to blow into it as carefully as he could. The perfect-looking embouchure resulted in a wavering tone with the occasional pubescent voice cracks reminiscent of a sixth-grade band Christmas concert performance of "Jingle Bells."

"Well, look what we got here," Languidus said, interrupting the performance and grabbing another silver flute from a nearby pile of junk. "Now, this looks like a ten-thousand-sesterces piece of equipment. Even engraved with a little love note from ol' Nero himself."

The jig was up, and the musician was about to lose his only good flute. "Please, that's the only working instrument I have left! It's all I have to make any money on the streets. I didn't even ask Nero to give it to me. I'm no criminal! Please, I'll do anything!"

The man's begging was quickly silenced by Tributus drawing his sword and tossing the flute into the cart. "Just be glad we didn't have to take it the hard way."

The two equites left the man's home with their first prize reclaimed. The next item on the list was located just down the block, belonging to another one of Nero's lower-class art friends. Just before the next knock on the next door, Tributus sighed. "Looks like it's three thousand sesterces worth of imported Egyptian oil. Here we go again . . ."

The knocking was met with a stretched-out "Come iiiiiin . . . Doooor's open," from a burly but tender voice. This time, there were no sounds of scrambling on the other side of the door. The equites pushed the door open to reveal a tall, well-fed man stretched across a fainting couch. His short tunic barely covered his thighs, and his chest hair poured out of the top. His skin was covered in a shiny sheen, and long curly body hair reached out to ensnare anyone willing to get close enough. After making direct eye contact with the two equites, he added, "I always love unexpected company."

"Uh . . . Good morning," started Languidus, reading again from the scroll he would surely memorize by the end of the day. "By order of Emperor Galba, the previous Emperor Nero has been declared a criminal by the state. According to Roman law, any gifts purchased with Nero's access to the imperial treasury have been declared illegal and must be immediately repossessed by the offices of Emperor Galba for instant auction."

Without looking at the list and maintaining eye contact with the man, Tributus spoke. "According to our records, you have three thousand sesterces of imported oil. We have orders to acquire the oil or nine-tenths of its equivalent value."

The man stretched and slinked off the couch into a standing position. "Hmmm, I do recall receiving that oil from Nero. Let me see." He walked into another room and shortly returned with a large, sloshing ceramic vessel. He brought it to the soldiers and set it down beside the armored duo. "Here it is, the Egyptian oil. I did hope to enjoy the rest of it, but the law's the law." The man shrugged.

Languidus took the jug and opened it, giving it a good sniff. "Yup, that's it alright. But the jug's only two-thirds full. We will require either another one thousand sesterces or the missing oil."

The man laid back down on the couch and stroked his exposed legs. "I don't have that sort of money on me. As for the remaining oil, you'll have to wipe it off me if you really want it back with those big, strong hands of yours." The man lay exposed and open to the equites to reclaim their oil.

Languidus approached the man and began beating him senseless with his sheathed sword. "That oil's resale value is garbage! Cough up the money!"

Languidus's strokes were only met with,

"Harder . . . Harder . . . Oh yes, that's the spot." After a good minute of striking, Languidus quit trying to reclaim the oil the hard way. There was no point when there was no money and no oil to reclaim.

"We'll be back for the rest of the money, and it better be here!" Languidus shouted before Tributus loaded the remaining oil—minus the glisten on the man's skin—onto the cart.

After slamming the door shut, Tributus looked at Languidus and said, "Well, that went about as well as I thought it would. Are we actually coming back?"

"Hades no, that dude's a creep. He probably wanted me to keep going. Can't give him the satisfaction. There's nothing wrong with being gay, but I draw the line at being a bottom! Disgraceful!" Languidus ranted before whipping the horse pulling the cart into a forward walk down the street.

"Now this is an interesting one," Tributus commented while reading the list of Nero's gifts. "This next one is an oil lamp on top of a sculpture of a lady's leg. I've never heard of anything like that before."

"Sounds hideous," responded Languidus as they walked to the next address. "How much could that even sell for?"

"Apparently thirty-five thousand sesterces," Tributus answered. "Nero custom ordered it for this guy. Here we are, anyway. Let's see how hideous it really is."

The two went through the motions, knocked on the door, and waited for the next victim to answer. This time, a loud, shrill woman's voice yelled, "Someone's at the door. I'm too busy taking care of YOUR children!"

The call was answered with an "OKAY, I'LL GET IT!" followed by mumbling, "Taking care of MY children, all she does is drink wine all day." A visibly tired man opened the door. "Yes, what is it? Hello? What do ya want?"

"We are here to reacquire illegal gifts from the late Emperor Nero," Languidus replied calmly, sensing the man's stress. "Supposedly, you received a leg-mounted oil lamp from Nero with illegally acquired funds, and we need to get it back or nine-tenths of the equivalent value."

"Oh, just when I thought that lamp caused me enough trouble, here I am continuing to pay the price. Gods, it was beautiful though . . ." The man paced his atrium, motioning for the equites to come in. "Honey! We've got two equites here looking for the leg lamp. You know, the lamp I loooooooved so much."

"That lamp was the worst-looking piece of trash I've ever seen. Good riddance. You're sleeping downstairs if you didn't get rid of it like I asked you to!" the loud, shrill voice responded.

"So, it's not here?" inquired Languidus.

"No, the wife made me get rid of the thing," answered the husband. "She said it didn't go with the rest of her decor for the villa. Really, she didn't like it just because I loved it so much, and she couldn't handle me being happy for once."

"Well, what did you do with the thing? You couldn't have thrown it away!" Tributus questioned.

"No, of course not. That lamp was a real thing of beauty. I gave it to a close friend so I could visit and see it from time to time," the husband explained. "Occasionally, it brings some joy back into my life. Ya know that feeling you got when you were a kid, just running around throwing rocks at slaves being marched into the city during a good ol' triumph? Like everything's just going great, and you don't have a care in the world? And your parents are probably getting back together? That's the feeling I got from that lamp."

"We need that lamp back by order of the new emperor! Where does your friend live?" Tributus interrogated, shaking the man violently.

"He lives three blocks north from here. It's a place just like this, and there's some old graffiti on the street's side wall," answered the husband.

"Most of these houses have graffiti in one place or another. How are we supposed to know which house it is?" Tributus continued to gather information.

"It's kinda long, I can't remember it all. It starts with some graffiti about how my friend is in love with a slave girl," the husband explained. "He hated it so much, but no matter what he did, he couldn't wash it off. Actually, he responded to the graffiti along the lines of how the 'OG (Original Graffiti-er) is just jealous of his good looks' or something like that. He's really sensitive."

"Right, we'll be off then to find this thing," Languidus said. Finding nothing else there, they left the husband and headed back to the streets.

"Please find a good home for the lamp! Every day with it felt like a new day walking through a field of bright green grass covered in crisp morning dew to greet the sun . . ." the husband described before being cut off by Tributus slamming the door.

"I didn't even bother trying to get money from that guy. I just want to see this lamp," Tributus told

Languidus as they made their way down the street.

"I know, it's gotta really be something special if that guy loved it that much. Shame his wife made him get rid of it," Languidus agreed, their enthusiasm for the task renewed.

The two equites traveled a couple of blocks before starting to look for the graffiti described by the husband. As expected, there were a lot of penises. Practically every major Roman politician from the last two decades was etched into at least one or two walls with an enormous dagger. Occasionally, there was an inscription of a dirty limerick or political propaganda, but nothing close to the description given by the previous leg lamp owner. Finally, the two equites came across an inscription that seemed to fit the bill:

Successus the Weaver is in love with the slave of the Innkeeper, whose name is Iris. She doesn't care about him at all, but he asks that she take pity on him.

Below the inscription was another block of text written in much different handwriting and color:

You're so jealous, you're bursting. Don't tear down someone more handsome—a guy who could beat you up and who is good looking.

After thirty minutes of wading through graffiti, dicks, and extremist political propaganda, and where and when to go for a good time, they finally found the correct graffiti. With the equites' morale restored, Languidus knocked on the door with vigor.

"I'm coming, I'm coming," the tenant responded. An athletic-looking man with medium-length matted hair and a tattered but well-fitting tunic opened the door. Without wasting time, the two equites began reciting.

"Good afternoon," started Languidus, reading

from his imperial orders. "By order of Emperor Galba, the previous Emperor Nero has been declared a criminal by the state. According to Roman law, any gifts purchased with Nero's access to the Imperial treasury have been declared illegal and must be immediately repossessed by the offices of Emperor Galba for instant auction."

Tributus followed up with the official description of the lamp. "According to our records, you are in possession of one oil lantern affixed upon a 2.5-cubit-long marble leg sculpture estimated to be worth thirty-five thousand sesterces. We have orders to acquire the lamp or nine-tenths of its equivalent value."

"I don't understand, Nero never gave me a leg lamp. I've never even met the guy," the tenant responded, panicked.

The two equites forced their way in, past the man. "Your married friend gave you up. He was very fond of that lamp and said he had to give it away to a close friend meeting your description. We don't want any trouble. We just need that lamp, or the money . . . but preferably the lamp . . ." Tributus attempted to calm the man down, but his aggressive body language made him more nervous.

"I don't know nothing about no lamp," the man answered, putting his hands up. "Never seen a leg lamp with ornately stitched tassels."

"We didn't mention anything about the tassels," Languidus responded. The cornered man looked Languidus in the eye, then Tributus, before darting between them and sprinting through the door.

"Oh, it's on," Tributus shouted before sprinting after the man. "You come back here right now or it's the arena for you!"

"I'm getting too old for this stercus," Languidus grumbled before building up to a clunky jog after him.

The younger Tributus was in much better shape and maintained pace with the escapee while Languidus disappeared behind the first corner. The athletic man plowed through carts and fruit stands, leaving a wake of destruction and angry citizens for Tributus to navigate through. Both men were nimble and quick, jumping over candlesticks of impressive sizes. After a minute of zigzagging through the marketplace and destroying a sufficient amount of produce, the guilty man turned on a sesterce into a narrow alleyway. About fifty cubits in, he found himself blockaded by an eight-cubit-high wall of garbage. Avoiding the loosely packed pile of refuse, the man hardcore parkoured against both sides of the wall and vaulted over the pile. Tributus knew he didn't have enough traction to pull off a street rat move like that and began pulling himself over the garbage. The act was taking so much time that the man was getting away for sure.

As Tributus peeked over the garbage, he saw the man nearing the end of the alleyway and yelled, "Get back here," before Languidus suddenly appeared at the alley's opening and clotheslined the runner to the ground with a massive thump.

"WHERE THE FUTUO IS THE LAMP?!" Languidus yelled, drawing his sword to the man's floored throat.

"I sold it, I swear! I needed the money! I don't have anything for you!" the man confessed to Languidus as an out-of-breath Tributus caught up.

"WHERE IS IT? Who'd you sell it to?" Languidus continued his interrogation, with Tributus as backup.

"Some North African merchant. He hangs out around the baths about a quarter mile from here, sells rugs and cotton. Please don't hurt me! I won't survive out here as a crippled beggar. I'm too beautiful," the man pleaded.

"We better be able to find that lamp or we'll be coming back for the money, and you don't look like you have thirty-five thousand sesterces of spare change on ya," Tributus threatened. As the two equites walked away, Languidus gave a parting kick to the man's ribs before sheathing his sword.

"I haven't felt this close to the prize in fifteen years. I never realized how much I missed the hustle," Languidus said as they briskly walked towards the nearby bathhouse.

"How did you know that alley was the place to stake out? I would've never caught him in a normal chase!" Tributus asked his older partner.

"Oh, when you've walked these streets as long as I have, you get to know the usual getaway routes for the runners. Experience comes with age. You'll get there, Tributus, you'll get there," Languidus mentored.

For hopefully the last leg of the trip, the two equites made it to the bathhouse to search for the merchant. There was only one who met the description, with a stand full of rugs and Egyptian cotton. Languidus and Tributus approached, hoping there wouldn't be another chase.

"Word on the street is, you have a very special oil lamp," Tributus inquired, going off the usual script. "From what I heard, it's the most amazing lamp. We would like to have it, and we're not taking no for an answer," Tributus stated, eyeing his own sword as a threat.

While the merchant began to look confused, Languidus continued the shake down. "Let me jog your memory: a beautiful stand sculpted as a leg in the purest marble, ornately sewed tassels, and an oil lamp that would light up a room as if the woman of your dreams just walked into your life. Sound familiar?"

"Ohhh, that lamp," the merchant replied, unaware of the dangerous beating he could soon be facing. "I flipped it for a hefty profit."

"GODSDAMNIT!" Tributus cursed.

"Oh, if you're looking for the lamp, it's right over there," the merchant said, pointing at a nearby shop. "I can't move high-class artsy merchandise like my friend can in his boutique. I recognized a masterpiece when I saw it and knew he'd pay the appropriate price. I'm sure he'd double or even triple—"

The two equites didn't have time for more explanations and left mid-sentence. They had reached the end of their patience and just wanted to cross the finish line. Walking into the boutique, they saw many sculptures and busts of famous men and gods. There were paintings and fine tapestries. The store was full of beautiful artwork, but nothing compared to the sight they beheld.

Standing in the middle of the boutique on a platform to feature the pinnacle of fine craftmanship was the leg lamp. Just as the legends had described, the oil lamp was bright enough to warn incoming ships of a densely fogged rocky coast. It stood atop a long slender leg of pristine marble, carved with every detailed muscle and tendon, showcasing athleticism, strength, tenderness, and elegance. It was not the leg you take a quick glance at, not the one you sleep with and forget, not the one you date a few times only to move on. This leg was the type you bring home to your parents for dinner during Saturnalia, build a long fruitful life with, and start a war over if anyone stands in your way. The tassels, far from being tacky, made the transition from leg to lamp a perfect fusion of form and function. Like a Kentucky Fried Chicken taco with Korean-flavored cabbage, this unlikely mutt of design was no monster. It was a miracle and the hallmark of craftsmanship.

"Can I help you? See anything you like?" the shopkeeper asked the two soldiers, who stood speechless at their long-awaited goal. "Oh yes, the lamp. One of my most prized treasures here in the shop. With as many suitors as it has, I'm not letting it go for cheap."

Tributus, without breaking eye contact with the lamp, shoved the shopkeeper to the ground. He and Languidus lifted the lamp off the stand and out of the boutique. Despite the floored man scrambling to his feet and shouting "THIEVES!", there was nothing he could do. The shopkeeper knew there was no recourse possible at this terrible and unexpected injustice.

By this point in the day, it was too late to search for more gifts. It was about to get dark. With no public street lighting, the drunks leaving the bathhouses, and the total lack of city planning producing the most confusing maze of curving and zigzagging streets, Rome after dark was no place to linger. Repossessing any more gifts would have ruined an already perfect climax for Tributus and Languidus's memorable day. They made their way back to the Praetorian Castrum with the cartload of reacquired merchandise from the dodgy tax collection scheme.

****

After a period of raking through the streets for more illegal gifts to repossess, the Praetorians, under Vinius's leadership, had accumulated a treasure trove of goods. It was now time to auction them off and refill the treasury. Word of the auction had been spread far and wide throughout the city for weeks, and there were high expectations from the auctioneers. Rumor had it that the great announcer of the annual games, Buccamus (Caldarius) Ventus, would be running the auction.

Buccamus C. Ventus, the windbag of great renown, was famous for his stentorian voice. His rise to public fame occurred amid a riotous crowd protesting food prices in the streets outside the forum. With a loud shout upwards of dozens of decibels, Ventus's voice pierced through the crowd, ordering them to "MAKE A HOLE" for the previous emperor Claudius attempting to cross the street. In this manner, Ventus single-handedly drowned out the overwhelming roar of the crowd and invoked obedience from the otherwise unruly congregation, and a path was duly made for Claudius. For this great action, Claudius immediately promoted him to the equestrian class, even though Ventus descended from a long line of plebeian shoplifters and cart drivers. While such a voice was meant for the battlefield, Ventus was cursed with flat feet and could not shout commands to the legions amid battle when his voice would be needed the most.

Claudius found another calling for Ventus. He turned out to be perfect for announcing and narrating the most prestigious games in Rome. Whether it was a gladiatorial match with the jeers of the crowd, a chariot race with the thunder of four-horse chariots sprinting for glory, or some esoteric Greek play eliciting widespread groaning from unwilling spectators of culture, Ventus would be heard over the additive noise of the event. Soon, Ventus had become a legend. However, becoming a legend in a city full of debaucherous temptations had a real cost.

While Ventus had not lost his edge when it came to his voice, he had lost his edge in pretty much every other category in life. He had grown too comfortable with his newfound wealth and took his success for granted. Fat, slow, and spoiled with an endless supply of wine, he had become a washed-up drunk. He used to have his pick of the ladies, but even with all his money, he barely saw any action in the last few years. It was getting harder and harder every day for him to get out of bed in the morning. His career as an announcer began to show his decline in life, with fewer jobs every month. He knew he needed a win today. If not for his career, Ventus needed a win for his confidence.

Ventus arrived at the outdoor amphitheater prepped for the auction to greet his now-current employer, Vinius. Catching his breath after the hike to the amphitheater, Ventus greeted Vinius. "Salve, Vinius, it's a beautiful day for an auction. Should have a good turnout."

"Yes, it is. We've promoted the event extensively," Vinius replied. "And we better have a good turnout and make some money. That's the only goal today. Rome is counting on this auction to get out of the red or black or whatever it is. We gotta get out of it."

"I've run auctions before," Ventus assured Vinius. "I've made plenty of money in the past at these sorts of things. I will say, they are usually only open to the patrician class. I don't know how much money we will find allowing all this lower-class riffraff into the amphitheater. Seems like we're just leaving the door wide open to nonsense."

"We need as many people to drive up the price of these items as we can. Additionally, some of Nero's gifts were of baser taste. That won't be a problem for you, will it?" Vinius questioned Ventus, sternly eyeing him down.

"No problem. If it gets rowdy, I'll be able to belt the bids through the crowd," Ventus defended his abilities.

"Okay, well, just know, we really need to get some heated bidding, or we'll be operating at a loss!" Vinius reminded him. Before leaving the auctioneering podium, he tossed a small bag of sesterces. "If you see any nice dining room sets, just set them aside for me. I could use an upgrade."

The mixture of plebs and patrician class filled in, leaving spotty coverage of the amphitheater seating. Many appeared to be just bored and came to watch the curious display of miserliness from the new emperor. Many had no intention of bidding. As the sun hit high noon, it was time to begin the proceedings. Ventus mounted the podium in front of cartloads of booty on display and unraveled a scroll with the list of items and their descriptions.

Upon Ventus's first booming words, the crowd immediately fell silent. "Welcome all to the auction! We have a lot of beautiful items and hope everyone finds what they're looking for. Don't be stingy with those purses, because you never know who might snatch up that dream gift of yours right from under your feet." Ventus paused to take a long, deep breath and then continued, "We have a lot to sell, so we'll be moving at a brisk pace here. Just raise your hand and shout out how much you'd like to bid when you see something you like."

The first item was now on display with the assistance of a beautiful woman. With the local plays on hold for the day, the auction had a full troupe of actresses trying to jumpstart their careers. The first woman, in a long flowing white dress, had mid-length curly brown hair. Practicing her show smile, she held up a large golden funnel about half a cubit in diameter. The funnel, of unknown purpose, had a sturdy wooden handle fixed to one side and was now on full display as the showgirl waved it around, attempting to demonstrate its many uses. She clearly didn't know what they were, but she kept up a good face.

"First up for auction is an antique ear horn, a perfect gift for your hard-of-hearing relatives," Ventus proclaimed. The woman began holding the horn correctly. "It was crafted in Athens over a century ago and has many stories to tell. Picture your favorite grandma or grandpa listening to their grandchildren's first words on this valuable antique. Its estimated value is one thousand sesterces. Let's start the bidding at eight hundred." Ventus's full description was met with an unenthusiastic crowd. Granted, most men's last desire was for their parents to hear again at the next family gathering only to lecture them about the old Augustinian ways or how they're not raising their children right. "How about seven hundred sesterces? It's real fine craftsmanship. You don't find pieces quite like this anymore."

"Three hundred!" shouted a middle-aged, balding man in the crowd. "I'm going to melt it down for scrap," he muttered to the crowd.

"Okay, bidding at three hundred. Do we have any other offers? This is a real bargain now," Ventus responded.

"You can't get three hundred sesterces of material off that piece of junk. It doesn't even look like real gold!" one man in the posse of scrappers spoke.

"You're right. Hey, sweetcheeks!" the bidder shouted, old-school and sexist. "Could you be a doll and bite that gold for me on the funnel? Tell me if it leaves a mark."

The girl timidly nibbled on the funnel with some force, observed the damage, and made a quick report to the man. "It looks like real gold but appears to be flaking off in tiny pieces."

"Good call, son. Looks like bronze underneath. I revise my bid, 180!" the man shouted to Ventus.

"You already bid; it's too late! You owe three hundred," Ventus responded. "And Julia, you're supposed to be on my side."

"Two hundred or I'm walking out of here. I can't make money off it for any more than that," the man bartered.

"Okay, fine, two hundred. But for everyone's awareness, all bids from here on out are final. I'm not haggling here," Ventus compromised.

"Are there any other bids?" Ventus paused for a full minute of nothing but a low rumble from the crowd. "Okay, final sale at two hundred sesterces from the gentleman in the front."

The "golden" funnel was then carried off for the winner, and the next item was on its way to center stage. It appeared to be a well-adorned vase etched with a well-endowed Nero. There wasn't anything else special about the vase; it was kinda boring. Even the etching of the full-figured, flexing Nero, while flattering to the late neck-bearded emperor, was quite cartoonish. The next showgirl, similar in appearance to the last, had unusually long eyelashes and knew how to use them. Showing the vase to the crowd, this girl had Miss-Mediterranean-level beauty-pageant suave. Batting her eyelashes like seductive Morse code at the front row, this girl was clearly looking for something more than an acting career. After a medium-paced twirl with the vase, she made it center stage, popped her hip to the left, and rested the boring vase on it in a serene pose.

"Next item is a vase commissioned by the late Nero from his favorite artist, other than himself," Ventus shouted, getting a handful of laughs at the Nero jab. He rubbed his head and groaned in early-onset frustration upon reading the information on the vase. "This vase is white, can hold a full urna of liquid, and is decorated with a portrait of our late emperor. This is a piece you can pass on from generation to generation. Its estimated value is . . . no, that can't be right . . . fifteen hundred sesterces. Do I have a bid for, I don't know, a thousand?"

The silent audience was still transfixed on the vase's accompanying showgirl. After about fifteen seconds of parting eye contact, a blown kiss landed square on the head of a well-dressed and clearly thirsty young member of the crowd. The man inquired, "Does the vase come with the girl?" The crowd laughed before Ventus responded.

"No, it's just for the vase," Ventus replied.

"Oh, I wouldn't mind. I could at least see the vase home," the woman announced to the crowd.

"Twelve hundred for the beautiful vase!" the thirsty man bid with a wink.

"That's twelve hundred to the man in the third row," Ventus said, excited at the prospect of making some money.

"Thirteen hundred," a man countered. The bidding war started for the most unremarkable vase in the city.

"Thirteen fifty." The thirsty man raised his bid. Back and forth, the bid increased little by little between half a dozen men until it reached two thousand as more bidders dropped out. Only two men were left bidding for the vase when it reached twenty-five hundred.

"Four thousand," a new, older gentleman from the crowd shouted, immediately bringing the bidding war for the vase to a halt.

Ventus eyed the crowd for thirty seconds of silence. The other two remaining bidders shook their heads in defeat. "Four thousand it is, to the older gentleman in the back." Ventus looked too old to be the owner of a vase like that.

The old man pushed his way to the front of the amphitheater and quickly chastised the woman. "Cornelia, what is wrong with you?" He escorted the lady and the vase off the stage and, before paying, shouted to the crowd, "This is my daughter. If you want her to bring you an ugly-culus vase, you'll have to talk to me first!" The most successful showgirl left one parting glance and then exited stage left, her arm locked by her father's strong grip, heading for a night of lectures.

"Looks like the vase is off to its wonderful new home. The next item up for auction is a real hot piece I'm sure will get everyone out of their seats," Ventus announced, trying to keep the excitement alive.

Approaching from stage right, powered by two black horses, was a war chariot like the audience had never seen before. Driving the chariot was the next showgirl, this time decked out in Amazonian armor. While stylish, the armor appeared to protect nothing more than a young boy's innocence. The chariot not only looked fast and sturdy but also had spinning rims on the wagon wheels and flames painted across the side, clearly making it much faster.

"This chariot, designed and custom-built for Nero's favorite gladiator, is a two-horse-powered, screaming-fast monster of a vehicle. Tremble at the power of such a beautiful war machine, built not only for function but for form as well. This wonderful vehicle is perfect for riding into battle, taking your son on his first hunting trip, Sunday drives up the

Appian Way, or just a short family trip to the temple. With comfortable handrails, reins equipped with adaptive cruise control, four cup holders, and plenty of arrow storage for your work trips, this slightly used chariot can comfortably seat four men, has only been driven two hundred miles, and looks and feels like new." Ventus, finding his pace once again, took a quick breath. "Starting at ten thousand sesterces, do we have a first bid for this truly luxury ride . . . horses and girl not included."

The crowd oohed and aahed at the most impressive piece of the auction. The showgirl in her video-game-style bikini armor smiled and waved as she lay across the chariot, not just to accent the beauty of the piece but to suggest what a man's life could be like with such a sweet ride. The crowd started bidding at the beginning price of the chariot. Luxury like this was hard to come by. They weren't buying it just for its function; they wanted to buy it for the lifestyle it offered. As all the middle-aged men caught in life ruts fought each other with the full power of their bank accounts, one angry voice rang out over the crowd.

"How about you give it to me with the ten thousand sesterces included, and I won't sue you?"

The irate voice, assumed to be from the previous owner of the chariot, brought the auction to a halt faster than the chariot could stop with its state-of-the-art antilock brakes. A contingent of sleeper cell men from the crowd joined in his outrage. "Yeah, this auction and all of its materials were illegally acquired," another man shouted. Outrage from the wronged men mixed with eager middle-aged bidders for the chariot, causing the energy of the amphitheater to grow to dangerous levels.

"We want our stuff back!" another angry man yelled.

A group of angered men, who presumably lost cherished items, started charging the auction podium, chanting, "Hey hey, ho ho, this auction's got to go." This contingent was a few crudely fashioned signs away from a brewing protest. They immediately became unavoidably disruptive to the auction and began attracting more and more members. Ventus attempted to shout through the extremely rowdy audience with no luck. Whether the new participants were just bored or outraged like the original protestors, the crowd was on the path to becoming a mob. Passersby, hearing the commotion, approached, and like any wild crowd, it was only a matter of time before someone got punched in the face, and the energetic crowd broke out into full-on fisticuffs. Soldiers, avoiding more carnage, escorted the showgirls and Ventus out of the amphitheater just before the mob grew even more dangerous.

"That's quite a commotion over there," Tributus mentioned to Languidus while watching the mob tip the chariot on its side and light another cart full of goods on fire. "Think we should get involved?"

"Futuit that," Languidus answered. "Doesn't look like it's worth the risk, and we were tasked with guarding this cart before the auction."

"I don't think the auction is happening anymore," Tributus commented, eerily calm as he watched the chaos unfold.

"Nope, that's above our pay grade, and we still need to guard these carts. Getting involved would be the perfect opportunity for men like those to steal all this treasure. Mobs are perfect distractions for looting." Languidus mentored the young Tributus while gesturing at a group of four men approaching the line of carts. Obviously up to no good, the men began perusing the collection of booty on the line of carts. Both equites knew they should do some preemptive policing.

They approached the opportunistic men and sidled up to a couple visually inventorying the contents of one cart. "Whatchya up to there, friend?" Languidus calmly questioned one man.

"Oh, uhh, nothing. Just curious. We're not thieves," the man answered, looking visibly nervous but also intrigued at the collection of goods. He then became transfixed on the leg lamp. "How much would I have to pay you guys to turn a blind eye to this beauty disappearing?"

"Yes, the leg lamp is quite a piece, but we are on orders. You can purchase all items at the auction as soon as it resumes." Tributus pointed to the amphitheater still in full brawl. At this point, the youths had arrived and began graffiti-tagging artwork and benches in the chaos. The auction was clearly not resuming any time soon.

Languidus pulled Tributus aside. "Tributus, let's not totally dismiss these guys. They are offering to pay. We haven't gotten our bonuses yet, and I have a feeling we may never get them. The way I see it, we're gonna have to take whatever bribes come our way till someone takes the throne who actually wants our loyalty. Ya gotta know how to thrive in the rough times, just business as usual."

"I see your point," Tributus listened. "But the leg lamp, it deserves a good home. At least."

The man offering money for the lamp looked

Tributus in the eye after overhearing their conversation. "I can tell this is a special lamp. I don't know what it is, but it puts me at peace like I'm walking into a cozy hovel lit by a warm fireplace with a hearty meal waiting for me on a cold winter's evening. Let me buy this lamp before some undeserving patrician puts it in a dining room used three times a year for special occasions. They won't appreciate it like I do!"

"We'll pay twenty thousand for the cartload and that cart over there," one of the other men offered Languidus. "We have the cash ready to go. No need to start anything, no need for anyone to go home empty-handed either."

"It's a deal," Languidus agreed before shaking on the arrangement. They made plans to deliver the money with a pouch of coins upfront and led the horse-powered cartloads of goods down the street and into a narrow alleyway. Tributus stared longingly as the goods he collected over the past week marched away to never be seen again. Just as suddenly as the beauty of the leg lamp entered their lives, it vanished.

Like that, the circle of corruption was completed. From a barely legal interpretation of a Roman law resulting in the thievery of thousands of treasured items to the men executing the plan taking what money they could. Substantial fractions of the funds collected through the auction were never directly routed to Vinius's treasury or the men enacting the law. Like the rest of Galba's taxes and policies, the scheme made very little money for the imperial treasury and only aggravated the people of Rome into apathy at best and traitorous behavior at worst.

8 THE STARS ALIGNED

It cost some boutique furniture and several thousand sesterces, but Otho was on his way to a very special place for a special meeting at the palace. Maybe Otho was blinded by nostalgia. Maybe the Oilatorium had lost some of its luster; Nero had not improved on the bath in the last ten years, and it felt like they ran it off bulk-bought oil. The aromas oozing out of the pipes smelled alright—but only alright. Sitting in the steam and the soapy suds was Vinius, resting his head on a pipe with a wet rag over his eyes. Otho took off what remaining clothes he still had on and stepped into the Oilatorium. Vinius, sensing movement through the rag, looked across the actively bubbling tub.

"Ahhh, so good to see you again, and I did receive your gift—very generous," Vinius greeted.

"Oh yes, you know how generous I am."

"That's why I keep inviting you back."

There was a pause as Otho immersed himself in the warm water he remembered as one of the highlights of his time with Nero. Vinius began to wake up, shriveling in the water.

"I get so pruned up these days with these fancy baths, especially this one. I could sit here for hours."

"You know, when I was here with Nero, I designed and built this thing," Otho bragged. "Yup, this was all my idea. Well, I got the idea from some other bath in some no-name facility, but they didn't get it like this."

"Oh, cool story, bro," Vinius responded. "Just a word of advice—the less you mention Nero, the better."

"Right, right, I know. You don't have to tell me," Otho recovered. "I don't think anyone hated him more than I do."

"Good, because if I'm gonna keep you around, you're gonna have to stop mentioning all those stories."

"Understood. So, how's the new administration spinning up? Any hot new positions you need filled?"

"Oh, you know how it is," Vinius leaned back and closed his eyes again. "There's absolutely no money left. We're having to tax the living daylights out of anything right now just to make ends meet. I made almost nothing—er, we made almost nothing the other day at a public auction. The whole thing's just backfiring. Luckily, Rome has true patriots like you, Otho."

"Yup, and any word of any positions?"

"Oh, nothing yet. The whole administration is really tight right now. There's nothing that immediately comes to mind; you'll just have to keep in touch. Keep this relationship going. I would recommend running for office."

"Oh, that's a shame. You sure there's absolutely no positions available, huh?" Otho became disappointed. "I suppose we would have to maintain this one-way relationship," he emphasized. "If there's nothing I can do to help the imperial administration, I suppose I would take my efforts elsewhere."

Vinius's eyes opened up; he knew he was losing a big fish. "Now, nothing immediately available is all," he jostled awake. "Have I forgotten to mention that Galba has yet to choose an heir? Someone patriotic and generous?"

"No, you haven't mentioned that," Otho replied, scratching the stubble on his chin.

"Oh yes, he has asked me for my opinions—Laco and Icelus, too, of course, but he does take mine a little more seriously than the others."

"Well, I suppose you are right. We will have to stay in touch."

***

"Oh my gawds, you're such a Taurus, Otho," a strange man yelled into the atrium of Otho's luxurious residence in Rome. The man wore a lengthy toga that draped nearly to the ground. The abundance of loose fabric accentuated every hand gesture and created downward gusts of wind, blowing up accumulated dust and dirt into the air.

"Look at this vase—this must be so expensive. This mural—so shows off your dominant planets," the man pointed from object to object, creating new eddy currents at every exciting object to point at, commenting on Otho's personality to nobody.

"Ahem," Onomastus interrupted the visitor. "Can I help you?"

"Wow, Onomastus," the man said with a hug. "Long time no see, my friend. Please tell me you remember me."

"Oh gosh," Onomastus broke the extremely unwanted hug, stared up at the ceiling in thought, and tried to match the loud personality to a name. He searched back because he just knew that he had met this guy before, years ago. It was on the tip of his tongue, so Onomastus went deep into his memory palace, quickly searching from encounter to encounter until he remembered. Three years ago, in service to Otho, he had gotten into a painfully intense conversation with an astrologer Otho had called upon. The man kept trying to explain birth dates associating with personalities and interpreting stars for prophecies, and, Jesus Christ, Onomastus just did not get it. Those things didn't seem linked at all. Yup, that's the guy. Onomastus exited his memory palace just before it turned awkward and looked at the man who was now a little insulted that it took Onomastus so much time. "Selucus . . . yeah, I remember."

"Where is Otho? I have to see him," Selucus asked.

With an audible sigh, Onomastus nonverbally complained.

"He's right over there." He led Selucus into a living room with spacious ten-foot ceilings, sparsely decorated with fine art. Otho had found the place fully furnished and didn't want to change a thing. In the living room, reclined on a couch, Otho was trying to read something.

They could tell he was distracted, continuously shifting positions until he got comfortable but then too comfortable, becoming too tired. "Selucus! I hoped you'd show up." Otho finally put the scroll down and got up to greet the astrologer.

"I got your letter," Selucus said with a hug. "I came as soon as I could. Also . . ." he paused, "I fuckin' told ya. Called this whole thing back in Lusitania."

"Called what?" Onomastus asked skeptically.

"That I'd survive Nero," Otho answered.

"It was incredibly clear you would," Selucus patted himself on the back. "After further dissecting the notes I wrote that night from the stars, this timeline makes way too much sense."

"What do ya mean?" Otho asked.

"Well, at the time, I knew you would survive Nero because Jupiter was the dominant planet of the night," Selucus explained, "but what I didn't realize until later was that Jupiter was descending southward. I eventually realized you would only need to survive Nero for less than a decade. It was so obvious I don't know why I didn't say anything that night."

"Wow, that's so cool," Otho responded. "Next time you read something cool like that, be sure to mail me about it. If I knew I only had a few more years to go, I would have been able to prepare more."

"So, how did you get ten years from the direction of Jupiter exactly?" Onomastus inquired.

"Well, it's not an exact science, but if it were easy to teach, there would be way more astrologers and I'd probably be out of a job!" Selucus laughed away the comment.

"I'm just happy it wasn't any later. Can you

believe how fast I bounced back? Look at this place!" Otho exclaimed.

"You certainly wasted no time. Your time spent in Lusitania was not unnoticed by the heavens."

"Is there any news from the heavens now?" Otho asked. "I'm flying blind here! I'm sure you've seen something."

"One week ago, before I even got your letter, I was posted atop a nearby mountain and noticed something very auspicious," Selucus said, drawing in his audience of one.

"Auspicious? I like the sound of that," Otho replied.

"You should," Selucus continued. "I saw Mars just crossing the astral plane and the Ursas in a particularly rare form. I had never seen such a sign from the heavens, so I pored through some textbooks the next morning at first light. That sign had not been seen since the return of a certain Roman from Gaul. I'm sure you've heard of Julius Caesar . . ."

Otho was so excited he didn't even know how to respond. There was no way he could be the next Julius Caesar. "Futuus," he commented in disbelief.

"I didn't know what to think of my findings, so I wrote it all up into a scroll and sent it to the greater astrology community for a professional peer review."

"So, what did they say?"

"The astrological consensus is that there are plenty of new movements afoot and this is going to be a glorious year for you, Otho," Selucus's news left Otho speechless. "I'd like to be the first to congratulate you on your fantastic future."

"Woah, so I'm, like, in . . . this is amazing

futuendi news, we should really go out and celebrate!" Otho rejoiced. Pleasantries continued for some time, including plenty of drinking. Casual drinking turned into getting-out-the-good-stuff drinking which turned into serious, spilling-into-the-streets-for-an-all-day-bender-style drinking. While Onomastus stayed behind at the villa, Otho and Selucus went out to celebrate. A few hours before dark, they both returned and continued drinking till sunset. After entertaining and boozing for a solid afternoon with Otho's favorite astrologist, Selucus was seen out of the villa before it got too dark. Otho could finally go back to reading that scroll—a thing he promised he would do when he got back. Well, maybe not; he was in a happy, drunk mood and decided to do something else he had been planning on doing for some time.

"Onomastus!" Otho yelled to Onomastus, who was just five feet away.

"Waddup?" Onomastus was tired and recovering from earlier drinking on a couch. Dealing with characters like Selucus wore him out. Onomastus, like most Romans at the time, did not like astrologists and thought they were a bunch of bull stercus artists.

"I've been waiting for a special occasion for this," Otho said softly, becoming emotional. "I think it's about time I make you a freedman."

"What?" Onomastus's mood perked up to Otho's level. "You serious?"

"Yeah . . . I mean . . . you helped me out in Lusitania and really helped me get close to the soldiers and everyone. Like, I couldn't have gotten into that carriage if it weren't for you remembering that one slave's name." Otho gave an impromptu drunken speech. "I've thought about this a lot."

"I'm honored," Onomastus replied. "Just trying to do my job."

"Of course, you'd be doing the same work, just with a fancier title and a lot more money. At this point, I need you as a freedman anyway, it's not strictly personal," Otho said. "We could get a lot more done, you and I. Work needs to be done, especially now; work I can't respectably send a slave to do."

"Oh Gods, what are you up to?"

"I promise, you've earned this, and I was planning on making you a freedman anyway. Don't think I just want something," Otho said.

"Oh, I believe you, but it sounds like the timing has to do with something you need." Onomastus questioned Otho's motive.

"Yeah, so . . ." Otho sat up on the couch with his elbows on his knees. He wobbled a bit back and forth until he managed to get his head straight. "I have to become emperor, and there's gonna be some politicking involved. Aaand a lot of money."

"Yeah, I mean, you're in the best position. Just need to get adopted," Onomastus replied calmly. "I know you got it. I wouldn't worry."

"No," Otho got a little calmer and more serious, "I HAAAAVE to become emperor. Otherwise, I'm futuero."

"Oh gosh, who's mad at you? We can figure that sort of thing out," Onomastus remained calm.

"It's not quite people being mad at me. It's more of, well . . ." Otho stood up. "Follow me, it'll probably be easier to just show you."

Otho then led Onomastus, first at a stumble,

then steadier as he got the right amount of blood back into his head, to a rarely used corner of the villa. Next to the kitchen was a locked door. Otho pulled out a key from underneath an adjacent rug. After opening the door, there was a box with another key. Walking over to another room, Otho moved furniture and some art cluttered in a corner, revealing another door.

"I've never seen you so secretive about anything," Onomastus commented.

"Well, you'll see . . ." Otho opened the second door, revealing several large boxes overflowing with gold. On top of the chest was an eye-patched skeleton draped over a jolly roger—not really, but it was the only thing standing between this closet and a Treasure Island amount of gold. This obviously wasn't the gold he came with.

"So, where did this come from . . . former master?"

"After a feeeew drinks, Selucus and I got to talking," Otho began recounting the events of the evening. "His interpretations of the stars sounded really legit, so we got to hashing out the details. That's when some investors overheard . . ."

"What details?"

"Oh, this star and that planet, which wasn't seasonable or something. I don't pretend to know his craft, but the stars are aligned, man! The stars are aligned!" Otho told a dumbfounded Onomastus.

"The stars are aligned? So, money just appeared here? Investors?" Onomastus attempted to follow.

"Yeah, so I ran into some rich friends, the investors. I hadn't seen them in a while, was like, 'Yoooo culus-hole,' and we got to talking. I told 'em the deal about me becoming emperor. Problem is, I'm gonna need some spending cash to deal with the soldiers. The soldiers . . . uhh, they want money. They told me on the trip. If I'm gonna have a peaceful transition of power, I need bribery cash," Otho explained.

"So, you borrowed all this money . . ." Onomastus grasped the details.

"No! No! Not borrowed. Invested, in myself. I told 'em I'd be able to pay them back as soon as I'm on the throne," Otho finished. "I figure I'll use this for spending money," he pointed at one chest. "This will be for bribing Vinius," he pointed to a couple of chests, "and all that in the back will be for the Praetorian Guard. There were some rough calculations I had to do on the spot. The lenders helped me with it. I think it should get me the throne for sure, no problem. We calculated it out . . . just enough."

"What if you don't?"

"What part of 'the stars are aligned' don't you understand?" Otho backed up his plan. "The position is as good as mine. It's in the stars! I've never, ever, been this set up! I just have to play the game now."

"I sure hope so," Onomastus worried, "and if we run into unforeseen problems?"

"Oh, I'd be as good as dead. They're the Sulpicii brothers, and there's a reason I haven't borrowed from them before. I lost a friend to them who needed some money to get through a divorce. They're serious," Otho calmly stated. "But that won't happen, because the stars are aligned! We're doing this thing, you and me."

"I . . . have some doubts, but, eh? I can't say

no," Onomastus rubbed his forehead. "I guess I could say no, now that I'm free, but . . . it's not my culus on the line for this cash. Of course I'll help ya!"

"You'll come around. With this and the stars, I'll be unstoppable!" Otho assured him. "I do need to find a safer place for this all. I thought of the double key trick on my way back, which should work in the meantime. I'm putting you in charge of handling the money, so it's all up to you. That's how much I trust you."

"Fun."

"And I don't even want to know where you keep it," Otho explained. "Some of the lenders may get impatient and want it back, but if I don't know where it is, they will have no way of squeezing it out of me. If someone comes askin' for me or my money, you say 'who's askin'?' and if it's one of them Sulpicii, say, 'I don't know what you're talking about.' "

"Right . . ."

"You, me, the stars . . . this is going to be our year," Otho wrapped his arm around Onomastus. "By the end of this year, you'll be an eques, maybe even a patrician. We're going to be opening a lot of doors soon."

"Alright, quite a position I'm in here,"

"We'll hash out more details in the morning. I feel a crash coming on." Otho closed and locked the door before falling back on the couch and tossing Onomastus the key.

After a few short juggles, Onomastus caught the key. His hands were trembling as if he had just ridden on a Six Flags roller coaster of changes in his life. No promotion in life ever goes unmet with new responsibilities you're not ready for. Except vice president—that title doesn't mean anything. Onomastus had a lot of work cut out for him, managing all that capital. There was one task he had to accomplish though: leaving some water for Otho to drink.

***

The next morning arrived after a busy, sleepless night for Onomastus. He had found a secure location for the gold and better organized it for distribution. Onomastus returned to find a very hungover Otho half awake in front of a tipped-over cup and a puddle. Of water. Onomastus sat heavily across from Otho with a different sort of headache.

"Morning. So, do you want to get to business now or later?" Onomastus greeted a pillow-creased face topped with greasy hair forming a half-mohawk that was sliding off his head. "There's only one right answer."

"Futuit," Otho responded. "That was some night, Freedman. Don't think I forgot about all that."

"Glad you remember some things," Onomastus replied.

"So, what'd you do with the money?"

"As if I'm ever going to tell you that," Onomastus responded, remembering the deal from last night.

"I swear, if you don't tell me what you did with my futuendi money, I will have you sent to the games so fast you won't have time to pack," Otho threatened, standing up and trying to look menacing while still being a bit wobbly.

"It's in your best interest if you don't know where it is, remember?"

"Good," he responded, readjusting his hair back on his head, looking more put together with real, not fake, hair. "Just testing. I was pretty under the influence, but I wasn't blacked out last night."

"I had a feeling," Onomastus responded.

"I will need to eat before we do get to business. The greasier, the better," Otho said, moving toward the kitchen.

The two entered an empty kitchen, hoping someone had left out some food to snack on. All they found was a half loaf of stale bread and some smoked meat. Otho sat down and began pounding on the table, "Food! Food!" he yelled repeatedly until his own commotion sent his headache spiking.

"Just hold on, okay?" Onomastus calmed Otho. He was not used to this level of toddler tantrum energy after so many years of emo Otho. Onomastus found one of the kitchen slaves and got him to start making breakfast. Luckily, there was already a fire smoldering.

"Breakfast is coming. It shouldn't be long." Onomastus sat down with Otho.

"Sweet."

"So, I've divided up the money," Onomastus began to brief Otho. "We'll have a good portion for Vinius access, and from my research, I'd suggest paying palace soldiers a hundred sesterces for good favor but to not raise suspicion."

"I suppose I should marry his daughter as well. That may save us some extra coin for the soldiers. Only a hundred?" Otho questioned.

"Yes," Onomastus explained. "It's a pretty typical gift without being perceived as a bribe."

"We can't just stop there, though. That's not good enough for exclusive loyalty. Everybody can hand out that amount of money." Otho thought out loud. "If we thought of a gift for the soldiers . . . that could go a long way. Not money, but something real nice. Classy, too."

"I don't know. We'll have to think of something good. It also can't be too obvious," Onomastus tried to brainstorm. "This bribery business is tricky."

"Pancakes!" Otho shouted.

"Oh, that's ridiculous. We can't secure the loyalty of the Praetorians with a well-balanced breakfast," he dismissed.

"Ha, no, I mean pancakes are here. Futuendi finally." Otho grabbed a platter with a grand slam of pancakes and poured honey all over his stack. He took a big bite and chewed with total satisfaction. "Ya know, I love pancakes more than anything. But after the first bite, it really goes downhill from there. The first few bites are bliss, then you eat another half of the pancake out of boredom. By the time you get to the last quarter, it turns into a real chore. You hate yourself by then, but you have too much pride not to finish the stack."

"How insightful," Onomastus said, becoming impatient with Otho's contentment and meditations on pancakes. "Can we get back to business here? What is a good gift for the soldiers? We'd never have time for something personal for all of them, so something mass-purchased would be perfect. It needs to be secret too; otherwise, we may as well just give them more money."

Otho's pancake pace was slowing as he approached the last quarter, and he stopped for a breather to speak. "Why not subligaculum? That's plenty secret. Hahaha."

"Subligaculum?" Onomastus questioned while Otho used more and more honey on each bite to power through the last part of the pancake stack. "I don't think we'll be able to secure the loyalty of Rome with loincloths."

"Hey," Otho burped as he sat back in bloated satisfaction. "One, don't underestimate a good pair of subligaculum, Onomastus, and two, I know a guy. What's the nicest pair of subligaculum you have?"

"It's all the same to me, really. Just some cloth around your junk. I can't imagine subligaculum ever being that amazing." Onomastus lifted his toga a bit, revealing his subligaculum, an unremarkable piece of boring fabric holding on, just doing the job subligaculum does. "This is all I wear right here. I'm not a fancy Roman just yet with your bougie subligaculum."

"That's where you are totally wrong. You are a fancy Roman now, and I'm about to show you a whole new world," Otho corrected. "Once I'm done digesting this food baby, I'm taking you to my subligaculum guy. Any good Roman has a subligaculum guy."

"Alright . . . I'll have to see it to believe it," Onomastus said skeptically, shaking his head.

"No, you'll feel it to believe it. You're getting a pair." Otho insisted, "It'll be my congratulations-on-not-being-a-slave-anymore gift."

"Oh, I can't wait to show it off to all my

friends. They're all gonna be so jealous." The eye roll almost sprained his face. "Ya know, most people get swords . . . something cool."

"One more thing," Otho's hangover was dissipating. "We need to set aside about the same amount of money for the movers and shakers as we have for Vinius. We gotta find who really drives the loyalty of the guards."

"We know who that might be?"

"No idea right now," Otho replied. "But we need to figure that out pronto. You're on it. We're not making up the whole thing as we go, just most of it. Anyway, I'm gonna nap off this food baby, and we'll be off."

Otho drank some water, napped for an hour and a half, and his food baby/hangover was gone. The two were on their way to the subligatorium (underwear store) as soon as he woke up.

9 SUBLIGACULUM

The subligatorium storefront was a small shop, nonchalantly placed in the middle of the city. It didn't stand out. Washed-out paintings of men in athletic poses adorned the weathered stone exterior, and one tiny window offered a glimpse inside. Above the door, a sign read *IT SUB TERRA* or "The Under World[8]." The interior was the size of a small studio apartment. Onomastus coughed as he entered. The sleepy shop was filled with smoke, illuminated only by the residual streetlight filtering through the doorway and window. In the back, a tailor worked fabric to specifications at a table. The front was cluttered with piles of subligaculum in various shapes and sizes. None looked particularly special—maybe a

---

[8] According to strict grammar teachers it actually read "Unspecified thing it goes under the ground", but few were well versed in grammar back then, particularly the shop keeper to which Latin was his second language. When people corrected his grammar, he told them to go somewhere else for their subligaculum.

leather thong here or there—but it all resembled discount bin underwear you'd find in a three pack at Target with the right coupon. Onomastus hadn't known what to expect, but he was still disappointed.

"Morning, tailor," Otho said.

"Uh, afternoon," the tailor replied. Otho had slept a little longer than an hour and a half. "What can I do for you?"

"It's been a while since I've been here. Do y'all still have the premium selection?" Otho inquired.

"Premium stock? I'm afraid I don't know what you're talking about," the tailor said.

"Oh, shoot, one sec. I think I remember this one," Otho remembered there was some passphrase to get in. He staired at the ceiling for ten or so seconds, grasping for the forgot-my-password button, and then remembered: "I see Lutetia, I see Gaul, I see Nero's Subligaculum. Y'all haven't changed it, have ya?"

"Haha, not anytime soon. It's funny every time," the tailor said. "Right this way."

It was either that or semper ubi sub ubi, Otho thought.

The tailor lifted a curtain at the back of the store, revealing a staircase lit by torches. Down one flight of stairs, Otho and Onomastus entered a large, vaulted basement illuminated by more torches. Lining the walls were exotic materials—rare animal fur, leathers, and dyed fabrics in every color. A sparse army of muscular slaves posed on pedestals, sporting luxurious looking subligacula, while a much older tailor fitted one pair to a full-figured statue of Mercury.

"One minute," the old man said to the eager buyers. "I'm almost done, and I'll be with you soon.

Feel free to check out the merchandise—no homo—that's why they're here."

The modeled subligaculum screamed comfort and style. Despite the weirdness, Onomastus, feeling curious, gently pressed the back of his hand against one of the slave's butts like a TSA agent. The subligaculum felt amazing, and Onomastus could now only imagine living every day in such comfort. "See anything you like?" Otho asked.

"Right now, just window shopping, but I see what you mean," Onomastus replied.

"Okay, all done here. Oh, Otho, I heard you were in town." The old man shook his hand. "What brings you to my subligatorium?"

"Magnus, always good to see you. Well, one, we have to treat this guy to something nice," Otho pointed at Onomastus, "and two, we need to find something good for a bulk order."

"Bulk order? I don't get a lot of those at my prices," Magnus said. "How large are we talking?"

"I think five thousand will do. And don't worry, I know your prices. For your quality, it'll be worth it," Otho replied.

"Who's this for?" Magnus asked.

"Soldiers," Otho answered. "I'm in command of some men now, and I'd like to treat them to something nice and functional. I want them comfortable and agile."

"Hmmm, soldiers," Magnus mused. "That's a new one. They must be some unit to deserve my work."

"Oh, they deserve the best!" Otho said with gusto. "Any thoughts?"

"Well, it needs to be flexible but durable. It

needs to breathe but still insulate for those cold winter marches. I think I have an idea." Magnus painted his artistic vision. "I have one subligaculum model that will stretch to most men's sizes and has been a favorite of the athletes. I happen to have it displayed right over here." Magnus pointed to a slave sporting the scientific peak of athletic-fit subligaculum technology.

Otho and Onomastus gazed at the masterpiece covering all the naughty bits of a slave posing and stretching his legs to show its superior flexibility. The base was smooth leather, blending seamlessly with red-dyed cloth sides that wrapped the slave's upper thighs. No matter what the slave did, the tightly fitted subligaculum stayed in place.

"POSITION 8!" Magnus yelled as the slave pulled one knee up to his chest, balancing carefully on one foot. The subligaculum held firm.

"POSITION 19!" he commanded, and the slave spread his legs as wide as possible, bending down between them.

"MOVEMENT 4!" Magnus shouted with majesty, commanding the slave to start running in place. The subligaculum showed minimal movement, and there appeared to be no chafing.

"I call it the Excellentia," Magnus said, handing two pairs to Otho and Onomastus. With the subligaculum in Onomastus's hands, he felt the leather thong portion lined with white fur. "You put a soldier in one of these, and he'll march for days with zero chafing! Show 'em! Show 'em your thighs!"

The slave stopped running and peeled back the subligaculum, revealing his pasty white skin.

"You did it again, Magnus. This looks

absolutely perfect," Otho said, clapping.

"Yeah, I think I'll take this one," Onomastus said without hesitation. "I don't think I'll go back to my old underwear ever again if I have a pair like this. I'll be wearing this out of the store." Onomastus began putting on his new Excellentia.

"Pair like that changes a man. Be careful," Magnus warned. "You may not like the person you become."

Onomastus slipped off his old pair under a long tunic and pulled up the Excellentia. The feeling was so otherworldly and decadent, he let out a faint "Mmmmmmm" as if he'd just put on pajamas straight out of the dryer.

"So, how fast could you do a bulk order?" Otho asked.

"Shoot, five thousand of the Excellentia? It's not gonna be cheap."

"That's no problem—whatever you need," Otho assured Magnus.

Magnus leaned on a nearby table, examined the stitching on a pair, and eyeballed some of the material before blurting out an answer. "Maybe three weeks," he guessed. "My fur suppliers are going to have to kill a lot of rabbits, but they always come through. That's why they're the best."

"Three weeks will work for me just fine," Otho said, sealing the deal. "I can always count on you."

"It's a sale. I better get to work then," Magnus agreed. "These slaves are gonna be busy doing something other than modeling for the next few weeks, I can tell you that. But don't worry, I've been training them."

"I don't know—are they ready?" Otho asked. "This is some technical work to match your fine craft."

"They better be. They're the best damn seamsters west of Athens. They don't call me Magnus 'The Dream Weaver' Tectrix for nothing! I wouldn't release a pair of the Excellentia unless it was of supreme quality."

***

It was a special day at the arena. Two gladiator superstars were set to face off, and the crowd was already swelling with cheers long before the main event. The long-anticipated climax between Marcus "The Thunder Hammer" Draquintus and Brutus "The Fury" Marcellus had finally arrived. Marcus, a seasoned champion in the arena for decades, was known for his adherence to the rules and his mercy. Brutus, on the other hand, believed everything was permissible and nothing sacred. He'd strike a downed opponent, throw dirt in your eyes—every dirty trick imaginable. Brutus was the gladiator Romans loved to hate.

To add to the drama, Brutus had recently stolen Marcus's beloved, Portia. Once, she had fought by Marcus's side, but she was seduced by Brutus in front of a live audience just last month. Unable to resist his bad boy charms, she left Marcus heartbroken and vengeful. Later, the town crier revealed that Portia had been placed under a love potion's spell, concocted with evil spirits from the East. The spell had since worn off, and she now wanted Marcus back. But to reclaim her, Marcus had to win her in one-on-

one combat to the death at the arena's upcoming RAW SMACKDOWN at the AREEENA THIS SUNDAY, SUNDAY, SUNDAY!

Vinius had box seats for the match, and Otho arrived well before the main event. The box, intended for the emperor, was nearly empty. The emperor found such base events, often rumored to be staged, beneath his refined tastes. Vinius sat at the edge of the box alone with his young daughter, Crispina. The arena was packed, every support structure filled to capacity. If the extendable shades weren't so high and flimsy, people would be hanging from them.

"Salve, Vinius. Thanks for inviting me. Is Galba not joining us?"

"Oh no, he's not a fan of these spectacles. His knees give him trouble, and he finds the idea of being carried by a slave up here more undignified than attending such base entertainment." Vinius mimicked Galba's high and mighty tone. "You know how he is. So, I'm having a daddy-daughter day. Have you met Crispina?"

"No, I haven't had the pleasure."

Crispina stood up, looking to be about half to two-thirds of Otho's age, though her presence alongside her father made her seem even younger. "Salve, Otho," she greeted softly, smiling politely.

"Salve, at last we meet. Vinius speaks highly of you."

Crispina giggled.

"Do you come here often?" Otho asked, waiting for her response.

She tilted her head away. "Oh, I live in the city."

"I mean the games."

She thought for a moment, smiling harder. "No."

Vinius stood back, watching the two. "Well, you two seem to be getting along. I'm going to say hi to a colleague. I'll be right back." He left them alone.

They continued avoiding unnecessary eye contact until the arena's performers stopped juggling flaming knives, leaving them with nothing else to look at. That bought Otho a couple of minutes.

"So, Crispina, tell me about yourself. What do ya do for fun?"

"I don't know. I'm not much of a hobby person."

"Ever try any?"

"Once." She nervously leaned against the wooden rail of their box seats and tapped her feet.

Otho waited a minute, not wanting to overbearingly hold the conversation.

"Some weather we've been having. Should be getting cold soon."

Crispina nodded. "Yup, that time of year."

Otho was suddenly reminded of his first meeting with Poppaea. He just had that effect on women. Some stagehands came into the arena, setting up small barricades and dragging around props for the main fight.

"You heard anything about this gladiator rivalry?"

"Honestly . . . I'm only here because my dad made me come," Crispina replied.

"Ah, I see." Otho got the hint and waited for Vinius' return. He was caught off guard and couldn't find any openings for conversation. Crispina just sat there, smiling and looking out into the arena. Vinius was gone for another twenty minutes.

***

Three weeks later, after twenty bolts of Egyptian cotton, six cows' worth of leather, three incentive programs due to unionization rumors, and 232 dead rabbits from "quality concerns," Onomastus sat outside the subligatorium, ready to pick up the shipment of Excellentia. His own pair had kept him sane while he managed Otho's finances.

Onomastus left an empty cart in the street and carried a chest filled with payment into the storefront. He wasn't the same man he'd been three weeks ago. Living the freedman's life, indulging guilt-free had changed him. The underwear, like his new position, gave him irreplaceable confidence. He held his head higher, stood straighter, and spoke more authoritatively, as if he owned the city—or at least a cash-flow-positive investment property.

He walked into the storefront, even smokier than before, and saw one of the slaves slumped over a table. The slave looked up and greeted him. "Ah, right on time. Bring it downstairs. They're expecting you." He jumped up and opened the curtain for Onomastus, who carried the chest with a waddling stride.

Downstairs, the secret panty chamber had been transformed into a workshop. Tables equipped with sewing equipment were scattered across the room. A tornado of productivity had hit the subligatorium to produce eight massive, fifty-pound bags at the base of the stairwell. Onomastus set down the chest to inspect the work.

All the workers, including Magnus, lay

motionless on the floor in Savasana pose[9]. Magnus rolled himself up with a grunt and slowly walked over to greet Onomastus and inspect the chest. "We just finished thirty minutes ago. That was quite an order," Magnus said.

"Your work and pace are impressive and much appreciated," Onomastus said, checking out a few Excellentia. "When these hit the market, I'm sure you'll get even more business."

"Oh, we won't be accepting any more business for at least a week after this," Magnus responded. "Looks like everything's here on your end." Magnus opened the chest and dug around a bit.

"As it is on yours," Onomastus replied, tying up the bags. "I've got a cart outside ready to go."

"Alright, boys," Magnus stirred his slaves to action. "One more task, then a long nap." Each slave groaned themselves awake, muscles stiff and aching. They grabbed a bag each and climbed the stairs, seeing the light at the end of the tunnel, followed by Onomastus and Magnus to the street.

"I'm sure y'all are gonna sleep well tonight," Onomastus said.

"Oh yes," Magnus replied. "We got the job done, and now it's time for a little R 'n' R"

Onomastus watched as the slaves loaded the bags into the ox-driven cart, grunting with effort. They moved quickly, eager to finish, but after all that work, their bodies protested. As the last bag made it into the cart, one young slave shouted for joy and grabbed the shoulders of two others.

Magnus pulled out a handful of Excellentias. "The stitching's all wrong on these—we're going to

---

[9] That one yoga move where you just lie down

have to redo them," he said, eliciting groans from the slaves. "Just kidding. It's all PERFECT!"

Onomastus walked up to the cart and made sure the bags were secure. "Welp, I appreciate the effort. I'm sure we'll do business again."

"You know where to find us," Magnus said, shaking Onomastus's hand before he climbed onto the cart and headed toward the Praetorian barracks.

"Have a good night," Onomastus called back to Magnus and the slaves. As he drove away with the goods, he heard Magnus shout, "Hey guys, we're getting drunk off our culī tonight!" followed by a roar of celebration.

Onomastus continued on his way to the barracks of the Praetorian Guard, the Castra Praetoria. The journey was uneventful, with nice sunny weather and little traffic. Even the jaywalkers did those little fake jogs with courtesy waves. It was just that pleasant of a day. He even passed some trees that had changed for the fall, making it unusually colorful too. There's a decent chance he even started whistling show tunes.

He arrived at the Castra Praetoria in a cheery mood and stopped just short of the gate. A scowling soldier leaning on a sputum greeted him. "What the futuus do you want?"

"I'm here with a gift from Marcus Salvius Otho," Onomastus said, snapping back into a more serious demeanor.

"Aight, well let's have a look then," the guard said. Two guards inspected the cart, one opening a bag and holding up a pair of Excellentias. "What is this? What's it even for?"

"It's a specially designed subligaculum for all

the Praetorians," Onomastus explained.

"We get so many gifts and bribes through these gates every day . . . and I've got to say, I've never seen subligaculum yet. This is a new one," one guard commented.

"I've never seen subligaculum quite like this before either," one of the guards who looked the most senior said. "Okay, you guys stay on post. I'm going to bring this in myself. I'm too curious now."

The older guard, decked out in full iron shoulder pads, motioned for the gate to be opened and hopped onto the cart. Onomastus led him toward the main barracks, where all the high-ranking officers and expensive rec room equipment were housed. Inside the Castra, a neatly aligned grid of wooden and stone two-story buildings surrounded a clean roadway and a training yard filled with newer recruits sparring with posts or each other with wooden swords. The gate closed and they proceeded forward under the guidance of the guard.

"My name's Onomastus, by the way," he said.

"Languidus. So, ya work for Otho?"

"Yeah, he's a good friend of the Praetorians. I'm sure this won't be our only time meeting." Onomastus attempted at building his professional network, reaching for a business card, if such a thing existed.

Languidus smiled and laughed with a phlegm resonating snort. ". . . Okay."

"What's so funny?" Onomastus asked as they approached the main barracks.

"Oh, just why I want to watch this. Everyone says they're friends of the Praetorians. Few can back it up," Languidus answered, hopping off the cart to fetch a couple of senior guards. "Wait here."

Moments later, Languidus returned with two other guards. "Onomastus, this is Barbius Proculus and Veturius," he introduced the two more senior-looking Praetorians with grey speckled hair and tanned, weathered faces. Barbius was taller and leaner, while Veturius had that extreme dad bod—he had a gut but moved with surprising agility. The pep in his step suggested he did cardio at least once a week to keep up with the younger recruits.

Both greeted Onomastus with small nods before opening the bags and examining the contents. They pilfered through and held up a pair of Excellentias, scratching their heads in confusion. Languidus watched the scene, silently snickering.

"They're subligaculum . . ." Onomastus explained, breaking the silence. "Called Excellentia. A special order."

"We've gathered that much," Barbius said. "What I can't figure out is why."

"What I can't figure out is if it's for me or my wife," Veturius laughed.

"It's some of the most functional and comfortable subligacula on the market," Onomastus assured them. "Just try one on. It's one size fits all."

"Maybe fifteen years ago," Veturius quipped, slapping his belly. He stretched the fabric a bit and then nodded with a smile. "Sure, I'll try one on. It goes down here, not up here, right?" he asked, holding it up to his chest like a sports bra.

"Yeah, yeah, it goes down there," Onomastus said.

"Who is this gift from?" Barbius asked.

"Marcus Salvius Otho," Onomastus answered

loudly and clearly, making sure everyone could hear the name. "He's back in the city and wants to show his benevolence."

"Oh, he's back, eh?" Barbius replied as Veturius awkwardly tried to change into the subligaculum. He tossed his sweaty pair onto the cart, intentionally close to Onomastus. "I remember him from back in the Nero days. What's it been, a decade?"

"Yes, he spent the last ten years in Lusitania as the governor," Onomastus said.

"Well, shoot, those were some fun times when it was him and Nero. Always having a good time and getting drunk. Sending us money, women, or some other gifts. I didn't understand most of the gifts, especially the art and performances, but I appreciated the cash and just the thought of it. It's been pretty stale since Galba showed up," Barbius reminisced.

"Damn, not bad," Veturius said, shifting around and doing a few stretches. "This is pretty futuendi nice."

"Really?" Languidus stopped laughing, surprised. Veturius was usually quick with a joke, never a compliment.

"You've got to try one of these. It's amazing." Veturius tossed a pair to Languidus and Barbius. "Otho, eh? How many of these Excellentias are in here?"

"That's right, Otho," Onomastus repeated. "And those bags should have about five thousand pairs, so it should be enough for everyone."

The other guards rushed to put on a pair, with Barbius being the fastest, tossing his damp subligaculum toward some poor unsuspecting trainee.

"Wow, it's like I'm not even wearing anything. But yet, I feel swaddled like a newborn," Barbius said.

"Futuit, this feels like a dream," Languidus said. "I guess I'll be seeing you again with goods like this."

"Told you. Pretty crazy you don't get subligaculum gifts all the time," Onomastus said.

"Yeah, usually it's some useless oil or art or something. We never know what to do with that stuff," Veturius said. "But this? We're gonna wear it until it falls apart. I get it's valuable and super nice, but why not just give us the gold?"

"Oh, he's not opposed to that either. I'm glad you're pleased—we knew y'all would love it. I'm wearing my Excellentia right now," Onomastus said. "Anyway, let's get these bags unloaded, and I'll be heading out."

"Oh, you can't leave without having at least one drink," Barbius insisted.

"I suppose I could stay for a drink or two before getting back to business," Onomastus agreed.

After a few hours of swapping stories and discussing everyone's favorite lady parts, Onomastus, and by proxy Otho, became good friends of the Praetorians.

"Oh man, you wouldn't believe the look on the guy's face when we took away his flute," Languidus was saying, recounting a story from the other day. Everyone laughed, then shared a moment of contented silence.

"So anyway," Barbius said, getting a little more serious, "we don't usually get gifts for no reason. So . . . what are you and Otho aiming for?"

Onomastus took a big gulp of wine. "There are a lot of things in motion. He's working to succeed Galba as emperor," he said.

"Ahhh, imperial ambition. Classic. The big leagues," Languidus replied. "Not a common goal, but not a rare one either."

"I don't blame him," Veturius added. "Being so close to Nero, that taste doesn't wash out easily. So, what's his plan?"

"Well, he's been friendly with Galba since the revolt and has been bribing the right people to stay close. Galba's pretty old and has no sons; he's gotta adopt someone soon, right?" Onomastus explained. "We figure you guys could get behind Otho. He's a lot more generous than Galba, so really, we're trying to save Galba from himself here."

"Gosh, that makes too much sense," Barbius agreed. "I'll tell ya what—no one's quite in charge of the guard. We've got leaders, but they're always one bad decision away from losing that position. It's really a popularity contest, and these Subligaculum are a good start."

"Any other suggestions on winning loyalty and keeping the peace?" Onomastus inquired.

"Other than the obvious bribery . . . hmm, well, there is one issue with one of the men, Cocceius Proculus," Veturius said. "He's in a boundary dispute with his neighbor, and it's gotten pretty litigious."

"Boundary dispute? What's the problem?" Onomastus asked.

"I don't really know, but knowing Cocceius, he's probably in the wrong," Veturius said. "Helping him out will earn you some favor. I can't think of anything else right now, but if I do, I'll let you know."

"Got it. Cocceius Proculus, boundary dispute. We'll get right on that." Onomastus made a mental note. "Well, I'm gonna head out now. Do stay in touch, alright?"

"Oh, we're definitely staying in touch," Veturius agreed.

"Get that boy Otho on the throne—he's OUR guy now!" Barbius shouted. "We're already SICK of Galba! Could really use a bro in charge."

"Oh, we think he'll be on soon. Talk to y'all later," Onomastus said, trying to leave on a high note as he made his way to the cart.

About twenty yards from the main barracks, Onomastus heard a quick pitter-patter behind him. Barbius hopped onto the cart, huffing and puffing after an impressive sprint, considering his dad bod. "Godsdamn, I haven't moved that fast since my thirties. This underwear is great."

"Barbius, come to say goodbye again or forget another favor?" Onomastus asked.

"Oh, just some more parting words," Barbius said. "Now, I don't have any particular legal requests; however, I happen to be the officer in charge of the password for the guard."

"What does that mean?" Onomastus asked.

"It means that while you may have the support of most of the guard, I can secure full loyalty for any action at any moment," Barbius explained. "The password works like a seal on a letter—it's legitimacy. Speak the right password on the right day, and the guard knows you have authority."

"I see what you're getting at," Onomastus said. "What would secure that password?"

"I think if I found thirty thousand sesterces a

month and a few other special items appeared at my estate, I could grant special access to a willing buyer," Barbius said as they passed the gate of the Castra Praetoria.

"Wow, you really don't give a stercus who knows that," Onomastus remarked, noticing the guards as they passed by.

"Oh, no one cares. That's just business as usual. I thought you already knew that," Barbius replied.

"I always suspected, and I don't know why I imagined it would be any different. Yeah, I get it. Send me a list of those special items, and I'll set it up," Onomastus agreed.

"I'll send you a list before the end of the week. I'm happy to be doing business with you. It's not the value of the items; they're just hard to find and of a more personal nature," Barbius explained.

"Oh, I'll getchyu covered, my friend," Onomastus assured him.

"Dude, thank you, and I gotta emphasize, that list is personal," Barbius said, his tone turning serious. "I trust you not to share it with anybody."

"I know how to keep a secret. It's safe with me."

"I knew I could trust you," Barbius said, hopping off the moving carriage and almost stumbling but managing a wobbly running landing for five cubits. "I'll send you that letter tomorrow."

Onomastus had a very successful evening. He made his way back to Villa Otho, having delivered pristine subligaculum and developed a good rapport with some senior soldiers. With a few bits of inside knowledge, he was well on his way to maintaining that relationship. He should speak at a seminar for networking. Onomastus hadn't even been a freedman in Rome for a month, and he was ankles deep in effective political corruption.

***

While Onomastus was out delivering goods and greasing some Praetorian hands with bribes and immaculately crafted subligaculum, Otho was entertaining company a few classes up. The room was fully stocked with wealthy patricians snobbing up the place, drinking the good wine, and eating all his best cheese while simultaneously criticizing its quality for their sophisticated palates. Subligaculum bribes would not work with this crowd.

"So, what do you need money for?" a thin, balding man asked Otho, his expression puzzled.

"I have accepted a position as Galba's heir and need bribe money for the guards," Otho replied. "Nothing nefarious."

"It's a coup?" the man asked, incredulous. "That really sounds like you're planning a coup."

"No, no, no, Galba is going to adopt me," Otho explained.

"Then what do you need the money for?" the man asked again.

"To gain access to Galba, secure the adoption, and bribe the Praetorian Guard for a peaceful transition of power," Otho said.

"That still sounds like a coup," another man, eavesdropping, put down his cheese and butted in.

"It's not a coup, that's the last thing I want," Otho said. "Think of it like you're investing in me and my future career. Money's tight right now—you know how Galba is—but I'll be thankful later, see?"

"I really don't mind if it's a coup. I don't like Galba or the men he confides in," the balding man said, expressing his concerns. "I'm just not sure what you're pretending it is."

"It's not a coup!" Otho snapped, losing patience.

"Well, whatever you want to pretend it is, I'm happy you'll be preceding Galba soon. I'm getting awfully tired of his strict fiscal policies and odd taxes. I'm okay with a little violence to overthrow him. If it isn't you, it'd be some other startup," said another old man, this one with a distractingly large wine stain on his toga. "You have my financial support; you seem like you're good for the money."

"Yes, a young, ambitious man like you— double our money not long after you assume office," the bald man concluded. "I've already added to my planned contribution, and my lawyer has looked over the loan. You should receive the aid you're asking for by the end of the week."

"Mine should have arrived this evening as well," the wine-stained man added. "Same deal—I use the same lawyer; he's very good. Are you getting the same tax write-off?" he asked the bald man.

"Oh, of course. You have to look for every loophole these days. Don't know how he clarified this as charitable public works, but the man sure is a miracle worker."

"Who?" Otho asked.

"Maybe if this works out, I'll give you his name. He's the best lawyer in the city for white toga crime, but he doesn't like to advertise."

"Oh, okay. Well, I'll let you know if I'm really in a bind. Thank you both so much," Otho said, finally giving up on convincing them it wasn't a coup. "Here's to the next dynasty of the Empire." He raised his cup of wine.

"I appreciate the sentiment, but I do need to be going," the bald man said, refusing to drink.

"Me as well, another time perhaps," the sloppy man said, clearly wanting to get out of there now that business was concluded. He did drink to the toast; he wasn't rude like the other guy. More likely, he just wanted to drink.

Otho called for a slave to show them out of the villa. As soon as the rich dudes had left, Otho lay down on the couch and began sipping his wine. That was a meeting he hadn't looked forward to, but he knew he needed to have it.

"Futuendi hate old people," he mumbled between sips.

He had a good thirty minutes of relaxation on the couch with his own thoughts before Onomastus returned from the Castra Praetoria.

"Hey, how'd it go?" Otho asked without getting up.

"Really freakin' well if ya ask me," Onomastus said, sitting down and pouring himself some wine. "Soldiers love the Excellentia. Got some good carousing in with a few of them and set up a bribe with the keeper of the password or something. I'm still not exactly sure what he does, but it sounded important, and we'll need him. Something about giving legitimate orders."

"Nice," Otho said, applauding.

"OH!" Onomastus suddenly remembered

something. "Hold on, name's coming back—Cocceius Proculus!"

"What about him?"

"He's one of the higher-up guards and could use some legal help with a border dispute with a neighbor," Onomastus explained. "I don't think I can handle it as a freedman—it's in the courts right now. The guy sounds like a culus, but he apparently holds some weight in the guard."

"That's awesome," Otho said, raising his cup in a mock toast. "I had some success myself."

"Oh yeah? How's that?"

"I practically doubled our money to work with through some loans from some rich dudes," Otho explained. "I started with the stars aligning thing and forgot that old dudes hate astrology. I had to explain my plan like four times—they were so slow. I gotta stop bringing that up unless I know they're cool. Freaking traditionalists."

"Otho, like no Romans like astrology. Most people think it's dumb. It's not just old people," Onomastus laughed. "Also, your plan doesn't make that much sense."

"What do ya mean? It's so simple!" Otho defended himself.

"It feels like you're just redistributing money without a lot of direction," Onomastus said. "I'm not exactly sure how that's going to get you adopted."

"We have Vinius, that's something," Otho countered. "That, the guards, and the fact that I've been involved with Galba since the rebellion—I can't see it going any other way."

"But you've been rarely seeing Galba since we got to Rome," Onomastus argued. "You really think

Vinius is going to be enough to change his mind? Also, why are we bribing the Praetorians so much? That doesn't make a lot of sense if the adoption's all in the bag."

"Oh, Vinius can get anything done in this town right now; he's kind of running the place," Otho explained. "Also, you should always have those guards on your side. No one will be able to dispute my claim to the throne if the troops love me. If I'm going to be emperor, I've gotta start bribing them sooner or later anyway."

"Well, I hope you know what you're doing," Onomastus said, finally giving up. "Because I don't know how you're going to pay off all this money as a private citizen. Do we have any income streams coming in from this venture? These monthly bribes are piling up, not to mention all these get-togethers you're having."

"Well, these get-togethers have an enormous return on investment because of all the new loans they've been bringing in."

"When do they expect their return on investments, though?"

"Oh, it won't take long. Things are moving so fast—probably early next year, I bet."

"But, even if you do get adopted, what if it takes longer?" Onomastus asked, staying loyal but critical.

"Don't worry about it," Otho said, waving his empty wine goblet. "The stars are aligned."

***

One night soon after, Otho had been invited to

the imperial palace for a dinner party, thanks to his continued bribing of Vinius. Before arriving at the party, Onomastus divided out thirty bags of a hundred sesterces for Otho to use as bribes for the palace guards.

He could have carried a chest or had slaves following him, but that would have drawn too much attention. That sort of show of power would just look too much like a coup, and it's not a coup.

Some would think—that's a lot of coins for one person to be carrying at one time. There's no way someone could do that casually without drawing that much attention to themselves unless they met with local smugglers to design special leg and body strapping capable of supporting twice that amount of cash underneath his toga. Would he be able to accomplish such an impressive feat of engineering? No, he didn't do that at all. Otho wanted the smugglers to design body straps capable of holding three times that amount of bribes because he knew he'd be using it all the time and would need room to grow.

The guards at the front of the palace heard Otho jingling two blocks away. He arrived at the street entrance and exited the carriage, only to jingle louder with each heavy step, testing the integrity of each city stone and a few railings. Luckily, there were guards at the front, and he could begin offloading coins immediately. It looked like the guards were in a good mood as well, so the tip should be well received. All the men were uncharacteristically smiling and relaxed.

"Evening, gents," Otho greeted four guards while reaching down to his ankles to grab the noisiest bags. "Here ya go. Doin' a great job out here."

"Hey, thanks, mister—you're pretty swell," one young guard said, accepting his tip. "That's pretty generous. I don't think I've seen you here before. Who am I thanking?"

"Marcus Salvius Otho," Otho said proudly with a stately grin.

"Hey, aren't you the guy that got us this subligacula?" another soldier asked.

"Ah, yes," Otho replied. "I take it y'all received your Excellentias. How are they? I'm wearing one myself right now."

"It's the best thing anyone's ever given me, and I'm counting my favorite son," one older soldier said. "I never knew just a pair of subligacula could make such a difference in my life. I have better posture, and I can't keep my wife off me when I'm home. I don't know if it's the design or the confidence it's given me, but it just turns her into an animal!"

"It took me a couple of days to stop getting random erections it is so futuendi soft," the younger soldier described. "Even afterward, I'm in ecstasy all day."

"I had chronic back pain that forced me to sleep on a wooden board," one older soldier said. "I thought it would never go away. But after wearing an Excellentia for a few days, it just disappeared. POOF! Now I can sleep however I want and feel great in the morning. It's like I'm twenty again."

"I went to a party a couple of days ago," the last soldier added, "and I've never been great with women. I never know what they're thinking or what to say. I just get so nervous. But ten minutes into the party, with this subligaculum on, I had two drop-dead gorgeous ladies hanging off each arm for the rest of the night. The legs on them! I did things that night, oh man, I've only dreamed of."

"Wow," Otho said, genuinely surprised. "I had no idea the Excellentia was such a big hit. If I'd known you all had these problems, I would've bought the underwear a long time ago. You've got to tell me these things!"

"Oh, we will," the young soldier replied. "You're the man with the plan and the goods."

"Y'all have a good night," Otho said, walking past the gate and into the palace. On his way to the dinner party, he made sure to stop at every guard he could until he wasn't so noisy. It took fifteen stops before he could enter the dining room without drawing attention with the clash of coins. During one out of every three encounters, he found a way to bring up purchasing the subligaculum, just enough to spread the word about how amazingly patriarchal he was. All it took was one night, a hundred men's lifetime wages, a nifty subligaculum design, and overworking Onomastus to gain the Praetorians's appreciation. With time, he would earn their total loyalty.

At the party, he saw the man his biggest bag of cash was meant for. There he was, sitting on a couch with his infamous scowl that was growing all too familiar.

"Otho . . ." Vinius said, barely glancing up as he nodded.

"Oh, it's been a minute. Any new openings in the administration?" Otho asked, sitting down next to him. "What's it been, a few weeks?" A slave approached and handed Otho some wine.

"Not anytime soon. Nope, no openings,"

Vinius said. "What on earth did you say to Crispina the other day?"

"In the arena? Not much; she isn't a very big talker."

"She told ME that you were mean to her," Vinius accused, "and that you didn't like her."

"But how? I hardly even asked her about the weather, let alone anything serious. She barely said anything!" Otho protested. "What did she say I said?"

"Oh, I don't think we need to go into specifics. So, is this arrangement still off?"

Otho reached into his cavernous toga filled with bribe bags, feeling around for the biggest one strapped to his hip. Vinius's eyes lit up like a cat spotting a small red bird perched on a low branch as Otho handed it over. He quickly snagged it and tucked it away.

"No, I don't think our arrangement is off. Whatever she thinks I said, it's a misunderstanding. She's, uh, attractive. I'd still marry her. She's quiet, nothing wrong with that."

"Okay, well, just treat her nice, okay? Glad to know you can keep a deal," Vinius said, holding the money close to his heart. "I've been trying to find her a husband for years. I don't know what it is that makes it so hard . . . she's a fine girl."

"I'm sure she'll make a fine wife, no doubt," Otho said, sipping his wine. They continued discussing the administration until Vinius suddenly had to go. It was one of those parties where you could tell by body language that no one wanted to talk to you. Everyone was standing or sitting in closed circles. But Otho knew what to do. Like an expert, he prowled around the room, waiting for someone to have drunk too much wine. The moment a man left for relief, Otho swooped in and infiltrated the group, waiting for and seizing every opportunity.

10 THE SULPICII

Fall turned to winter, and Otho's stash of cash vanished along with the leaves. By leveraging the infrastructure to package subprime mortgages as non-risky financial assets, he managed to keep borrowing just enough money to maintain his plan. According to the stars, he only needed to sustain the bribes for about a year. But as he bribed more people, he found others who also needed to be on his side, and he couldn't resist adding them to the take. After all, what harm could it do? There was something about a man who handed out seemingly endless amounts of money that attracted a certain crowd.

"Hey, add three hundred thousand more sesterces to the Cornelius account," Otho shouted.

"Loaning or taking?" Onomastus yelled back from the records room.

"Loaning," Otho replied.

"Oh, thank the Gods," Onomastus muttered.

"Does that cover everything?" Otho asked, entering the small room to find Onomastus hunched over a long scroll, its edges worn from constant use. Onomastus grabbed a white stone and glanced at a wall covered in names and numbers. The fifty or so names and numbers were interconnected by string from one name to another.

"Futuit, hold on, this is getting complicated," Onomastus said, adding a few ticks to one name, then erasing and redrawing numbers connected to Cornelius by string. He stepped back, tracing the strings with hand gestures. "Yeah, I think we're good for another week." He then cast a handful of dice into a corner, their scattered numbers indecipherable. "Maybe two."

"Wow," Otho said, trying to grasp the accountant black magic Onomastus was performing. "That deserves a drink."

"Let me balance a few more things, and I'll be out for that drink," Onomastus replied, flicking beads back and forth on an abacus with increasing speed. He was on the brink of completing the day's calculations and could almost feel the final numbers falling into place.

"Wait, I may have more money coming in tonight," Otho said, leaving the room. "One of our investors is stopping by soon, and I think we can stretch things for another few days."

Otho knew one of his oldest investors was due to arrive a few hours after noon, and it was about that time. He headed toward the front door to greet him, only to be intercepted in the dining room.

"Otho, where's my money? I want it back!" An angry man with jet-black hair stood up from a couch, emerging from the shadows.

"I don't have it, Decimus. It's all tied up,"

Otho replied. "I won't be able to earn a profit for you until after I become emperor. You still have time to invest more."

"I've spoken with my father, and we're no longer interested in investing—only collecting," Decimus said.

"Your father's missing out on a golden opportunity to secure a foothold in Rome's political landscape for decades. He must see that," Otho argued.

"No, he doesn't," Decimus replied.

"Has ol' pater Sulpicii lost faith? Does he really not think I'm gonna to make it?" Otho asked rhetorically.

"No, he doesn't," Decimus said sharply. "Rumor has it Galba's about to pick his successor, and the rumors have been sayin' you ain't it."

"That can't be right," Otho said, a shred of doubt creeping in.

"It's from a very reliable source I've heard, and I'm here to pull our money out," Decimus stated.

"You'll have to come back. I don't have it here," Otho said. "You should consider yourself lucky because pulling out now would be a terrible mistake."

"That's a risk my father is willing to take," Decimus said, heading for the door. He paused and looked back, "We'll be back at the same time tomorrow."

"We'll?" Otho echoed. Decimus left, casting a potent stink eye over his shoulder. "Onomastus!"

"What?"

"No extra money, and I need a meeting with Vinius tomorrow!"

"Alright, I'll be out for drinks in a minute,"

Onomastus called back, sensing Otho's worry. "Did the meeting go okay?"

"What? I can't hear you!" Otho yelled back, peering into the records room at Onomastus.

Onomastus didn't respond, focusing intently on his bookkeeping before he lost those intricate thoughts that took hours to put together. It's been taking longer each day to balance Otho's budget, and he couldn't afford to lose his train of thought. Scribbling furiously, he finally finished, and after what felt like a month of living in that stuffy room, he stepped out. The place smelled like dude in there, and Onomastus was the only dude.

"That's a shame we didn't get more money from the Sulpicii—they've been one of our more stable lenders," Onomastus mused, still caught up in his work. "But we'll be fine. One week of funding has been typical for us."

"We may only need another week," Otho said.

"Oh? How's that?"

"Sounds like Galba might finally be picking his successor soon," Otho said, "or so the rumors say."

"That's great! You're on the short list, right?" Onomastus asked.

"Oh yeah, I just need to meet with Vinius tomorrow to plan out the rest of the budget," Otho said as Onomastus grabbed a drink. "We're futuendi finally going to see some payoff for all this work." Otho said energetically while lying down on a couch and drinking wine.

"Seriously," Onomastus said, kicking back. "We'd be cutting it super close otherwise."

"How that?"

"Well, most of the contracts expect a payout in a month or so," Onomastus explained. "We actually started hitting some of those return dates a couple of weeks ago. Didn't you say you took care of those?"

"Yeah, we got the loans extended and expanded."

"Oh, stercus, like you just borrowed more money?" Onomastus asked, peeling back another layer of the onion.

"We pay off the interest over time. Most of the creditors were kind enough to lend me more money," Otho elaborated.

"That explains some of the numbers you've been sending me," Onomastus said. "So, how many times can you do that?"

"Depends on the creditor and my credit rating. Since I'm about to become emperor, I've got a really good credit rating," Otho said. "That's actually how we ended up living in this magnificent villa."

"What? But we've been here this whole time!"

"Yeah, I told one creditor I was going to be emperor and came from a very prestigious family. This place turned out to be quite affordable given my credit limit, with a small initial price. I floated the down payment with the money we had left over from our journey here," Otho explained.

"That's pretty tenuous," Onomastus said, trying to wrap his head around it. "And that was before the astronomer even came."

"Well, I always knew I was going to be emperor, or at least successful," Otho said. "Even if I didn't, I probably could have gotten this place. Just having a good family name here means creditors will lend you almost anything if you know what to say."

"It is weird though, I still haven't met your family."

"Oh, they don't visit often."

"I don't know how you live like that. Thank goodness Galba's finally making up his mind, because I think you'd have been borrowing a lot more against your own debt in the next couple months otherwise."

"I wouldn't worry about it," Otho said. "My credit is still great. My interest rates are so low, I'd be an idiot not to borrow more money."

"Is that why you were throwing down all that money at the races the other day?" Onomastus asked. "Those were some huge bets!"

"I had a really good feeling about those bets. It paid off, didn't it?" Otho said. "We tripled our money that day!"

"But what if we lost?" Onomastus asked. "We'd be in the hole right now!"

"We'll never be in the hole as long as I have this credit," Otho said. "And it's going to get even better when I'm adopted."

"Why would you need good credit then? Won't we start paying off the debt at that point?"

"There'd be no point to that if my interest rate is lower than it is now," Otho answered. "They were already low when I got here, and as soon as I told my creditors I had the Praetorian Guard on my payroll, my interest rates halved!"

Onomastus was speechless.

"Just keep the stash safe. I'll talk to Vinius tomorrow, and we'll be fine," Otho said, taking another drink of wine.

***

Otho walked to his meeting with Vinius on a cold, overcast day. The streets were quiet, dim, and speckled with puddles, the air thick with damp smoke. Every man huddled around a fire or moved briskly, seeking warmth. As Otho rounded a corner, he noticed two men standing by a basket fire. They looked up, as if recognizing him, but Otho didn't know them. Avoiding eye contact, he kept walking, not in the mood for handouts.

"Otho, over here!" one of the men with buzzed hair called out. Otho's hand went to his dagger.

"It's Octavius, of the Sulpicii. This here's Nonus," Octavius said, pointing to Nonus, who had slicked-back, oily black hair, "and I believe you met our youngest brother, Decimus, yesterday,"

"What a coincidence it is running into you," Otho said, relaxing his grip as he approached the two Sulpicii brothers, both wrapped in long cloaks with their hands stretched out toward the fire.

"Not a coincidence," Nonus said. "I think you know why we're here."

"Why here? You know where to find me," Otho replied.

"Don't worry, we know how to find you wherever you are," Octavius said. "Our father wants you to know you're cut off for good."

"Decimus told me that last night," Otho said.

"And unless you're adopted by Galba by the end of the week, we'll be back to collect what ya already owe," Octavius continued. "From what I've heard, you'd better start collecting that money now."

"That would be pretty stupid," Otho replied "For the paterfamilias of the Sulpicii, your dad is inept at making money."

"Bull stercus," Nonus spat. "We've been watching you for a month now, you ain't making any futuendi money."

"No, no, no, hear me out," Otho said, his voice taking on a desperate edge. "Galba should be picking his heir this week, maybe even today. I'm on my way to arrange everything with Vinius right now."

"We all know you're not going to be the heir. We're onto you," Octavius said. "You're going to Vinius, huh?"

"Yes, on business. Everything's going to be fine. Things are in motion. I won't be able to pay y'all back for at least another month, but that's no big deal. Your father will get nothing if you're impatient. He'll understand; he's a businessman like me."

"That's not what I meant," Octavius said. "If you're going to Vinius, you're carrying. How much of my father's money are you bringing that snake? A hundred? A thousand? Hand it over." Both Octavius and Nonus reached inside their cloaks, and Otho took a step back. The three stared at each other for a tense fifteen seconds until Nonus moved to grab Otho's sack of coins. Otho kicked over the basket fire and bolted down the street, coins spilling from his cloak like blood from a shot deer.

"Futueō you!" Nonus yelled as Otho fled, leaving chaos in his wake. Otho glanced back to see the brothers frantically stopping the burning logs and embers from igniting a nearby hay pile.

"What the futuit is going on out there?" residents shouted as they emptied chamber pots and whatever water they had on the fire.

"Hey, watch where you're tossing that

stercus!"

"I wouldn't have to if you didn't set my neighborhood on fire!"

"Futueō you and your stercī neighborhood."

After running for twenty yards, Otho slowed to a walk, flipped the brothers the bird, and calmly continued on his way to Vinius. He was supposed to meet Vinius just outside the baths near the palace. Though he encountered no more Sulpicii brothers, Otho remained vigilant, eyes scanning every corner and alley. How many Sulpicii brothers could there be?

He arrived a little early and decided to wait out of sight in the shadow of an alley. He kept watch for Nonus and Octavius, but they never appeared. After about thirty minutes, he spotted Vinius with the other pedagogues and whistled. Vinius slipped into the alley, approaching Otho with a nonchalant air.

"Well, I tried, but Galba doesn't seem interested in adopting you as his heir," Vinius said.

"Just keep trying, and I'll keep sending the cash," Otho replied, handing Vinius a thick and chunky bag of sesterces. "I should be a shoo-in. No one has been more faithful to Galba than I have."

"Convincing Galba of anything isn't that simple," Vinius said. "Maybe if you found some ancient, nearly forgotten ancestry and weaseled into one of those old Roman families, you'd have a decent shot. You could marry someone from a good family?"

"I'll look into it," Otho said, already scheming. "Just remember, I can keep that gravy train going for you if you get me adopted. But in the meantime, we'll be in touch. And I told you, I'll marry Crispina after the adoption. That's the plan."

"This coin's a little light. You may have to pay

up front on that deal sooner rather than later."

"I'll need to find a good lawyer to arrange that—someone who isn't her father."

"Hey, what's with the alley?" Vinius asked. "Too good to be seen with me in public?"

"I saw an old girlfriend in the area," Otho lied. "She's the clingy type. Didn't want to deal with her. You know how it is."

"Haha, okay, gotta keep you single for Crispina," Vinius laughed. The two shook hands and parted ways until their next not-so-shady back-alley meeting.

***

Galba sent a man named Vitellius to become the governor of Germania. He was annoying and an ineffectual leader, and Galba saw this as an opportunity to kill two birds with one stone: get rid of a nuisance and prevent powerful men from gaining influence in distant regions with large military forces. This proved to be a prudent move, as some soldiers up north, angry over not getting paid after crushing Vindex's revolt, rebelled. Unfortunately, Vitellius joined their revolt, becoming their leader. This marked Galba's first major crisis of legitimacy as the new ruler.

Rumors of Galba choosing an heir began circulating days after the revolt in Germania. Despite the growing concerns among investors that Galba might pick someone else, Otho kept the optimism alive. He maintained his credit and kept enough cash for a week or two runway budget [10]to continue bribing the right people, with some leftover discretionary funds.

"You really shouldn't be spending that on remodeling the guest bedroom," Onomastus lectured as Otho reviewed his finances in the records room.

"I'm not a barbarian, Onomastus," Otho replied. "I can't let my guests sleep in a subpar room when they visit. I have to project power with my nice things—it's not just about bribery!"

"Yeah, but you only have a few guests staying over each month," Onomastus protested, waving his growing book of ledgers and IOUs. "And when have they ever asked for a private botanical garden and a heated bird bath?"

"It's January! I don't want the birds to get cold!" Otho argued back, but their debate was cut short by a loud knock at the door.

"Go get it," Otho ordered a nearby slave.

The interruption helped cool tempers. "Anyone scheduled to come by tonight?" Onomastus asked.

"No, no one," Otho replied. "Maybe an investor? Usually, we get some warning." His suspicion grew. "Could Galba have finally picked an heir?" They exchanged a glance, excitement brewing.

---

[10] Referring to an airport runway, this was how much more financial runway Otho had for his success to takes off. Accounting for the medium sized staff working for Otho, repeat bribes and certain investors that expected a more immediate return, Otho had a good idea on his cash burn through rate which was about enough to maintain three Greek Theater troupes. Otho made sure to continually borrow enough money for about a week or two of that burn through rate so it wouldn't suddenly collapse when employees didn't get their pay checks.

"Otho, come quick, I couldn't stop them!" the slave yelled as he ran back.

"What?" Otho asked.

"They're ransacking the place!" the slave responded.

"What the futuit?" Otho and Onomastus said in unison as they rushed to the door. There, three men in their late twenties, with the signature black, oily, greasy hair of the Sulpicii brothers, were ordering a troupe of slaves to carry off everything not bolted down from Otho's villa.

"Annoying-culus Sulpicii brothers! I should have known!" Otho shouted. "It's Quintus, Sextus, and Septimus. What the futuit are you doing here, so far from a wet nurse?"

"Ha, good one. If it isn't our favorite deadbeat, Otho, and his lackey, Onomastus," Quintus, the eldest, taunted. "What are you doing so far from a rich cougar?"

"Oooooh," Sextus and Septimus echoed.

"Anyway," Otho said, regaining his composure. "Would you mind making like a tree and getting the futuent out of my villa?"

"Not until we get enough," Quintus answered. "We heard that Piso is going to be Galba's heir. There's supposed to be a big scene at the Senate tomorrow to make it official. Our father wants his money back. Now! While he can still repossess something . . ."

"Hee hee, time's up, Otho, hee hee," Sextus, the weird middle child, snickered.

"If y'all don't get out of here after returning everything you verpus-heads have taken, I'm gonna beat your culus, then sue it," Otho retorted gracefully and with much less cursing than he felt.

"Un-futuendi-likely. This is all collateral, and we're just reclaiming it," Quintus said before Otho silenced him with a swift right hook to the face before shaking his knuckles in pain. Septimus lunged to grab Otho from behind but was interrupted by Onomastus's swift kick to his groin.

Otho stepped back, regaining his balance and taking a menacing stance. Quintus wiped blood from his nose, which now squeaked with each breath. Sextus and Septimus moved in beside him, rubbing dirt in their wounds as they stood up.

The three brothers drew matching five-inch pugio daggers, shifting their weight like wrestlers ready to pounce. Onomastus revealed his piercingly slim nine-inch dagger and grabbed a nearby rounded table, using it as a shield. With much gusto, Otho drew a fat, seven-inch pugio, longer and thicker than anything the Sulpicii had. He performed a few kung fu style moves swiping his dagger through the air, swinging it around like a maniac, and landed in a defensive stance. No one knew the name of the stance, but it was definitely named after a predatory animal. He had the larger dagger, and he knew how to use it.

Despite outnumbering Otho and Onomastus, the Sulpicii brothers grew more nervous. "Get the futuo out of here," Otho commanded forcefully.

"Fine, you can put your verpus away," Sextus said. "I mean di—daggers." The three brothers retreated with whatever loot they had managed to grab.

"We'll be back," Quintus shouted over his shoulder. "It's over for you, Otho. You've got one week."

Otho spat in Quintus's direction. House slaves quietly reentered the room, cleaning up the mess and bringing back a few pieces of furniture left just outside the atrium. Otho and Onomastus sat down on two heavy couches that would have been taken last.

"What do they mean, Piso is going to be the heir?" Onomastus broke the silence.

"Rumors, just rumors," Otho replied.

"You knew about this?" Onomastus asked.

"Yeah, some investors are getting nervous and want to pull out. It's so futuendi stupid," Otho grumbled. "I'm gonna give Vinius an earful over this. If he doesn't do anything to make me the heir in the next week, we're cutting him off. These rumors are going to ruin my credit."

"How are the rumors so widespread if they're not true?" Onomastus asked. "It's concerning—there's no smoke without fire."

"Unfounded, it's nothing," Otho insisted. "However, in case you weren't paying attention tonight, if we don't do something about it, the rumors themselves are going to get us killed if we're not careful!"

"Agreed," Onomastus nodded.

"Tomorrow, we need to pay the Praetorians a visit and arrange for some security till we settle this."

The overcast skies above Rome cleared, revealing a blinding sun on another frigid day. It was the kind of day where only the truly dedicated would brave the cold for an early morning jog. Otho and Onomastus began their brisk walk to the Castra Praetoria, their eyes squinting against the glaring sunlight. The sharp wind made their noses run and numbed any exposed skin. They kept up the fast pace, partly out of fear of running into more of the Sulpicii brothers, but mostly because it was too cold to be outside without at least two large animals' worth of fur. The brisk pace kept their blood circulating, a small defense against the harsh elements.

They rounded corner after corner, moving at an aggressively fast walk, scanning the mostly empty streets for threats. Otho had been jumped before and made sure to avoid even the homeless huddled around basket fires. "With these rumors going around, we may not be safe until we reach the Castra," Otho told Onomastus.

"How many more people are you worried about?" Onomastus asked.

"I don't even want to think about it. If my investors don't believe I'm going to be emperor, my credit is in the trash!" Otho panicked. "You're an accomplice too, Onomastus. If we're not careful, we could end up at the bottom of a galley. I'm going to futuendi kill that Vinius." Otho huffed, pushing through his speed walk.

"Have you heard of many investors wanting to pull out?" Onomastus asked. "If even a few pull their money, we won't have anything."

"Enough are interested that we're futuentur," Otho replied. "If we don't take care of this today with the Praetorians, we're as good as dead."

"I'm afraid we might be too late," Onomastus said as they rounded the last corner to the Castra.

Blocking their path was a group of twenty armed mercenaries, led by the oldest four Sulpicii brothers.

"Mater futuit," Otho muttered, stopping short.

"What the futuo do you want, Primus?"

"First, I want you to apologize for what you did to Quintus," Primus[11] said, the eldest. "Second, we're not letting you go until we have all our money back—with interest."

"Primus, your entire family is so short-sighted, it's no wonder your father had so little creativity he numbered you all instead of giving you proper names," Otho said. "Let me guess, you must be Secundus, Tertius, and Quartus."

"Shut up," Primus snapped, regaining control of the conversation. "It's officially over, Otho. Galba has picked Piso. He just held a comitia to make the announcement public."

"Wow, if you're going to make something up, you could at least choose a believable word," Otho retorted. "What the futuo is a comitia? There's no way that's real."

"Well, does this look made up?" Primus held up a sesterces coin. "It's the Comitia Commemorative Coin. Right here, it says Piso is the heir to the throne."

"You can't believe everything you read on a coin, Primus," Otho said. "You're dumber than you look, you know that?"

"Why am I even arguing with you? Seize him," Primus ordered. His mercenaries surrounded Otho, seizing both his arms. Onomastus tried to slip away but was caught in a pincer maneuver and was grabbed roughly. The two struggled, but the mercenaries were too strong. Maybe they shouldn't

---

[11] In large families with many sons and uncreative parents, Romans would often name their children *First/Primus, Second/Secundus* and so on. The Sulpicii were one of those families.

have futuatis Quintus and Septimus so badly the night before.

"I have to hand it to ya, Otho," Primus said, approaching Otho's blistered red face, firmly held back by the mercenaries. "It was pretty difficult finding mercenaries after you paid off the Praetorian Guard so well. Damn unions. I thought you might have amounted to something."

"The Praetorians don't work for verpī," Otho spat in Primus's face.

"Where the futuo is my money?" Primus growled, punching Otho in the gut.

"Somewhere your lackeys will never find it," Otho answered. "I don't even know where it is, because I knew I'd eventually meet a thug like you, Primus."

"I wasn't talking to you," Primus said, turning to Onomastus. "You don't have to die for this man. Where is the money?"

Onomastus remained silent.

"I said, where the futuo is the money?" Primus barked, and the mercenaries began roughing up the quiet freedman.

"Leave him alone!" Otho yelled. "He didn't do anything wrong."

"Not quite in a position to talk, are you?" Primus ordered more beatings for Otho. Then he pulled a mercenary's sword and held it to Onomastus's throat. "Last chance, where's the money? Before you accidentally drown in the Tiber . . ."

Onomastus gulped, unsure what to do while being stared down by a mingētur Sulpicii. Ten seconds passed before Onomastus heard a commotion, and suddenly the grip of the two mercenaries loosened. The men fell to the ground with javelins in their backs. Arrows rained down on the remaining mercenaries as a group of Praetorian guards sprinted in to finish the fight. Languidus and Tributus tackled the four Sulpicii brothers to the ground before they could escape.

All twenty mercenaries were defeated in under twenty seconds after a brief scuffle. Languidus and Tributus held the Sulpicii brothers down while the units retrieved their weapons and arrows from the bodies.

"Man, can you believe these thieves were so well-armed?" Languidus asked Tributus. "You two were really lucky we happened to be in the neighborhood."

"It's really crazy. They just get better equipped every day," Tributus replied. "What would these streets do without us patrolling them?"

"Gosh, if it isn't our good friends Otho and Onomastus," Languidus added.

"Languidus!" Onomastus shouted back. "Thank the Gods you came when you did. These Sulpicii were about to kill me."

"Ahem," Languidus grunted, allowing the Sulpicii brothers to get up and dust themselves off. "All I see here are four men caught up in an armed robbery. I don't know how the courts would condemn such fine young men. Better get out of here and go back home to your fellow patricians before more thieves come and we can't stop them."

"Yes, thank you so much," Primus said before running off with his brothers.

"I'm not going to push my luck," Languidus

said as they walked away. "They're too rich. It's not worth the headache of killing them."

"What the futuo are y'all doin out here so exposed?" Tributus criticized.

"We were going to ask for a little protection," Otho answered. "Almost made it to the Castra. That family has been harassing me for the last week."

"What for?" Tributus asked.

"Rumor is Galba picked Piso," Otho replied. "They want to rob me blind now that I'm not as powerful."

"Damn, that's just not right," Languidus said. "That's your money. You'll be safe from now on. We'll take care of it."

"Thanks," Otho said. He bent down and picked up the Comitia Commemorative Coin that Primus had dropped after being tackled by Languidus. He wiped some mercenary blood off and read the inscription:

"LUCIUS CALPURNIUS PISO FRUGI LICINIANUS"

"ADOPTED BY GALBA"

"Futuus," Otho muttered. "This coin looks legit. I think we need to stage a coup now."

11 THE COUP

Languidus and Tributus escorted Otho and Onomastus into the Castra, followed by a small unit of Praetorians who had taken out the Sulpicii mercenaries. Languidus led the two straight into the administrative building and quickly shut the door behind him, allowing only Tributus to follow. The office was sparse, decorated only with some armor and weapons propped against one wall. Against another wall, desks overflowed with loose scrolls, and in the center of the room sat a large, bare table surrounded by wooden stools. The table was marred by red ring stains from countless cups of wine, unprotected by coasters. Otho and Onomastus took seats on one side of the table, while Languidus, without a word, exited to an adjacent room. Tributus closed all the shutters, leaving the room dimly lit by a fireplace and a few candles scattered across the large table.

"Onomastus," Otho whispered while Tributus continued to secure the room, "how much money do we have left if we don't spend anything else?"

"I think we have only a hundred thousand sesterces left," Onomastus whispered back.

"That'll have to do," Otho whispered.

Languidus returned, this time accompanied by Cocceius Proculus, Barbius, and Veturius. The five guards sat down opposite Otho and Onomastus, silent and stern, arms crossed. Onomastus and Tributus looked around, waiting for action. Otho stared straight ahead, avoiding eye contact to keep from being the first to speak. Everyone knew the agenda. This wasn't a meet and greet, a job interview, or even a business meeting—it was a negotiation.

After a minute of tense silence, Languidus broke it. "So, you mentioned that you were looking for some protection," he said, his patience thinning.

"Yes, it appears I may need to cash in on some favors from the past few months," Otho said.

"The big issue I foresee is that the Praetorian Guard only provides protection to the emperor," Barbius noted. "Are you trying to start a coup?"

"Yes, that would be the plan," Otho answered.

"Coups aren't cheap, Otho," Veturius responded. "Even with your previous contributions."

"I wouldn't think they would be. Otherwise, we'd change leadership with the seasons," Otho joked, trying to lighten the mood. "Do tell me, how expensive are imperial coups? Do you think I haven't been generous in the past?"

"If you have to ask, you can't afford it," responded Veturius.

"No, no, no," Barbius replied. "We'll give you the friend price, of course. Among the men here in this room, I believe we can put you on the throne by the end of the week for . . . a . . . erghmm . . . ahhhhh, two million sesterces." Barbius looked to his fellow guardsmen, who nodded in agreement.

"Big oof, Barbius," Otho said, clutching his heart. "I thought we were all friends here."

"The last coup was way more expensive," Languidus pointed out.

"Oh, yes, I'm sure," Otho agreed. "What you don't realize is the difference between a one-time payment and long-term income."

"Do enlighten us," Veturius said.

"Well, it's one thing to get your cash in one lump sum. But if you take a little less and invest with me, you'll get a long-term return."

"Long-term?" Languidus asked.

"Yes, most men go for the quick payment without considering the more patient, but lucrative, approach," Otho explained, talking down to the guards. "Let me ask you, what were your pay increases like under Galba?"

"Hahaha, what pay increases?" Barbius laughed.

"Exactly. Now, what did they look like under Nero?" Otho pressed.

The five guards thought for a moment and began nodding their heads. "Okay," Veturius said, starting to understand. "I suppose we could help you out for a million instead."

"For a million, I could just escape to the countryside and live a quiet, peaceful life," Otho countered. "I've always wanted to take up sculpting."

"Okay, half a million," Barbius offered.

"I hear Alexandria is a nice place to move to," Otho mused. "You could buy an entire city along the

Nile for that price—rich cotton, beautiful African women, fresh fruit, perfect weather . . .”

"Quarter mil, final offer," Barbius said, dropping to an eighth of his original price.

"A quarter?" Otho asked. "I think I can do a quarter."

The five guards nodded in agreement. "Yeah, we can arrange it all for a quarter, no problem," Barbius settled on the price.

"Okay, it's a deal." Otho shook Barbius' hand. "Fifty thousand now and two hundred thousand next week when you're done. Okay?"

"Got it," Veturius said as they all shook Otho's hand.

"I can fork over another fifty thousand now for any bribes you might need," Otho added. "While I'm sure you're all capable of pulling this off, let's not cut corners. This needs to be quick and as bloodless as possible."

"Agreed," Veturius said. "This should be easy. Galba couldn't have made himself an easier target with all his policies."

"Okay, I think we have an accord," Otho said, closing the deal. "If you can lend me a protection unit, I'll pick up the money now."

"No problem, I'll lead it myself," Languidus said. "And don't gossip about this to anyone outside this room until the plan is in place. Close contacts only," he warned. "We won't be able to pull it off if anyone sees it coming."

***

Over the next week, the Praetorian guards

Otho had paid spread the word to close conspirators. Once a signal was given, everyone would stop supporting Galba and back Otho as the new emperor. Although word of the coup spread among the upper ranks of the guards, many ensured that no rumors reached Galba. On one occasion, Galba did hear of the coup against him, but Laco dismissed it as nonsense with no legal precedent. Despite Otho's visible bitterness and anger, particularly toward Vinius, Galba and his advisors suspected nothing. They thought he was just jealous of Piso.

About a week later, on the ides of January, Otho joined Galba and his advisors in an official sacrifice at the Temple of Apollo. Otho stood with Vinius at one end of the altar, while the imperial party impatiently waited for a slave to coax a sheep up a flight of stairs to the altar in front of the temple's large columns. Everyone watched as the slave tugged at a rope tied around the sheep's neck, but no one offered to help. The sheep clearly didn't want to go. He had seen what was done up there.

"So, what happened anyway?" Otho asked Vinius.

"Whatever do you mean, Otho?" Vinius responded coldly.

"You said you'd get me adopted. What exactly happened?" Otho pressed.

"I never said I'd get you adopted. I said I'd try to get you adopted. It's no guarantee," Vinius said. "It's over now. Nothing I can do at this point. So, where's my money?"

"Money for what?" Otho asked.

"Money for access," Vinius said. "You're still paying for influence and imperial access. How do you think you got invited here? Don't tell me you're going to short me."

"Why would I pay for access now?" Otho asked. "Clearly, I'm not going to get anything out of it. Your access is a terrible investment."

"You can still gain influence, and that's worth a lot around here," Vinius insisted.

"Well, consider my imperial influence subscription canceled," Otho said. "Don't bother inviting me to any more imperial events. Our last meeting was your last bribe, Vinius."

"Okay, well, the wedding's off. Crispina never liked you anyway."

"Good, because I wouldn't have wanted to marry her anyway. She's a terrible date, and I can pull far more beautiful ladies who don't have fathers ready to futuit me in the culus."

"You'll regret shorting me, Otho," Vinius threatened. "But enough of that, it looks like they've finally got the sheep up to the altar." Otho left to join the imperial party, positioning himself behind Galba to observe the sacrifice to Apollo. Vinius, however, lingered and had a word with the priest of Apollo, Umbricius.

"Pssst, hey," Vinius whispered as the slave wrestled the sheep onto the altar and Galba began another long-winded speech about patriotism, devotion to the gods, or some other drivel.

"What? Now is not the time Vinius," the horseshoe-bald priest, fattened by the constant access to sacrificial meat, whispered back. "Dude, I'm in the middle of a sacrifice, Vinius."

"I need you to declare an omen," Vinius demanded.

"You know I'm not that kind of priest," Umbricius said, frowning. "Don't confuse me with the augurs."

"No one cares, man. Just do it. Who even knows the difference?" Vinius slipped a chunky bag of sesterces into Umbricius's hand.

"I have a reputation to uphold. What if the union finds out I'm breaking rules again?"

"Tell Galba he's about to be betrayed. Imply it's Otho. I don't care how you do it, just do it." Vinius patted Umbricius on the shoulder and rejoined the imperial party.

Five more agonizing minutes passed as the crowd endured the sheep's pitiful bleating. Finally, Galba concluded his speech, which no one had been listening to. Umbricius picked up a ceremonial dagger, bedazzled with jewels, and plunged it into the sheep's belly, slicing it open from end to end. Warm entrails spilled over the altar, the blood steaming in the cold winter air. Umbricius pulled out a kidney and examined it against a strand of small intestine. His mouth went agape, and he shouted, "Noooo! What a terrible omen!"

"Oh no, what could ever be the matter?" Vinius asked flatly.

"Galba, you must be careful," Umbricius warned. "These entrails show signs of great commotion. You are in the midst of a betrayer! He could be right behind you."

"Oh my," Galba murmured, looking distressed. "I had a dream recently where Nike took away my fortune. I knew it!"

"Hey, you're not an augur," another priest interjected.

"Shut up," Vinius snapped.

Vinius gave Otho the evil eye, then nudged the other pedagogues, turning Icelus and Laco's attention to the still-bitter Otho. Galba moaned in lamentation at the news of the betrayal. Otho's face reddened with nervousness.

"I wouldn't worry too much," Otho said, trying to calm Galba without giving himself away. "My cousin's an augur, and he taught me a few things. That kind of kidney is easily misinterpreted as commotion when it really signals a bountiful harvest."

"Really?" Galba asked, perking up.

"Yeah," Otho assured him. "I went to a seminar the other day. Apparently, augurs in Rome only need to attend a forty-hour correspondence course. It's practically a pseudoscience. You can't trust everything they say. It's insane that augur evidence is still admissible in court, considering how unreliable it is."

"I've never heard that before," Galba said, cheering up.

Onomastus slunk into the crowd and nudged Otho. "Sir, uhhh, your architects have arrived. I'm afraid you need to leave right now if you don't want to miss them."

"What architects?" Vinius asked, narrowing his eyes.

Onomastus and Otho paused, awkward silence hanging between them as Otho scrambled to explain. "Oh, architects to appraise a property I'm thinking of buying. It's in a great neighborhood."

"Architects for an appraisal?" Vinius questioned. "I've never heard of such a thing."

"The owners are very old and couldn't give

me a proper price on the building," Otho said, gaining confidence. "I wanted to do my due diligence before buying. I have to go; these guys are good and hard to get ahold of. I hope the rest of the sacrifice goes well. I'm not feeling great anyway—probably a fever. Shouldn't be hanging around you all." Otho said as Onomastus dragged him away before he could spew more nonsense.

Once they were a safe distance away, Onomastus spoke freely. "What the futuus was that? You nearly gave the whole plan away up there!"

"How was I supposed to know Umbricius would tell Galba someone was going to betray him?" Otho snapped. "He's not even an augur, just a priest. Big difference."

"Well, lucky for you, it wouldn't have mattered much. It's time." Onomastus led Otho through the palace of Tiberius. The temple and much of the imperial party were eerily quiet, with guards absent or giving Otho nods of approval while tugging at their underwear.

"Yeah, I heard your signal," Otho replied. "I was so thrown by the omen I barely remembered what you meant by 'architects arriving.' Where are we meeting?"

"The soldiers are waiting at the Golden Milestone," Onomastus answered.

"Perfect, that's a great starting point. I can't wait for this charade to be over," Otho said. "No more sucking up, Onomastus, can you believe it?"

"No, I can't," he replied. "If you'd told me two months ago we'd be launching a coup, I'd have said, 'What went wrong?' " He laughed.

"Ha, well, there's more than one way to skin a

cat," Otho responded. The two exited the palace, where a litter was waiting to carry Otho to the soldiers awaiting his arrival.

"You get the imperial treatment now," Onomastus said, waving him into the litter.

"Oh, okay," Otho said, stepping into the man-powered carriage, typically reserved for upper-class women.

The pole bearers made their way toward the Milestone at the Temple of Saturn, where all roads in the city began. You can't miss it because of all the tourists and all of the merchants trying to sell souvenirs to the tourists. The litter moved at a moderate pace, but after two blocks, it began to slow to a crawl. "Hey, speed it up," Onomastus urged the bearers. "We have men waiting, and a good distance to go!" he whispered.

"I'm sorry, these things aren't made for middle-aged men," one of the pole bearers responded. "Usually, we only get women. This is as fast as we can go with Otho's weight."

"Fine, but you're getting no tip if we don't make it there by noon," Onomastus snapped. "And I'll be spreading terrible reviews."

The litter traveled a few more blocks over fifteen minutes, but they weren't speeding up. They weren't going to make it. "Hey, Onomastus," Otho called down.

"Yeah? Enjoying it up there?" Onomastus replied.

"Not at all," Otho said. "This is slower than stercus and really boring. Plus, it's freezing today. This was a bad idea."

"I'll plan better next time," Onomastus said.

"We can always walk the rest of the way."

"Yeah, get me off this thing," Otho ordered. The exhausted pole bearers set him down, and Otho stretched his legs to warm up. "You all seriously need to find a different job. That was awful." He continued to chastise the pole bearers.

Otho began to run toward mile marker zero, with Onomastus following close behind. They ran through the city streets, eager to reach the forum's main square. They could almost see the opening to the square, aglow with cold sunlight in contrast to the dimly lit roads and alleys. Just before they reached the square, Otho's right shoe came untied and flew off. He stopped, hopping on one foot shouting "futuendi damnit" as Onomastus circled back to retrieve the shoe.

"Today couldn't get any more complicated," Otho grumbled as he retied his shoe. He then walked into the forum square like he owned the place. Without any more serious complications, he would own it by the end of the day.

There were more pigeons than people in the forum. The square was surrounded by towering columns and buildings, and at the far end stood the monument at mile zero, from which all distances were measured. The milestone, a proud twelve feet tall, was covered in gilded bronze, shining in all directions—wherever bird stercus hadn't sullied it.

Approaching the mostly shiny column, Otho found twenty-three soldiers waiting for him. They were in full armor and greeted him with an enthusiastic, "Hail, Emperor!"

As soon as he heard his first imperial greeting, Otho froze. Collecting himself, he turned to

Onomastus. "Where the futuo is everyone? We can't overthrow the empire with twenty-three futuendi men! What the futuo happened?"

"This isn't everyone, dude, calm down," Onomastus replied. While Otho's back was turned, the soldiers sat him down lifted him onto a chair like a Jewish boy at his bar mitzvah. They drew their swords and began cheering.

They hollered and chanted, proclaiming Otho as emperor. The loud men made sure to attract as much attention as possible, marching their new emperor toward their headquarters in a rowdy procession.

"Otho, this is it," Languidus said, leading the small unit.

"It doesn't quite feel like it. I was expecting more people, to be honest," Otho replied. "Where are we going?"

"To your temporary headquarters at the Castra. We'll keep you safe there until the coup is over," Languidus answered.

"What did you expect it to feel like?" Tributus asked Otho.

"I don't know, more people at least, maybe some fighting or something," Otho said. "At least an argument with Galba or Vinius."

"I wouldn't worry about any of that. Why do you think we're making so much noise?" Tributus said. "Gotta kick this thing off somehow."

As the chanting, singing soldiers rounded a corner of the mostly still city, they caught the attention of another small group of soldiers patrolling in a loose gaggle. Either out of excitement or curiosity, the on-duty soldiers approached and joined the formation, waving their swords. This alone doubled the size of the crowd.

"Hey, who's that? What's going on?" one of the new soldiers asked Languidus.

"That's Otho, the new emperor. Ya didn't hear? We're having a coup today!" Languidus answered.

"About damn time. Who's Otho again, do we know him?" the soldier asked.

"He's the subligaculum guy," Languidus said.

"Oh, futuo yea, that dude's the tits. First time in my life I've been able to run without chafing," the soldier said, joining in on the procession. "How many people are in on this?"

"EVERYONE!" Languidus shouted, grinning ear to ear. "All of the Guard is okay with the new emperor."

"Oh geez," the soldier said, drawing his sword with the others. "Martialis at least knows, right?"

"Uh, shoot, I forgot about him . . . No futuendi idea, we're about to find out," Languidus shouted with excitement. "What's he gonna do?"

"Good point," the soldier said, joining in the chanting.

"Wait, who's Martialis?" Otho asked.

"Don't worry about it. He's just the Officer of the Day," Languidus said.

"Sounds important," Onomastus commented.

"Eh, what's he gonna do?" Languidus said.

As they rounded more corners toward the Castra, another group of twenty Praetorians joined. This group was more hesitant, and their officer ran up to Otho's growing party while the others kept their distance.

"What the futuo is going on?" the officer shouted at Languidus through the chanting.

"It's coup time, son. Otho's the new emperor as of twenty minutes ago," Languidus answered.

"I didn't hear about this. How much?" the officer asked.

"The annual bonuses haven't been negotiated yet, but more than zero," Languidus said.

"How do we know we're not gonna get screwed again? I don't like the sound of that," the officer replied.

"Hey, there's no futuendi chance of bonuses with Galba, and I know this guy—he's a bro," Languidus said. "He's the subligaculum guy! Now either follow us or get the futuo out the way!"

"Oh shoot, the subligaculum guy, now that's something I can get behind!" the officer said. "Alright, men, we're joining in. It's another coup!" he ordered his men, who until now had been keeping their distance.

With every corner they rounded, more soldiers joined the celebratory march. About a third had prior knowledge, and the rest joined out of curiosity, peer pressure, or because it just looked like a good time. The subligaculum was wildly popular, and none of the guards who intercepted the formation were willing to stand in the way of progress and, hopefully, better bonuses.

By the time they approached the Castra, the unorganized formation had grown to over a thousand men. Many didn't even know what was going on, as Languidus was only able to explain the situation to the first few groups. The rest had to rely on whatever information passed through the ranks via hard-to-coordinate chants. Many of the men marched with swords out for intimidation, creating quite a scene when they reached the gate.

At the top of the gate stood the Officer of the Day (OD), Tribune Julius Martialis. Even in modern military units, the Officer of the Day serves as a babysitter while all the responsible adults are out. They're supposed to be in charge in case anything urgent happens. Because of the immense responsibility shouldered by this position, they are often the last to know of such shenanigans.

"What the hell is going on down there?" Martialis asked Barbius and Veturius at the top of the gate, as the formation waited for it to open. He was supposed to be the roadblock to prevent shenanigans, and overthrowing the government was about as much of a shenanigan as you could possibly see.

"Oh yeah, I heard the coup was happening today," Barbius said. "Otho, right?"

"Yup, Otho," Veturius said. "Hopefully he's better than Galba. Pretty low bar there."

"A coup?!" Martialis said, flummoxed. "This is an enormous crime! You can't just replace the emperor on a whim! There has to be voting, committees, an agreed replacement!"

"I don't think they know that," Barbius told Martialis as the chanting and violent sword waving persisted. "I'd say go down there and let them know, but they don't look too willing to learn about rules, procedures, and political norms right now."

"Besides, Otho's pretty popular around here. Makes sense," Veturius said. "The troops are way more loyal to him than they are to Galba. Especially after that subligaculum thing."

"When did that start?" Julius asked.

"A few months ago," Veturius said. "Combination of Otho being a bro and Galba being, well, the opposite of a bro. It was only a matter of time."

"Out of all the days I got OD duty, it had to be today," Martialis lamented. "Well, what are we going to do?"

"I see two options here," Barbius said. "Option one, we let them in and let the coup run its course. Option two, we don't, and wait them out, and hope they lose interest before they kill us. It'll take them at least a few hours to build ladders or something."

"I don't know if we can even do that," Veturius said, criticizing option two. "Like half the guards in here are pro-Otho. Probably take them fifteen minutes to get out here and let everyone in."

"Godsdamnit," Julius said, frustrated. "I'll never live this down! If I give up just like that, no one will take me seriously again, but you aren't giving me many options here."

"Tell you what," Barbius said. "If anyone asks, just tell them the truth. You'd just be a small roadblock at the cost of your life. I'll back you up." Barbius patted Julius on the back.

He thought for a moment, staring down at the raw USDA choice shenanigans chanting at the gate. It was a heaping mass of undisciplined soldiers, the kind you see at the end of a close sports ball game with a trophy at stake, moments before easily tippable cars end up on the sidewalk. "Fine, let them in," Julius said, motioning to the men below to open the gate. "I really don't like this, but whatever. Just, futuo. Hey, just knock me on the head. I can say I was overpowered. I gotta save some face."

"Sir, I'd lose my position if anyone found out I struck a superior officer," Veturius replied. "I'm only three months away from retirement."

"You're useless," Julius said. "I hate you guys."

"Just doin' our jobs, sir," Barbius replied.

The gates opened, and the guards outside brought Otho into the Castra, still carrying him on his throne but careful to dip low enough so as not to bump his head on the top of the gate. Inside, the remaining guards either celebrated or rushed in to find out what was happening. Otho was now safe from sudden and unexpected retribution—the coup had secured the package.

Otho was set down on the ground and greeted by the whole camp with a few boisterous cries of "Hail Otho!" He responded with a confident smile, waving and shouting "Thank you!" before Languidus and Tributus led him to the headquarters of the Castra. The headquarters was filled with officers, including a grumpy but silent Martialis. Everyone gathered, and the first meeting of the new administration began. Around the main table were the primary instigators: Otho, Onomastus, Languidus, Tributus, Cocceius, Barbius, and Veturius. Men crowded into the room, gathering around the doors and windows. It was drafty, but the room was so packed with bodies that it wasn't cold.

The walls were lined with men discussing what had happened, what might happen next, Otho, the subligaculum guy, local sports, and how cold it was, because people will never stop talking about the weather. As the room grew louder, everyone began to compete in volume, until nobody could hear themselves think. Celebration wine was passed around, and the noise escalated further.

Once everyone's cups were filled with the good stuff, Languidus stood up and hushed the room with a piercing two-finger whistle. "ALL HAIL THE NEW EMPEROR!" Languidus toasted. The room echoed with another hearty "Hail Otho!" so loud that Otho could feel it rattling his stomach, followed by cheering and table banging. Languidus sat down and motioned for Otho to speak.

"Thank you, everyone," Otho began, collecting his thoughts. "It is a good day for Rome and a good day for the honor of the Praetorian Guard, but the day is far from over before I can start allocating those well-deserved bonuses . . ." More cheers erupted, cutting him off.

Otho waited for the crowd to calm down before continuing. "How about a toast to our organizers: Languidus, Tributus, Cocceius, Barbius, and Veturius," Otho raised his wine, prompting more cheering. When the noise subsided, he moved on to business. "What is the status of Galba and the pedagogues? Do they suspect anything? Are they still alive? When are we going to boot him off the throne?"

"About that," Cocceius spoke up, "we had to make a trade-off for today's plan."

"What did we trade for what?" Onomastus asked.

"Well," Cocceius said, "we had to decide whether it was better to spread the word about the coup to all the guards or keep everything on the down-low to take Galba by surprise."

"So, let me guess," Otho said. "The march through the city was how we got the word out, and now Galba knows about the coup."

"He's holed up in the palace with the guards who didn't hear in time, and we can't get anyone to come out," Cocceius explained. "At least, not without blood, as you requested. We're at a stalemate."

"What are we gonna do now?" Onomastus asked.

"We can't have Galba in command for long," Otho added. "He could escape or, worse, get word to an outside army. Any ideas?" The room fell silent as the crowd pondered and sipped their special occasion wine. "Anybody?" Otho asked again.

"What if we—no, never mind, that's stupid," Veturius began, then paused. "We'd never have enough time to build a wooden horse that big."

"Well, suppose Galba believes you're dead," Tributus suggested.

"Why would he believe that?" Otho asked.

"Simple," Tributus said. "I just go to the camp and tell him I killed you."

"What if they ask for proof?" Onomastus inquired.

"I'll just kill someone on the way and get some blood on my sword," Tributus said. "I'll say it's yours. There's not much risk, so it's at least worth a try."

"There's no way anyone will be that stupid," Onomastus commented.

"I don't know, they're all pretty stupid. They got themselves into this mess in the first place," Languidus agreed. "That might actually work. I don't think any of them have a clue what's going on. I'll lead some guards and wait nearby in case they come out, and we'll finish the job. What about the other pedagogues? Kill, capture, what?"

"Capture them," Otho said. "They won't have any power, so I'm not too worried. Also, don't forget to kill Piso—could be a power struggle otherwise. And kill Vinius. I hate that guy. Plus, the empire could sure use all that money he's hoarded."

"Consider it done," Languidus replied. "I'm not sure if this plan will work, so maybe think of a backup plan, just in case."

Tributus and Languidus downed the rest of their wine and left the room to execute the scheme. They slipped through the gates of the Castra, which were opened just enough for them to squeeze through, before shutting them tight again. It was a short walk from the Castra to wherever Galba was holed up. When word spread that a coup was in the works, everyone shut themselves in, and the streets were as empty as an office on a Friday afternoon just before a three-day weekend. Not completely empty, but those outside didn't have their priorities straight.

"Hey, what are you doing out here? Don't you know there's a coup going on? You could get hurt!" Languidus asked a lone street vendor. The vendor was tending to a wheeled cart full of fruit and vegetables, waving away flies.

"Oh, it's not dangerous yet," the vendor replied. "Besides, my master would kill me if he knew I took a day off without asking. That's the fear I know."

"Well, do you know where the emperor's holed up? We've got a message for him," Languidus asked.

"I think by the temples, so I've heard. I'd start looking there."

"Hey, how are we going to prove we killed Otho?" Tributus thought out loud to Languidus. "I figured we'd find someone that looked like him or get some blood or something."

"Yeah, shoot, I don't know," Languidus looked around. "Usually, there are at least some dead bodies lying around, especially at a time like this. It's just desolate out here—except this guy . . ." They both glanced at the slave nervously holding up a goat.

"Please don't . . ."

"We're not going to kill you; you look nothing like him," Languidus assured the workaholic slave. "But that goat will have to do. Rome thanks you for your sacrifice," Languidus said before taking Tributus's sword and slaughtering the goat, getting it nice and bloody. "Yup, that ought to do just fine."

"Hey, why couldn't you use your own sword?"

"Oh, I don't want to rust it unnecessarily, fine thing like this. That sword of yours, though—its days are numbered anyway. Got it nice and stained for ya. You get to take all the credit!"

The two soldiers began walking briskly toward the temples.

"Hey, but it makes no difference if I get credit from Galba . . ."

"Shut up . . ."

Languidus knew the entire guard corps and easily talked their way toward Galba with Tributus's bloodied sword. The guards had made a temporary fortified area with a large mass of soldiers blocking all entrances, watching the rooftops and doors carefully. The three pedagogues paced around an open area in front of the temple while Galba clutched his head, muttering about how it was all over. Languidus nudged Tributus, who raised his sword in the air, drawing everyone's attention. It was a quick walk, and all eyes on him made him subtly shake.

"I have news for Galba—Otho is dead. I killed him, and this is his blood." Tributus centered his breath after delivering the critical news to the emperor in person. But something was not quite right with the news or the soldier.

"Wait a moment, son," Galba said, locking eyes with Tributus. "With all the chaos in the streets caused by Otho's betrayal, there's one thing I don't quite understand." He paused, collecting his thoughts. Tributus stood there, nerves betraying his unease. Should they have found someone who looked like Otho? Maybe brought more men to back up the story?

Tributus glanced at Languidus, whispering, "Back me up." Nothing.

Galba drew closer, scrutinizing him. *Where even is his commander?* Galba now realized what felt off. Tributus was on his own.

"Who even gave you the order to kill Otho?"

"Nobody. I was just trying to protect you, the rightful emperor," Tributus replied to the skeptical old man.

"How can you call yourself a soldier if you don't follow orders?" Galba's anger was visible, a lone vein briefly appearing through his wrinkles. While the pedagogues celebrated Otho's supposed death, Galba could not believe the audacity of this soldier who would kill Otho without receiving any order to do so. He knew if he let this slide without a stern lecture, none of his troops would ever take him seriously again. There was nothing Galba hated more than people taking initiative and thinking for themselves.

"I have never seen a soldier as incompetent and nearly as disrespectful as you! Do you understand what terrible things could befall an army where soldiers just willy-nilly decide to make their own decisions?!" Galba chastised, his tone mocking, his gestures exaggerated.

"I was just trying to help. The decision seemed so obvious I didn't think I needed an order," Tributus defended himself, though Galba remained firm in his military discipline. He glanced back at Languidus, who shook his head at Tributus's audacity.

It was clear now that it didn't matter what Tributus said in response to Galba's rhetorical questions—he was in for a humiliating public lecture, and there was no getting off the ride until Galba finished grandstanding.

"Of course, you don't know what would happen to an army because you've never been in a command position in your life and have never dealt with free-thinking worms like you."

Tributus hadn't been a soldier for long, but he'd been around long enough to know that the only thing he could do was endure the lecture and look as sorry as possible so it would end sooner. "No, sir . . . ."

"I'll tell you what happens. The army falls apart, does their own thing, and the Roman Empire falls to the barbarians. Do you think Julius Caesar conquered Gaul because of soldiers with 'good ideas'?"

"No, sir . . ."

"No, he didn't. He won Gaul with discipline and soldiers who knew how to follow orders to the letter. Do you know what it means to follow orders to the letter, soldier?"

"Yes, sir . . ."

"Following orders to the letter means you don't do anything unless ordered, you don't think anything unless you're told to, and you certainly don't come up with any half-brained schemes on your own. Do you understand what I'm saying here, soldier?"

"Yes, sir . . ."

"Good, because I'd hate to find out that our army has gone soft and started teaching soldiers to think for themselves on the battlefield."

"No, sir . . ."

"Then who in Jupiter's name made you think it was okay to kill a man without a direct order from your commander?"

Noticing a pause in the pace of Galba's lecture, Tributus saw an opportunity to save himself and end the tirade. He hadn't asked for any of this; he just wanted to deliver the news to his emperor and put his mind at ease enough to get him to leave his position. But now, he just wanted the public lecture and the show of power to stop. This was his one chance to shorten his ordeal. With the right response, maybe Galba or the crowd would take pity and end the spectacle.

"No one ordered me to kill Otho, but my oath of allegiance to the empire did. The man claimed to be emperor and was, therefore, a traitor," he said with resolve.

Members of Galba's entourage, eager for the

lecture to end as much as Tributus was, began to slow clap. A few cheers and a faint "Yeah . . . Yeeeah, for Rome," rose from the crowd. Tributus had played his one card and won. There was a surge of public approval.

Galba finally relented. "Well . . . next time, wait for the order. But for killing Otho, which was something you would have been ordered to do soon . . . thank you for your service." He conceded.

Tributus cut his losses and walked away from the camp as soon as he heard the applause. It was finally over. Languidus slipped away discreetly to join him in the streets for the walk back to the Castra. The streets were still empty, with even less traffic now. Once the merchants realized there would be no business today, they decided the risk to their safety wasn't worth it.

The two soldiers spotted a couple of their coconspirators standing half hidden behind a column at a corner of the temple. The men began waving, signaling for confirmation of the ruse's success. Languidus gave a big thumbs-up while mouthing, "He bought it," and the two soldiers darted off toward the Castra to deliver the news. Languidus and Tributus, trying to still look nonchalant, did not run with them.

"Gods, I'm so glad we went with Otho," Languidus said. They were far enough away now that they didn't need to be that discreet. "I've never seen anything like that before. What an absolute tool!"

"Really? Never? There's gotta be someone. I mean, that's the biggest tool I've ever seen, but it didn't feel *that* bad."

"No . . . well . . . let me think." They ambled along. "There was this guy I used to serve under years ago. While we were drilling, he made us memorize and recite verbatim laws, regulations, and choice quotes from Virgil. The dude was a tool and a nerd."

"Yeah, that dude's the biggest tool. What happened to him?" Tributus asked.

"There was an 'unfortunate training accident' a few weeks after he took command. The dude tripped and fell on a spear—if you know what I mean."

***

It all still looked clear. Everything still seemed normal as Galba left in his litter, heading through the streets of Rome. But once he had cleared his fortifications and the protective reach of his military force, a large group of cavalrymen and soldiers descended upon him. They stopped just short of Galba's defenseless entourage and launched a volley of javelins at his litter. Though they missed the emperor, they disrupted the formation of men tasked with transporting Galba to the palace. He fell to the ground, defenseless, with no German cohort or any of his men positioned to protect him from Otho's surprise attack.

If his faithful men or army weren't going to save him, Galba's only remaining hope lay in the one lone centurion Densus who, for reasons unknown, remained loyal despite increasingly poor odds and even poorer pay. Perhaps he was truly brave and loyal, perhaps he had a death wish, or maybe the man just didn't like Otho's subligaculum. Whatever the reason, he stood alone in front of an entire cohort of Praetorians.

Throwing down his shield, the centurion

picked up another gladius, wielding two swords. He threw one soldier off his shoulder and engaged another. Blocking one blow with his gladius, Densus hooked the attacker's leg with a swift kick, dropping the soldier to the ground and running him through with the spear. Then, picking up yet another gladius, he presented a formidable defense between the cohort and Galba's helpless body as more of Otho's men advanced.

As one of Otho's soldiers lunged for a killing blow, Densus parried with a left-hand block and delivered a fatal thrust with his right, driving the sword through the eye slits of the soldier's helmet. Blood pooled on the ground. Though clearly on the losing side, the centurion deserved a medal for his bravery. While he simultaneously thwarted two more of Otho's troops with expertly placed blocks, a third soldier delivered a devastating kick to his crotch. His greatest asset was also his most vulnerable point. With that knock out, but not quite fatal blow, Galba's last defense was gone.

Galba was now at the mercy of superior bribes. He would never pay a soldier more than his senate-approved stipend, and he spoke his last words while presenting his neck. "If it is your order . . . Just do it."

On paper, Galba was the perfect candidate for emperor. In practice, he lost his throne in seven months. Despite winning the election to the purple[12],

---

[12] The purple references the Tyrian purple toga which was so expensive it became a status symbol. It was often worn by generals in triumph or higher Roman magistrates. It is an incredibly pricey dye because the only known method for making it involved milking mucus from a rare sea snail. Tyrian

he had murdered entire families who had supported
Nero. He alienated all his support in the city with a
series of tone-deaf, stingy policies. Despite Otho
commanding the loyalty of the Praetorian Guard,
Galba picked Piso as his heir based on his superior
family name. Finally, Galba refused to pay his own
soldiers. Rome is a city that will turn on you
quickly—whether for lack of influence, cash, or
might, any man in Rome is one well-placed bribe
away from being murdered in cold blood. Galba was
the first of four emperors to sit on the throne during
the year of 69.

***

The action had subsided for the day, and Otho
made his way to the Senate to claim his well-earned
position. All the senators in the city had gathered at
the Curia, waiting for him. Unsure of the city's
current state, Otho traveled with a strong force of
Praetorians but could finally take his time crossing the
city. He no longer had to race from one place to
another, fleeing some ill-gotten fate. He had made it,
and now he was going to take his time.

But he couldn't do it. His whole life, Otho had
walked quickly and didn't know how to slow down.
After a brisk stride, he entered the Senate, uncertain
of the mood. Even though the doors were closed,
Otho could hear the noisy room waiting inside. Two

---

purple eventually began to exclusively signify Roman royalty for
its decadence and became illegal to wear unless you were the
emperor.

guards opened the large twelve-foot-tall bronze doors, releasing a gust of debate, shouting, and cumulative chatter. The dim January sunlight framed Otho's staunch silhouette as he entered, and the crowd hushed.

Otho kept his composure and walked confidently to the other end of the room, with a hundred senators on each side watching his every step. In the dead silence, his footsteps echoed against the marble floor and the hundred-foot-high ceiling. Upon reaching the end of the room, Otho turned to face the four hundred patriarchal eyes fixed on him.

What was I going to say again? he thought.

12 LANGUIDUS PREVENTS ANOTHER COUP

"Afternoon," Otho greeted the Senate. "Many of you may not know me." He paused, attempting to read the room, but the senators gave him nothing. Searching for non-verbal cues, Otho found himself grasping at straws. "My name is Marcus Salvius Otho . . . and I am the new emperor?"

The room erupted in complaints and shouts. Cries of "Can any Roman buy the throne now?" and "Why you?" filled the air, along with "What the futuo is going on?" and a fair amount of "I knew Galba would futuit this up. I TOLD YOU!"

Otho raised his arms, trying to hush the room. It took a couple of minutes, aided by guards whistling sharply, but he eventually managed it.

"The Praetorians grew too tired of being neglected by Galba and chose me as the emperor," Otho said plainly. "I'm afraid Galba and Piso were killed by the guards not two hours ago, and I will humbly accept the position of emperor thrust upon me."

The shouting began again. A short, stocky senator walked off the first step into the center aisle of the Curia[13], commanding the room with his arms until the noise subsided. It took dozens of seconds for the crowd to quiet down, but it was getting quicker each time. They were adult enough to understand they needed to speak one at a time now. They didn't even need a talking pillow[14] to pass around. "I have heard you were . . . VERY close with the guard," the senator said. "It looks a lot like you planned this whole thing yourself."

The senator stepped back, and Otho responded. "I won't deny the crime of being friends with the Praetorians. I'm no idiot—you must be on good terms with the guard if you want to get anything done in this city," he said, prompting murmurs of agreement. "The guard planned it themselves, as they were getting no support from Galba. It was only a matter of time before someone else claimed the throne with more sinister intentions."

Otho paused, trying to draw the audience in. "What happened was, I was on my way home when I ran into a couple of guards I've done business with before. I went over to say hi, and before I knew it, they lifted me up and proclaimed me emperor. You know how they are. I couldn't say no. A few hours

---

[13] The Curia, at that time the Curia Julia, was the meeting place for the Senate in Rome

[14] During Roman group therapy sessions and senatorial meetings in the early 3rd Century BCE to 2nd Century AD, talking pillows were used during heated debates so that one member of the senate could speak at a time. There is no historical or archeological evidence of this cultural practice, but I like to imagine it's true.

later, they killed Galba, and now . . . here we are. True story . . . can't change the past."

Snickers spread through the Curia as another senator stepped forward. "We're not primarily concerned with whether you organized the coup, Otho," he said. "We're concerned about the empire's stability, that you're of sound mind, and that you're not up to no good. We don't want any violent men oppressing families out of jealousy—or worse, paranoia. Such a violent start is not typically a good sign. This isn't a good beginning; there could have been more discussion."

"Understood, understood," Otho replied with a single laugh. "Ha. I have no sinister intentions. Many of you may remember I was a close ally of Nero, and some of you may hold that against me. But I'm not him. I assure you, I'm just a stoic Roman like any of you who wants a stable empire ruled by a just leader. I will hold no grudges, no one is getting exiled, and I am far from paranoid. My immediate plan is to restore wealth and status to all patrician families who lost property or were exiled during Nero and Galba's reigns." Otho paused again. "And there will be absolutely no mandatory art viewings, plays, choir concerts, water organ performances, or hour-long lyre concertos."

The crowd began to shift in his favor, murmuring in agreement. Otho then fielded questions like a pro, quickly discerning the popular stance on each issue and committing to agreeable actions while Onomastus took down meeting notes in the corner. He accumulated a long list of grievances that had been ignored by Nero and filtered away by the pedagogues. By the end of the meeting, the Senate, though still holding some reservations, was relatively okay with Otho being in charge. Otho didn't seem to have many other ambitions and compromised easily.

The apparent easygoing nature of Otho calmed the senators, who were concerned they'd have to learn the eccentricities of another psychopath. Many had lived through the whims of both Caligula[15] and Nero . . . Galba had been easy to control and predictable, like a high-fiber diet. They were worried about another man with such youthful energy. But at least Otho wasn't a moody teenager, and for many of the senators, that was enough for now. Otho knew what he had to do: accomplish as many of the popular actions Onomastus had written down as he could, avoid getting too weird, and he could keep the throne for a long time.

Once Otho had finished speaking to the Senate and easing their concerns, he exited the Curia with the guards and Onomastus. Two guards opened and closed the large bronze doors, letting in the stinging January air. "Well, I think that went well. You got that list?" Otho asked Onomastus.

"Yup, right here," Onomastus replied. "I got all the requests down. How much of this are you actually planning on doing?"

"As much as I can," Otho replied, exhausted.

"Sir, your sedan," a group of slaves offered Otho a luxurious ride home. They looked much

---

[15] While Nero was hated for being artsy, Caligula was hated and feared for old fashioned crazy emperor reasons. He was normal then after a near death experience re-emerged as maniacally dangerous crazy. Not only did he politically persecute half his family and most of the senate, but he made a horse a senator among other strange *Emperor has no clothes* type loyalty tests.

stronger than the last group.

"No, thanks," Otho declined. "It's way too cold to be sitting down, and I've been carried around enough today." He gripped his stomach. "Anyway, yes, I'm going to try and get as much of that done as possible."

"Wow, Otho the benevolent emperor," Onomastus teased. "I thought you were just in it for the money."

"Well, you're probably not completely wrong there," Otho agreed with a hint of qualification, "but I'm not quite done securing the job. Unless I play this right, I've got the most dangerous job in the city. Gotta at least be popular and competent till things calm down. If you haven't noticed, the mechanism for being replaced . . . ahem," he coughed, "isn't exactly forgiving. Not gonna rock that boat."

"Ah, that's true," Onomastus responded dryly.

As they approached the palace to begin settling into the imperial lifestyle, a crowd of poor people appeared from the wild. With the commotion over, the city began to reemerge and observe the aftermath. The crowd saw the royal escort and assumed it was Galba's deposer. "Hail Nero!" they shouted.

Otho politely waved back and kept walking past the crowd. "Did they just call me Nero?" Otho asked his entourage.

"Yes, they most certainly just called you Nero," Onomastus replied. "You are not mistaken."

"Why would they . . ." Otho wondered aloud. "Do I look like . . . I feel like someone would have told me if I looked like Nero before."

"Well, the plebs haven't seen Nero in a while;

maybe they forgot and assumed because you're young?" Onomastus speculated.

"I don't know how I feel about that," Otho said. "You know why I'm being called Nero?" Otho asked Tributus next to him.

"Beats me, could be a rumor," Tributus said. "If it bothers you, we can find out and put an end to it—ya know, the kind of ending we do for those sorts of things."

"No, no, no, no, don't do that. I have a feeling that would make things worse right now. That's definitely something Nero would do, and I have to be the good emperor for at least a year or two," Otho said aloud. "Although I really hope the senators don't hear about that. I just spent an hour convincing them otherwise, and I'll never hear the end of it."

"Alright, if you change your mind, you know where to find me," Tributus said. The imperial entourage continued to the palace, hurrying through the streets until they could warm up inside with fire and wine.

Otho and Onomastus entered the palace atrium and saw a group of slaves struggling to put up a full statue of Nero. The palace was in chaos—pieces of weaponry and papers were strewn about the hallways, meeting rooms, and dining areas. Scraps of wood, linen, and trash littered the floors. It was as if everyone had paused halfway through a monster home makeover.

"I don't look anything like that," Otho said, eyeing the Nero statue.

"Hail Nero," the slaves said, taking a break to greet the new emperor. "Sure, you do. You look great," one slave told Otho. "Just a little older and wiser."

"Okay, why does everyone keep calling me Nero?" Otho asked the slave. "Stop."

"You're not? I heard Nero overthrew Galba and was coming back to the palace," the slave said, equally confused and afraid.

"Yes, I'm the new emperor and overthrew Galba, but no, I'm not Nero. Please don't call me that," Otho said, trying to contain the rumor. "Well, I didn't overthrow anyone—the Praetorians did, and they chose me! It doesn't matter. I'm Marcus Salvius Otho. Clear? Where did you hear I was Nero?"

"Oh, oh, oh, oh, oh! Sorry! Apologies, sir. This actually makes way more sense," the slave said. "I thought Nero killed himself. But you can't believe everything these days. A lot of us thought he made it out to Alexandria and was waiting for the right, opportune moment to return. Anyway, I heard it from the chef. He said we were basically serving Nero now."

"Okay," Otho said. "You're fine—not the only person to mix that up today. Just trying to figure out where it started. And STOP SPREADING IT AROUND!"

"You want us to take the statue down, then?" the slave asked.

"No, it's fine. Maybe I'll swap out the head sometime. Actually, no—yes. I mean, take it down. Or maybe just get an artist to swap it out," Otho said, admiring the statue's generous proportions. "Something similar. Where's the kitchen? No, don't tell me—I remember."

The kitchen was a few rooms over, and Otho moved through some of his old stomping grounds.

Each room brought back memories—partying it up, being married, drinking, abusing servants, living the high life.

He thought he'd be getting plastered by now, not on his way to confront the chef. Maybe soon he'd get everything settled and squash the rumors.

"These rooms are spacious," Onomastus commented, taking in the tour.

"Oh yes, we threw a lot of crazy parties here before I got exiled," Otho said, pointing down a hallway. "Right over there's where Nero shot that dude right in the middle of the party."

They reached the kitchen, where the chef was preparing some of Otho's favorite dishes for his first meal as emperor. "Hail Otho!" the chef greeted him.

"First, I'm excited about the food. It looks amazing," Otho said.

"I remember what you liked, Otho," the chef replied.

"So, you know me, and you knew I was coming?" Otho paused. "But you told everyone I was Nero?"

"No, no, no, I didn't. What?" the chef defended himself. Before Otho could get angry, the chef tactically placed an olive and lamb kebab in his hand. Otho took a bite before replying.

"Just how I remember them. I remember your cooking—so good," Otho said, savoring the flavors. "So why did the slaves in the atrium call me Nero, then?"

"They said what?" the chef exclaimed. "Ohhh, I know what happened. Gosh, this is funny. I told all the house slaves to get the place ready because we were getting a new emperor and that you'd basically be like Nero. That was dumb. I'm so sorry."

Otho, now seated, munched on the lamb and olives during the apology. The chunks of lamb were perfectly browned and speckled green with a secret blend of herbs and spices. "Forgiven. I'm not that much of a tight-culus like Galba was. That is kinda funny . . . Basically Nero?" Otho asked the chef.

"Compared to everyone else the staff has served, it was the easiest way to explain who you were and what to prepare for."

"Huh. That traveled fast," Otho said. "Just like this city."

"Is that a bad thing?" Onomastus asked, digging into dinner. It had been a long day.

"Not really. I don't think I'm going to fight this at all, actually," Otho said. "This might even work in my favor."

"How so?"

"The people loved Nero," Otho said. "Only the Senate hated him, and they know I'm not Nero— at least, I hope I convinced them tonight. As long as I don't kill a bunch of people, I think I'll be fine. Also, I have a feeling the Senate's out of touch enough not to hear these rumors." Otho celebratorily fist-pumped in the air. "If anyone snooty asks, I'm really angry about it. Brief the slaves."

"Gotcha, I can't imagine that'll be too hard," Onomastus said, rolling his eyes. It was too late to think about political fallout—it was time to enjoy dinner. Between Otho's easygoing demeanor and his good mood, the chef's apology would have been accepted no matter what with those lamb kebabs. While Otho ate, the chef gave him the rundown of the kitchen and got reacquainted with the new emperor, discussing what types of food to keep in stock from now on. Otho took another kebab, his body signaling it was time to eat and rest before being interrupted.

"There you are," Languidus barged in with Barbius and Tributus. "What are ya doing in the kitchen when you have the whole palace?"

"Eating. What else do you do in a kitchen?" Otho replied. "What's up? Something wrong? Sit, eat!" He snapped mid-bite, prompting the chef to snap at a slave, who started pouring wine as Otho spoke through a mouthful, "Wine!"

"We know everything seemed to go well in the Senate today, but we've been hearing rumors that there are still mutinous senators," Barbius reported. "You shouldn't trust them, Otho. They're bad news."

"I appreciate it, but you can never please the entire Senate. I'm not too worried about it," Otho said, dismissing their concerns. "If it makes you feel better, keep an eye out for me, okay? That's your job anyway, right?"

"Oh, we'll do more than that," Tributus said aggressively.

"Whatever you do, just be smart about being stupid, okay?" Otho requested. "I have a solid position in this city right now. I don't need any of y'all screwing that up for me."

"We can be discreet," Languidus replied.

"Yeah, like when you shouted all over the city, and we didn't get the jump on Galba?" Otho said.

"Totally different situation. That was the only way it was going to work. We game-planned it for an hour," Languidus said. "Anyway, you'll be safe. We have your back. Just don't get too close to any of those senators."

"Whatever. Futue off—I'm eating. It's delicious," Otho said. "Join me or leave—I'm not in the mood to work."

The three Praetorians grabbed some meat and exited with a "Hail Otho." They left the palace, munching on their kebabs as they walked in double file. Finishing as they stepped into the dimming streets, they tossed their sticks aside and made their way to the docks.

"I guess it's up to us to hold this thing together," Languidus said. "I can't believe Otho is that naive."

"Are the senators really that rebellious?" Tributus asked.

"Oh, they're the worst," Barbius said. "They're politicians. You can't trust any of them."

"Yeah, absolute liars who only care about money, keeping it for themselves and from the people like us who do the real work," Languidus said. "It's a shame Otho doesn't realize the danger he's in, especially since he just led a coup himself."

"Pretty strange, right?" Barbius said. "We'll have his back whether he likes it or not."

"Right. Keep your eyes open," Languidus told Tributus.

"What for?" Tributus asked.

"Anything suspicious. Unscheduled troops in the city, secret meetings of senators, large weapons caches," Languidus listed. "You've been around long enough; you'll know it when you see it. Trust your instincts."

***

As soon as Otho stepped into the office, he was immediately overwhelmed with the task of fixing Galba's mistakes. From sunrise to sunset, he worked tirelessly—releasing property that had been illegally seized by either Galba or Nero, freeing men imprisoned in the recent chaos, and keeping generals and governors loyal across the empire.

"Bring him in," Otho shouted to the guard outside his office, inviting a stern-looking, middle-aged man to enter. Marius Celsus, a military expert and consul-elect, walked in. His short hair and upright posture exuded stoic Roman values. Just by his demeanor, he seemed like the type who would jump on a hand grenade for patriotism alone before intimidating his daughter's husband for never being good enough.

"Hail Otho," Marius greeted. "My deepest gratitude for releasing me from prison."

"Salve," Otho replied, trying to put Marius at ease. "Yes, I must apologize for the whole imprisonment nonsense. Take it more as a compliment, if anything."

"A compliment?"

"Yes, a man as loyal and competent as you—I had to make sure you were safe during the chaos. Really, I had no choice but to pretend to imprison you," Otho explained. "The guards were set on staging that coup, and I was just trying to prevent a bad situation from getting worse."

"I've never heard that one before," Marius said. "But you seem like an honest man, so I'll take your word for it. I do plead guilty to being extremely loyal, ya got me."

"I appreciate that," Otho said. "I'd like to

make up for the inconvenience by making you head of military affairs."

"Thank you. Whatever you need, I aim to better the empire."

"Don't thank me just yet. We're in a bit of a pickle," Otho told Marius. "You know about the Vitellius situation?"

"Yes, I've heard the rumors, and I discussed the situation with Galba before the coup. Anything new?"

"Unfortunately . . . nothing good," Otho replied. "I've received letters of loyalty from the generals in the East, but not from Vitellius. He's marching on Rome as we speak."

"That's not good," Marius replied.

"They're marching through the Alps in the winter!" Otho exclaimed. "Do we stand a chance against the Germanic legions?"

"I don't know. Those German troops are tough. We can find a way to beat them before they get too close to the city, though. We've got time. Ideally, we should avoid that fight if we can," Marius said.

"That's exactly what I was thinking," Otho said. "I just sent a letter warning him not to have more than a soldier's ambition. Galba is dead, Vinius is dead, and we're correcting their mistakes. I've also offered him positions in government or a city to govern. Hopefully, it won't turn into a major problem."

"Wise actions," Marius said. "But don't be surprised if Vitellius doesn't back down. This could be a power grab fueled by the Senate. We need to prepare for all possibilities. I would immediately send for the Seventeenth Legion from Ostia for support.

We need to mobilize now. If we wait and Vitellius doesn't back down, it'll be too late."

"Just why I hired you," Otho said. "That'll be your first task. Coordinate with the other military leaders in the city and set up a game plan."

***

Marius arranged the transfer of soldiers from Ostia within a few days. Given the proximity to the city, the operation was swift, and all the right parties were coordinated with supreme bureaucratic efficiency. While the Praetorian guards didn't need to be involved, Marius could have avoided a lot of trouble by informing them.

Two of those Praetorians heard rumors about the troop transfer and discussed the matter at the western gate.

"What do ya mean they're moving weapons into Rome?" Languidus asked Tributus.

"I swear, I have a very reliable source. Varius Crispinus is heading to Rome right now with a large weapons cache," Tributus answered.

"Crispinus? Right now?"

"Yeah, right now!"

"I don't trust that guy," Languidus said. "He's one of us, but he's a tribune, so who knows where his loyalties lie."

"Why would he be transferring weapons from Ostia, and might I add, under guard?" Tributus said, adding to the shock.

"Futuo, that can't be good," Languidus said. "Good work. This is exactly the sort of thing we needed to watch out for. How close are they?"

"They should arrive in the next couple of hours," Tributus answered.

"Futuo, okay, no time to discuss. If they get those weapons into the city, there's no telling where they'll hide them. Grab some men on horseback and come back here. We'll have to intercept them, fast!" Languidus ordered. "Go!"

Languidus stayed at the gate, keeping a careful watch for Crispinus and the weapons cache, hoping Tributus would return before Otho's enemies did. He paced nervously until Tributus returned with a dozen men and an extra horse.

"Thank the Gods you're back. They haven't arrived yet."

"Awesome. Are we waiting here or going out to meet them?" Tributus asked, gripping his sword.

"Oh, we're going out. There's no telling who's in on this. Best to take them by surprise," Languidus shouted, grabbing a spear and mounting his horse. Without further commands, the group rode off, Languidus leading the charge.

"How far do you think they are?" Tributus shouted over the billowing dust.

"From your estimate, any moment now. Ostia isn't far away," Languidus shouted back over the galloping hooves.

Sure enough, they crested a hill and spotted a group of armed men escorting carts of weapons toward Rome. Just like the rumors suggested, Crispinus was at the head of the formation. Languidus raised his spear, signaling the attack, and the Praetorians increased their speed, charging forward.

Two dozen men scrambled to defend the carts, but it was too late. Otho's loyal Praetorians took out half with a volley of javelins and finished six more with spears. All that was left were three limping soldiers, two centurions driving the carts, and Crispinus, who managed to raise his shield in time. But with the shields already pierced by javelins, they were useless. The remaining forces scrambled to defend themselves against the final attack.

The mounted Praetorians began circling, waiting for an opening. Dust filled the air, clouding visibility. With each revolution of the cavalry, one guard would spot a weakness and charge in, picking off the limping soldiers first. The hardened centurions and Crispinus were left for last.

In a final swooping attack, Crispinus fell to the spear of Languidusas his lance wavered. "You idiots," he gasped. "We're on the same side."

With only two left, it took just two more charges of the Praetorian horsemen before they all fell. The guards slowed their pace and dismounted. "Get these bodies off the road," Languidus shouted. "We'll send slaves later to bury them. Let's secure these weapons before anyone else dies."

The Praetorians gathered the loose weapons scattered from the skirmish and loaded them back into the carts. Three of them mounted the carts, while the others led their horses back to the city, slowly trotting toward the west gate.

"Take these arms to the Castra," Languidus ordered. "We need to tell the boss."

Tributus and Languidus hurried back to Rome, their horses still fresh. "Heading to Otho?"

"That's right," Languidus said. "Get ready for one hell of an 'I told you so.'"

"I still can't believe it's been less than a week

and someone's already tried to overthrow him," Tributus shouted. "I wouldn't have suspected the weapons shipment if you hadn't told me to look out for it earlier."

"Once you've seen as much as I have in this city, you learn to see it coming a mile away," Languidus said. Both guards fell quiet for the rest of the ride, smiling in their victory. When they reached the city, they slowed their pace to avoid trampling civilians or getting yelled at by the traffic cops. They guided their horses at a brisk walk the rest of the way to the palace and dismounted at the entrance.

"Waddup," one of the palace guards said as they tied up their horses. Each made hyper-specific gang signs at each other.

"Yo, you won't believe what we just did!" Tributus exclaimed, loud enough for everyone to hear. He had been waiting the whole ride to boast about how awesome he was and couldn't wait any longer.

"Finally get laid?" the guard replied.

"Haha, no," Tributus said. "I mean, I get some all the time, but no. We just stopped a coup."

"Nice, dude. I'm sure Otho will be happy to hear that," the guard replied. "Heard there might be another one soon."

"See ya." Languidus and Tributus left the guard and entered the palace.

"Oh hey," the guard yelled after them. "If you're trying to see Otho, he's with like eighty senators right now for a dinner party. I'd try again later."

"Eighty senators?" Languidus asked.

"Yeah," the guard confirmed. "It's a big-culus dinner party. I don't know what it's about. Not my place."

"Tributus, do you know what this is?" Languidus asked.

"Um, no," Tributus said as Languidus paused long enough to make him think. "Wait . . . was this where the coup was going to happen? The timing is just way too suspicious to be anything else."

"Not just that," Languidus said. "We're not just stopping the Senate from deposing Otho right here and now. Those eighty senators must be the defiant ones planning this whole thing. If we play this right, we can take out all of Otho's enemies right here! Right now!"

"Futuo," Tributus said. "Eighty is way too many for just us. Let's get some men together."

So, they did.

***

The main hall of the palace was set up for an imperial-sized dinner party. The typically open room was now a sight under construction as palace slaves scrambled to clear existing furniture and fit in as much table and seating space as possible. At the insistence of the catering company, many of the tables were centered around a pseudo-stage at the hall's center for entertainment.

Colorful linens lined the walls, and large torches were carefully placed to avoid fire hazards. Couches and tables were packed around the stage, hoping to seat everyone. At the center of it all, on a platform just slightly elevated above the rest, was Otho's throne, overseeing the hall and the stage.

"I don't care what centerpiece you use, just

make sure it's ready in the next hour!" Otho yelled at one of the caterers, who held up two arrangements of mountain flowers. "Just make a decision for yourself for once. Onomastus!"

"Yes," Onomastus answered.

"Godsdamn, I just want tonight to be over," Otho fumed. "Is everything set up on your end? I have way too many important things to do than decide what flowers to put in the centerpieces."

"Yes, it looks like most people will be arriving soon. I've got the list of all the senators you need to schmooze with," Onomastus reported. "Entertainment and food are good to go, according to the caterer."

"Fantastic. If tonight goes well—really well— I can finally stop trying so hard," Otho said. "It's exhausting proving to everyone that I'm past my youthful Nero days, at least to the upper crust here. This is going to be one boring evening. I'm going to do a lot of complaining in the Oilatorium tonight when this is all over."

"I had a feeling," Onomastus responded. "I've already given the order to have it ready at the end of the dinner."

With all the preparations made and the slaves scrambling to set up the room for more people than the fire marshal would ever recommend, Otho took a moment to relax and wait for his guests. There was nothing more he and Onomastus could do but wait. This wasn't just going to be a dinner party; it was a banquet—a true marathon to test Otho's endurance for boring conversation with Rome's elites. He had to appear as normal as possible for the next ten hours.

Soon enough, the senators began filing in— some individually, but most in groups arriving from the baths. A handful of senators even brought their wives, though no children were allowed; it wasn't a company picnic. However, the amount of kissing the new boss's culus with tactically careful greetings and a generous serving of compliments was very similar to one. The shoe was on the other foot for a change, and thankfully, Otho knew what that was like, or he might have believed he was wielding a massive dagger.

Otho was typically greeted with the casual "Hail Otho," followed by generic comments about how great the banquet hall was set up or how delicious the food smelled. But every fifth senator would use the greeting as an opportunity to subtly mention some issue they were having—one that only a man with extreme executive power could fix without spending a fortune in bribe money. Otho caught nearly all those remarks and had Onomastus write down the not-so-subtle requests in his big book of popular demands. It was an intimidatingly large document with tons of notes scribbled in margins that were getting larger by the hour.

An hour into the banquet, the vast majority of senators had arrived. Otho had mounted his throne on the slightly elevated platform and relaxed, participating in politically fueled banter with the bolder senators. After a few glasses of unwatered wine, Otho became very approachable, and all the guests were having a good time. The not-so-low-key event of food, wine, and fun made everyone feel like they were back in the days of Claudius when the craziest thing that happened was Vinius stealing those plates.

Three hours into the banquet, even the most

straitlaced senators had drunk enough watered-down wine to relax. This was the cue for the entertainment to begin, starting with a flute player. A scrawny man in an oversized tunic took center stage, his head adorned with a crown made from backyard weeds and a few flowers that were days away from wilting from a French's-mustard yellow to a Dijon.

The flute player confidently took the stage and began playing a ballad with long, drawn out notes and resonant pauses. He had the tempo down, and his showmanship was impressive, even adjusting the dynamics to draw in the crowd. But what he didn't have was intonation. Five minutes in, the audience began heckling him for his inability to hold perfect pitch and the awkward cracks in his tone caused by his low-quality flute. While they didn't know it was his pitch that was off, they knew he sucked. They threw dinner rolls at the musician until he got off the stage to jeers of, "You suck, get a better flute!"

That's why any good catering company books three times as many entertainers as you think you'll need. It's always a tough crowd at a six-to-ten-hour banquet. The next entertainer was a male contortionist.

"Jesus Christ, that's disgusting. So unnatural. I kinda wish I could reach that area, though," Otho said to a senator. "Anyways, yes, I'm rolling back all the taxes Galba introduced. I can't afford for my administration to choke out all the business that props up this city."

"I'm so happy to hear you say that," the senator replied. "Aren't you worried about the deficit Nero left behind affecting your office?"

"Not at all. Tanking the city's economy with

unnecessary taxes would be way worse than freaking out about some debt. Have you not heard of the Laffer curve? Governments are supposed to take on debt during chaotic times to prevent bear markets from exploding into a depression. It's all about your debt-to-GDP ratio and balancing out the . . . eh, I'm not going to get into all that made-up economic stuff. But I got a guy to explain it all to me last night that seemed very smart," Otho replied with anachronistic Keynesian theory. "I'm a stoic Roman just like everyone here, well, most people here, not like Brutus and his gambling problems." Brutus was a nepo baby who everyone liked to make fun of. Otho tactically joined in on the arbitrary social trash talk to fit into the elitism club. So what if the guy had a drinking problem and only had wealth because of his parents? He was an okay dude who might say the wrong thing every so often. That didn't matter; making fun of his problems was a way of signaling to the in-group.

"I know, I wish he could just get some help already," the senator replied.

"All I want for Rome right now is for everything to stabilize so we can tackle important issues like the grain crisis and the large deficit," Otho said. "We're going to need everyone on the same page to get this done. I'm a law and order guy," he added, throwing out as many buzzwords as he could muster.

"Spoken like the steady leader Rome needs," the senator complimented. "What help will you need?"

"Right now, I could use some heavy senatorial support dealing with Vitellius," Otho said. "He may be the biggest threat to the stability we all need to get this whole mess behind us."

"I've heard he is still in rebellion."

"You heard right. Did you also hear that he's headed down to Rome this very moment with his army?" Otho asked. "Unless we find a way to a peaceful diplomatic solution, we'll see an unnecessary and costly battle between Romans that no one wants."

"We can arrange a meeting among senators with Vitellius to try and work something out," the senator offered. "There's not much more we can do at this time other than pose a hard target to discourage an attack."

"I'm already handling the creation of a counterforce for that very purpose, and I hope we don't have to use it in battle," Otho said. "You'll have your work cut out for you. I've been in correspondence with Vitellius for a few weeks now, and he does not sound like a reasonable man."

"What do you mean?"

"I warned Vitellius not to have more than a soldier's ambition and offered him a high position if he backed down. I've even ensured that his family in the city is safe," Otho commented. "Next thing I knew, he replied with a letter full of so many insults and unbecoming language that unless you all intervene, it will come down to bloody, senseless violence."

"In my honest opinion," the senator lowered his voice, "from what I've heard, I don't know how much we can do to help you on the diplomatic front. The reports I've heard are that they're coming, and there's not much we can do to stop them."

"I was afraid of that," Otho replied. "You don't think you'll be able to talk Vitellius down?"

"I am very skeptical," the senator said

apologetically. "We'll do what we can as fast as we can. In the meantime, I highly recommend mustering as many forces as you can and sending them north."

"I was afraid of that," Otho responded. "I'll get with my military advisors tomorrow and start accelerating the plans for war. I hope you're wrong."

"I hope I'm wrong too. I'll do what I can diplomatically and set something up," the senator assured him. Just as their conversation wrapped up, a big ruckus unfolded. The male contortionist finished his performance, and just when he was to be replaced by exotic female dancers, the banquet hall filled with armed guards.

"What the futuit," Otho said in disbelief. The guards surrounded the drunken, lounging senators. They killed a few guards, senators, and entertainers blocking the path before the remaining senators near the ambush could dart to the other side of the banquet room. Senators at the other end of the room erupted in an uproar, shouting, "Where are the girls? You're not exotic, dancing, or wearing tasteful outfits befitting a performance!"

Languidus stepped forward and shouted over the eighty senators, "Enemies of Otho, you thought you had it all figured out . . ." Chills swept over the crowd. Husbands protected their wives. The rich protected their gold. There's only so much one man can do to stop such uncalculated chaos. Wine was spilled that night.

"What the futuit, Languidus?" Otho shouted.

"Sir, you are in danger!" Languidus shouted back.

"I am in no such thing," Otho stated. "Everyone, I'm terribly sorry for the mess and this awful disturbance. I owe everyone here another dinner party, my treat," Otho announced to the senators who hadn't already fled. "Everyone, exit stage left, and Languidus, stand right *futuendi* there and don't even think about it!" Whatever *it* Languidus was thinking about, Otho wanted him to stop. The senators and remaining company filed out as if they were in an elementary school fire drill, half afraid of the Praetorians and half afraid of Otho's apparent power over their safety. "Y'all too," Otho ordered the guards. "Get out of here!"

The room emptied swiftly at Otho's command. Left behind were Otho, Languidus, Onomastus, Marius Celsus, a few new advisors, and some slaves, who quickly started scrubbing wine stains from the upholstery before they set in permanently. Otho's pale, scrawny advisors slithered to his side, standing to his left.

"These men were plotting to kill you and crown their own emperor," Languidus said.

One advisor whispered into Otho's ear. "I don't need your help, back off, ya nerd," Otho snapped, shoving the weak-mannered man away. "What evidence do you have of this plot? You'd better have something good because you're ruining a perfectly good evening."

"Just this morning, some Praetorians and I uncovered a plan to smuggle in a legion's worth of weapons from Ostia and stage a coup," Languidus explained. "We have evidence!"

"Did that shipment of weapons happen to be transported by Varius Crispinus?" Otho asked.

"How did you know?" Languidus looked baffled.

"Because I ordered him to bring the Seventeenth Legion into the city to muster forces against Vitellius," Otho said, rubbing his forehead in frustration.

Languidus paused, realizing his mistake. He came in red hot but started cooling down, a little unsure of what was going on. "Oh, well . . . what about these senators—"

"I'm hosting a futuendi dinner party, Languidus. That's what emperors do," Otho cut him off, verbally swatting down his dagger into its place. "Now tell me, how did you know it was Crispinus?"

Languidus flushed with embarrassment, unsure of how to respond.

"Well?" Otho pressed. Languidus stepped closer to the throne. Some of Otho's men moved to intervene, but Otho waved them down. "I know him, he might be dumb, but he's loyal."

Speaking in a low, humble voice, Languidus continued, "We received intel that the weapons from Ostia were meant to fuel a coup against you."

"And what did you do with this very faulty intel?" Otho asked.

"We intercepted them."

"What exactly does that mean?"

"We killed them. Crispinus and the twenty or thirty men he was with are dead," Languidus admitted. "No longer a threat. We thought they were coming for you; we didn't have time to confirm."

"Godsdamnit," Otho sighed. "Get yourself and your men the futuo out of here. I'll figure out how to clean up your mess in the morning."

"Yes, sir," Languidus said, pausing as he considered warning Otho about the senators. But this was not the time or place, so he wisely backed off and motioned for his men to leave. "Sir?" he added before departing.

"What now?" Otho asked, slumped on his throne. "Make it quick."

"The soldiers are pretty hot right now," Languidus began, kneeling.

"Hot? Like how hot? Why?" Otho asked, sipping his wine while dripping a shotgun pattern of droplets on his toga. He was too exhausted for anger.

"We got everyone all excited about killing your enemies and it's pretty wild out there. In between the soldiers looking for a fight and the rumors of another coup, after we killed those men heading here this morning, there may be a minor amount of looting," Languidus admitted, trying to ease into the news.

"Languidus," Otho said, leaning back and closing his eyes. "Y'all basically have two jobs: keep me alive and keep the city under control. Is that so hard?"

"It's not as easy as it looks, sir," Languidus replied. "We can probably handle the looting and riots, but it'll be easier with some incentive."

"So, you want me to pay everyone extra money for the problems you all caused?"

"Ahem, I mean . . ." Languidus cleared his throat. "You know how we operate."

Otho leaned forward, glaring at Languidus's bold suggestion. "I'm just trying to hold this empire together. I can't give you an infinite amount of top cover," Otho said, contemplating whether to give in or risk dealing with an uncontrollable guard. "Futuendi fine, Languidus. We'll bribe the men again. Say it's for calming the riots and looters. But there's a catch."

"Very reasonable, sir. What's the catch?" Languidus asked.

"Y'all aren't getting away with this stercus unscathed. If I don't do anything, one of you will crash every banquet, temple sacrifice, political meeting, and garden party I throw. Worse, I'll look weak. Find a dozen scapegoats and execute them tomorrow. I don't care who, just make sure everyone knows why. No more coups . . ." Otho sighed. "And if you do suspect something, please tell me about it before you get the top one percent of the city killed over a wild hunch, okay? If it happens again . . . just . . . let's talk it over first."

"Yes, sir," Languidus agreed.

"Discuss the details with my advisors," Otho ordered, motioning to his two administrative experts. "Get it done and make the executions public. You've got one week."

Languidus left with the advisors, waiting until they were outside before starting their discussion. Otho slumped back in his chair, closing his eyes. He sipped his wine for a moment.

"Onomastus," Otho said softly, "Is the . . ."

"The bath's ready, man," Onomastus answered.

"Thank you. I don't want to be disturbed tonight," Otho said. "Get a big breakfast ready for tomorrow and call all my advisors in. We've got a lot of work to do. Apparently, we have a war to wage."

13 THE MARCH NORTH

As if a tropical storm had swept through the city, Rome emptied in the chaotic winds of the Praetorians, only to fill back up the next day as if nothing had happened. The following morning, Otho visited the Castra and delivered a stern lecture until order was restored. He then turned his attention to preparing for the incoming attack. Somehow, perhaps by leveraging his strong line of credit, Otho managed to keep the city from spiraling into complete chaos—just the usual turmoil that kept business moving, though not of the violent kind.

It was a tumultuous three months. Otho's early reign wasn't just about taming rambunctious Praetorian guards and bracing for the Vitellian army. There was also severe flooding of the Tiber River, stranding many in the upper floors of their homes, and rumors of ghosts of every Scooby Doo variety. None of the apparitions—especially the large ones running about the city—were ever captured, so we'll never know if they were actual ghosts, stressed-out citizens,

Old Man Jenkins trying to save his theater from an industrial capitalist, or just Plutarch fabricating omens again. It was probably Old Man Jenkins.

Otho's transition to power was far from smooth, and though most of the problems weren't his fault, he held the city together through sheer financial might despite violent, natural, and supernatural disasters. That, however, was Rome; Germany was another story altogether.

"I don't know how Vitellius managed it this time," Otho remarked in a quiet but bustling administrative office. "But he's somehow more disgustingly insulting than ever. I have to respond, and I need some good zingers from everyone." He read more of the letter from Vitellius, cringing and wincing. "This doesn't even make sense; he must have been drunk when he wrote it. I can almost gauge his drinking by his punctuation. I didn't fight my way to this position to be drunk texted by some buffoon."

"Otho, why do you keep corresponding with that snake in the grass?" Onomastus pleaded. "Y'all are getting into a mingendi contest, and all you're doing is trolling each other." Since Otho's rise to power, he had maintained constant correspondence with the rebellious Vitellius. At first, the exchange was polite, with Otho even offering olive branches—zero consequences, money, and a career if Vitellius would quit his rebellion. But then the insults started flying. Every week, Otho received a new letter filled with increasingly crass accusations, and he responded in kind. The arms race of comebacks and criticisms had turned into weeks of trolling, like two people lost in the comments section of a spicy election year reddit thread.

"It's a mingendi contest I will win!" Otho shouted, still intently reading the rage-baiting letter. "I cannot wait to rid ourselves of this ungrateful piece of stercus."

A group of patrician-looking folks walked in. "Oh, you're back," Otho greeted, his eyes still glued to the infuriating letter. The senators had just returned from a diplomatic mission to Vitellius. "Any luck with a nonviolent solution? After what I just read, I'd be surprised if your conversation lasted more than a minute."

"It lasted a while," the lead senator replied, clearly exhausted. "All night, really. He's surprisingly fun—too wild for my taste, but we talked. He hates your guts way too much to stop. We didn't reach a peace agreement. He should be nearing the top of the boot any day now. Luckily, their army is too large to move swiftly. Well, I guess that's not exactly lucky. I'm afraid it's war, sir."

"Well, I could've told you that," Otho responded. "Have you seen what he's been writing me?"

"Yes, and your responses as well," the senator said. "Where's all this beef coming from?"

"He didn't tell you?" Otho asked, his frustration mounting. "Apparently, he thinks I'm a pelusia magna and all sorts of other lies. I haven't even met the man. He's an animal and has no place in Rome. We're marching out to meet him in battle tomorrow."

"He is some kind of animal; I could see him saying that . . ." the senator muttered under his breath. "Sir," he added quickly. "The main force won't reach us in time by the looks of it. A force should be sent to

Cremona to intercept them." He pointed at a large map in the room.

"That fast?" Otho exclaimed. "Celsus, I trust you to take what men we have and head there as quickly as possible. We need to get the jump on them before they establish a foothold in Italia."

"Understood, sir," Celsus responded enthusiastically. "Who will command the main force then?"

"I can do that myself. Why?" Otho asked. "Do you have a suggestion?"

"Why not your brother Titianus?" Celsus suggested diplomatically, as if ready to backpedal at any moment.

Otho looked at Celsus in confusion. "Why would I do that? He has no military experience. I'm sure Rome has someone more qualified."

Celsus took Otho aside, away from the other officers and politicians. "Your family's been bothering me nonstop the last few weeks to get you to include your brother. I'm sure he'll be fine. He won't be making any important decisions; we just need someone with an important-sounding title."

"Why are they being so insistent? Titianus does perfectly fine for himself," Otho said quietly. "He can get along just fine without me involving him in imperial affairs. Maybe a position once this is all over."

"I'll make sure to include some seasoned generals. Think of it as a dynastic loyalty thing. It's not a terrible idea," Celsus argued quietly, his voice barely above a whisper.

"You think I'd have a loyalty problem otherwise?"

"Well, you've only been on the throne for three months," Celsus pointed out. "Anyone would have loyalty concerns after such a sudden change in leadership."

"You and the Praetorians keep saying that. Rome loves me, and I've been good to them," Otho responded defensively. "There's no reason to worry about another coup." He gritted his teeth, wrestling with Celsus's suggestion. "I just hate working with my brother. But I see your point. I guess I can trust him more than most men in Rome." He paused, wrestling with himself. He knew the right answer but didn't want to say it. "Fine. I think I can handle dealing with him for one campaign."

"Thank you, sir. I'm just trying to help. Your family can be more persistent than you are," Celsus admitted candidly. "I see where you got your drive."

"Okay, it's settled," Otho announced to the room. "Celsus and Gaius Suetonius will lead an army north to intercept the Vitellian forces, and Titianus and I will follow with our own."

Everyone present agreed and got to work. The room became even more lively as each man erupted into quick-paced planning around the map. They all detailed routes and supply plans. Onomastus peeled away and spoke to Otho, who was silently listening and agreeing to the advice given by the military men.

Otho sat down in the corner of the room, seeking a moment of mental rest. Onomastus noticed the opportunity for a private conversation and approached him.

"We've been friends for a long time," Onomastus began. "You usually tell me just about everything."

"Yeah, we've always been open," Otho agreed. "Even when you were a slave."

"In all these years, you've never really talked to me about Titianus," Onomastus said, curiosity in his voice. "I mean, you've mentioned that he's your brother, but that's about it."

"What's there to tell?" Otho responded curtly.

"It just seems like something's up," Onomastus pressed, trying to draw out more information. "Is there something wrong with him? He hasn't been involved much since we got to Rome."

"Gosh, how do you even explain," Otho muttered, stalling for time.

Onomastus waited in silence.

"Well, Titianus has always been the golden child, being the oldest and all," Otho finally said, though he stopped himself from saying more. "Eh, this isn't the right place for this talk. Maybe tonight."

"Okay, one last drink in the Oilatorium before we head north for the campaign tonight," Onomastus suggested.

"Agreed," Otho said, and they shook hands. "Back to work. We've got a lot of planning to do before tomorrow." The two of them returned to the planning committee. The room buzzed with activity, filled with spirited debates, deals between generals thirsty for action, scribbled down logistical calculations, and orders scribbled down and dispatched by a line of spritely messengers at the entrance. While 90 percent of the orders were concerning the war and 5 percent were to nosy wives wanting to know when their husbands were coming home, the most hotly debated 5 percent was what food to order for the room.

Everyone was working from dusk to dawn with little to no breaks. This was the night before the final school project was due and no one could leave until that one thorough worker who had to ace the project said you could leave, and nobody had any more concerns. Just like a school project, there was also that kid that came in at the last minute to contribute a small amount of effort and share in the credit.

Amid the intense planning, Titianus finally arrived. He stood tall above many of the stout Romans in the room, his presence commanding attention. Despite his middle age, he was still classically handsome with a well-defined jawline and jet-black hair speckled with gray. He probably even had six-pack abs without dieting or exercising. Seriously, futuit this guy.

"Glad you could make it," Otho greeted his brother with a firm handshake.

"Wouldn't miss it for the world, brother," Titianus replied in a strong voice. "I wish you'd reached out to me earlier when you came back to Rome."

"Well, I've been pretty busy," Otho said. "I haven't had much time for socializing."

"I know. I could have helped you out, though," Titianus replied, patting Otho on the shoulder. "I'm not a senator anymore, but I still have plenty of connections that could've made that crazy transition of power easier."

"Oh gosh, I know," Otho nodded silently. "But I managed just fine without ya, so no worries. You're here now, and that's all that matters."

"Yup, that's crazy though," Titianus

commented.

"What's crazy?" Otho asked.

"You as emperor. I never would have thought of it, man," Titianus said. "Too awesome, real proud of ya."

"Thanks, bro," Otho responded slowly, the resentment bubbling beneath the surface. Despite the critical work that needed to be done, Otho decided to make an exit. "Anyway, Celsus, why don't you catch Titianus up on everything." Otho began walking away, tapping Onomastus on the shoulder to follow. "Guys, I trust everyone here to finish planning. I need to prepare myself for tomorrow's march. Everyone is doing an admirable job. I believe we'll save Rome from that pelusia magna, Vitellius. See you on the road." Otho left to a chorus of "Hail Otho."

Onomastus and Otho made their way to the Oilatorium, having sent word ahead to ensure it was ready for their arrival.

"I wouldn't feel guilty," Onomastus said as they approached the palace's inner sanctum.

"Guilty about what?" Otho asked. "Leaving early? I was just slowing them down at that point."

"Yeah," Onomastus agreed. "It seemed like most would've left long ago, so you're good. I'm surprised we haven't had more issues with the leadership. Must be a big improvement from Galba or Nero."

"I'm not surprised. From what I've heard, Galba really sucked," Otho replied as they entered the Oilatorium. Despite losing some of its former luster, the bath was still as cozy as it had been on day one. The elaborately crafted tiling and piping were now coated in years of oily residue, creating a subtle rainbow of dark greens, reds, and pinks. Geologists could have estimated the age of the bath by counting the rings of oil.

"And Nero, bless his heart, that kid had issues. Anyone would with a mom like his. She was a handful," Otho continued as they settled into the bath.

"I've heard some of the Agrippina rumors, and she's been dead for years," Onomastus said before relaxing into the warm, gurgling water.

"Gosh, this place was where I first heard Nero complain about his mother. Brings back memories," Otho said, letting the room's warmth take over. "Boy, if these walls could talk."

Onomastus wasn't ready to let the conversation slip away. "So, what's the deal with you and Titianus? I've got to know, especially after that sudden escape from the war room."

"Oh gosh, where do I even start," Otho sighed. "It's a story as old as civilization."

"Which story? We've got time," Onomastus pressed.

"Okay, I'll get to it," Otho said, his pace still slow. "He's the older brother, and I'm the second oldest. Nothing wrong with my family, but the eldest always gets the land, the wealth, the social prestige—generally just all the attention from the family, especially from the pater. Always a little jealous of all that. The second son is always the backup."

"Haha, just that, huh?" Onomastus chuckled. "That's pretty normal."

"Titianus has always had the family's praise, and I've just kinda fended for myself," Otho continued. "It's just going to be annoying. You don't realize those dynamics until after you grow up. Even today, he was weirdly positive no matter what. It always feels like he's talking down to me. Not exactly the vibe I want to put out there as emperor."

"I'm sure it'll be fine," Onomastus said, trying to reassure him. "He'll get the idea."

"Yeah, he will. Worse things have happened; it's just going to be annoying," Otho agreed. "Man, I might even have to yell at him, and that'll be weird. I just can't wait for all this to be over so I can actually start ruling. I didn't think the chaos would last long after the coup. It's just senseless violence, all of this."

"I think this is ruling," Onomastus laughed. "Why did things blow up so much anyway? With Vitellius?"

"I . . ." Otho gathered his thoughts. "I have no idea. The guy kept insulting me, and I couldn't resist responding in kind. I'm not even sure what he was trying to accomplish. I got rid of the corrupt people. Maybe he's just jealous he wasn't here to do it himself, or he wants the power for himself, but that's not the impression I've gotten from him. He's got no chance, though—he's going up against Rome!" Otho speculated. "Unless we parley or something, we may never know. I've never met him in person, so I have absolutely no read on the guy beyond his drunken letters."

"His loss," Onomastus said. "You gave him plenty of chances."

"Yeah, I just hope it's resolved quickly with the least amount of violence possible," Otho said. "I want to get back to this Oilatorium and not spend my first year on the frontier. At least the campaign will give me some legitimacy, I suppose. There's one last thing."

"What is it?"

"I want you to stay here and look after things while I'm up north," Otho ordered. "You won't be in charge on paper, but you essentially will be."

"You don't have anyone else?"

"No one I trust," Otho replied. "This could be a dangerous time while I'm gone. At the first sign of trouble, ride north. At that point, you probably wouldn't even be able to trust the Praetorians."

"Stercus," Onomastus said, feeling the weight of responsibility. "You don't think it'll come to that, do you?"

"Probably not," Otho replied, a bit more calmly. "I've distracted most of the ambitious types with the campaign, so I'm not sure how anything could happen. Those sorts of men are only dangerous during peacetime. I'll have an army behind me, and that's much more power than a throne. Just be careful."

"You don't have to worry about me. I'll be spending most of my time here, where no one can bother me."

The Oilatorium was always a special place, and Otho felt his troubles melt away before he'd have to face them all again in the morning. This was the last moment of peace they'd have before the constant meetings, marching along the road, speeches to the troops, and the awful quiet on the eve of battle.

***

At first light, Otho woke up and went about his usual morning routine, rubbing bread on his face to get a good natural glow, among a few other beautification rituals. He then put on his custom travel model subligaculum. This morning, instead of grabbing his imperial toga, Otho donned a full set of armor—breastplate, helmet, and tunic. He had it all except the shield. From this point until after the campaign, Otho was no longer a politician but a general. He wanted to impress, so he made sure to wear the armor with the highest helmet plumage and the most gold and silver embroidering. He had to be the most extra. It was a stiff and clunky walk out of his bedroom.

Escorted by his contingent of Praetorians, including Languidus, Tributus, Barbius, and Veturius, Otho walked out to the street, painfully aware of how he looked. They all mounted horses standing by for their arrival. Once they entered the main roads of the city, their path was flagged out and marked by a clear logistics chain. Every man able to haul goods, every man willing to muster, every soldier in full armor, and anyone who needed some soldiers' pay to catch up on back taxes was marching north and out of the city. Many side streets and minor roads acted as tributaries spilling out onto the Via Flaminia.

Luckily, Rome had legalized lane splitting, and Otho entered a medium-paced trot. "Y'all ready for a fight?" he asked the Praetorians.

"Oh yes," Tributus said, a little unsure.

"My life is a fight," Languidus said, dead serious in an overly masculine tone. "It'll be a nice change for my enemy to meet me in the field."

Everyone stared at him, even though he looked serious.

"Good, because it's gonna be a good one,"

Otho shouted over the clamor of the lines of soldiers and rolling carts loaded with weapons and supplies.

Tributus and the other Praetorians burst into laughter. "Bro, I'm just joking, dude. This isn't even gonna be a fight. They'll give up before we even meet shields!"

The laughter and conversation died down as it was too much effort to shout over the noise. The group was now separated as they weaved through the heavy traffic. Commuting out of the city was the worst on the first day of a major campaign.

With expert lane splitting and Otho's small personal entourage looking important enough for everyone to get out of the way, it wasn't long before they exited the city gates. The supply line had thickened through its city tributaries into a river of mass exodus. There were no women or children, just soldiers and some slaves pulling carts. The various sizes of formations of men intermingled with slow-moving carts and horses appeared to go on for miles. With the brand-new legions consisting of very fresh recruits, the formations were scattered with a mix of colored cloaks, armor of differing materials, shields and helmets of varying sizes, and previous lives as kitchenware beaten from pots into shoulder pads. Pre-industrial revolution, uniforms and armor were sometimes standardized, but only when they had time. In this case, everyone scrapped together what they could at the last minute. It wasn't a sea of red but a multi-toned rug of faded colors. Zooming past the formations, Otho inspected the army practically created overnight . . . well, over a month. It's impressive—be impressed, reader.

Otho hit his last speed bump before driving to

a fast gallop, which he maintained until reaching a forward command tent. He dismounted to check on progress. His brother was there, working on food supplies, intermediary camps, and general logistics. "Hail Otho," the men greeted Otho, who was walking a little stiffly in the armor he wasn't used to wearing.

"Salve, how goes the march north?" Otho inquired.

"We have all the intermediate camps planned out and are working on the final details regarding the food," one general responded. "Celsus is already far along the march and will be reaching Cremona any day now with his men. He's sending back messages regularly from scouts to assist with the planning."

"Sounds like y'all have everything under control," Otho said. "Good to know I have competent men in charge. I won't bother y'all unless I need something."

"We're running a real tight ship. We haven't run into any logistical problems so far, my brother," Titianus assured him. "That armor looks a little uncomfortable. Is it new?"

"Yes, I haven't needed it until today," Otho replied. "It'll loosen up by the time I get to Cremona. You know, they want me to wear all this special stuff because I'm emperor and all—so lame, right?"

"I wouldn't know," Titianus said. "I've got a friend who runs a business breaking in new sets of armor. He pays slaves an extra salary to do physical labor in the armor until all the leather is stretched out. That stuff looks way better when it's a little worn in, like it's seen some action. Just adds some credibility—food for thought."

"I don't need that, or a stranger's body odor in

my armor," Otho replied. "No worries. I have all the credibility I need. That sounds fake, too—might be worse."

"I've acquired a carriage so we can ride up with the march and stay close to the action," Titianus said. "Should be a nice ride up. I can't wait to catch up on everything going on."

"Uhhh, ya know what," Otho said, "I was thinking I'd ride up to the front of the line and march with the men."

"On foot? Why?"

"It'll be great for morale," he answered. "Besides, I won't break in this armor sitting in a carriage."

"Fair enough, but you'll know where to find us," Titianus replied.

****

Seeing that there was no more business to attend to, Otho remounted his horse and headed north with his guards.

"We're gonna walk?" Languidus asked, trotting beside the soldier-filled road. "The whole way? That's a bit much for morale, isn't it?"

"I suppose it is," Otho replied. "But we don't need to sit in a carriage anyway. You're here for protection, so I don't know why you're complaining. Besides, it's better than spending a week in a carriage with my brother."

"Yeah, I can see that," Languidus added. "I don't know what your brother was like growing up, but he seems like a tool."

"You have no idea," Otho said. "There's a

reason you haven't dealt with him yet." He then turned to Tributus. "You've never been on a campaign before?"

"I have, but I don't miss the marching," Tributus replied. "Don't worry, we'll keep a close eye on you from up here."

As they entered the largest forward mass of the march, a thick, suffocating dust cloud surrounded them, and traffic on the Via Flaminia slowed to a crawl. Otho rode off-road, weaving through the troops until they reached the front of the army's march—the source of the standstill. A convoy of wagons, laden with merchandise, was moving south.

"What in the futuus is this?" Otho muttered, puzzled by anyone heading south. He rode up to the front, his Praetorians following close behind. The leading wagon was inching past the soldiers, but the real holdup was a heated argument between a merchant and an officer.

"We're marching north. You need to move aside for the imperial army," the officer demanded.

"Listen here, buddy," the merchant snapped. "I've been traveling these roads my whole life, and there are laws protecting my right to use them. Besides, what's the harm in sharing?"

"Don't let them pass!" the officer shouted to his men as the merchant's convoy attempted to push through the army.

"I've got sixty thousand sesterces's worth of goods that'll go bad if I don't make it to Rome tonight," the merchant argued. "This delay is cutting into my bottom line."

"What the futuo is going on here?" Otho barked as he rode up.

"This man won't let me use the road," the merchant said, exasperated.

"Emperor Otho!" the officer exclaimed, prompting a loud and unexpected "Hail Otho!" from the troops. Both Otho and the merchant winced at the noise.

"My apologies, Emperor," the officer explained. "This merchant's convoy is clogging the road, and he won't move."

"Wait, Emperor Otho?" the merchant asked, clearly out of the loop. "I've been in the sticks for six months. What happened to Nero?"

"Nero got bullied into suicide and was replaced by Galba last year," Otho replied.

"Galba? What happened to him?"

"He didn't pay anyone, so there was a violent coup. He got killed, and I was elected emperor," Otho said flatly. "Now, will you please move before I have to get violent myself?"

"Can I at least be compensated for my goods? They'll spoil at this point," the merchant tried to bargain, sensing the temporary nature of Otho's leadership but quickly realizing he was pushing his luck. "Actually, never mind. We'll wait. Wouldn't want to hold up the march, Mr. Emperor."

"Thank you," Otho said. As the merchant began turning his wagons around, Otho asked, "What are you transporting, anyway? And how much is it worth?"

"Mostly wild game from Germany—rare birds, bear, elk, boar—you name it. Worth sixty thousand sesterces, maybe up to 120,000 with the right buyer."

"How are you keeping it fresh?"

"A special blend of herbs and spices, but it won't last much longer."

"Tell you what," Otho said. "I've got a hungry army camping a few miles north tonight. I'll pay you eighty thousand to turn around, deliver it, and have it ready for these men." He snapped his fingers, looking around until a competent centurion arrived. "Get the coordinates for tonight's camp and give them to these men."

"How many soldiers are we talking about?"

"Enough to eat that much meat. Deal?" Otho stuck out his hand. "Worst case, we smoke the rest for leftovers."

The merchant shook on it, and the wagons turned around with some help from the soldiers, heading north to camp. With the convoy out of the way, the officer asked, "Otho, what brings a man as important as yourself all the way up here? You could be getting drunk in luxury right now!"

"As much as I love luxury, I'm not a fan of long carriage rides with boring company. I may or may not be avoiding that," Otho quipped, drawing laughs from the officer.

"Haha, that bad?"

"Oh, not the worst I've experienced. Riding with Galba and Vinius—now that was the worst! I'm joking a bit, but not entirely about Vinius," Otho laughed. "What kind of emperor would I be if I didn't lead from the front? You're all fighting for me, aren't you?"

"Yes, sir, we are."

"And you are . . . ?"

"Titus," the officer replied. As the wagons cleared out, Titus barked marching commands, and the army resumed its advance. Over the next thirty minutes, the traffic jam eased, and the soldiers returned to a steady march.

Otho walked alongside Titus at the front of the formation. Ahead lay the northern half of the Italian Peninsula; behind them, the full might of the lower half, assembled through weeks of planning and one frantic night. With the emperor in their midst, the soldiers at the front tried to maintain straighter formations and more serious expressions, their thousand-yard stares a testament to their effort to look professional. It was dull. Even more dull than most long marches. This lasted for about five minutes.

"So, Titus," Otho eventually asked, "know any good jokes?"

"Uh, no, sir, not off the top of my head."

"Does anybody know any good jokes?" Otho called out to the troops until one brave soldier spoke up.

"Is it okay if it's dirty?" the soldier asked.

"Yeah, I'm not your mother. Go for it," Otho replied.

"Why do so many Greeks have beards?" the soldier asked.

"I don't know, why?" Otho responded.

"So their women have something to hold on to," the soldier answered, making wild tongue motions. The joke landed well, and Otho laughed, which made everyone else feel more comfortable and loosen up.

"How long have you been serving the Empire?" Otho asked Titus.

"Fifteen years now," Titus responded proudly, "and I wouldn't trade the experience for anything."

"Where have you been stationed?"

"Mostly down south, sir. I've been really lucky—amazing wine, weather, and women down there," he said with a grin. "To be honest, aside from a few skirmishes with runaway slaves and some road bandits, I haven't seen much action. This will be my first real battle."

"It's my first too, and we'll be fine," Otho admitted. "We've got plenty of experienced men leading the charge, and I have complete confidence in them. I doubt we'll even need to fight—we're so much stronger than Vitellius."

"Oh, I'm not worried. I can't wait," Titus said. "I've been disrespected my whole career by the old soldiers who've seen all the action. Now it'll be my turn to stercus on the younger ones with my experience. I hear it's life changing."

"Well, I'm not that excited, to be honest. I wish this were a battle for new territory or defending against invaders," Otho said. "Roman-on-Roman conflict is senseless. I wish I could have avoided it . . . but I had no choice. We have to do what we have to do."

"If only you could've handled it like you did with that merchant," Titus said.

"Believe me, I tried. What went so wrong with that guy?"

"I don't even know," Titus replied. "He was set on getting to Rome on time, and I've got a giant army behind me. Next thing you know, it's either win or back down and look like a pelusia magna in front of everyone."

"I know the feeling," Otho said.

"If you hadn't come down to sort things out,

we would've had to force them off the road, and I don't know how that would've gone."

"That would've been a shame. Think of all that wild game waiting for us up ahead," Otho said, his mouth watering. "Good thing."

14 THE SIEGE OF PLACENTIA

Otho continued marching northward with his men toward the Vitellian army. Other than reports of naval conflicts near southern Gaul, there wasn't much news from the front. Soon enough, the Vitellian forces and Otho's forward troops, led by Celsus, began clashing. These clashes started as small skirmishes involving hill people pressed into supporting either side. Afraid of losing their land and families to the civil war, some Northern Italian farmers decided to fight. None survived.

Vitellius's army gained a strategic foothold in the plains at the base of the Alps with the arrival of the Germanic troops. At this point, the time had come for the two forces to meet. Otho was still marching north with four legions at his back when a leather-armored messenger arrived, bearing news at the speed of a well-maintained post office. But it wasn't union pressure or an overbearing postmaster general fueling this rush—it was a different kind of urgency.

The messenger maintained a lightning pace,

only slowing as he came within shouting distance of the legions and Otho. "The Vitellians are approaching Placentia!"

"How far are they from the Po River?" Otho shouted back.

The messenger slowed to match Otho's pace. "Three days, and Vitellius is gaining more and more support on his march, sir," the exhausted messenger reported. "There are already a thousand men and some cavalry at Placentia, but we need more support if we're going to prevent the Vitellians from establishing a foothold on our side of the Po. Celsus is requesting urgent reinforcements—whoever you can send to reach there in time. Currently, a forward Vitellian army led by Caecina is making headway."

"Stercus, that sounds serious," Otho muttered, turning to Languidus. "You're always itching for a fight. Take three Praetorian cohorts and go support Celsus."

"Yes, sir," Languidus replied. "You don't need any guards on your march?"

"I've got three legions, futuo!" Otho cursed. "If they can't protect the river, we don't have much hope in this war. Besides, Celsus can't reinforce Placentia. We can't lose that river crossing. Take Titus Vestricius Spurinna and secure the position."

"You heard him—get going," Languidus ordered the officer leading a nearby cohort. "I'll gather the others and catch up." Languidus and Tributus rode off to inform the remaining cohorts. They weren't far behind the front, and the two Praetorians reached them within minutes.

Languidus rode up to the officers and shouted, "We have two days to reach Placentia and meet our enemy in battle. We'll have to double-time it if we want to get there before the enemy—the time for battle is upon us."

After a collective groan from some of the men and enthusiastic battle cries from others, the officers ordered the double speed. They set off, rushing past the other troops and toward the Po at a grueling four miles per hour. The unmounted cohorts were in for quite a ruck-run[16]. Thankfully, the men had already crossed the Apennines and traversed inland enough that the rest of the journey would be through the plains of Northern Italy.

Languidus and Tributus, luckily on their mounts, led the men to the front. "Godsdamn, I knew we should have gone faster," Languidus complained. "I hope we have at least three days or everyone's gonna be gassed by the time we get there."

"How could we have known when the Vitellians would arrive?" Tributus shrugged.

"I had a feeling. I bet the Senate even invited Vitellius and Caecina into Italy. I knew we'd be betrayed!" Languidus yelled to the marching troops. His call to loyalty spurred the men to pick up the pace even more, reaching a blistering five miles per hour.

"You've been saying that since the coup—I guess you were right."

"You've grown a lot, but Roman politics is the toughest thing you'll have to learn if you're going to be a Praetorian," Languidus lectured. "If we'd been

---

[16] For those fortunate enough to avoid military service, a ruck-run is when you run with a heavy backpack on. Fortunately for Ruck-runners, at the end of the run, most participants get a higher disability rating upon retiring from service as it will destroy their back.

knocking down doors like I wanted, we might've had more time or even prevented all this mess. It's way too convenient for all this to be organized from outside Rome."

"Freaking hindsight," Tributus grumbled. "I'm sure Otho will believe you after this is all over."

"For sure. He'll figure out we have his best interests at heart," Languidus said. "I love the guy—great emperor, very generous, the type I like to see in charge. He's just a bit naive, so we've gotta help him through that."

The soldiers marched on.

Despite being spoiled by exclusive service in the city, the troops managed to keep up the pace along the inland road to Placentia. The first day was grueling, but they made progress into the northern plains and reached the Po River. They had another day's march to reach the ever-encroaching front. The hills flattened out into beautiful, bountiful plains, dotted with farms and villas. As they passed each rural home, the legions received dirty looks from the homeowners, unsure of what was going on or who could be trusted in such violent times.

The men of the country hadn't been following politics—all they knew was that soldiers were running amok. *Are we under attack? Which side am I on? Is that soldier going to steal my food to fuel the war machine—or worse, my daughter?* Needless to say, everyone was on guard in the Po Valley as soon as the armies arrived without warning.

The soldiers were hot and eager to fight. Due to the quick pace and the lax leadership of Languidus and the other tribunes and centurions, the goal wasn't discipline but speed. The cohorts spread out across the road and countryside at differing speeds. Who were they to tell the faster soldiers to slow down? The combination of relaxed discipline and the men's thirst for combat gave the rural farmers of the plains a very real reason to fear the soldiers.

While the vast majority stuck to the march, a group of more athletic men grabbed a standard and headed toward a nearby farm. "Where do you think you're going?" Languidus shouted at the group of twelve spritely, armed teenagers.

"We're going to check that farm for Vitellians!" one acne-covered soldier yelled back before jogging off with the others.

"What the futuo? Get back here!" Languidus shouted. It was like calling to a dog fixated on a squirrel let loose in the backyard—there was no recalling them. Their ears were clogged with testosterone, and they wouldn't hear anything. The soldiers were on their way to harass the farm. Nothing short of violence could stop them.

"We goin' after them?" Tributus asked.

"No time, I'm afraid," Languidus replied. "Oh, those poor souls."

A few hundred yards away, Languidus and Tributus watched. Predictably, the farmers saw the soldiers running toward them. Grabbing whatever farm equipment could pass as weapons, they prepared to defend themselves.

"Yeah, I do not see this ending well at all," Tributus commented.

The two watched from a distance as the farmers followed the tenets of Cobra Kai, their lives depending on it. The farmers struck first, they struck hard, and there would be no mercy.

"That was a dumb move," Languidus said, watching the scene unfold. "But I don't blame them. What would you do if a bunch of soldiers charged at you?"

"It's the only respectable thing they could've done," Tributus replied. The two watched as the farmers' weapons were easily deflected, and the soldiers slaughtered four men in broad daylight.

"Oh gods, just don't come back with anything," Languidus muttered, hoping the soldiers wouldn't compound their stupidity. But the men entered the farm buildings, looted them like Link in a pottery shop, and returned with extra food. As they rejoined the formation, Languidus shouted, "Were there any Vitellians there?"

There was a pause.

He shouted again, closer this time, "Were there any Vitellians there?"

"I don't think so," one of the soldiers replied, slightly out of breath. "But they attacked, so maybe they were."

"Y'all are dumb stercī," Languidus chastised. "They were just farmers. Now get the futuo back in formation."

The men rejoined the ranks, slowing down to the four or five miles per hour the rest of the troops were marching. Most focused on their pace, though not all. It was a mostly peaceful march. Mostly.

Eventually, the Praetorian cohorts reached the river Po with what looked like two hours of sunlight left. The leaders shouted orders to set up camp. Most of the men were exhausted, but they were disciplined enough to set up tents, start dinner, and dangle their feet in the icy water of the Po. The river had been snow not long ago, but nobody cared. They were just happy to be done with the day's march, tending to their blisters. Many hadn't marched this much since boot camp, and it showed. They'd just pulled a twenty-five-mile day with a similar day ahead.

"I can't believe it took them this long to march," Spurinna said, arriving with Languidus. "These men are soft." While Languidus was in charge of the Praetorian cohorts, Spurinna was the general. Once united with the thousand or so men at Placentia, he would take overall command from Celsus. He rode quietly for most of the march, letting Languidus lead, only stepping in if he saw unnecessary risk. Now, he looked with tired eyes at the naked camp and then at Languidus. "Night's coming soon, and we have no idea where Caecina is." Spurinna didn't say another word and went back to overseeing the troops.

Languidus knew exactly what Spurinna wanted. He needed to become a bit of a hard-culus now. Frustrated, he charged over to the reclining soldiers. "What the futuo are y'all doing sitting down?" he yelled.

"Camp's set up, just waiting for dinner and the rest of the cohorts," one soldier replied.

"You're not even close to done. Do you want us to be slaughtered in the middle of the night? There are Vitellian armies running all over the place," Languidus lectured the inexperienced city soldiers off their culi and into action. "We need fortifications before we can even think about sleeping. Y'all, take those axes and start cutting trees for a wall." He shoved a dozen men off the ground. "And you dumb culi, get the shovels, dig a trench, and start piling up dirt for fortifications. What the futuus do you think we brought all those tools for if we weren't going to use them? Do you remember anything from your training?" He gave one man a swift kick in the culus for being slow to stand.

While they were undisciplined on the march, their attitudes were quickly beaten out of them by the experience of the older members of the cohort under Languidus's lead. The men groaned and complained but got to work. "We'll have to retrain most of these men when we get back to Rome. They're useless!" Languidus told Tributus.

"I'm not surprised," Tributus said. "I don't think most of these men have ever built a marching camp before."

"Yeah, you're right. I'll supervise the trench digging. You get more men for the lumber," Languidus ordered. "You know what you're doing. Let's get this thing built before we lose daylight."

Languidus wasn't being overly harsh. In hostile territory, building a fortified camp after a day of marching was standard practice to avoid nighttime attacks. The marching camps consisted of a surrounding trench with the soil used to construct walls and four gates to be guarded through the night.

The soldiers grabbed their shovels, standing around cluelessly until Languidus placed flags marking the camp's corners. "What are y'all waiting for?" Languidus barked. "Start digging. You don't eat until it's done."

Like that, the tents were surrounded by men digging a four-foot-deep by four-foot-wide trench and piling up the dirt. The men led by Tributus began deforesting a nearby grove of evergreens, industriously transporting lumber to the camp like an army of beavers. Within an hour, the walls began to take shape. Another hour later, the encampment was done. The soldiers waited nervously as Languidus walked along both sides of the barricade, inspecting their work. They wouldn't eat until it was finished, and they could smell the stews of local herbs, meat, and porridge waiting for them. Only one man's opinion stood between them and their dinner.

"I can't believe y'all took so long," Languidus said, delivering his criticism. "We could've been attacked! Anyway, this will do for the night. Go eat."

The men swarmed the pots brewing dinner. The sun had set, and there was just enough orange light from the scattered clouds and cooking fires for them to find their bowls. They filled their bowls and consumed the contents of each cauldron until nothing was left. Everyone enjoyed fifteen minutes of feeling full before darkness and sleep overtook them all—except for those unlucky enough to pull the first shift of night guard.

***

The next morning, every man felt yesterday's march in their stiff, aching muscles. Those slow to rise were awakened by Languidus and the other tribunes making noise like an annoying dad trying to get their kids up for Saturday morning pancakes. They banged on pots, yelled, and kicked people awake until the inside of the camp collapsed, and everyone had their fifty-plus-pound packs back on their backs for the day's march.

"Ha, this is my favorite part," Languidus told

Tributus. "If y'all aren't packed up and on the road in the next five minutes, I'm burning this camp to the ground with you in it!"

"That should get 'em going," Tributus replied.

The men scrambled to gather their things until nothing was left in the camp except for three slowpokes struggling with a tent. The wind caught the fabric, and one held on desperately while the other two tried to catch the flailing corners. They were done in ten minutes flat. Languidus handed Tributus a torch before mounting his horse and grabbing another torch from the last night guard. Tributus took the cue, and both began burning the camp to the ground. With the camp ablaze, the slowpokes gave up on perfection and got the hell out of there with their tent folded incorrectly.

"We gotta burn it anyway," Languidus said as he and Tributus exited the camp. Other tribunes joined them once they had finished setting fire to the remnants. "Can't leave anything for Vitellius."

Spurinna rode toward them with five cavalrymen. "Languidus," he called, "you did well with the troops last night. Take charge of the rest of the march to Placentia. I'm going to push ahead and see what work I can do while y'all finish up."

"Yes, sir," Languidus replied, watching Spurinna gallop away with his men, their figures silhouetted against the red sunrise. Languidus felt a swell of pride. Maybe his men stood a chance in combat after all. They were rusty, but they were rising to the challenge.

The three cohorts packed up and set off for another grueling twenty-five-mile march to Placentia. Some looked back, a little sad to see all that work go up in smoke, but most just focused on the road ahead, marching down the Po River toward the battle.

For many of the younger soldiers, the day's march was much like the one before. But for the older soldiers, it was different. Every few minutes, they scanned the horizon for signs of trouble. Reports from the front suggested that Vitellian commander Caecina was lurking nearby, and they could run into his forces at any moment. The real concern wasn't spotting Caecina's army—it was not spotting them until it was too late, and they were ambushed.

"Does that look like a group of men to you?" Languidus asked Tributus, pointing toward some distant trees.

"I don't think so. Looks like just trees to me," Tributus answered.

"That's what they always look like from this distance," Languidus said, narrowing his eyes. They kept walking until Languidus, still uneasy, hummed nervously. "I don't like it. Send up a scout."

He ordered a scout to check out the suspicious shrubbery, watching intently until the man returned. "See, nothing," Tributus said.

"We're at the front now; you can't be too careful," Languidus said. "If I were them, that's where I'd hide for an ambush."

Every grove of trees, every hill, every valley came under the scrutiny of the experienced soldiers. Fortunately, the Po Valley's flat terrain offered few opportunities for an ambush, so scouts were rarely deployed. Still, there were some suspicious spots.

The pace of the march was slightly slower than the previous day, thanks to a few men not yet conditioned for a soldier's life outside the city. The rest of the troops helped pick up the slack, and soon enough, early in the afternoon, they spotted their destination: Placentia, a large, walled city on a bend in the river. The sight of the city renewed their energy, and the pace quickened. They just had to push a little further, and they could rest before the battle. No more marching camps—they'd be protected by the city's fortifications.

Languidus was relieved too. They'd made it, and for now, it seemed safe from the Vitellians. But as they drew closer, his relief turned to concern. "Oh no," Languidus muttered.

"What? You see Caecina and his men?" Tributus asked.

"No, thank the Gods," Languidus replied. "But . . . just look at those fortifications."

The city was still far off, but Languidus could see the cracks in the walls, the missing towers. "What about them? They look sturdy enough," Tributus said. "What do you know about fortifications?"

"Well, for one, they don't look like they're in the best shape," Languidus began. "I can see cracks from here. And second, there isn't a single tower along those walls. Either someone half-culus'd this city's defense, or it's so old we're looking at a relic, not a fortification." As they got closer, Languidus spotted more flaws. "No parapets either. Damn, we've got some serious work to do."

"I don't think this place has seen an attack in a while. Peace made the city soft, vulnerable," Tributus said, agreeing out of habit.

"You got that right," Languidus said. "It's a good thing we got here before the enemy." The army crossed a tributary to the Po and entered the city, which was starkly Roman in its grid layout. In an effort to look disciplined, the men reformed ranks. They were back in the public eye and had to appear at least somewhat like a trained unit. They marched to the center of town, where Spurinna had set up a temporary headquarters.

"Nobody leaves formation," Languidus ordered the officers.

"Languidus," Spurinna greeted him more warmly than he had on the march. "Glad y'all made it as fast as you did. I think we have one, maybe two days before Caecina crosses the river."

"They're close," Languidus replied. "The three legions Otho is leading are too large and tied down by logistics to speed up. We'll have to hold out a little longer before they get here."

"Celsus and Gallus are approaching with forces from the Balkans, but they might not make it in time either," Spurinna said. "We only have about a thousand men here in addition to your cohorts. They've sent scouts north and caught a glimpse of Caecina's force. They're slowed by their size, but Caecina is in the valley, eager to establish the rebellion past the Po before the main forces clash. They outnumber us five, maybe ten to one, with legionnaires and Germans. We haven't gotten much help from the locals—they're apathetic toward both Otho and Vitellius."

"Damn, they could have been useful. We need to start work on the—"

"Yes, we're working round the clock and could use help with the city's defenses," Tributus interrupted.

"We'll get right on it," Languidus said,

smirking at the first sign of competency in days. "I'll go tell the men."

Languidus left the command tent and faced the three cohorts, who more than doubled the city's forces. The men were grumbling, itching to rest, eat, and pitch camp before the battle.

"All right, men, I know how much y'all love wall building," Languidus shouted, drawing groans from the city soldiers. "It appears we're going to fight the Vitellians here any day now. Until we see them crossing that river, we'll be working round the clock to make sure these city defenses are abso-futuendi-lutely perfect. Do you hear me?" Languidus shouted until he got a resounding and unified "Yes, sir." "If these decrepit, crumbling walls don't look like the ones y'all are used to in Rome by tomorrow, we'll meet them in the field, and trust me, y'all don't want that," he threatened. "We're outnumbered ten to one, and those German troops have more experience than most of y'all combined. I want parapets, I want towers, and I want any projectile you can lob over that could smash a helmet." Languidus paused, making sure he had everyone's full attention. "Now, let's get to work!"

The soldiers quickly fired up and scrambled to find tasks before the centurions gave orders. The mission was laid out, and the troops were reinvigorated. It was frustrating to keep working after a fifty-mile march, but this time, everyone knew their efforts weren't just a precaution—they were necessary. Men cooperated with such enthusiasm that almost every completed task was followed by high fives, fist bumps, or encouraging words.

Craggy sections of the wall? No problem.

They patched and reinforced them. Missing parapets? Easy—they built them, there's not much to that one. There wasn't anything Languidus and Spurinna's soldiers couldn't do with their overwhelmingly positive attitude. The positivity was absolutely sickening; it seemed inevitable something would go wrong. But nothing did. Even the construction of the towers, a massive undertaking given the necessary speed, proceeded smoothly. Cartloads of stone were hauled from city streets and other sources, enough for four large towers on the walls most likely to face action.

Tributus led a group of men around the city to gather projectiles for the impending battle. They collected arrows, spears, and other sharp objects in one cart, while another was piled high with stones to rain down on the enemy. They went from house to house, gathering heavy, tossable belongings from locals who were indifferent to the conflict between Otho and Vitellius. Tributus, eager to avoid any missteps in his first combat experience, promised the citizens that everything would be returned or reimbursed. At the mill, the workers were reluctant to part with the millstone, a significant loss. Tributus swore on his honor that he'd bring back an equal or better millstone after the battle, and the mill workers believed him. He did actually swear on his verpus; that's what Roman's did, just look up the etymology of "testify."

After a couple of days, the city was ready. The walls were repaired and fitted with parapets for protection. Towers were built and loaded with heavy objects to drop on the enemy. Languidus was finally proud of his men. By noon, two days after their arrival, the job was mostly finished. It would never be fully complete for months, but all the critical fortifications were in place. Some sections of the wall still needed attention, but there was no longer time. Done was better than perfect. Just as Languidus was inspecting the fine work his men had accomplished, the horn blew from the tallest tower: "Everyone to your positions—Caecina is here." The horn's tone was low and menacing, unlike the "dinner's ready" horn.

Every soldier rushed to their temporary barracks, donned full armor, grabbed weapons, and prepared for battle. Languidus, Tributus, and Spurinna took their positions atop the city gate, watching as Caecina led his Vitellian army across the Po River. Troops marched across the bridge in units, regrouping on the other side to form a besieging force.

"Why didn't we fight them on the bridge?" Tributus asked. "Isn't that what you usually do in this situation?"

"Normally, yes," Spurinna replied. "But not this time."

"Why's that?"

"Because those men have been fighting on the German front for years while we've been guarding old men at dinner parties. If we fought on the bridge, we'd lose," Languidus said.

"Oh stercus, really?" Tributus said, worry creeping into his voice.

"Don't worry," Languidus said. "Neither of us has been involved in many sieges. Defending a city wall gives us a good shot."

"Especially since I doubt Caecina knows how many troops we have here," Spurinna added. "This is going to be his first tough target since leaving Germania."

The Vitellian troops formed up, a mix of somewhat-organized Roman legionaries and German barbarians of varying degrees of nudity, stumbling into loose formations of their own. The Germans, shield-smashing and singing, were clearly having a better time. They stopped three spear-throws away and began loudly carousing.

Their leader, presumably Caecina, rode forward to within one spear-throw of the gate. He was accompanied by two men and a tall, full-figured woman on horseback wearing a purple dress. The woman caught everyone's attention first. "What the futuus is he doing on the battlefield with a woman?" Spurinna muttered.

"I don't know, but if I had a wife like that, I wouldn't let her leave my side either," Languidus made hand motions commenting on her huge chest. Spurinna didn't reply because he's a culus man and therefore much more civilized and overall a better person.

"Between the distance and her loose dress, I can't really make that out to be fair," Tributus said, trying to sound polite because he's a personality guy.

Caecina, however, was a close second in drawing attention with true Broadway flair. He was tall, broad with a growing gut, and wore trousers— one leg red, the other green. His cloak was a patchwork of fabrics, each a different color. It looked like a multicolored dream coat. "Wow, what a culus," Languidus commented, though he was secretly jealous of that style.

"Hello, this town—*hic*," Caecina interrupted

himself, yelling to the gate, ". . . is under the control of Vitellius now. No need to fight—just give up and we can all have a—*hic*—great time tonight." He finished his gesture of goodwill and began ogling his wife with an oily glance.

"I don't think we will," Spurinna called back. "This town is under the control of Marcus Salvius Otho, true emperor of the everlasting Roman Empire, and it's going to stay that way." Spurinna's sobriety contrasted sharply with Caecina's slurred speech.

"What happened to—*hic*—Galba?"

"He's dead; Otho replaced him!" Languidus shouted.

"Oh right! *Hic*—I keep forgetting. Hey! *Hic*— we don't have to fight, alright?" Caecina called back. "We've captured tons of towns with no—*hic*— problem aight. We're not gonna kill anyone—don't worry, we're just on our way to Rome."

"I don't think y'all will be killing anybody," Languidus shouted, followed by the men atop the walls chanting in unison, "Long live Otho!" along with some other smackdown chants they A/B tested on each other while building the fortifications.

Caecina grabbed his head at the noise. "Fine, *hic*—have it your way." He and his purple-clad mistress rode back toward the army. There wasn't much delay between the brief negotiations and the battle. The Vitellians saw Caecina retreat, and it was go time.

At the blast of a Vitellian horn, all units charged forward in unison. The legionnaires stuck together, raising their shields in tight formations, but the recruited barbarians just charged. On the open field, nothing was more terrifying than a bunch of armed, half-naked Germans running at full speed. But this wasn't an open field. With the Othonians safely behind the city walls, the sight was less intimidating.

As the Germans reached the wall, the Othonians began pelting them with stones, arrows, and spears. The shielded Romans weren't much of a target compared to the exposed barbarians. Despite the onslaught, the Germans charged through the pain. Some fell to stone-induced concussions, but others kept going until they reached the wall and gate, where they set the reinforcements aflame or tossed back the stones. The high ground proved merciless to the Germans, who could only hurl insults while trying to shield themselves as best they could.

"What are a bunch of pansy Roman actors and musicians doing on a battlefield anyway?" some taunted the Othonians. Their insults were met with more stones. The Germans kept beating against the wall, though their intel was out of date. The defenses held firm, but that didn't stop them from trying. Everything in front of the wall was set ablaze, and heavy armaments were deployed against the defenses in a desperate attempt to create an opening.

Eventually, the Roman legionnaires reached the wall with their ladders. They maintained their discipline as best they could but lost men as they waded through the bodies piling up at the base of the wall. As they got closer, the ground grew red with German blood, the thuds of stones, and the wooshes of arrows and spears creating an ominous backdrop to their final approach. When they made it, sixteen formations began hoisting their hastily constructed siege equipment up the twenty-foot walls. Some ladders were shoved off, and the onslaught continued as they scrambled to raise them again.

The remaining Germans, anxious for combat, began scaling the ladders only to be pelted all the way up with all manner of projectiles. Even with teamwork holding the ladders steady, most didn't make it more than eight feet before falling. A few reached the top, only to be prodded back to a dizzying fall with spears and swords. Each climb grew more dangerous and slippery as blood and guts coated the rungs. After an hour of the fruitless assault, with their pre-battle buzz worn off, the Vitellians retreated back across the Po—sober and defeated. Some limped, others were intact, but their overinflated confidence had taken the hardest blow.

As they retreated out of range, the men atop the walls cheered and shouted insults. "Yeah, go and tell Vitellius to go back to Germany while he still can!" Tributus shouted in excitement. The battle was over, and the newly refurbished defenses had proven their toughness. As the field cleared, masses of bodies were scattered before the wall. Guts and corpses accumulated where each ladder had been. Broken weapons and shields lay among the smoking ruins of everything wooden that had burned during the assault.

One particular column of smoke reached the heavens, rising from the town amphitheater. After the battle, the magistrate climbed to the top of the gate to survey the damage.

"Did y'all win?" the old man asked as he groaned his way up the stairs. The seventy-year-old magistrate, dressed in a conservatively white toga, maintained a calm, unflappable demeanor. He had looked after Placentia for years, and while he wasn't thrilled about war on his doorstep, there was little he could do to stop it.

"We won today, but they'll be back tomorrow," Languidus replied.

"I guess that's good," the magistrate mumbled, reaching the top of the gate. "Congratulations, you should be proud of yourselves." His tone changed when he peered over the parapet at the smoking wreckage left by the Vitellians. Uncharacteristically, he began cursing and shouting in anger. "Fiends! Those merdae!" he yelled. "Those scumbags from Cremona must have come here and burned down our amphitheater!"

"It was the Vitellians. Almost everything burned in the chaos," Spurinna broke the news.

"As long as I've lived, those idiots in Cremona have been jealous of our amphitheater," the old man ranted. "It was the pride and joy of this city, and now it's gone. Biggest in all of Northern Italy. People used to travel hundreds of miles to see our plays."

"It's war, sir," Tributus tried to calm him. "We watched the whole thing. Everything got burned. It can be rebuilt. It's just an amphitheater."

"*JUST* an amphitheater?" The magistrate's voice trembled. "I saw my granddaughter's first performance there, the night before I lost my wife. I never saw Flavia so happy." Tears welled in his eyes before turning back to anger. "There's no way it's just a coincidence. The first chance Cremona got to burn it down, they took it.

"Well," the magistrate kept ranting. "It was those good-for-nothing northerners. Whatever you need, we will provide, no question!"

"Yes sir, we're going to have many more preparations tonight before the next assault," Spurinna said. "Anything that can strengthen the wall—metal to melt down, weapons, projectiles—"

"Slow down," the magistrate interrupted. "Talk to my men. They'll arrange it. I'm going to inform the elders. I have a feeling you'll get a lot more recruits tomorrow."

After the beloved amphitheater burned down, every able-bodied local man joined the fight. If there was going to be a battle at Placentia, they wanted the defenders to win. The locals were distrustful of most outsiders, especially their neighbors from Cremona. Like die-hard sports fans, they were loyal to their own town, and no one from Cremona was going to burn down their amphitheater and get away with it.

The Placentia-Cremona rivalry was all too real. Cremona was the foothold to the north of the Po, and Placentia to the south. It didn't matter what the eyewitnesses said, nothing could convince the locals that it wasn't all Cremona's fault. From that moment on, the Othonians had 100 hundred percent of the city's resources and efforts in fighting off the Vitellians.

***

The next day, Spurinna had all the able-bodied men at his disposal. Unfortunately, there wasn't much the Othonians could do at this point except wait and prepare more projectiles for the next battle. The top of the city wall became crowded with armor and heavy or sharp objects ready to be thrown. The town even donated all available metal for the effort. When day broke, the people of Placentia saw a very different sight as the hordes of Vitellius crossed the river.

It was impossible to tell how many of Caecina's forces were bearing down on the walled city because every single soldier was covered by a screen, mantlet, or some hastily constructed wooden structure wheeling toward the city. The wood of the siege equipment was so fresh that some still had greenery flapping in the breeze. This was a real overnight job. Not only could the defenders not tell how many men approached, but they also couldn't determine what their intentions or weaponry were. The squeaky wooden wheels drowned out the thoughts of the defenders as they watched Placentia's first ever morning rush hour of wheeled vehicles make its way from the bridge to the wall.

"I don't like the looks of this," Languidus said, eyeing the bus-sized wooden screens inching closer to the walls and gates. "Do we have anything that could break those up?"

"I think I have an idea," Spurinna replied. "Tributus, get some men to bring up those millstones. I doubt those screens are as strong as they look."

Tributus raced down the stairs with some Praetorians and made for the cart full of millstones. Rolling them to the stairs was easy enough but getting them to the top of the wall was grueling. One by one, step by step, the Praetorians heaved and ho'd each millstone to the top of the wall. As slow as the Vitellian siege engines rolled, it wasn't as slow as lifting up four-hundred-pound-plus mill stones on a staircase wide enough for two normal-sized men or one especially large one. At least three people would need chiropractic care afterwards.

The squeaks of the siege engines' wheels

echoed against the walls, intermingling with the thuds of stones and the whips of arrows and javelins. The Vitellian shields held firm as their archers set up to pin down the defenders. Arrows were retrieved and fired back, with sturdier ones swapping sides a dozen times throughout the day. Languidus and Spurinna watched in anxious anticipation as the shielded Vitellians reached the wall and started their slow, methodical work—breaking through or over the defenses without getting whacked in the head. Some soldiers probed the wall for weak points with sledgehammers, while others began piling dirt at the base of the wall to create a siege mound. A ladder could be shoved over, and a siege tower could be destroyed, but a dirt ramp was nearly impossible to destroy without a backhoe.

One group of Vitellians, determined to breach the gate began attacking it with crowbars and pickaxes. The gate had been reinforced as much as possible the night before, but what was under that screen remained a mystery.

"Here they come," Languidus said calmly, watching the screen survive an endless barrage of stones. The projectiles did nothing, and the Vitellians reached the gate. Despite the relentless assault, Languidus and Spurinna remained calm. They were waiting—just a few more moments—while the city's silver, gold, and bronze supply finished melting. Then, they poured the molten metal through a small hole at the top of the gate onto the unsuspecting attackers.

"Well, here we go," Spurinna said, signaling the soldiers to pour the molten metal. Screams of pain pierced the siege screens, much to the defenders' grim satisfaction. The attack on the gate halted as the Vitellians reeled from the searing metal. But when they thought the danger had passed and resumed their assault, they were met with another wave of molten metal. That was enough to dissuade any further volunteers.

The gate was the only part of the wall equipped with the special molten metal defense, but the other attackers were making progress elsewhere. Weak spots were under attack by sledgehammers, and several dozen men were hard at work digging the siege mound. After thirty minutes of pelting the Vitellians, the Othonians realized they weren't making a dent in the siege equipment. They tried torches next, but the wood was too green and fresh to catch fire. The pelting slowed to an occasional toss as the few men with a good arm and good aim attempted to pick off those who felt too safe behind their shields. Millstones were still a ways off, and anxiety began to morph into boredom as the shock troops stood idly, watching the legionnaires pile up dirt.

In a lull in the fighting, one of the Vitellian soldiers shouted up out of boredom, "So, where were y'all stationed before this?"

Typically, opposing armies didn't share a common language, but civil wars were an eerily special circumstance in ancient warfare.

"Rome, third cohort of the Praetorian Guard," Tributus replied, overseeing the millstone transportation. Some stones were over the stairs and rolling into position, but it required coordination to determine targets and navigate the narrow, crowded walls. "What about y'all?"

"Twenty-First Legion!" the soldier shouted

back proudly. "Predators: first strike, first kill!" His men echoed the phrase in unison, as they always did whenever someone mentioned the number twenty-one—a good morale booster, though it quickly became cumbersome anytime the number twenty-one happened to come up in casual conversation.

"Ha, Twenty-First, huh—"

"PREDATORS: FIRST STRIKE, FIRST KILL!"

Tributus was interrupted by the loud battle motto. "So, where have y'all been stationed?"

"Up north in Switzerland and Germania," the soldier replied. "Have y'all even seen a battlefield?"

"Well, some of us."

"Haha, I figured. So, what are y'all, actors? Dancers? Not much else happens in that city, right?"

"Oh, we've seen some action."

"Yes, I know y'all have plenty of games and athletic events," the soldier teased. "I can tell y'all are professional spectators, just watching us do the real work. Looks like all that training's paying off." He laughed and got back to digging.

"Futuo you, man," Tributus yelled back, only to be flipped the bird by the soldier. He tossed a stone but was too slow and only heard more laughing.

"Okay, let's futuendi do this," Tributus said angrily. He peered over the wall, eyeing the siege mound. It was already forming quite a ramp. "Get the board and that stone ready." Two men picked up a long wooden board just the width of the parapet opening and lifted it into place. "Everybody else, get ready to focus all your fire when their shields get destroyed."

The two men pushed the board over, forming a

ramp onto the earthen siege mound, and four others quickly rolled a five-hundred-pound millstone onto it. The board bowed and arced but miraculously held. The millstone rolled down, shattering the shielded siege engine and crushing several unsuspecting diggers. The commotion forced men into the open as the millstone kept rolling across the field until it came to a stop and thudded into a two-inch-deep dent in the ground. The exposed men were then met with the return of the endless volleys of stones, javelins, and arrows as they scrambled for new cover.

The other stones were dropped onto the remaining screens, shattering and disabling them, crushing some men underneath and leaving others stranded at the wall or retreating under the Praetorians' coordinated fire. "Yeah, how do you like that, Twenty-First?!" Tributus called out, but there was no response from the men.

***

The siege dragged on for three more days. The taunts from the Twenty-First—PREDATORS: FIRST STRIKE, FIRST KILL—invoked a murderous rage in the Praetorians. Calling them actors was a step too far. Between the insulted Praetorians and the Placentia locals mourning the loss of their amphitheater— thanks to those Cremonans—there was nothing Spurinna and Languidus couldn't ask of their men.

Each day brought new and improved siege engines from the Vitellians, but none were strong enough to withstand the millstones or the ingenuity of the Othonians. Eventually, Caecina capitulated and

retreated to Cremona with the Twenty-First—
PREDATORS: FIRST STRIKE, FIRST KILL—
where they were to be reinforced by Valens, who led
the Fifth Legion. (Their real battle motto was
"CRESTED LARK—MORE THAN A BARK.")

The important thing was that Spurinna,
Languidus, and the Praetorians had prevented the
Vitellians from taking Placentia and gaining a
foothold south of the Po. Word was immediately sent
to Celsus, traveling with the Batarian forces and the
other incoming legions, that the battle was won and to
hurry on up for the main event.

15 MILITARY COUNSEL

Otho, at the head of his army, arrived at the fortified camp where his three generals—Gallus, Celsus, and Paulinus—were gathering their forces. Gallus, initially marching straight for Placentia to aid Spurinna and Languidus, halted at Bedriacum upon hearing news of the successful repulsion of Caecina's forces. Bedriacum lay on the northern side of the Po, east of Placentia, with Cremona halfway between the two cities, where Caecina had been reinforced by Vitellius's other general, Valens. Hold on, let me draw a diagram.

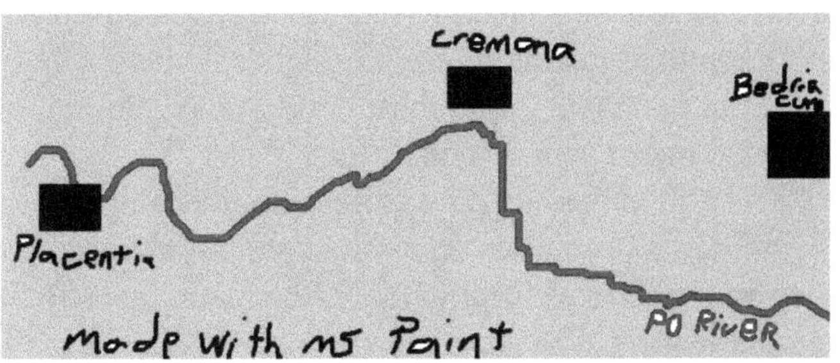

Okay, much better. Up is north, one mile is one mile, and this has not been drawn to scale.

By the time Otho reached Bedriacum, Gallus and his men had already erected a large fortification. Otho entered the wooden-walled camp with much pomp and circumstance. He graciously waved to his men, projecting the image of a confident leader despite the weariness of the long march. After a quick "Hail Otho," the soldiers returned to their tasks, preparing for war. The camp, though vast, was cramped, dusty, and smelled like a middle school locker room. Wooden walls enclosed the quintessential experience of a soldier's hard life on the front.

In one corner of the camp, centurions drilled men on shield wall tactics. Another busy centurion yelled at soldiers with inadequate armor and shields. Most had little to no armor, while a few sported gear so elaborate it was deemed impractical. Experienced soldiers carried large scuta that offered adequate protection while the inexperienced ones either didn't know what to buy or couldn't afford proper gear, resulting in shields of every shape, size, and color.

Finally, it wouldn't be a Roman camp without some enforced discipline on the new soldiers who acted up. Most misbehaving recruits were disciplined with the pickaxe, forced into hard labor. Others faced harsher punishment—marching around the camp in either too much gear or none of it.

Otho's men began settling into the camp, expanding its borders to accommodate the increasing number of soldiers. Meanwhile, Otho made his way to the command tent to meet his generals. Inside, he found Paulinus and Celsus poring over maps and organizing supplies. His brother, Titianus, hovered over their shoulders, trying to contribute to the campaign. In another corner, Languidus and Tributus were drinking and discussing the condition of their troops with the other Praetorian prefects: Cocceius, Barbius, and Veturius. The whole gang was there—except Onomastus. Titianus would have to serve as Otho's extra eyes and ears outside.

"Salve, Otho. Glad you made it up safely. Anything interesting on the march?" Paulinus greeted him.

"Nope, pretty boring on my end," Otho replied, scanning the room. "Where's Gallus?"

The tent erupted in snickering. "Oh, Gallus," Languidus laughed. "He's injured. Couldn't make it."

"What happened?" Otho asked, confused by the laughter. "The Vitellians didn't attack him, did they? What's the joke?"

"He . . ." Paulinus struggled to compose himself. "He fell off his horse."

"Hahaha, what? How?" Otho asked.

"He won't say," Celsus chimed in, still laughing. "But I heard a rumor he was swatting at a bee and got spooked."

"Wow," Otho said, grinning. "He's never gonna live that one down. What a dumb-culus."

With the story shared, Otho shifted to more serious matters. "So, how's the campaign going? What's the state of affairs?"

"The men are very anxious for war," Celsus reported. "Gallus apparently could barely get them to stop here and wait for everyone else to arrive. It's good that they're eager, but I'm worried about their discipline."

"You can't fault them for being eager," Otho replied. "But I'm sure you can solve the discipline problem. What's the current situation?"

"We've had success in Narbonese Gaul with an overwhelming naval victory, securing that front and cutting off enemy supplies," Celsus began. "We secured Placentia and stopped Caecina's southern advance." Languidus raised his wine cup in self-congratulation. "Thanks to the Praetorians and Spurinna. However, we've kind of lost control of Macer—he's leading his unit of gladiators directly south of Cremona. We can't seem to get him to do anything useful."

"Isn't he supposed to protect our flank?" Otho asked.

"Probably not now," Celsus sighed. "They're just harassing the Vitellian forces around Cremona, not really accomplishing anything. They've had some success, but I don't know what you'd expect from gladiators. Gallus had similar trouble keeping his men under control."

"Eh, what can ya do?" Otho shrugged. "I guess them being an annoying distraction is the most we can hope for. What's the enemy's position?"

"Valens and Caecina have combined their forces in Cremona. They're not in a good position to invade, especially after Placentia. They won't be crossing the Po anytime soon."

"Well, that's fantastic. But the big question is, what do we do now? Can we finish this? I don't want a prolonged war. I just want this over with so the empire can return to normal."

"We're evenly matched with the Vitellians in

numbers," Celsus said. "We may even have the stronger force because of the shorter march."

"But that doesn't necessarily mean we should rush into battle right now," Paulinus interjected.

"Why not?" Otho asked. "They could dig in and cause more problems for the empire."

"There are many reasons to delay the attack," Paulinus began. "First, according to our current information, the Vitellian army isn't getting any bigger. Valens and Caecina are united now, and there are no other forces approaching. The German and British troops can't leave their posts without forfeiting territory to the barbarians. There are zero forces in Spain, and our naval victories in Narbonese Gaul have cut off their access to the sea for escape or supplies."

"So, what's the difference between attacking now and later?" Otho asked.

"They've already devastated Italia north of the Po, and they're cut off by the Alps," Paulinus explained. "They have no access to the sea and won't be able to maintain their forces for long. If we wait until summer, the northern troops will be fighting in a warmer climate they're not used to, and we'll have more support ourselves. We have access to Rome, the sea, and the East, which still supports us. More soldiers are also on their way to reinforce us."

"So, you're saying we should wait here until summer?" Otho asked. "That's so long."

"Yes," Paulinus replied. "There's no reason to attack now when waiting is so advantageous. It's a low-risk strategy with a lot of potential reward."

Otho, despite the sound argument, hesitated. "I get what you're saying, but I really want this to be over so the empire can get back to normal. And what about everyone north of the Po? They'll continue suffering until we end this."

"Sir," Celsus interjected. "I agree with Paulinus. Given our extensive military experience, this is the commonsense path forward." His insistence was palpable.

"We can beat them, and we can beat them now," Languidus countered. "I was at Placentia, and I watched these guys fight. They're garbage soldiers. They couldn't even get on top of the wall once! We could probably crush them in the open field."

"That bad, huh?" Otho considered Languidus' proposal of just YOLO'ing it.

"Waiting till the summer is a stercus move," Proculus added.

"Gallus believes we should wait," another soldier interjected.

"Who the futuo are you?" Tributus asked with a burp.

"I'm Gallus's delegate while he recovers from his injury," the man answered. "He was adamant about waiting for summer and the extra troops."

"See? That's a stercus move from a man afraid of a bee!" Proculus gestured wildly with his wine.

"Let us fight, let us fight!" the other Praetorians began chanting, wine splashing everywhere. "LET US FIGHT!"

"The Placentia siege is not a fair comparison to how they'll fight in the field," Paulinus shouted over the rising chants. "The northern troops are well trained for open-field combat, not siege warfare. The Germans didn't have cities to besiege. They're as inept at it as the Praetorians would be in an open battle outside Rome."

"Futueris you, Paulinus!" Barbius countered. "We're the best anywhere—siege or field! Anytime, any day!" The chest-pounding resumed.

"Come on, we got you this far. We can finish the job, Otho," Languidus urged.

"They called us dancers and actors before retreating from Placentia," Tributus added. "We can't wait them out after that. Besides, we all just wanna get back to Rome and kick it."

"Yeah, well, oof, that's a lot to consider," Otho said, thinking over the two proposals. "Uh, could I discuss this privately with my chief commander?" There was a pause as Titianus, lost in thought over the map of Northern Italy, needed a verbal nudge. "Titianus . . . my chief commander . . ." Otho prompted.

"Oh, right, yes. Let's discuss," Titianus said, leaving the tent with Otho. They strolled down the main road of the camp, deep in conversation about the pros and cons. The camp was loud with drilling, but not so loud that they couldn't converse as they walked down the dusty paths.

"It's not just about finishing this," Otho began, a barrage of questions at the ready. "Every day Rome isn't whole, the senators turn against me. What do you think? You've been here longer than I have. What am I missing? Can we just take 'em now? I like the part about them running out of supplies, but do we have the time?"

"Gosh, it's a tough one for me too," Titianus replied, wishy-washy. "There's a lot of arguing in that tent between the Praetorians and the generals, so it's hard to know. Both sides make good points."

"Not surprising, considering how divided

everyone is," Otho said.

"There was one thing I heard that's a bit disturbing," Titianus added.

"What?"

"Languidus thinks the generals are stalling until Vitellius gains the advantage and influence in the Senate."

"That guy always thinks someone's out to get me. You sure?" Otho asked.

"At first, I was skeptical, too, but I've been getting weird vibes from the generals. It's strange they don't want to attack. It's almost too convenient, ya know?"

"I'd like to get this over with," Otho wavered. "It does seem like a risk, but those generals have way more military experience than the Praetorians."

"There's a rumor going around that if we delay long enough, the Senate might choose another emperor to avoid a wasteful battle between Romans. Some think Paulinus might be positioning himself for that."

"I don't like the sound of that one bit," Otho said. "I lost a fortune becoming emperor. I'd be finished if the Senate took it away."

Their conversation was interrupted by the sound of quick footsteps. Of course, it was Languidus, Tributus, and Proculus. "Titianus, did you tell him yet?" Languidus asked.

"Yes, I was just explaining your theory about the generals," Titianus replied.

"Otho, I don't trust a man who won't drink with me, and those two are squares," Languidus added.

"Not everyone drinks, especially not as much

as you," Otho said. "But never? That is a bit weird . . ."

"I know they sound reasonable with their strategy, but I think they're hiding a plot," Languidus insisted.

"This isn't like the last time you thought someone was out to get me, is it?" Otho asked.

"No, it's different," Proculus said. "I've been watching them closely. They're very secretive about their correspondence—burning letters and all. Who does that? They're definitely hiding something for sure!"

"So, Otho, the way I see it," Titianus jumped back in. "From the numbers and what Languidus has told me about Caecina's forces, we have the upper hand. If there is a plot, attacking now could foil it. It's a win-win."

"Who else feels this way?" Otho asked, though he already knew the answer.

"We all agree the generals seem shady, and we should move forward with the invasion," Proculus confirmed.

"Fine, but y'all better win this thing," Otho relented.

"Oh, don't worry," Titianus said. "There's something else I need to discuss with you."

As the Praetorian prefects left, Titianus continued, "We don't think you should join the battle. Stay back south of the Po."

"Why?" Otho questioned. "I marched all the way up here with my troops. Why can't I join them in battle?"

"Everyone thinks it's an unnecessary risk," Titianus explained. "If something happens to you, the battle would be pointless. You haven't named a successor, and with you dead, Vitellius would have just as much legitimacy as anyone else."

"That's a good point," Otho conceded. "It just sucks. I came all the way up here for the battle, only to stay back. I might as well have stayed in Rome."

"We'll be in close contact the entire time. We'll send messages on the hour," Titianus assured him.

"Just in case the rumor about Paulinus is true, don't give him any real authority. I'll trust the army to Proculus and you," Otho instructed. "And if anyone asks why I'm not there, tell them I couldn't bear to see Romans killing Romans or some stoic stercus like that, alright?"

Otho returned to the command tent with Titianus and briefed everyone on his decision to wait out the conflict in Brixellium. That day, the information spread across all the units in the camp at Bedriacum, and an air of seriousness settled over the ranks as everyone realized they would be marching to battle the next day. As day turned to night, the noisy drilling and military preparations gave way to the crackling of campfires. The soldiers ate a big meal, laid by the fires, and stared at the sky sleeplessly until their bodies succumbed to the fatigue of the day.

Once the military affairs concluded, Paulinus and Celsus joined the troops in retiring for the day. However, the Praetorians, Otho, and Titianus stayed back. "We can't go to sleep sober on a night like tonight," Proculus said, shoving wine toward Otho and Titianus.

"I owe y'all one last drink anyway," Otho agreed. "It's wild we haven't even been in business that long."

"And we only saved your life three months ago," Languidus said. "I knew as soon as I tried on that subligaculum that you were good people."

"You should never underestimate a good pair of subligaculum," Otho said, drinking his wine.

"Must have been a crazy time back in January," Titianus said, trying to fit in.

After a brief silence, Otho asked, "What's it gonna be like tomorrow?"

"I don't rightly know," Proculus replied. "Supposedly Vitellius has seventy thousand men. I don't think Rome's had a battle this large in a while, let alone one where both sides are led by Romans. Honestly, I don't think anyone involved has experienced anything like it. Most of the troops haven't even been in a real battle."

"If I could have avoided this, I would have," Otho said with a heavy sigh. "I tried, I really tried. But Vitellius is being a culus, and there's no getting around it. He might have been okay as a governor, but right now, he's causing too much harm to the empire. We've got to stop him for the good of Rome."

"And we will," Tributus raised his glass.

They all clinked their cups and downed their drinks, sharing a few more while reminiscing about the action they'd seen, providing a real season-finale vibe. One by one, they retired for the night, leaving Otho alone with his brother.

*****

The next day, Otho woke at the crack of dawn to the noisy commotion of an army scarfing down breakfast and marching like a great stampede through the camp. The miniature city had completely emptied onto the road facing Cremona and the Vitellian army. He stepped out of his tent to see his brother and the Praetorians discussing plans for the day. Otho wouldn't be completely alone; a small contingent of twenty bodyguards and a horse was ready to take him south below the Po.

"Y'all ready?" Otho asked Titianus as he mounted his horse.

"More than ready. I'll let you know as soon as we've won," he replied.

"Don't you futuendi worry, Otho," Languidus added. "Just kick back and relax in safety."

Otho began riding and looked back before reaching a gallop. "Good luck. I'm counting on you." With that, Otho rode south to Brixellium to nervously await the outcome of the battle.

16 THE FIRST BATTLE OF BEDRIACUM

The fateful day had begun. It was a clear spring morning, perfect for a march. The Othonian legions were on their way west towards Cremona, advancing in tight formation along the main road. Despite leaving their heavy equipment behind at Bedriacum, the sheer number of troops created a slow crawl towards their destination, stretching for four miles. The soldiers were fully committed to the battle ahead with no plans for overnight camps—just a straight march to combat.

The generals, Praetorian prefects, and tribunes rode on horseback alongside the army, scanning the road for any sign of an ambush or the Vitellian army so they could form up in time. Scouts were kept to a minimum to avoid alerting the Vitellians to their approach.

Despite being on the same side, Celsus and Paulinus kept their distance from Titianus and the Praetorian leaders, clearly displeased with Otho's decision. "They're angry, but there's not much more they can do about it," Proculus said.

"Who cares? They're just a bunch of stuffy desk jockeys," Languidus replied over the rolling thunder of eighty thousand marching men. "There's no way they can prove we convinced Otho. If anything, it proves they just wanted to delay to take the throne."

"Hey, I just realized—how are our men going to tell each other apart from the Vitellians?" Tributus asked after a pause.

"They're all in the same units; they should know who's who as long as they stay together," Languidus answered.

"But do they even know everyone?" Tributus pressed. "A lot of these guys have only been in for a month since we started rapid deployment."

"Hmm, stercus, you might have a point," Languidus admitted. "All the more reason to keep our formations solid."

"Maybe," Proculus chimed in. "Say, Titianus, are we planning on parleying with Caecina or not?"

"Gosh, I hadn't thought about that," Titianus replied. "Is there any point in trying to settle this?"

"Might be worth a shot," Tributus said. "But wouldn't that tip him off that we're coming?"

"Could, but it might also distract him if it drags on long enough. Plus," Proculus added, "if we somehow succeed, we might make some money out of it."

"Now you're speaking my language," Languidus said. "Low risk, chance for coin—why not?"

"I'm up for a ride," Tributus agreed as they both began to speed up.

"Sounds like a plan. We'll catch up with you guys later," Languidus called back as they galloped ahead. Paulinus, watching closely, squinted in confusion.

"Where the heck are y'all going?" Proculus shouted after them.

"Scouting ahead to find a suitable battlefield," Tributus yelled back.

Languidus and Tributus sped towards Cremona like they were on a mission to deliver a pizza in thirty minutes or less, their speed making them feel invulnerable. After all, who would see two riders as a threat? In no time, they crossed the four miles west of Bedriacum, reaching the familiar sight of the Po River and Cremona in the distance. Even from afar, it was clear the Placentians were right about the city needing a good amphitheater.

The city was buzzing with military activity. The vast number of troops had stripped the nearby fields of crops and the forests of trees. Cremona clearly wasn't equipped to support the seventy thousand men boasted by the Vitellian army. "How do we even get a meeting with Caecina?" Tributus asked.

"We just walk up and ask," Languidus replied. "Everyone respects a good parley. We look official enough, don't we?"

They slowly trotted up to the most important-looking tent amid the hustle and bustle of Vitellian preparations. It was guarded by a few idle soldiers and adorned with the most flags—clearly their best bet. They parked their horses and approached.

"Can I help you? Who are you?" a centurion asked.

"Yes, we've been sent on behalf of Otho to

parley," Languidus announced. "May we speak with Caecina?"

"Parley? I was wondering why there was no communication," the centurion replied. "Sure, he's down by the river. You two, follow them and make sure they behave." He gestured to two guards, who mounted their horses and escorted the Praetorians to the river.

There, they saw an enormous work area filled with lumber and workmen. The Romans were at peak industrial capacity, sawing, axing, and constructing wooden frames or pillars. It was odd to see such large frames being built so far from a city to siege. Upon closer inspection, it became clear: they were building a bridge across the Po.

As they arrived, another grumpy centurion greeted them. "What is it? Is more wood coming?"

"We've come to parley with Caecina," Languidus repeated. "We've been sent by Otho."

"You'll have to wait here," the centurion said. "He's very busy, so this might take a few minutes."

The group dismounted and tied up their horses, watching the bustling work area. The centurion, instead of fetching Caecina, busied himself with soldiers who were slacking off or doing an inadequate job. Caecina, in his flashy clothes, stood out like he did at Placentia—still accompanied by the woman in the purple dress.

"Dang, there she is again," Tributus said.

Languidus whistled. "Yup, hard to forget her."

Caecina was indeed busy, and the centurion, distracted by his own tasks, wandered further away from him. "At least we've got some company," Tributus said. "So, how's the camp?" he asked the guards watching over them.

"Don't tell him," one guard warned the other. "They could be spies."

"Oh, come on," Languidus said. "You think we're going to exploit the quality of your dinner against you?"

"I suppose not," the more defensive guard replied, softening. "It's okay, for now. The wine and food are better here than up north, so I can't complain. It's much warmer too," he added, getting friendlier. "Between you and me, I kinda hope we're down here for a while. I could get used to this."

"Yeah, we've been down here our whole service," Tributus said. "Can't imagine being stationed north of the Alps. I hear you get more action though."

"It's not as exciting as you'd think, but it's definitely crazier than not being on the frontier," the guard replied. "I'll probably finish my service up there. At least we'll get a break from the cold and the frontier action this year."

"I don't blame you," Languidus said. "But I hate to break it to you—we don't think you'll be down here much longer."

"Yeah, why's that?" the guard asked.

"Well, we're either going to reach a settlement today, or the battle's gonna be soon and we'll settle it then," Languidus said.

"Wow, sucks for you guys," the other soldier remarked. "Rumor has it that none of y'all are even real soldiers—just a bunch of commoners mustered at the last minute. It was good knowing you guys."

"Bull stercus, I was there at Placentia," Tributus argued.

"That doesn't count," the guard shot back.

"What about the gladiators? I heard they were giving y'all trouble." Languidus mentioned.

"They're not a problem anymore," the guard said. "Took them out a few days ago."

"Eh, took y'all long enough—they were just gladiators," Tributus retorted, salvaging what he could of his trash talk. Before the exchange could escalate, a large group of scouts rushed into the camp, shaking up the entire vibe of the workshop area. Caecina looked shocked by whatever they reported—it had to be news of the approaching army or something serious. The centurion returned to the two Praetorians, who were already mounting their horses.

"Caecina's not able to meet," he said.

"Not now, but later?" Tributus asked.

"Not now or anytime soon. I think you know why," the centurion replied. "No parley—battle's on."

"Ah, whatever," Languidus said. "Guess that's our cue to leave. Tributus, let's get out of here." They both mounted their horses and, before anyone could say goodbye, took off at full gallop back toward the Othonian lines. As they sped away, they noticed the work camps transforming into a hive of activity, soldiers swarming about, falling into ranks, grabbing gear, and preparing for battle. Orderliness quickly dissolved into chaos, but as they made more distance, the chaos faded back into organized movement.

"Hold up," Languidus ordered, bringing them to a halt at the edge of a field. They had put about a mile between themselves and the camp and looked back to see the Vitellians forming up. With a momentary sense of safety, they watched the sharp battle units of cohorts marching down the road toward them.

"Futuus, that was fast," Tributus commented.

"They were ready for this," Languidus said. "So much for the surprise. Not like we had much chance of catching them off guard. They look too sharp for that. Let's get back and tell the others to be ready."

The two Praetorians resumed their gallop down the road, taking about forty minutes to reconvene with their generals. "They're mobilizing—probably two hours out!" Tributus yelled to everyone.

"All of them?" Titianus inquired.

"That's what it looked like when we left the camp," Languidus confirmed, addressing both groups of generals.

"Left the camp?" Celsus asked, incredulous. "What the futuus were you doing in the camp?"

"Uhhh, spying. Don't worry about it," Languidus replied. "We need to get ready."

"Okay, this is it," Celsus said, shifting into command mode. "Everyone start fanning out across the road, and I want our reserves in the fields guarding the flanks." He began issuing orders to the centurions, who quickly organized the men. The main road was soon covered by the center formation of the cohorts, creating a large mass of men three-cohorts wide on each side, extending into the surrounding wheat fields. A large reserve force gathered behind the center to support the front lines.

If you're imagining neat, systematic lines of well-equipped soldiers, you'd be mistaken. This was a mass of men forming a rudimentary shield wall in a blocky formation, a far cry from the precision of imperial-age armies. The column of men gradually fanned out into a battle line, their ranks stretching across the landscape like a transposed operation in action.

The Vitellian lines began to march in a long, curving formation that followed the rolling hills of Northern Italy. Gaps were made for trees and rocky outcroppings, and the slow, deliberate advance toward the Othonians began.

Meanwhile, Proculus remained with the generals and Titianus, sending Languidus and Tributus up to lead the Praetorian cohorts. The Praetorians, maneuvering through rougher terrain away from the road, moved quickly and efficiently despite the challenging landscape. The formation process took about an hour, and by the time Languidus had led his men through a small grove of trees, rumors began to spread among the soldiers.

"I heard they're not even gonna fight—abandoning Vitellius, I heard," some said. But as they emerged from the grove and saw the Vitellian army across the field of tall grass, those rumors were quickly put to rest. The front lines peered over a field of tall grass to see that the Vitellian army was very real. Despite this seemingly convincing evidence, the rumors did not go away.

"Yeah, I bet they don't even fight. They'll break contact before this even begins," one soldier said. The Vitellians were a few stone's throws away in rows of tighter formations at the edge of a vineyard. With a visual of the Othonians, they began fanning out into their own formation to counter, piercing into the long, fertile, green rows of grapes. "Yeah, they're definitely gonna run away," another soldier spread more gossip or trash talk. Maybe both?

Who knows, but the wishful thinking for sure made everyone more relaxed than most would be facing down an army.

Atop their horses, Tributus and Languidus caught their first full glimpse of the Vitellian army, obscured by the landscape. There was no telling how many men they'd face that day—the Vitellians stretched over the hills and beyond the horizon. With contact imminent and the two sides less than a fifteen-minute slow march away from clashing, Tributus and Languidus dismounted, handing their horses to senior soldiers at the rear, and took up their shields and swords. They began moving up the lines between two of their four cohorts.

"I don't care what you've heard . . . be ready for a fight . . . do not run after them . . . hold the line at all costs!" Languidus shouted, his voice cutting through the noise of two thousand marching men. As they reached the front of the formation, the Vitellians, now just thirty yards away, formed their own shield wall. "LOCK SHIELDS!" Languidus ordered, tightening the formation.

They were now within volley range. The Othonians held their shields close, leaving no gaps as the first wave of Vitellian javelins arced overhead. The tightly packed shields absorbed the blows, and the Othonians kept marching steadily forward.

Languidus, positioned at the front, ensured there were no gaps in the line. With his vision obscured by shields and bodies, he marched over the uneven terrain with his men, the shouts of both armies growing into a deafening roar like the final moments of a close sports game. The formation tightened further, as they closed in on the enemy. The Vitellian battle cries grew louder until the Othonian advance suddenly halted.

A wave of silence rippled through the ranks, followed by the sounds of clashing shields and the metallic clang of weapons striking armor. The pressure from the ranks in front pushed Tributus backward until he was trapped by the men behind him. The two sides had made contact, and the battle began in earnest.

Like a four-thousand-man rugby scrum, the two armies pushed against each other, gaining ground only as men in the front fell and were replaced quickly by another soldier, ceding inches in the exchange. Tributus could feel the pressure building as he neared the deadly front line.

The sure footing of the Praetorians in the deadly scrum proved successful as they began gaining ground until they reached the interior of the vineyard. That's when things got messy. Tributus began nearly tripping over bodies of his own men and the Vitellians. He and the other men began slashing and shoving through the fighting of either side, even slower and more cumbersome. With the added resistance to movement, a stalemate set in. At the center of the cohort, there would be no retreating. Now, there was only one direction: forward.

Tributus, now just five ranks from the front, felt the weight of the situation. Trapped between his comrades in front and a shield behind, he had no choice but to prepare for the fight. Everyone knew that, so they all just moved forward. The men of the cohort stood there pressed against each other, silent and afraid. Staring straight ahead, all they could do was imagine if they would end up on the front line.

What would they do when they got there? What would they encounter? They could only wait to see in between their fellow brothers. On his way up, Tributus began stepping over more and more bodies fertilizing the vineyard.

"Futuo! You ready for this?" Languidus asked by his side.

"How long do you think?" Tributus shouted through the ever-growing grunts of the front lines as soldiers shoved their shields against each other.

"No telling," Languidus replied. "As long as the center holds."

Anticipation grew as one rank, then two, then three fell. Sometimes a line held for twenty-five minutes, sometimes for just five. With no clear movement forward or backward, any progress against the Vitellians could only be guessed at. As the line inched closer, the air thickened with sweat and anguish. By the time they were one rank away, all they could do was stumble over the piling corpses, lean against the shield at their back and keep pushing forward. Tributus and Languidus were one rank away from the fighting, they could now occasionally catch glimpses of the combat between the shields. But they couldn't look for long; most of their efforts were spent pushing the frontline soldiers forward with sure footing. Trapped between the front ranks and the pressing shields behind them, they relied on the noises from the men ahead to gauge the battle. They dared not look above their shields.

Tributus heard grunts, slashing, and the clanking of swords against armor. The grunts grew weaker, strained by heavy breathing and occasional shouts of pain. Every so often, Tributus felt the tension in front of him relax, only to snap back with the force of a wall, followed by more heavy breathing and grunts. Each cycle of relaxation and tension grew longer until it didn't snap back at all. The shouting directly ahead grew louder. There was no relief, no stepping back—only one direction: forward.

Tributus felt the man in front of him give way, and to relieve the pressure at his back, he sprinted two feet forward, shield first, into the gap until his arm reverberated against his shield with a heavy *thunk*. The man in front of him was gone—now, he was that soldier. After a slight give from the other side, he was met with equal force. What was left of the man before him was a fading corpse among the many on the ground. Tributus was at the front.

Paralyzed by the sudden responsibility, Tributus stood there, leaning against the shield behind him and pushing forward, keeping his head down. WHACK—a sword came down on his helmet. Moments later, he caught a glimpse of the same sword thrusting inches from his face. Every muscle in his body ached as he forced himself to stay locked in place. He couldn't retreat even if he wanted to. At this rate, a cramp might defeat him before the man in front of him could. There was only one direction: forward.

Fully realizing this, Tributus summoned the courage to peek over his shield between sword thrusts. He locked eyes with his enemy—a fellow Roman, inches away. Brown and dead, the tired eyes of the soldier stared back, and Tributus quickly ducked as the gladius thrust forward again, closer this time. Adrenaline surged through his aching body. He gripped his sword, and in one motion, he peeked up, saw the top of the enemy's helmet, and stabbed over the shield. He felt a flinch on the other side, and when he pulled his sword back, it was stained with blood— a lucky first blow in the scrum. He followed up with another overhead swipe, glancing quickly to confirm the hit, and felt the flinch grow stronger. For the first time in what felt like hours, Tributus felt the shield in front of him lighten. One more thrust, and his sword found the shoulder of the Roman before him. The man went limp, and Tributus surged forward.

Before he could advance further, another thud shook his left arm. A new Vitellian was now in front of him, fighting for ground. The force from this soldier's shield was far greater than anything Tributus had faced that day. He pushed back with all his might, locking his body in place. This was a fresh man, eager for the fight. Tributus peeked over, saw the ferocity in his eyes, and immediately ducked to dodge the man's sword. There was no way he could let this man gain ground. This was a zero-sum game. There was only one direction: forward.

The enemy continued to slash and stab wildly, his sword scraping across Tributus's armor. He stood firm, taking the blows, while the man to his right wasn't so lucky. The soldier beside him grew pale, blood oozing from a wound, and as he was crushed by the weight of the formation, Tributus panicked. He looked around, but the formation was breaking. Just as the man fell, Languidus slammed the Vitellian back into place, locking the line once more. Now, both were on the front line. Languidus gritted his teeth as he adjusted to the new pressure.

"Futuo!" Tributus heard his friend and mentor grunt through the pain.

"This futuendi sucks," Tributus growled,

ducking and dodging the enemy's sword while pushing forward through cramping muscles. The air grew muggier with sweat and blood. He could taste the bitter iron.

Tributus relied on the soldiers beside and behind him to keep him propped up against the line until he could make a move. Languidus, though older, maintained his energy and ferocity. He protected not only his own men but also Tributus beside him. How long they'd have to hold the line was anyone's guess. With the shield walls tangled together, retreat would mean massive losses. There was only one direction: forward.

Just as they felt the shield pressure wave ripple through the cohort on first contact with the enemy, the pressure at their backs began to decrease. They were holding the line themselves, losing ground with diminishing support. With each decrease in pressure, the Vitellians pushed harder, forcing the Othonians to back up slowly over the bodies beneath them. Holes were forming left and right. The formation was breaking, and there was nothing they could do but hold on long enough to create a clear path for retreat.

"Futuendi don't stop now!" Languidus called out, not knowing how many men were left in front of or behind him.

"The formation's breaking!" Tributus shouted. "We're not going to make it—we have to retreat!"

"If we retreat, we die, Otho dies, the empire dies!" Languidus grunted back, digging his heels into the dirt. "There's no going back!"

Tributus glanced over his shoulder and saw daylight peeking through the ranks behind him. The formation was gone—what had happened to it? He was alone against the army. He couldn't stay there and survive, but he couldn't leave without abandoning Languidus. Then, the man to his left tripped on a corpse, and the soldier to Languidus's right cried out in pain as his shield arm was struck. There would be no one to replace them—that was the end of the line. Tributus dropped his shield and sprinted away over the corpses and through the slower retreating men. In all directions, he saw Othonians running for their lives as Vitellians broke through. It wasn't just the Praetorian cohorts; the center of the Othonian army had been shattered long before, and the flanks were just now realizing it. But he didn't see Languidus running beside him.

Panicking, Tributus searched for his horse—any horse. He had no time to wait; he had to get out of there. Gaining height and speed, he saw the full extent of the defeat. The enemy army remained intact, while Otho's fled in desperation, scattered across trampled fields, destroyed vineyards, and groves. The landscape was littered with running men. The center of the retreat was so bloody and chaotic that he had to avoid the main road for a mile.

Thirty minutes later, the only men left were those who had retreated early or the officers with horses who had escaped the front lines. The Othonian army's long retreat back to Bedriacum had begun. As the sun set, Tributus had to return to the road to avoid getting dangerously lost. He spotted lights along the road, hoping they were friendly.

The retreat had found some semblance of order, with men marching together, though the units were broken and overflowing onto the road. It wasn't as orderly as it seemed. Tributus recognized the broken spirits and the lack of shields—it was indeed the Othonians, and he was among friends. He rode at a faster pace until he caught up with Titianus and Celsus.

"Titianus," he greeted them. "What the futuo happened?"

"Tributus, good to see you made it out. Where's Languidus?"

"We were at the front when the line broke," Tributus paused. "I don't think he made it out. It collapsed too fast."

The others had nothing to say, so they just muttered, "Futuo."

"What happened?" Tributus asked again. "Where are Proculus and Paulinus?"

"Our center was too ambitious and advanced too far in chase of an early victory," Celsus explained. "They couldn't hold long after the counter-push. The road and surrounding area were so clogged with dead that we couldn't successfully retreat or reform."

"Proculus and Paulinus ran off in shame," Titianus added. "They couldn't keep their men under control and felt it was their fault. All we could do was get as many men out of there as possible. It's going to be a long march back. We'll have to surrender."

"Is Otho going to agree to that?" Tributus asked.

"He won't have a choice," Celsus responded. "I haven't done a count, but it looks like we've suffered major casualties while the Vitellians have maintained most of their force. I don't see how we can recover."

"We should meet him at Bedriacum," Titianus added. "We still have fresh troops, so it's not completely over."

"If we surrender, what happens to Otho?" Tributus asked again.

"I don't know," Titianus answered. "Nothing good."

17 BURNED LETTERS

Otho was already anxiously awaiting news from the battle. He was so restless that he summoned Onomastus to travel north to help with administrative duties. The lack of updates gnawed at him, and he was also preoccupied with the endless tasks of mustering more troops in case the battle didn't prove decisive.

As rumors of a massive defeat spread, it wasn't long before some disoriented troops made their way south of the Po, seeking safety from the Vitellians. Word of the devastating loss traveled fast, and soon, even before hearing from his generals, Otho's soldiers were begging him to launch another attack. "It's not over until it's over," they insisted. Though this was likely just the typical sucking up, Otho knew he had to travel to Bedriacum himself to learn the truth from his generals.

In just a short afternoon, Otho sped back north to his main forces at Bedriacum. The quick carriage ride brought him face-to-face with the grim reality as he arrived at the camp at sunset. As he entered, Otho was greeted with a hearty "Hail Otho," though from fewer and less-enthusiastic men. The camp was a quarter of its original size, with the remaining soldiers battered beyond recognition. Many were wounded or bandaged, and there was no drilling or equipment preparation—just men licking their wounds around campfires. The only activity that could be called productive was the preparation of dinner.

Otho headed straight for the command tent to assess the extent of the loss. Inside, his brother Titianus, Celsus, Tributus, and Barbius stood over a map, discussing the Vitellian troop placement. Titianus nodded along to whatever Celsus was saying, while the two Praetorians stood silently, arms crossed, with expressionless faces.

"How bad is it?" Otho asked, inserting himself into the conversation.

"Not good at all. That might have been it, Otho," Celsus answered truthfully.

"We don't have to give up now. We still have plenty of men left," Barbius answered delusionally.

"How bad?" Otho pressed, growing frustrated. "Where are the Vitellians, and how many remain? What's the state of our troops?"

"Between the deserters and the dead, we have about a third of our men left," Celsus admitted, rubbing his forehead. "The Vitellians stopped about five miles short of Bedriacum. We sent a delegation to discuss peace and saw that they'd brought the heavy machinery for a siege. They're almost as strong as they were at the start of the battle. Maybe they lost a few thousand, but I'm not sure."

"We still have troops finding their way back," Barbius added. "And more men are on the way. It's far from over, Otho! We can still win this—we shouldn't give up! You said it yourself, Celsus—we have the logistics chain from Rome and the sea."

"We're not going to last long here, Barbius. They have the will and the means. Once they cross the Po with those troops, it's over," Celsus argued, waving his hands in frustration. "Between the rout and the battle itself, I'm not sure how many are still making their way back or who fell on the road. We may have lost as many as forty thousand men. I doubt anyone else is coming."

"Futuo, that many?" Otho was shocked. "In the rout? I thought they'd just be captured. Isn't that usually what happens?"

"Not this time," Celsus said grimly. "The only reason to capture someone is to sell them as a slave. But nobody's buying former Roman citizens as slaves. They slaughtered anyone in their way. The most merciful thing they did was stop short and let us surrender."

"How did it go so badly?" Otho asked, feeling the full weight of the loss. He had a feeling it didn't go well but had no idea it went that poorly.

"Well, it wasn't the Praetorians' fault," Barbius interjected unhelpfully. Otho rolled his eyes, and Celsus shot him a look that could have cut through stone.

"Our center quickly destroyed the first ranks of the Vitellian forces and captured their standard," Celsus explained.

"That sounds like a good start. What went wrong after that?"

"They overextended, and the second line of the Vitellians hit back with a hard punch. They must have really wanted that standard back. At that point, they just outfought us," Celsus said. "Once the center broke, all the lines broke. It was a mad dash back here . . . at least for those fast enough."

Otho sat down on the ground, overwhelmed. Barbius started bickering again about how they couldn't give up, how they had to keep fighting, while Celsus debated the futility of it all. But Otho wasn't listening. He was stuck on the part about forty thousand men dying in a battle that didn't need to happen.

As he sat on the dirt floor of the tent, Otho reflected on the chaos that had led him to the throne. He thought about all the letters exchanged with Vitellius that had led nowhere, all the lives disrupted and destroyed by the chaos he had unleashed. Would this be his legacy as emperor if he continued? This wasn't about change—it was about him. How many Roman lives was his life worth?

"What I'm trying to say is," Celsus's voice brought him back to the present, ". . . yes, we could keep going, hold them off until more fresh troops arrive, maybe corner them until they run out of supplies—but now it's going to take months and tens of thousands more lives, not to mention the locals, whose lives and property will be destroyed by a massive rebel army! Continuing now would be idiotic!"

"We give up. Final word," Otho said with quiet authority after a moment of thought. "Can we at least hold off another day or two to get a few things in order?"

"Yes, we have enough time for that," Celsus confirmed.

"Otho, why are you throwing your life away?" Barbius argued. "This is just a setback."

"Shut the futuo up, Barbius. This is final," Otho snapped. "I'm going to need some space to get things in order."

"We still have your tent ready, with an office and a bed," Celsus said.

Otho nodded and left the command tent for his own. Inside, he found a well-furnished space with a couch, a desk, and a bed. A slave entered to light a couple of oil lamps, casting a soft yellow glow in the tent as the evening light outside faded.

"Would you like me to bring you anything, sir?" the slave asked.

"No, thanks. I'll be fine for the night," Otho replied, sitting down on his bed. The slave left, and Otho was alone. He didn't even bother to undress, just lay there on his back, absorbing everything. It was all over, and he lay there, prostrate in resignation. For the first time in a long while, he had given up. As soon as he stopped thinking about what he would do in the next week, month, or year, and focused only on what he would do tomorrow, the thousand screaming voices in his head went silent. Otho slept better that night than he had in over a decade.

***

Otho woke the next morning to the chirping of birds and a figure at the entrance. He groggily stirred in his bed, blinking against the beams of light piercing the tent. "Who's that? What is it?" he asked.

"I rushed up as soon as I heard," Onomastus's

voice replied.

Otho sat up, disheveled. Onomastus had seen a lot of the real Otho, but never the early-morning version: tired eyes, askew wig, and a toga barely hanging on by friction alone.

"I'm glad you made it," Otho greeted his friend. "The work we do today could save dozens of lives."

"I had a feeling you'd need me more up here than in Rome," Onomastus said, shaking Otho's stiff hand. "You don't look your best; I always forget you wear a wig[17]."

"Right now, keeping up appearances isn't as important as surrendering gracefully," Otho replied. He stepped outside and called to a nearby slave. "Bring all my correspondences and what Onomastus traveled with. I'll also need some wood for a fire. Set up a fire right there," Otho said, pointing just outside his tent. He and Onomastus reentered the tent, leaving the entrance flaps open to let in some light. Otho sat on the stool next to his desk while Onomastus settled on the couch.

"So, what's the plan for the campaign?" Onomastus asked. "I've heard mixed rumors. Some say you're regrouping for another attack, others say surrender."

"We're not continuing this slaughter. We're surrendering tomorrow," Otho said. "We need to tie up loose ends today, and then that's it."

"That's it? That can't possibly be it," Onomastus replied in disbelief. "Don't you have a

---

[17] Author's note: you are not crazy, Otho just wore his wig so well that no one ever noticed he had one on, with the sole exception of Onomastus.

backup plan? An escape plan, something?"

"No, I have to surrender," Otho said, surprisingly content. "If I don't, thousands more will die in my name."

"But everything we've been through, all the deaths already . . . They'll mean nothing?" Onomastus asked. "Didn't you say Vitellius was just a culus? What about all the Romans who will suffer under his reign?"

"One bad emperor is better than another battle where forty thousand Romans die at the hands of their brothers," Otho stated firmly.

"Futuo, so . . ."

"Yes, I'm basically a dead man," Otho responded. "There's no way Vitellius lets me live after this. All I can do is take the honorable path and be remembered well."

"This isn't like you. You always have a plan, you never give up."

"I know," Otho said. "Just help me out, alright?"

A few slaves began filling the tent with boxes of scrolls and letters. They also brought in Onomastus's administrative work and a reserve of currency he assumed Otho would use to continue the campaign. Two others started constructing a small campfire just outside the tent.

"So, what are we doing?" Onomastus asked, eyeing the massive pile of letters and paperwork from months of planning.

"I'm going to write to friends and family," Otho said. "You're going to help me comb through these letters and destroy anything that speaks ill of Vitellius."

"This is going to take all day," Onomastus said. "Isn't there something you'd rather do . . . ya know?"

"No. If Vitellius or his men get their hands on those letters and see the nasty things everyone said about him, they'll be exiled or executed as soon as he gets to Rome. That includes correspondence with your name on it," Otho replied. "It's the least we can do."

Onomastus agreed and began sorting through the letters one by one. While many went into the keep pile, the burn pile grew steadily. As the day wore on, Onomastus quickly became adept at skimming each letter, finding the obscene comments, and tossing the stack into the fire, pressing down with a poker to ensure the complete destruction of each letter.

Meanwhile, Otho cleaned himself up a little and got to work writing nonstop. He barely made a sound as he penned his final words to his sister, his nephews, his contacts in Rome, everyone he had worked with, and anyone he cared about who wasn't in the camp. He only paused for visitors.

"Onomastus, I'm glad you made it up. Can you believe we're giving up?" Barbius greeted Onomastus.

"Futuendi stupid if you ask me," Tributus added. "They killed Languidus, you know! We can't give up."

"Good to see you too," Onomastus replied, looking up from the letters. "Yes, I couldn't believe it either when I heard."

"Hey, salve," Otho greeted the two Praetorians. "I know you don't agree with the decision, and that's okay. You're going to be fine once this is over. I'm sending a letter recommending you both to Vitellius to keep your posts."

"I just can't believe you're going to roll over like this," Barbius said, still agitated but calming down, cued by Otho's demeanor. "Thanks, though . . . It'll be a loss having Vitellius in charge. We'll miss having such a generous emperor."

"You still have one for now," Otho replied. "Here, take this, both of you." Otho handed them two chests of silver and gold. "It's the least I can do for all your loyalty and hard work. And take these too," Otho added, offering them rings from a bowl of expensive-looking jewelry.

"This is awfully generous of you," Tributus said, accepting the hard currency. "Aren't you going to need this?"

"This will do me no good where I'm going after this," Otho said. "Just take it. I don't know if Vitellius will pay you what you deserve."

Barbius and Tributus left with Otho's gifts, confused and disillusioned by his quick decision to surrender. Throughout the day, Otho was visited by many soldiers and officers from his close circle. Each begged him to fight Vitellius, but Otho continued to refuse, responding by giving away more money and possessions.

Late into the night, Otho finished writing his letters to family and recommendations for all the loyal men who had served under him. Onomastus stayed late, reading months of correspondence, filing harmless writings, and burning the rest. It was like a frantic last-minute audit, desperately trying to avoid an impending disaster.

The late-night cram session turned into early morning as an orange glow began to brighten the eastern sky.

"Onomastus," Otho said, breaking the silence. "I want you to leave first thing today with Celsus and Titianus."

"You don't want to have one last day?"

"No, too dangerous. You saw how the soldiers are acting," Otho replied. "Any longer and we risk more bloodshed."

"What's the harm?"

"What's the point?" Otho said. "No need to delay the inevitable. I have to surrender today, and I don't want you around if it gets nasty."

"I just wish it could have ended differently," Onomastus said.

"Me too," Otho replied. "Just know that it's all going to be fine without me, and make sure all these letters are delivered." Otho handed him a bound stack of letters. "Now get out of here."

The two shook hands and said their goodbyes. Otho sat down on his stool to watch what might be his last sunrise while Onomastus stirred the general and Otho's brother to action. Before the camp could rise to another day of waiting between a massive army and surrender, a motley crew of slaves and soldiers working under Celsus scrambled to pack everyone's things into a cart, mounted their horses, and slipped out of the camp, leaving without a word.

"MUTINY! LONG LIVE THE EMPEROR!" a voice cried out not even a moment later. Praetorians, fresher soldiers, and hyper-devoted men eager for war began running about, grabbing unit standards and rallying the camp into formations.

While most of the soldiers were not in favor of continuing the campaign, the loud minority clamored for action. Even those weary of living on the edge of total defeat had to join in, fearing retaliation from the architects of the mutiny. Many still refused, but most joined in. The camp was in a frenzy, and Otho was on the brink of another coup.

"What are those dumb culi going to do? Force me to continue leading them to their deaths?" Otho muttered to himself, watching the men approach his tent, led by Barbius and Tributus. Otho walked out, clad in his toga, wearing a fierce grimace, and holding a sword.

"We won't let you surrender!" Barbius shouted, leading the confused troops toward the center of the camp at Bedriacum. "We'll take it from here, just like we always do."

Otho said nothing, standing ten yards away from the mutineers. Sticking the hilt of his sword into the ground.

The mutineers rushed in but were too late. Otho fell forward onto the blade. He lay bleeding out for the next minute, motionless and at rest, as his men watched in shock. The campaign was over, and with it, the life of the second emperor of the year 69 AD